Dublin in the Rain

A Novel By

Andrew Critchley

To Kim

My muse, my inspiration, my true friend

With Special Thanks

There are so many people that I would like to thank. I have been blown away by the numerous kind and supportive messages from people this year – whether it's been via Facebook, LinkedIn, personal e-mails or face to face discussions.

Although it's sadly not practical to thank you all individually in these pages (as much as a large part of me would love to do so), what I can say is that collectively you are the reason why this book exists.

As motivated as I have been around *Dublin in the Rain* – there were times when the endless edits, proof reads, plot-hole management, etc. were quite life sapping and soul destroying.

In such moments, the messages of positivity, enthusiasm and support were what carried me through, inspired me to put in the extra hours and work harder every day!

So a massive thank you, beyond words, to anyone who has supported and encouraged me on my journey as a writer.

**

Man cannot live by literature alone – even if it is a nice thought.

As such, special mention should be made of Coffee #1 in Pontcanna that has been my office and working/creative environment this year (Basil Fawlty-esque rants at my computer included) along with Mulberry St restaurant in Llandaff, my after-hours watering hole of choice as Gee treated me to some really rather delightful wines given my limited budget.

A quality red will always nourish the soul and inspire the creative juices!

God bless you all and many thanks.

**

And last, and most definitely not least, my very special thanks to my dear old ma and pa without whose simply wonderful support this year would have been a very different story.

**

I sincerely hope that anyone reading this book enjoys it as much as I did writing it (well, most of the time anyway!).

Andrew Critchley, ISOG.
October 2013

Preface

A Tragic Tale of Woe

It was April 1947.

Dermot and Rose were blissfully happy as they walked home from Phoenix Park with their son. Now the lighter nights had come, Dermot loved to come home early and play football in the park with his son whilst Rose, or Rosie as Dermot always called her, watched happily as her beloved man and son played together.

Dermot and Rosie's background could not have been more different. He was one of nine children from the impoverished backstreets of Dublin. Rosie, in contrast, came from 'serious money' to the south of Manchester.

They had met just after the outbreak of war when Dermot had come over with the Army to be stationed near where Rosie lived.

To the despair of Rosie's sole surviving parent, her domineering and controlling mother, Katherine, they had fallen in love. To her mother's even greater horror, Rosie became pregnant by Dermot.

For all Katherine's reservations and prejudices, Dermot Flanagan was a very good man. A decorated hero in the war, he had returned safely in 1945 to take his woman and son back to Dublin to build a life together.

Dermot was an extremely gifted ball player, wonderful Irish dancer and, above all, a man with an excellent head for business and an almost super human capacity for hard work. In only two years, he built a thriving timber business from nothing and, with Rosie expecting their second child, now living in a delightful town house, there seemed nothing but good times ahead for the happy couple.

Once Rosie had given birth, they were finally planning to marry.

Not being married had never previously bothered them as they were both rebels in their own way – Dermot rejecting the Catholicism of his background and Rosie rebelling against the social and behavioural expectations of her upper class mother.

They were so in love, and that was the only thing that mattered to them.

It started to rain as they walked home – they didn't care as they huddled together as their son ran on ahead, ball in hand.

**

Kenneth Braherty was a highly successful financier in his mid-forties.

He'd started the war rich and ended the war even richer. Kenneth had all the trappings of wealth – a beautiful home, a beautiful wife and three children.

He was a big drinker, and not uncommonly for the times, sexist to the core. He doted upon his two sons, and no expense was spared in ensuring that they both went to the best possible schools and universities. However, he largely ignored his daughter; no effort whatsoever was made to ensure she received even a half-decent education.

Despite all these things, his daughter adored him – far more than either of her brothers, who merely took their father's wealth and commitment for granted.

Braherty was driving home in his beloved car, a Rolls Bentley. He'd been drinking again, as he often did straight after work, before returning home. But that night, even by his standards, he'd had a skinful and was driving far too fast as the rain came down – oblivious to the world around him.

The young boy dropped his ball in the street and despite the shouted pleas and screams of his mother, chased after it into the road.

Kenneth Braherty didn't see the boy, and as his car hurtled towards him, Dermot Flanagan reacted immediately to save his son.

As with most things that he'd done in his life, Dermot Flanagan was successful – but this time he was to pay the ultimate price.

Braherty's car hit him full on at speed as he pushed his son clear and to safety.

Despite efforts to revive him, as Rosie and her son looked on with heartbroken and anguished tears, Dermot Flanagan died by the roadside that rainy Dublin evening.

**

Worse was to follow; three days later a distraught and devastated Rosie miscarried in the night – lacking the strength to move and with her sleeping son not hearing her cries for help, she also died.

7

The son's first awareness of his mother's plight was when he entered her bedroom the next day to find her motionless in blood covered sheets.

The authorities tracked down Dermot's and Rosie's parents and, after no little discussion, it was agreed that the orphan boy would return to England to be brought up by Rosie's mother, Katherine.

It was a decision of duty, not love, by Katherine, and the poor boy's childhood was a miserable one, devoid of any affection or warmth and coupled with rigid, remorseless discipline – almost to the point of cruelty as the slightest wrongdoing would invariably be met by the stiffest and most brutal of punishments.

**

Kenneth Braherty had been full of remorse after the accident and pledged to help Rosie and her young family in every way possible – money would be made available to ensure that they would want for nothing.

Upon hearing of Rosie's death, Kenneth's remorse turned to devastation. He offered to help but Katherine brutally rejected his advances.

Kenneth, already a heavy drinker, descended into the alcoholic abyss and over the remaining 15 years of his life, lost virtually everything – his money, his wife and was even ignored and treated as an outcast by his two sons.

Only his daughter stood by him, unstinting in her dedication and support as he sunk further and further.

He died of sclerosis of the liver, his daughter at his bedside, unable to ever forgive himself for what had happened with Dermot and Rosie. Unpunished by the authorities because no laws existed at the time regarding drink driving, he punished himself instead.

His dying words were, "May the Lord forgive me for what I did; that somehow my wrongs can be put right."

**

Nearly 50 years after the tragic events of that rainy Dublin evening, a fed-up. lonely, somewhat grumpy and tetchy man found his way to a hotel bar in Dublin on April 17 1996.

This is his story.

In a Hotel Bar

It was raining. It always seemed to be raining when I visited Dublin.

As my ferry arrived at Dún Laoghaire and its two granite piers late afternoon, it was, on the surface at least, an unremarkable April day.

I disembarked and undertook the mundane task of going in search of a taxi. As I stood in the long taxi queue, I cursed under my breath.

"Why does it always sodding rain here every time I forget an umbrella?"

Finally I was at the front of the queue. A middle aged taxi driver, whom I remember most notably for his short build and truly awful teeth, ushered me into his cab.

"Where do you want to go to, my good man?"

"The Midlothian Hotel."

"Where, sir?"

"The Midlothian Hotel, Dublin; it's south of the river. Winter Street, I believe."

"Oh, that Midlothian Hotel, sir."

"Sorry, I didn't know that there are more than one in Dublin," I commented.

"There aren't, sir. That's the only Midlothian Hotel I know of."

I shook my head in disbelief and cursed quietly,

"God I hate this place."

"Sorry, sir, what did you say?"

"Nothing. Nothing at all," I replied.

As the taxi driver put my belongings in the boot, I slumped on the back seat of the car.

"Spring is in the air, sir," said the driver.

"More like winter if you ask me. It always seems to rain when I come here."

"To be sure though it's a glorious city when the sun shines, sir."

I met the poor man's efforts to cheer me up with a stony silence.

"Will you be going into town tonight, sir?"

"No, is there any reason why I should?"

"Ah, sir the craic is great in downtown Dublin."

I said nothing.

"Do you come to our fair city often, sir?" continued the driver.

"Around every three months."

"Are you here on business, sir?"

"Yes."

"Do you always take the boat, sir?"

"Yes."

"Why don't you fly, sir?"

"Because I hate flying, that's why."

The taxi driver switched the radio on. It was almost exactly five o'clock and the news had started. I wasn't paying any real attention, but do remember hearing in solemn tones that the sea rescue services had abandoned their search for a family of three that had gone missing in their boat off the coast of Galway in a very bad and unexpected storm two days earlier.

"How terrible," said the taxi driver.

"Yes," I replied.

"And in such a wonderful place as Galway, sir."

"I've never been there."

"Oh, you should go there, sir. It's truly God's own country."

**

We arrived at The Midlothian Hotel, situated to the south of one of the main drinking areas in Dublin, Temple Bar. As a hotel it was a little pretentious, with what can best be described as an eccentric interior design based solely around purple, red and green colours.

However, if one ignored the visual aspects of the décor, it was clean and quiet – and despite its location, seemingly miles away from the craic of downtown Dublin.

After checking in, I had a bath and changed into fresh, dry clothes and then did a little work preparation for the business of the next day. It was now gone six o'clock in the afternoon, and I felt a little sleepy after a long drive from my home on the outskirts of Sheffield to Anglesey, subsequent ferry journey and drenching in the taxi queue.

I lay down on the bed to rest and slipped into a late afternoon snooze.

**

I awoke with a start; disorientated I noticed that the television set was on and blaring.

11

I had a glass of water to help me re-orientate and saw on television the same report as in the taxi of the rescue services abandoning their search for a boat containing a family of three that had gone missing off the coast of Galway.

An enormous sense of loss filled my body and soul.

**

I wandered downstairs in the hotel for an evening meal. The big old clock in the entrance hall chimed eight. I entered the deserted hotel bar and saw the barmaid all alone; I had an eerie, overwhelming feeling of restlessness sweep over me.

"You look as though you've had some bad news," said the barmaid.

I saw her sweet and gentle smile coupled with striking long flowing blonde hair and, as I reached the bar, her kind deep blue eyes. Even a particularly badly designed red, purple and green bar uniform could not detract from her obvious charm and beauty.

"It's been one of those days," I replied.

"What you need is some rest and relaxation, what would you like?"

"I'll have a red wine, thank you."

"What's your name?" she asked.

"Whatever you want it to be," I said.

"You look like a Jonathan to me."

"My God, that's astonishing. My name is Jonathan. Jonathan Melton. What's your name?"

"Maolíosa," she replied in a soft voice with a delightful Irish lilt.

"I'm pleased to meet you, Melissa."

Despite my words, sadness swept over me. Hearing the name of Melissa always bit hard in the pit of my stomach.

"Do you not like the name, Jonathan?" asked the barmaid.

"No, quite the contrary – I love the name; it just reminds me of events in my life that I would rather forget."

"Do you want to talk about it?"

"Not really. Seriously bad shit happens; that's life, I guess."

"That's my task for the evening then."

"What?" I asked.

"To give you some good memories to go with my name."

There was still no one else around in the bar and a silence now passed between us.

"I bet you a drink that you can't spell my name correctly," she said.

"That's the easiest drink that I'll ever win. It's M-E-L-I-S-S-A," I replied with naïve confidence.

She laughed.

"I'll join you in taking a glass of house red wine. As you can taste yourself, it's not the greatest drop of wine on this planet, but it's very palatable – particularly when free!"

"OK, how do you spell your name then?" I asked.

"Easy peasy, lemon squeezy – it's M-A-O-L-I fada-O-S-A."

I looked bewildered.

"It's Irish Gaelic. Do you like Dublin?" she asked.

"Next question!"

"Ah, it's a grand city to be sure – full of life and laughter and music and fun. There's no finer place to be in the world for a great night out."

"It must be in my DNA. There's just something about this city when it's raining that bugs me. And when I say bugs me, I mean really, really bugs me. I can't put my finger on it."

"Oh dear, a problem with my name *and* Dublin – this simply won't do, young man!"

We continued talking for ages and found that we shared a genuine passion and love for literature. The bar was still empty except for the two of us and the enchanting conversation flowed effortlessly.

After a couple of hours, I realised that I was starving and that the restaurant in the hotel was soon to close. I very reluctantly left the bar to make my way to the dining room.

I can't remember what I ate at all, only that I was thinking of Maolíosa throughout the meal. It had probably been five years since I'd talked at any length with a woman in a non-business environment.

She made me feel good about myself. More than that, she made me feel good about life. Being around her gave me a positive energy – energy that dispelled the grumpiness and tetchiness that had increasingly come with the lethargy and mundanity of my life.

Being with Maolíosa, I no longer felt quite so alone in the world.

**

After finishing my dessert I rushed back to the bar, hoping that Maolíosa would still be there. To my delight, she was, smiling and looking radiant.

The bar was still totally deserted apart from her.

"Who on earth designed this bar?" I asked.

"Probably the same eejit who designed this bar uniform. I normally love the colour green but the shade they use here is rather, how can I best say it, eccentric. Either that or colour blind."

I laughed and replied,

"I'm glad you said it and not me. Eccentric is the word I often use to describe the décor at the hotel."

"From what I understand, I think that the owners wanted to attract American tourists and make them feel at home. The problem is that it's neither beast nor fowl. I think that the brochure says the hotel has a unique 'Irish American' character. Unique pretty much sums it up – although not in a good way. "

I smiled and said,

"There's a good quote if I can remember it. Ah yes, 'it's impossible to have bad taste, but many have none at all'."

"I like that. Whose quote is it?"

"No idea, I just remember reading it once and it struck a nerve. It's almost like an Oscar Wilde quote, but it isn't."

"No, definitely not Oscar, I'd have recognised it. Changing the subject, I bet you didn't know that Maolíosa was a male name for most of its history, did you? It meant the servant of Jesus."

"You're joking, a male name? You're taking the Michael out of a poor Englishman," I replied.

"On my dear Ma's soul, that is the truth. I wouldn't lie to you. I think that there was once even an Earl of Orkney called Maolíosa."

"You do realise that you look about as un-male as it is possible to look?"

I cringed, very self-consciously, at the ineptness of my attempt at a compliment.

Maolíosa smiled and said,

"It's my first night working here you know – the regular bartender is off-sick."

"Did you get wet today?" I asked.

Maolíosa looked at me rather perplexed, perturbed even.

"I got soaked today in the queue waiting for a taxi," I said, hoping for sympathy.

"You poor thing."

There was a biting sarcasm in Maolíosa's voice.

"You're right. It's just me being a miserable old grump as usual and feeling sorry for myself. My apologies!"

"I'll forgive you. Only this once mind."

"I certainly shouldn't be complaining anyway. The weather in Dún Laoghaire was clearly nothing like as bad though as what's been going on this week on the west coast of Ireland. What with that family's boat going missing in the storm and all that."

Maolíosa's eyes clearly moistened as she spoke the words,

14

"How could such a thing like that happen in such a peaceful and picturesque place? For me Galway is the most magical place on this planet."

A single tear ran down Maolíosa's face.

"That's what the taxi driver said to me," I replied.

Maolíosa's face brightened before she said,

"I'm sorry but it's closing time."

"But it can't be. It's only…"

"…One in the morning. I was told very strictly that the bar had to close at one in the morning," she added.

I could not believe it. The hours with Maolíosa had passed in what seemed like minutes. Even more scarcely believable, I'd genuinely enjoyed being with a woman – something I'd not felt in a long, long time.

"It's been nice to meet you, Jonathan."

"You too, Maolíosa."

"See you then."

"Hopefully, yes," I said.

Maolíosa smiled and said,

"Oh, I'm sure we'll meet again."

I thought about kissing her on the cheek and then thought better of it.

Parents and Childhood

I was born in Berkshire, England – Reading to be precise – to parents Robert and Mary Melton on September 20th 1966. They christened me Jonathan Paul. "Good names from the Bible", my mother used to say even though I never remember her as a religious person in the slightest.

My early pre-school childhood was an enjoyable one. As a family, we were comfortable financially, living in a pleasant part of Reading in a semi-detached house with a small garden.

We were a happy family in those days, or at least that's how I remember it; arguments in Reading certainly seemed few and far between.

I particularly loved how my father and I used to play regularly together in the garden.

I was the only child – something that I never gave any thought to at the time, but in later years, I came to understand that it was something that had a very significant impact on my parents' marriage.

During my initial years at primary school, I wasn't a healthy child, like many children who ultimately become very healthy adults. It seemed that I was off ill every school term at one point – mumps, chickenpox, measles, German measles, scarlet fever, and shingles even. You name it – between the ages of five and seven, the odds were that I had most common illnesses and ailments at some point.

And through every illness, I remember my mother being there – tending to my needs, caring for me, looking after me.

As a child, I viewed my mother as an angel of kindness, my very own 'Mother Mary'. Like myself, my mother had dark brown curly hair and deep dark brown eyes to match. I felt that she could do no wrong and I only had to look into her eyes or feel her warm embrace for the world to seem a better and safer place.

**

Shortly after my seventh birthday, my parents decided to move house to somewhere bigger in Taplow, a nice enough village located between Maidenhead and Slough – it had more bedrooms, a bigger garden and all the usual middle class suburban trappings. To the outside world, everything was how it should be.

However, my world and perspective on life changed overnight – in that almost from the very first moment that we stepped into our new house, my parents seemed to do nothing but row and argue. My father was increasingly never there; he would always leave for work early and return late in the evening – usually after I'd gone to bed.

Some nights I only realised that my father had come home when I was awoken by the sound of my parents arguing. Weekends were generally the same story with my father either spending more time at work or locked away in his study at our new house – not speaking to either my mother or me and certainly no longer spending any time playing with me in the garden.

Things became so bad between my parents that my mother left home to stay with her sister.

I couldn't go with her due to school, and I missed my mother deeply. Those 14 days seemed like an eternity, and I remember lying awake at night frightened that she would never come back. At times, I worried that my mother had left because of me, and the reason that my father never came home was because he didn't like me.

As an eight year old, I simply didn't understand what was going on in my life as my parents' marriage disintegrated in front of me.

I felt paralysed by fear, isolated and abandoned.

I even wet the bed one night.

**

My father persuaded my mother to come back with promises that he would change and that he'd be home more often. For a while, he was true to his word. However, less than six months after my mother returned, my father was back in his old routine.

My mother and I did not doubt that he was working very hard, but, to us, work had come to consume and dominate his life.

As spring became summer in 1975, in my father's absence, I would spend hours in the garage on my own throwing a ball against the wall and hitting it with either a tennis racket or a cricket bat. Given the hours and hours of practice, unsurprisingly I became very adept with a cricket bat or tennis racket.

Come the summer holiday, I had no friends and was, to all intent and purpose, a loner, with my mother as the sole focal point of my life. Sadly, though, my mother was clearly feeling as isolated as I was. I often saw her crying privately to herself.

17

As the summer of 1975 drifted by, I increasingly started to listen to the arguments that my mother had with my father. Sadly, the arguments followed a depressingly similar pattern.

"I'm totally fed up with this, Robert."

"Fed up with what, for God's sake, I just don't know what you want, Mary."

"I want the man that I married back in my life."

"I'm the same loyal, faithful, honest man that I've always been."

"That isn't what I mean, and you know it."

"Yes, I know. I know it's my fault. Everything is my fault!"

"I'm not saying that."

"Yes, you are."

"No, I'm not!"

"Well, what are you saying, woman?"

"I'm saying I want more from life. I want a husband that I see and do things with. Robert, we've not even had a holiday this year! I'm fed up and poor Jonathan's so miserable without you around. He's no friends at all."

"And I suppose that's my fault as well?!"

"It's this house. Ever since we moved to this house, you've got worse. We used to be happy."

"Don't be stupid, Mary. For God's sake, I just don't know what's the matter with you. You have a house that scores of women would give their eye teeth for, and yet all you do is complain. Nag, nag, nag. All the time."

"Sod the house, Robert. I'd live in a cardboard box if it meant that you ever gave me your time – I need to feel that you do actually want to be with me – that I'm your wife and not your skivvy. I'm like a leper in my own home."

"I've had enough of this melodramatic crap. I'm going to my study to work."

**

At the end of February 1976, not long after Valentine's Day, it was my mother's 31st birthday. While I was at school, she'd started going to a local gymnasium and was looking as fit and healthy as I'd ever seen her.

For her birthday, I'd saved up my pocket money for weeks to buy her a nice card and a bunch of flowers. As I walked into the kitchen to give her my card and flowers, I saw my mother clutching a card to her chest and smiling. The smile grew wider when she saw the flowers that I'd bought her.

"Are they for me, Bub?" she asked.

"Of course they are. I love you, Mum."

"They're beautiful, so beautiful. I'm so lucky to have you as a son."

"What did Dad get you?" I asked.

"Nothing. He didn't even say 'Happy birthday' to me this morning. He forgot Valentine's Day, which was bad enough, but now he's forgotten my birthday."

"Didn't he send that card that you're holding now?"

"No, someone else sent that. Someone who actually seems to care about me," she replied.

"Maybe Dad will bring in something with him for you tonight," I replied.

"And pigs might fly."

**

Sadly my mother was right. There were to be neither flying pigs that evening nor any birthday card or present from my father.

Instead, my mother calmly announced over dinner,

"I'm leaving you, Robert. Now, today."

"Is this some sick joke, Mary?" responded my father.

"No, Robert. Our marriage has become a sick joke. You don't even remember my birthday anymore."

"Shit, Mary, I'm sorry," a rare apologetic tone to my father's voice.

"No, you're not. You're wrapped up in your own pathetic little world of self-pity. You're not sorry at all. You need help, Robert. You're sick."

"I'm not sick. Don't say that."

There was stony silence from my mother. My father continued,

"For God's sake Mary, you're not going to leave us just because I forgot your birthday."

"No, Mum. Don't leave. Please. PLEASE," I injected panic stricken with fear.

My mother turned to me and said,

"Bub, I love you so very, very much but I cannot continue living like this with your father."

I began to cry – I was almost frenetic with fear.

"Mum, I beg you. Please don't leave me."

"Mary, please, if not for me then for the boy. Please stay," added my father.

My mother came over to me and gave me the biggest hug. She looked into my eyes.

"Now listen to me, Bub. I love you and I'll still see you, and I'll always want to see you but I've got to leave. For my own sanity, I've got to get out of this God-forsaken house. I can't spend a minute or a second more with your father. He's destroying himself, and he'll destroy me with him if I don't leave."

I could see tear upon tear rolling down my mother's cheeks. She gave me one more very big hug. She then collected her belongings, which she'd clearly packed before my father came home, and calmly walked towards the front door.

"Don't go, Mary. I beg you. I'll get on my knees and beg if you want."

"I don't want you to beg. You need help Robert. You're sick. You know you are."

"How many times do we have to have this bloody argument? I'm not sick, woman. There's nothing wrong with me, for God's sake. All I need to do is be home a bit more. I'll do that Mary. I promise. I really mean it this time."

"I've had enough of your false promises. I've taken as much as I can take from you. I don't see why I should suffer because of your pathetic self-pity and ridiculous, totally unfounded insecurities. All I want is a little love and happiness in my life, that's all."

"Please, Mary. Please!"

Before my mother closed the front door behind her, she said,

"As long as I live I'll never step into this house again."

I prayed every night for months for my mother to return but my prayers went unanswered.

After a time, I simply assumed that there was no God.

**

Inevitably, my parents' divorce was messy and prolonged. It was clear that my mother wanted nothing financially from my father. All that she ever wanted from the divorce was for me to be with her.

However, my father fought the custody battle with an aggression and steely determination that wasn't seen in him before or after. He hired the best, most expensive lawyer – a horrible, creepy man with very greasy slicked back hair called Mr Bennett – and I remember the first meeting between my father and Mr Bennett at our house vividly.

"What do you know about the man that your estranged wife is now living with?" asked Mr Bennett.

"He's a fitness instructor," replied my father with some distress.

"Excellent. And where do they live?"

"I understand that it's a small bedsit located above the gymnasium where he works."

"Even better."

"Why?" asked my father.

"The way that I see it, the way that I'm sure I can *facilitate* the jury to see it, is that your wife chose to leave of her own free will a hard-working, upstanding, pillar of the community for a muscle-bound fitness instructor with limited prospects."

"Sounds good to me," replied my father with a rare glint in his eye.

"We'll look into this man's background as well. If we're lucky, we'll find that he's moved around a lot in the past few years – possibly a few ex-lovers. It shouldn't be too difficult to portray this man as a complete 'fly by night'."

"So you think I have a good chance of gaining custody of Jonathan then, Mr Bennett?"

"I'd say that you have a very good chance indeed. The point that I will make very strongly in court is that if your estranged wife truly loved Jonathan then she wouldn't have abandoned him for a life of sin and debauchery in a bedsit above a gymnasium. I think that we won't have too much difficulty in *persuading* the court that your estranged wife is a selfish, wanton home breaker not worthy of having the custody of a child."

"But Mum didn't abandon me, and she's not a home breaker. Mum still wants to see me. She promised. Dad, why won't you let her see me?" I interjected.

"She can see you anytime she wants," replied my father.

"Only if she comes to this house."

"Yes, I think that's reasonable."

"But you know that she'll never come here. She's frightened that you'll destroy her. She said so."

"I wasn't trying to destroy her. I know that it's painful, son, but she abandoned us both."

"No, she didn't. She left you, not me. You were trying to destroy her."

I was by now screaming.

"Jonathan, I think that you should leave the room. Go and play in the garden or something."

"No, I won't."

"I said leave the room," the firmness in my father's voice all too evident.

21

"No," I replied.

With that, my father picked me up screaming, dragged me to my bedroom and locked the door. I screamed and shouted for a while, but no one listened.

Mr Bennett never came to our house again.

**

My father took a couple of months on leave from work to spend time looking after me during the summer holidays. During his extended leave, he kept saying to me over and over again,

"While we've got each other, son, we'll be OK."

At the beginning of September, to look after the two of us, my father hired the first of what would prove to be many housekeepers.

Even on my tenth birthday, my father refused to let me see my mother. He heaped a mass of birthday presents on me but the present that I most wanted, above anything, was to see my mother.

The sad and sorry divorce settlement between my mother and father was finally reached on November 17th 1976. My father won custody of me and it was decided that my mother would only have access to me one day a week.

I would spend every Sunday with her – she would pick me up at 10 in the morning and then drop me off at six in the evening. To my considerable frustration and anger, I had no say whatsoever in the matter. Whenever I tried to speak to my father about my mother, he merely kept repeating the same words.

"She abandoned us both. We've just got to get on with our lives. While we've got each other, we'll be all right."

From the day that the courts made their decision, my father always referred to my mother as 'she' or 'her'. I used to cringe inside when I heard the way that my father spoke about my mother.

My sole consolation at the time was that at least I would finally get to see my mother again. I kept telling myself that she would reassure me – that somehow she would make things better.

A Solitary Child

I remember vividly the first day I spent with my mother after she had left. Although late autumn, it was a nice day and the two of us happily walked around a local park and she took me for a Wimpy hamburger for lunch.

"Dad said that you abandoned us both."

"He shouldn't say that. It's not true," my mother replied.

"That's what I said, Mum. You left because Dad was trying to destroy you."

My mother looked shocked at my words.

"You shouldn't say that either."

"But that's what you said the night that you left, Mum."

"Maybe I did but I was very emotional that night. I didn't want to leave you. It's simply that your father and I couldn't live together anymore. He made me so very unhappy, and I think, to be honest, I made him unhappy. There are things that I'll tell you when you get older that will hopefully help you understand."

"Tell me them now. I want to understand now."

"No, Bub, it's not right."

"But Mum."

"No buts, Bub. I get so little time with you I want us to have nice days together, not to talk about your father."

"OK, if you say so."

"Yes I do say so. Do you want a big ice cream for dessert?"

"You bet."

**

As my mother dropped me off at the gates of the house in Taplow, she gave me a big hug. We were both crying.

"Now go in to your father."

"I want to stay with you, Mum," I pleaded.

"I'm sorry, but you can't."

"You don't want me, do you?"

"Now look at me. I want you more than anything in the world but the courts have made their decision. If you don't go to your father now then they'll never let me see you again. You don't want that, do you?"

I shook my head.

"Go on, Bub, be brave. Wipe the tears from your eyes and I'll see you next weekend."

**

On the weekend before my eleventh birthday, my mother brought a man with her. She introduced me to him, but I was too bewildered, too annoyed, to remember his name.

All I could see was this enormous man with jet-black hair towering over me like Man Mountain. I also couldn't help but notice how facially similar he was to my mother.

Although Man Mountain was always kind and polite to me, I immediately decided that I didn't like him and there was to be no changing my mind.

"Happy birthday, Jonathan," said Man Mountain as he handed me a parcel.

"We'd have got you more but we don't have a lot of money at the moment," added my mother.

I opened the parcel to find a new tennis racket. It was precisely what I wanted – but the fact that Man Mountain was there undeniably totally spoiled it for me.

"Thanks, Mum."

I gave her the biggest hug I could muster.

"We both bought it for you."

I doubt if I said more than five words all that Sunday as my mother and Man Mountain walked around together hand in hand.

For the first time, I wasn't in tears when I left my mother at the end of the day.

**

Whereas the previous year my father had showered me with presents, there was nothing that year from him on my birthday – not even a card.

I was very angry with him.

The following Saturday I was playing, as usual, in the garage with my new racket smashing a ball against a wall again and again when my father came in.

"Where on earth did you get that racket?"

24

"Mum gave it me for my birthday last Sunday."

I could see the look of horror immediately on my father's face. He put his head in his hands and rubbed his head up and down in frustration as he said,

"God, I'm really sorry."

"Don't worry, Dad."

My father came over and held me tightly. There was real emotion in his voice as he said,

"You're a good boy, Jonathan. I'm just really struggling since she left me for that muscle-bound wanker. But while we've got each other, we'll be all right – yeah?"

"Yes, Dad, we will. What's a muscle-bound wanker?"

"Not a nice person, that's all, son."

As I looked my father in the face, I could see that he'd been crying. All my annoyance that he'd forgotten my birthday turned in an instant to sympathy.

To try to put things right my father took me out to the shops that afternoon and spent hundreds of pounds on me.

I can't remember a single present that he bought me.

**

The next day I was waiting as ever at 10am at the front gates of our house for my mother to collect me. Man Mountain was once again in tow when she arrived.

As with the previous Sunday, my mother and Man Mountain were very loving, caring and affectionate towards each other – very different from how she had been with my father.

I did think to ask my mother and Man Mountain what a 'muscle-bound wanker' was but thought better of it.

Over lunch my mother asked me,

"What did your father get you for your birthday?"

"He forgot – but he bought me loads of presents yesterday."

"Sadly that's your father all over. He's wrapped up in his own little world of self-pity with no care for anyone else, and he thinks the occasional grand gesture somehow makes it all right. He's not well. My one hope is that I could get you away from that destructive environment. You're a young boy. You should be enjoying life."

"Dad's fine. His only problem is that you left. You have no idea of how he feels or how I feel."

"So tell me how you feel. Talk to me, Bub, I'm your mother."

"You're not my mother, you're a home breaker."

**

As 1977 became 1978, little by little, Sunday by Sunday, my resentment turned to genuine anger at my mother and Man Mountain. Like my father, I began to think of my mother as 'she' or 'her'. I also started to share my father's sense of abandonment.

To make matters worse, children can be very cruel at that age and many of my classmates at school were making my life such a misery, often reducing me to tears.

If you show weakness then some children will pick on you all the more and that's certainly what happened to me. Playground chants would increasingly come to haunt me.

"Melton's lost his mother
He doesn't have a brother
He's got no friends at all
'Cos his willy's very small."

After a while I stopped crying at the various chants and darker, angrier emotions, all directed at my mother and Man Mountain, began to replace the hurt inside of me.

**

One Sunday shortly before Christmas, for the first time in ages and ages, my mother came to meet me on her own.

"I've something to tell you," she said.

"What, are you coming home to Dad and me?" I asked.

My mother looked at me bewildered.

"No, I'll never come back to your father. Never ever – I love you so much and miss you so much, but I simply cannot live with your father."

Disappointment showed clearly on my face.

My mother took a deep breath and said,

"Actually, I'm going to have another baby."

"How could you do this? Playing happy families with your Man Mountain friend whilst you have left Dad and me in such misery and loneliness – I hate you for what you've done to us."

My mother started crying. It didn't bother me one iota.

"I never meant to hurt you, Bub. I love you. Your father's not well, and there's simply no helping him. I so wish it didn't have to be like this. I want us to be together."

"Well, I don't!" I shouted back with a snarl in my voice.

My mother put her head in her hands.

After my outburst, my mother and I said little more that Sunday.

**

My father was doing his best to look after me but the reality was that he was struggling to look after himself. Our situation wasn't helped by the fact that housekeepers continued to come and go with ever increasing rapidity, some staying as little as a couple of weeks.

My father's solution was to send me to boarding school in the spring of 1979.

Boarding School

The boarding school wasn't somewhere select like Eton or Harrow but located in the South West of England on the edge of Tiverton. It was nice, homely and friendly.

It was like a fresh start for me.

Most of the teachers were kind and, unlike in Taplow, my fellow pupils were not cruel to me at all. At Tiverton, I became stronger, more resilient and confident by the day.

I was lucky in that the first full term I had at the school was the summer term. Unlike my previous school, at Tiverton they played both cricket and tennis. These were without doubt my favourite sports and the school had such excellent facilities for cricket with proper practice nets and a small picturesque ground. But most of all, it was the quite delightful tennis courts that captured my heart.

There were around 13 or 14 of us at the school who played cricket seriously and we all got on well as friends whereas the tennis was somewhat more select as only four or five of us played to any sort of decent standard.

But whatever sport I was playing, the weekends that summer term were like a holiday as we'd play from dawn till dusk – always encouraged, always cajoled by the ever present sports master John Tasker.

John Tasker was and is a quite splendid man, an English teacher in addition to being the sports master. Over six feet tall with dashing moustache and sideburns, John made an immediate impression the first time I met him at cricket nets.

"Pads on, Jonathan!" he said.

"Yes, sir," I replied.

"It's yes, John."

I was taken aback.

"Jonathan, I will always treat you like an adult. All I expect you in return is that you behave like an adult."

"Yes, John."

"Now get in those nets and show us how good you are."

And if John Tasker was not enough to lift my spirits, then there was always my fellow pupil and tennis and cricket Captain for my year, David Pritchett.

From the very first moment that I met him, I liked David. With flowing blonde hair, even at 12, David had enormous charisma, confidence and self-belief that was infectious.

"Jeez, you can bat!" he said to me.

"Thanks," I replied.

"And you play tennis?"

"Yes."

"As well as you can bat?"

"Probably better."

"Brilliant, we're going to take on the world – and if not the world, then at least most of Southern England. What's your name again?"

"Jonathan."

"Everyone in the team has a nickname. Do you have another Christian name?"

"Yes, Paul."

"Perfect. From now on you will be J.P."

**

That summer I played in every Under-13 cricket game for the school. I was helped by the fact that my mother and Man Mountain drove hundreds of miles to come to watch me play. I quickly worked out that the longer I batted in the game then the less that I would to have to speak to them. I scored a lot of runs as a result.

It was also proving to be a truly excellent summer for my tennis. As a team of two, David Pritchett and I successfully made our way to the semi-final of the South West England Under-13 tennis competition – the final of which was to be held at Tiverton School itself.

Each match would consist of David and me each playing a game of singles and then a game of doubles against the opposition. To my enormous pride, throughout the entire tournament, I had yet to lose a singles match – something that I was told had never been achieved before in the history of Tiverton School.

The semi-final was early in June. Before the match, my mother's Man Mountain came up to me and said,

"Do you want to knock up before the match, Jonathan? I played tennis for Essex a few years ago."

"I'm sure that was very nice for you," I replied with the most sarcastic tone I could muster.

"Please don't be like that, Bub, it was a kind offer. He's a very good player. Maybe he can give you some tips," said my mother.

"Will the both of you just leave me alone? I need to focus on my match. I'm playing soon," I shouted.

I convinced myself that I wasn't being rude, merely that to 'knock up' with Man Mountain would have been disloyalty of the highest order to my father.

Much to our delight, David and I both won our singles games to march triumphantly into the final and, to add to the elation, the following three Sundays my mother and Man Mountain did not make the long journey down to Devon as my mother was giving birth to her 'wonderful' new baby.

Such was my state of mind that those three Sundays were amongst the best three Sundays of the whole summer term.

**

The next time that my mother and Man Mountain came down to Devon, it was for the tennis final itself.

To my considerable surprise my father had also decided that day to come and watch me play for the first time that summer. My mother was clearly shocked to see my father there. I took enormous satisfaction in her embarrassment and discomfort over the matter.

The new baby was there as well and this merely added to the already fraught atmosphere. The baby seemed to be permanently crying and, as a result, my mother was always giving it a big loving hug.

As she and Man Mountain were doting together over the baby, pandering to its every need, quite oblivious to my father's presence, my father was growing more and more agitated as the day wore on. My earlier pleasure was now turning to anger.

David Pritchett was to play the first game of singles and to be honest I hardly watched his game as my attention was focused on my father and my mother's new family clan.

As it was, David won easily enough and now it was my turn. A personal victory would see our school win the tournament and for myself, establish a record of having never lost a match throughout the entire tournament.

A sizeable crowd of support from the school had gathered to watch the final. However, with what was going on with my parents I couldn't focus on the game – no matter how hard I tried.

My opponent served first. He was very big for his age and carrying more than a few extra pounds over his optimum weight.

"Move him around the court, Jonathan. He's not going to be particularly mobile," was John Tasker's excellent advice.

However to put that into practice I needed to get the ball into play and, for the first game at least, this proved an impossibility as four booming first serves flew past me. Matters didn't improve in the second game as I lost my serve to 15. Another four booming serves and there I was – three-love down.

My opponent may not have been mobile. There again he didn't need to be.

"Don't worry, Jonathan, he'll burn himself out. He won't keep serving like this. Slow the game down and remember to move him around," said John as I slumped in my chair.

"OK," I responded.

My mother's new baby continued to cry.

"I wish she and her whole bloody family would just sod off," I muttered before taking to the court again.

Little more than 10 minutes later, I'd lost the first set by six games to one.

The second set began little better and I quickly found myself a break of serve down, and although I improved a little, I was staring defeat in the face at 5-3 down.

What John Tasker had said was true, my opponent has started to burn himself out, the summer sun was sapping his energy and his serve had lost its bite and venom. However, instead of taking John's advice of slowing the game down and moving my portly opponent around the court, I was trying to outhit him.

All I felt on court was anger at my mother.

Finally, at the jaws of defeat, I started to take John's advice. I won my own service game easily and then broke my opponent's serve by, for the first time, using a touch of subtlety rather than the previous battering ram approach.

I held serve again and suddenly I felt that the set was in my control at 6-5 in front and with a set point on my opponent's serve.

I played a very nice approach shot to my opponent's weaker backhand side and it left me with the easiest of volleys to clinch the set. Unfortunately, my mother's scrawny little monster of a child chose that very moment to let out an ear-piercing shriek.

I netted an awful volley.

My dreadful error was compounded by two thunderous serves from my portly opponent to make it six games all.

"Again, Jonathan, again," urged John,

"You've won the set once now win it again."

The little monster, however, continued to bawl.

I started the game with a double fault and that was followed by more careless and loose shots. As another tame forehand found the net, my serve was lost.

I threw my racket hard to the floor in anger and frustration – bringing words of admonishment from the umpire.

As I sullenly picked my racket from the floor it was evident that the frame was smashed and of no further use.

"Take my racket, J.P. But please don't break it," offered David as I slumped for the final time in my chair.

John Tasker was silent but I knew him well enough to know that he was decidedly displeased. I slunk out almost apologetically for what was the final game. By now, I was completely demotivated as my mother's baby screamed on and on and on. Inevitably I lost the game for a 6-1, 8-6 defeat.

After shaking hands with my opponent, I wandered towards David and John and handed David his racket back.

"Bad luck, J.P. We'll win the doubles together. We can still win this. No problem," said David full of confidence.

John Tasker was, however, somewhat less sympathetic.

"I'd like to talk to you, Jonathan – in private!"

We walked out of earshot of everyone and then John said what he had to say,

"That was unacceptable behaviour. No matter how frustrated and angry you were, at Tiverton we will not tolerate you throwing your racket to the floor in that manner. You are not only representing yourself, you are representing this school and such actions are not acceptable in any way whatsoever."

"I'm sorry. You're right. It won't happen again when David and I play the deciding doubles game."

"I don't think that you fully understand me. When I say that such actions are unacceptable and will not be tolerated, that is exactly what I mean. Paul Davenport will play the doubles decider with David."

"But John."

John Tasker has the sternest of looks on his face. It became clear any negotiation on the matter was out of the question.

"Yes, John," I responded.

"That's better. Now go and take a shower, cool off and come out and cheer David and Paul to victory."

As I walked alone to the changing rooms, I was close to tears.

Once in the changing rooms, as I kicked out brutally at the shower wall, I imagined in my mind that I was kicking out at my own mother.

Freshly washed and in my school uniform, I went over to stand with my father. The fact that David and Paul Davenport were being soundly beaten and that poor Paul Davenport was having a veritable nightmare of a match did little to lift my spirits.

"That screaming brat of hers made you miss that easy volley on set point didn't it, son?" asked my father between games.

"It most certainly did – I'm convinced that I'd have won if I'd have put that volley away."

"I'm sure you would as well. Just look at her, doting on that child. She barely watched any of your game."

"I know, I know. She doesn't care about us. Never did. I'm sorry Dad, but I need to go and sit with the team."

"You go on, I'll see you later."

Although I did my best to cheer on David and Paul and although John Tasker did his best to offer his good advice and encouragement, our school team ended up losing the final.

**

After the awards presentation for winners and runners-up alike, the crowd made their way away from the tennis courts. As the crowd dispersed, my mother and Man Mountain came towards me with the baby in tow.

"Bad luck, Bub. Can I have a look at your medal?" asked my mother.

"You can keep the bloody medal. I don't want it. It would have been a winner's medal but for that screaming brat of yours."

"Don't speak to your mother that way. You break the racket we bought you and now you shout at your mother when she asks to see your medal. You need to learn some discipline and manners, young man," said Man Mountain.

"Oh, sod off, you muscle-bound wanker, just leave me alone," I shouted at the top of my voice.

My father rushed over – in time for my mother to launch a tirade at him.

"Here's the problem, I tell you. Honestly Robert, you're turning my own son against me. It's your poison that I hear coming out of his mouth. You want everyone to be as miserable as you are. You're sick, Robert. You need help. I've said that for years. "

"No, he's not," I responded.

33

"You're young and impressionable, Bub. I don't blame you."

"For God's sake, stop calling me Bub. I'm nearly thirteen and I hate it."

"I'm sorry but all I want you is for you to be happy and have a chance in life. And you won't, not surrounded by all his sick poisonous nonsense. Trust me, I know," replied my mother.

"I'm fine. I really like it here. I have friends now. In fact, the only thing that makes me unhappy is you, him and your screaming bloody baby. I'm fed up with you coming to see me. I'm fed up with you saying Dad is sick. I just wish you'd stay away and leave me alone."

My mother started to cry and the broadest of grins crossed my father's face.

My mother saw this and, clearly incensed, screamed,

"Look at you, Robert – Mr Bloody Self-righteous. You say you love your son but look what he's becoming. You're not a father to that boy."

My father's grin disappeared.

"Fuck off, Mary. Just fuck off. I love my son."

"He's your son when it suits you, isn't he, Robert? But only when it suits you."

"Leave it, Mary. It's not worth it. Leave the idiot to his world of self-pity," said Man Mountain.

"And what's it got to do with you? Just sod off. Leave Dad and me alone," I interjected.

"You ungrateful little shit. We drive hundreds of miles every weekend to see you. What little spare money we have, we spend trying to please you and…"

"Sod off, you wanker. I've told you twice now. Just piss off, you stupid muscle-bound wanker," I shouted.

Man Mountain was incensed by my outburst and moved as though to strike me. Although he undeniably pulled back at the last moment, I slipped whilst moving to defend myself and caught his arm in my face as I fell to the ground.

"Shit, I'm sorry, so sorry. Are you all right?" asked Man Mountain.

However, the words were barely out of his mouth before my father charged Man Mountain and they both fell to the ground, grappling together.

"Don't you ever, ever, ever fucking hit my son, you cunt," screamed my father.

"All right, all right, calm down. I don't want to fight with you," pleaded Man Mountain.

Seeing the melee and fracas from afar, John Tasker sprinted over to break up the two men sprawling on the floor. Man Mountain was only too willing to pull himself away, but John had to restrain my father.

"What on earth is going on here?" asked John.

"I'm Jonathan's father and that cunt there hit my son," screamed my father.

"Is that true, sir?"

"No, it isn't. I didn't mean to anyway. It happened by accident – when he slipped, I made contact with him. I'm truly, truly sorry," replied Man Mountain.

"Then, sir, I must respectfully ask that you leave the school grounds immediately."

"Please, Mr Tasker, it's a family quarrel that got a bit out of hand, he meant no harm," pleaded my mother.

"When I say immediately, I mean immediately. Now if you want me to call the police then I will do. Otherwise be on your way and be very prompt about it."

"Come on, Mary, let's go," said Man Mountain, the air of resignation in his voice all too evident.

The two of them and the baby went on their way. The baby, who seemed to be permanently crying during the earlier tennis match, had been silent whilst the madness of the previous few minutes had been going on.

As they walked away almost out of earshot, my father shouted a few parting words,

"My solicitor will be in contact with you tomorrow. Think on that during your journey home."

**

After the madness of that day, my mother, Man Mountain and the new baby stopped coming to see me on a Sunday.

Some months later, my father told me, almost in passing, that they had moved to a part of East Anglia – miles away from Taplow and even further away from my school in Devon.

However, my mother's words "He's your son when it suits you, isn't he, Robert? But only when it suits you," were to linger long in my mind.

Memories of My Father

I returned to Taplow at the end of summer term. It was a glorious warm summer's day, but the house was unwelcoming – immaculately clean but devoid of soul, without a single picture or photo in sight.

As soon as my father and I arrived, we were greeted by the housekeeper, who had a face like thunder as she tore into my father,

"I've had enough of you, Mr Melton. I've had enough of your foul moods. I've had enough of cooking for you and you not coming home. I've had enough of your ungrateful manner. But most of all, I've had enough of your drinking. There isn't enough money in the kingdom of China to keep me here a moment longer. Goodbye!"

The housekeeper slammed the door and left.

"Kingdom of where?" asked my father.

"China, I think."

"Looks like a take-away then, son."

**

The next morning there was a knock at the door. My father answered it. A blonde woman of medium build in her mid-forties was there with an enormous smile on her face.

"You'll be needing a new housekeeper, I understand," said the woman in an accent I'd not heard before.

"Yes, as it happens. Who sent you?" asked my father.

"Does it matter?"

"Not really. The kitchen is through there. Lunch would be nice. There should be enough food in the fridge for you to put something together."

Lunch was indeed wonderful and while we were eating, the new housekeeper asked me,

"And who might you be, chiseler?

"Chiseler?" I asked.

She smiled before saying,

"Ah, it's what we Dublin people call little people."

"I'm Jonathan."

36

"And I'm Annie and very pleased to meet your acquaintance, chiseler."

My father sighed as his mood visibly darkened.

"You're here to be a housekeeper, not to speak during meal times and certainly not befriend my son with your Irish nonsense. Is that clear?"

"Yes, sir, it is," replied Annie.

**

As July came to an end, I grew ever more lethargic. Most days I wouldn't get out of bed at all – after all, there was nothing to get up for – particularly if there was no cricket or tennis on television. I remember permanently lying in bed listening to either my father's collection of Beatles records or the sound of the rain beating on the window.

It seemed to rain an awful lot that summer.

I wandered down to the kitchen one day for a drink of water. With Annie's arrival, the kitchen had become the one room in the house which was warm and welcoming.

"Chiseler, can you keep a secret?" she asked.

"Yes," I replied.

It was a rare moment of excitement for me.

"Can we talk occasionally? I won't tell your Da if you won't."

"I won't tell. I'm really bored!"

"Don't you have any friends, chiseler?"

"Not here. All the kids around here hate me."

"Ah, that is sad. I'll be your friend if you'll let me."

"I'd like that."

"That's grand. You've got a friend now."

"I've a friend at boarding school in Devon as well," I said.

"What's his name?"

"David. David Pritchett."

"Where does he live?"

"He lives in Devon – on a farm!"

"Fair play!" said Annie.

"He gave me his address."

"So, chiseller, your Auntie Annie thinks you should write to him."

"I should?"

"Yes, you should."

**

As Annie suggested, I wrote a letter to David and was delighted when I received a reply from him inviting me to spend a couple of weeks on his parents' farm near Barnstaple. After weeks, days and hours of boredom, I was so excited that I rang my father at work.

"Dad, Dad. David's invited me to his farm."

"Jonathan, is that you? What's the matter?"

"Nothing's the matter. It's David – he's invited me to his parents' farm in Devon."

"Who's David?"

"He's the school tennis and cricket captain."

"Oh yes, I remember."

"Well, can I go, Dad? Please Dad."

"We'll talk about it when I get home."

"Oh, Dad."

"I said we'll talk about it when I get home."

**

As soon as my father walked through the door that evening at around 8 p.m., I was at him.

"Can I go then, Dad?"

"Show me this letter."

My father read the letter at length.

"I need to ring David's father to check this is OK with him."

"Please can you do it now. The number's in David's letter."

"I'm tired and hungry, Jonathan, and I want something to eat. Then I've work to do in my study. I'll do it tomorrow."

My patience snapped with him.

"Yes, Dad and I'm bored and lonely sat around this house on my own. Why can't you do it now? It will only take a minute."

"Don't speak to me like that, young man! I said I will do it tomorrow, and tomorrow I will do it."

"Sorry."

"Now come and eat your dinner and let's have no more of this nonsense."

**

The following evening, my father arrived home much earlier than expected.

"I've bought you a new tennis racket, Jonathan. It's a much better one than the one that your mother bought you."

"Thanks, Dad."

"Do you want to try it out with me now then?" asked my father all excited.

"OK then," I responded with a shrug of the shoulders – more in bewilderment and surprise than a lack of interest.

We played together for a good hour or so. I'd forgotten that my father was a decent player, and as time passed I began to enjoy myself more and more. I even laughed at times and, perhaps more remarkably, so did my father. For once, our spirits were high.

"Dinner's ready!" shouted Annie

"Great, Annie. We'll be there in five minutes!"

It was the first time that I'd heard my father call her Annie.

Over dinner, my father spoke up.

"I called Brian Pritchett today."

I was decidedly taken aback – my father never spoke during meal times. I was perhaps more stunned that he'd actually called David's father.

"I must say that everything seems in order and if you want to go down to Devon for a couple of weeks then you have my permission. If you still want to go, that is. "

I jumped up from the table and flung my arms around his neck as he sat in his chair.

"Thanks, Dad, when can I go? When can I go?"

"After the Bank Holiday weekend, just before the new term is due to start. Now sit down eat the rest of your dinner."

When Annie came in later to serve the dessert, she gave me a wink. I smiled.

**

It was the Bank Holiday weekend before I was due to travel down on the train to see David. My father spent that whole three-day long weekend with me – he did no work at all nor did he step once into his study.

Many years later, I still treasure that gloriously sunny weekend.

On the Saturday, the two of us went to watch Middlesex play Surrey at Lord's Cricket Ground, a place with such a real aura and history to it.

As a young boy, along with the hope of being Wimbledon Champion, I used to dream of playing at Lord's Cricket Ground myself one day. The players pavilion is a truly majestic building and as the players walked down the Pavilion steps onto the playing field, I wished that one day I could be one of them.

**

On the Sunday, my father and I spent the day relaxing and playing around. Annie had taken the weekend off so we were all alone together. For a large part of the day, we played cricket in the garden as my father bowled to me for hours and hours as he'd done in Reading years before.

The two of us pretended that I was batting at Lords and when I'd made a hundred off his bowling, my father applauded and said,

"Well batted, son".

I raised my bat in acknowledgment of an imaginary crowd.

As it started to go dark and we couldn't play any more, my father cooked a barbecue. It had been a truly glorious day and I went to bed that night as happy as could be.

Little did I know that better still was yet to come.

**

I awoke on the Bank Holiday Monday and when I opened my bedroom curtains, I saw that my father had marked out the whole of the back lawn into a tennis court complete with tennis net, seats and everything.

I rushed downstairs with excitement.

"Dad, it's out of this world. You must have been up all night."

"Not really. I got up this morning as soon as it was light. It looks pretty good, doesn't it?"

"It's wow. Just wow," I replied.

"Play commences at midday today. It is the Men's Final of the Taplow Wimbledon Event," announced my father in a very official voice.

"Who's playing in the final?" I enquired.

"This year's final is Melton versus Melton – to be more precise R.V. Melton versus J.P. Melton – over the best of five sets. I expect no quarter to be given, young man. Now let's have a hearty breakfast of bacon and eggs to prepare for the big game."

Once again, my father displayed his unexpected culinary skills in the kitchen and, having allowed our breakfast to fully digest, we took the court for a warm up at around 11.45 a.m.

"Great shorts, Dad," I said observing with amusement his remarkable capacious and lengthy sportswear.

"1962 classics, son."

I couldn't contain my laughter. My father smiled a big, broad smile that I'd not seen for such a long, long time.

The match started precisely on time and, despite the absence of any crowd it proved to be a classic encounter. My father was true to his word of no quarter given and it was clear from the first few games that he was determined to win.

The first set was his comfortably at 6-2. I improved markedly to take the second set 6-4, but a run of four games enabled my father to take the third set 7-5 having been 5-3 down.

"There's life in the old dog yet. I should have made it a three set match," my father roared after a booming forehand return winner flew past my racket on set point.

The heat began to tell on my father and the fourth set was easily mine at 6-1. However, my father found a second wind to take a 3-0 lead in the final set only for me to produce the best tennis of the match and my life up to that point to take six of the next seven games to finally secure the match 2-6, 6-4, 5-7, 6-1, 6-4.

I can still remember virtually every point we played in the match.

After my winning shot, my father still found the energy to jump the net and give me an enormous hug after shaking my hand firmly.

"Quite superb young man, I thought that I had you there but you came through like a true champion – now for the Cup and presentation."

My father disappeared into the house and brought out an enormous silver trophy. I was speechless.

In an official tone, my father announced,

"And this year's winner of the Taplow Wimbledon Men's Championship is Mr J.P. Melton."

After handing me the trophy, my father stood and applauded.

I smiled the broadest possible of smiles.

"Well played, son!" shouted my father at the top of his voice.

**

My father took me to the station at Reading and he sat with me waiting for the train to come.

As I finally boarded the train, he said,

"Behave yourself now, Jonathan. And if you've any problems or want to come home early then, please, you know where I am."

"Thanks, Dad."

As the train pulled away, my father waved and smiled at me. It was a very forced, brave, smile. Most of all, it was a sad, weary, smile.

I felt as though I was some sort of rat deserting a sinking ship.

41

A Death Is Announced

My train arrived in Tiverton around lunchtime and David and his father were there at the station to meet me. David's father was a giant of a man – rather like my mother's Man Mountain, the only difference being that David's father was blonde rather than dark.

Unlike Man Mountain, however, I took an immediate liking to David's father.

"You must be Jonathan. I'm Brian Pritchett. Welcome to Devon."

Brian had the broadest smile, one that lit up the day and conveyed a genuine love of life. There were few occasions when I saw Brian without a smile on his face.

"Hello, J.P.," chipped in David.

After a 40 minute drive from the station in Brian's dirty old pickup truck, we were at the farm. In the heart of north Devon, the farm had been in the Pritchett family for nearly two centuries but it had been very well maintained.

The old farmhouse itself was a splendid building, full of character – but most of all, it exuded the warmth and the aura of a family content and at peace with itself.

David introduced me to his mother, Alison. Like Brian, she was a big, big, warm human being and she made me feel very welcome from the first moment I met her.

Shortly after arriving we all tucked into a hearty lunch of superbly cooked bacon and eggs – like Annie, Alison's cooking was very good, and within only a few minutes I felt more at home than I ever did in Taplow.

As I ate, David explained to me the rules of the farm.

"All visitors have to pull their weight around here, J.P. – you included."

"Fine by me."

"That means getting up at five thirty in the morning."

"OK!"

Over those 10 days, I learned how to milk cows and how to milk a goat by hand. They had been growing rape on the farm that summer, and at the end of every hard day's labour, I'd take Brian's sheepdog,

Dolly, for a walk on my own after the evening meal to watch the sunset come down over the fields.

And how glorious those bright yellow fields looked at the end of a summer's day. It was a new world for me.

David also had a brother and sister, Graham and Sarah, 18 months older and two years younger than him respectively. Both Graham and Sarah were very different from David – not least because David was much brighter and sharper than his siblings. Although Graham was the older, it was almost as though David was the elder son.

Even at 13 years of age, David's charisma filled a room when he walked in.

Graham was very much his father's son – a warm, friendly, practical child of average intelligence. Sarah meanwhile was similarly her mother's daughter, always in the kitchen, tidying the house and dreaming of marrying some local farmer when she grew up.

In contrast, David had won a scholarship to become a weekly boarder at the school we both went to in Tiverton. During my short ten days' stay on the farm, it was all too evident how much pride Brian took in his son's scholarship.

During my weekend there, David and I went to watch the local village cricket team – the two of us sat on the boundary edge, throwing the ball back to the players every time it came our way. While the players had their teas, David and I played around on the outfield with a bat and ball having fun.

**

Within a day of being back in Taplow I was once again in the old routine of life on my own, not communicating with anyone other than dear Annie and learning more of her Irish slang.

I couldn't wait for term to begin – although it was only a few days, the time waiting to go back to Tiverton dragged more than ever. All I wanted to be was back in Devon, either at Tiverton School or on the Pritchett Farm, and not stuck in boring, dull old Taplow.

The difference was most apparent at evening mealtime. Down on the farm in Devon, all six of us would be around the table, laughing and joking. The family dog, Dolly, and Harry the cat were always fighting and making a nuisance of themselves; whilst back in Taplow, we ate oppressed by the silent, almost funereal, atmosphere demanded by my father.

After dinner, my father and I would sit and watch television, exchanging only the occasional comment. I appreciated that my father

43

was very tired after a long day's work but then again Brian and Alison worked incredibly hard as well – yet the atmosphere at the farm was so very different.

**

It became the pattern of my life throughout 1980; weeks of enjoyment at boarding school together with occasional weekends of fun as a guest on the Pritchett Farm – milking cows and goats and walking dogs, fresh country air in my lungs and a spring in my step – punctuated by the boredom of being in Taplow.

In the summer holidays, I was able to spend four weeks on the Pritchett Farm. Every day seemed like an adventure, and my lasting memory was of seeing crops that I'd helped plant the previous autumn grow and be harvested.

Harvesting crops was hard work but with the sun shining it was great work – Graham, David and I always used to beg Brian for a chance to sit with him in the big combine harvester.

Looking back it always seemed to be raining in Taplow yet the sun always seemed to shine in Devon, even on a cold December day.

**

I particularly remember that the sun was shining when I heard that December that John Lennon had been shot in New York. I pondered to myself how inappropriate it was that the sun could shine at such terrible, terrible news.

That evening a few of us huddled around an old clapped out cassette player in our boarding school dormitory and played Beatles albums until the House Tutor, Reverend Brownley, arrived at our door.

I'd already come into extensive contact with Reverend Brownley earlier in the summer, since, sadly, he had taken over responsibility for the tennis team from John Tasker.

Unlike John, who would always pick the best team, Reverend Brownley believed in giving everyone a chance. This meant that David and I played on a rota basis. It also meant that our school team, which had won nearly every match the previous year now lost far more than it won.

Reverend Brownley was in his mid-forties of medium build, and with very short cropped grey hair. I could never imagine him having ever been a boy or young man – that somehow he would have come out of the womb already in his thirties and with his dog collar firmly in place.

As *Tomorrow Never Knows* played majestically to huddled masses on the cassette player, we heard Reverend Bromley's familiar pompous tones,

"Time for lights out, boys."

"Can't we play the second side of *Revolver* one more time, sir?" I asked.

"Tell me, why should I allow you to keep playing music after lights out time, Melton?"

"Because John Lennon died today, sir."

"If that's the case, then you should definitely turn the music off immediately. When I was a young man I remember John Lennon as a very arrogant long haired heathen who said that his little pop group were bigger than the son of the Almighty Himself."

"I think that you'll find, *sir*, that The Beatles were somewhat more than a *little pop group*," I replied.

"I'm not here to discuss the merits of The Beatles or John Lennon, I said lights out," commanded Reverend Brownley.

"All right then, you pompous old tosser," I muttered.

"I heard that, Melton. Rather like on the tennis court, you think that you're that much better than anyone else and that normal rules don't apply to you?"

I shrugged my shoulders.

"Don't you, BOY? I think an hour in detention reading the Book of Job might teach you some much needed respect and humility."

**

The depth of my father's problem truly hit home that Christmas. Annie's request that we have a festive tree was met with the most brutal of rebuttals from him.

My father was working on Christmas Eve and I wandered down to the kitchen to talk with Annie. She was putting a mass of empty alcohol bottles in the bin.

"Why does Dad drink so much?" I asked.

"People drink for many different reasons – to be happy, to live, to love, to share, but sadly also to forget, to take away pain. It depends on the person. My own Da drank terribly. It killed him in the end."

"Why did he drink?"

"To forget and take away the pain. Same as oul fella."

"Oul fella?" I asked.

45

"It's Dublin for your father."

"What did your father want to forget?"

"To try and forget that he'd done something terrible. He'd been drinking one day and was driving home when it was bucketing down. A chiseler ran into the road chasing a ball. My Da was too fluthered to stop and though the chiseler's father ran out and pushed him away, my Da ran into the chiseler's father and killed him."

"That's terrible," I said.

"Sadly there was more. The chiseler's Ma was there and she was with child herself. The shock was too much for her. She lost the baby and died herself in the process. My Da wanted to try to make amends but the chiseler was taken back to England by his grandma. My Da wanted to be punished but there were no laws on drink driving in those days. If he'd have been sent to the Joy, he'd have been better about it."

"What's the Joy?" I asked.

"It's Mountjoy Prison in Dublin. Anyway, he wasn't sent there and I watched him drink himself to death over fifteen long years. On his deathbed, he was still full of regret. If I have one hope it's that his poor soul will find some peace."

"What does my Dad want to forget?" I asked.

"The same thing, I suspect."

I was silent.

"The Lord helps those who help themselves. Remember that, chiseler. You'll be a young fella soon but never forget that the Lord helps those who help themselves."

**

My father arrived home very late on Christmas Eve. Not only was there was no tree in the house but there were no presents to be seen.

On Christmas Day morning, my father handed me an envelope containing a Christmas card and £200 – no little money back then.

"Sorry son, I didn't know what to buy you. It's better that you buy yourself something that you need."

"Thanks, Dad," I replied trying to conceal my disappointment at having not a single present to open.

"I've got you this," as I handed my father a bottle of vintage port with some Stilton bought from a mixture of saved up pocket money and money that Brian Pritchett had given me for helping out weekends at the farm.

"I don't know what to say," replied my father.

"Merry Christmas, Dad."

46

"Merry Christmas, son"

Annie came in and gave us both a card.

"I know you don't approve, Mr Scrooge, but it is Christmas, after all."

Even my father laughed.

However, the moment soon passed and by mid-afternoon, my father had descended into a drink-induced darkness and melancholy from which there was no escape.

I looked out of the window at our back garden – the white lines of the tennis court had long disappeared. Part of me wanted to give my father a big hug, like the one that he'd given me after our tennis match, but I felt as though I was intruding on his own private little world.

We barely spoke a word during the whole afternoon and evening.

By the end of Christmas Day, the bottle of port was empty, the Stilton untouched.

**

Early in the New Year, my father took me on the now familiar drive to Reading station to return to boarding school.

The car journey was silent.

As I boarded the train, I said,

"Bye, Dad."

"Bye son. Take care."

They were the last words that we would say to each other.

**

As January became February in 1981 on the seventh of the month, a cold winter's Thursday morning, I was taken out of class and walked over to the Headmaster's study by John Tasker.

I was greeted by an ashen faced Headmaster, Mr Parkerton. In his early fifties, well dressed with immaculately cut grey hair, Mr Parkerton had an aura that was undeniably kind. However, at the same time, everyone at the school knew that he was not a man to get on the wrong side of.

He invited me sit down and John joined the two of us.

"I'm very sorry, Jonathan, but in the early hours of this morning your father was killed in a road accident," said the Headmaster.

I sat there numb, senseless – unable to speak. It's true that the strangest things cross your mind at such points and all I could think about was that the Headmaster had never called me Jonathan before.

47

"If there's anything we can do then please let us know. All our thoughts are with you at this terrible time."

"Thank you, Headmaster."

I didn't cry at all but do remember that my legs started to shake uncontrollably.

A New Family, A New Life

Brian was an absolute rock following the death of my father. He was kind enough to accompany me to the inquest, held in East Berkshire Magistrates' Court in Maidenhead.

An elderly coroner presided over the sad events of the day as the inquest took evidence from a variety of sources.

A balding middle aged policeman, who attended the scene of the accident, was the first to give evidence,

"There was no indication whatsoever that other cars were involved in the accident, nor any skid marks to indicate that Mr Melton had lost control of the car before crashing through the barrier and down a large bank and into a small lake on the edge of Taplow. There were no witnesses to the accident. A Mr Fairburn saw the car when walking his dog around the lake at around six a.m. in the morning. The estimated time of death was around two a.m. on the morning of February twenty-first. It has been determined that Mr Robert Melton left his place of work at around eight p.m. on the evening of February twentieth. His whereabouts until the time of the accident are unknown. We have tried to contact Mr Melton's housekeeper but without success. However, we have concluded that it is highly unlikely that she would have anything of relevance to add to our inquiries."

The pathologist who conducted the post mortem was next on the stand.

"Mr Robert Melton suffered a fatal head injury in the accident, and it is very likely that death was instantaneous. Although only an approximation, the post-mortem would indicate that Mr Melton would have been around three times the legal limit for alcohol when driving at the time of his death."

And finally, there was my father's family doctor,

"Mr Robert Melton was suffering from severe depression at the time of the accident. He had developed a very severe drink problem and suffered significant damage to his liver."

After a short amount of deliberation, the coroner for the inquest delivered an open verdict on my father's death.

I remember feeling angry with my father as his death had confronted me with the very real possibility of having to live with my mother, Man Mountain and their infant child.

I could think of nothing that I wanted to do less in my life.

**

A few days after the inquest, Brian took me to see my father's solicitor, the greasy and rather unpleasant Mr Bennett, at his offices in Marlow for the reading of the Last Will and Testament of my father.

As we sat down with a cup of tea, Mr Bennett read the Will. It made no sense to me.

Thankfully Brian intervened,

"Can we have things in plain, simple English, please?"

"Mr Robert Melton's finances were not in a good position as he had accrued significant debts from, according to hearsay, an unfortunate mixture of excessive alcohol consumption and too much time spent in houses of ill repute. His Life Assurance Policy is rendered effectively null and void due to the open verdict delivered by the Coroner at the inquest."

"Can't we do anything about that?" asked Brian.

"I see no legal basis to challenge the decision," replied Mr Bennett

"Bloody insurance companies – never trusted them."

"That's as maybe, Mr Pritchett, I can only advise on the legal realities of the situation. It is, however, not all bad news. Following his wife's departure, Mr Melton was the sole owner of the house in Taplow. Based on a current valuation from Harmston Estate Agents, the house has increased in value significantly versus the purchase price seven years ago."

"What sort of money are we talking about?" asked Brian.

"I would estimate the net worth of Mr Melton's estate will be £20,000 to 30,000 after his debts are paid off. As per the Will, this money will be placed into your trust, Mr Pritchett, with the intention of funding Jonathan's education, both currently and possibly university in the future if needed. Any money remaining will be paid to Jonathan, along obviously with any interest accrued, on his thirty-fifth birthday."

"That's exactly what Robert told me when I spoke with him shortly after Christmas," said Brian.

**

Brian and I sat in his pick-up truck after the meeting with Mr Bennett.

"It's an awful business. I don't know how much you understood of what was said in there," said Brian.

"Most of it I think."

"You'll be looked after, don't worry."

"I hope so."

"If there's no place else for you to go, you know that you'll always be very welcome at the farm for as long as you need – whether that's ten weeks or ten years."

"Really!"

My spirits improved.

"Alison and I have come to view you as the sixth member of our family."

I hugged Brian tightly and started to cry.

"Thank you," I said through my tears.

"However, you do realise that you'll need permission from your mother if you're going to live with us," added Brian.

**

They buried my father on February 26th at Taplow Church. It was a cold, wet Tuesday morning. It was also my mother's birthday – exactly five years to the day after she'd left my father.

Apart from my mother, Brian and me, around 15 of my father's business associates turned up for the funeral. I'd never met any of them nor did any of them seem to know that I existed, never mind my name.

At least my mother, thankfully, had the decency not to bring Man Mountain with her. She even looked genuinely upset as she stood there dressed from head to toe in black in the grey and the drizzle of the graveyard.

I sobbed as the coffin was lowered into the ground.

**

I met with my mother outside the church after the funeral.

We had not spoken a single word to each other since our argument at the school tennis match over 18 months previously and my mother was clearly nervous.

We went inside the empty old church and sat down beside each other on the wooden row of seats that were at the back.

"You've grown so in the past couple of years. You're a very handsome young man," she said.

I was silent and my silence only served to make my mother more nervous still.

"Are you doing well at school?" she asked.

"OK," I said shrugging my shoulders.

"What are your favourite subjects?"

"French."

"You like languages then. Say some French for me."

"What's going to happen to me?" I asked.

My voice was abrasive and confrontational.

"What do you want to do?"

"I want to move in with Brian Pritchett and his family. I really like being at Tiverton."

"You could stay at Tiverton and come and spend the school holidays with us in Norfolk."

"What an absolutely fantastic idea. Why didn't I think of that? Oh, how *wonderfully super* that would be, being hit by that muscle-bound wanker that you live with."

"He is not a muscle-bound whatever. He's a good man. And he didn't hit you that day. You slipped and he barely caught you. Anyway, you were so rude to him. I don't blame you – spending time with your father influenced you negatively. Such poison, such madness, Lord knows, I spent enough time with him myself to know what he could be like."

"Leave Dad out of this. He's dead."

"But there are things that you should know. He was a sad, ill man. I'd like to sit down and talk to you about him rationally. You're a young man now. You can begin to understand such things."

"I'm not interested in what you have to say. He's dead and that's all that matters. Don't you feel guilty about that?"

"No, I don't. I only feel very sad."

I shook my head in disbelief.

"Look, your father had issues that he couldn't come to terms with. He had problems with, how can I put it…"

I was furious and interrupted my mother, shouting,

"I really don't give a flying fuck about what you have to say about Dad. I just want to know what's going to happen to me."

"I so desperately want you to come and live with us – if only during the holidays. Can't we start again? You and I used to be so close. I always wanted you, I truly did. Not like your father."

"I said leave Dad out of it."

"All right, not one more mention of your father. Please though think about starting again – starting afresh. I do love you. I truly do. More than you can imagine."

"But it's not just you and me though, is it? There's him, and there's your other child, as well. I'm not part of your new, *oh, so happy family*."

"You could be if you wanted. Yes, I am happy for the first time in years and I feel no guilt about that. But, and it's a very big but, you're the missing piece, Jonathan. I wish that you'd please give it a go. I'll beg if you want. Please."

"Why should I give it a go? Just give me one good reason."

"For me."

I looked my mother straight in the eyes, summoned up all the anger that I felt towards her in an icy stare and then shook my head slowly three time as I said,

"No, no, no."

"So what do you want to do?" my mother asked in a sympathetic tone.

"I told you already. I don't understand why we're having this conversation. I want to live with Brian and his family. Brian's has said he's OK with that. It's what I want. You got what you want, and now I want what I want. If you love me so very much as you keep telling me then that's what you will let me do."

"All right, I'll sign the necessary papers. But if you ever change your mind, you'd be so very welcome to come and live with us. I'm your mother and you're my son. I want you in my life."

There was a weary sigh to my mother's voice.

"You just don't get it do you? I cannot think of anything worse than moving in with you and your *oh so wonderful, oh so happy* family. I'd rather live on the streets," I said.

"You've made your point Jonathan. I'll sign the papers today."

Tears were running down my mother's cheek – her voice breaking with emotion as she said the words.

I stood up to go.

"Give me a hug before you go. Please Jonathan, please. Don't do this to me!"

I was unmoved.

"Look, I've got to go. Brian's waiting and I want to get back to school."

I ran off around the back of the church and when safely alone, stood there and sobbed.

As I wiped the tears from my eyes, I made a vow to myself that I kept repeating again to myself like a mantra.

"Nobody, just nobody nor nothing is ever going to make me cry again. Nobody, just nobody nor nothing is ever going to make me cry again. Nobody, just nobody nor nothing is ever going to make me cry again."

I was going to be strong.

After five or 10 minutes, I went to find Brian and kept muttering my new mantra under my breath as I found him outside the main door of the church.

Brian looked very solemn.

"I've just spoken with my mother," I said.

"Yes, I know. She told me all about it."

"And you're still OK that I spend my school holidays on the farm? I'll work hard, I promise," I asked full of trepidation.

"More than that – you can become a weekly boarder like David and spend your weekends with us if you want. I said before that you're welcome for as long as you want and I meant it."

Brian then smiled.

The broadest grin crossed my face and didn't leave it during the whole journey back to Devon.

My delight was matched by David's when we arrived back at the farm, the farm with its beautiful meadows, orchards, panoramic views and many different animals that was now to become my home with the warm and caring Pritchett family.

"You mean J.P.'s going to live with us, Dad?" asked David.

"Yes," said Brian.

"Brilliant!" screamed David at the top of his voice before jumping on my back in excitement.

"When, when, Dad?" added David, almost hysterical with excitement by this point.

"Immediately," said Brian.

"I need to collect some stuff from Taplow," I interjected.

"We can go to Taplow this weekend if you want," suggested Brian.

"Can I come, Dad? Can I come?" screamed David.

"Yes, David, as long as you promise to stop behaving like an over excited five-year- old," said Brian in a slightly exasperated but very loving manner.

**

That weekend, Brian, along with a still highly excited David in tow, took me to my father's old house in Taplow. Most of my belongings were at the boarding school in Tiverton and it wasn't a massive task.

With a weary sigh, I went through my father's old record collection in the living room and took out all the old Beatles records that I wanted to keep, along with his old record player.

I very much wished that I'd been able to say goodbye to Annie, who had always been kind to me – but she'd clearly moved on.

After that, it was up to my bedroom – the previous scene of seemingly endless, boring and wasted hours lying in bed listening to the dull pitter-patter of the rain against the windows.

The only thing that I wanted from my room was the cup that my father had given me after the game of tennis we played during our last great weekend together. As I picked up the cup, I could feel the emotion well up inside of me.

I gritted my teeth as I remembered my mantra from the previous day.

"Nobody, just nobody nor nothing is ever going to make me cry again."

Again and again I repeated this to myself, until I felt the emotion subside within me. I felt good, I felt stronger – as though a battle had been fought and won.

As we drove out of Taplow village, I said to myself silently "I'm sorry, Dad, so very sorry," and took a deep, deep breath before pushing all the air out of my lungs.

"You all right there?" asked Brian.

"Thank you again for letting me stay with you. I don't think that I could ever repay your kindness," I replied.

"Jonathan, friends don't have to pay back something that is given freely."

I smiled.

"It's going to be brilliant, J.P. You'll see. I still can't believe that you're coming to live with us," said David.

The 'Good' Reverend Brownley

I may have escaped the boarding house and Reverend Brownley at weekends for the sanctuary of the farm, but the 'good' Reverend was still there to haunt me during the week.

If I close my eyes, I can still hear his voice ringing in my ears, spouting pompously his favourite quote from Job 19:25.

"I know that my redeemer liveth, and that he shall stand at the latter day upon the earth."

It was bad enough that theology was a compulsory subject up to O-Level at Tiverton, but I also had to put up with the tiresome 'good' Reverend during every tennis lesson. The 'good' Reverend was only interested in improving those of very limited ability – highly laudable in itself – but of no value to either David or me.

Worse still, unlike John Tasker, the 'good' Reverend was against any form of representative sport – be it representing the Devon County School Team, or heaven forbid, the English Schools Tennis Team.

I had one final try to persuade the 'good' Reverend to change his mind on the matter. I knew it was a forlorn hope but I cared deeply about my tennis and knew that I had to try.

I knocked on the door of the small, pokey teacher's office that was adjacent to the changing rooms.

"Enter," said the 'good' Reverend.

I went into the room. As always for a tennis lesson, he was dressed in ridiculous white capacious shorts, black socks and his usual black shirt and dog collar. Although I'd seen him dressed like that on many occasions, I still struggled not to laugh upon setting eyes on him.

"Reverend Brownley, sir, I've heard that the Devon Schools Tennis Association are holding trials next week. I would really like to attend if possible, sir."

"That is quite out of the question."

"But why can't I attend the trials, sir?"

"Because, Melton, tennis at this school is about 'Sport for All'. It is about everyone participating, it is about the love and beauty of the game and about pupils being given the opportunity to improve their skills. It is not, contrary to what you, and Pritchett for the matter, believe, it is not and never will be about elitism, do you hear me? All the two of you care about is win, win, win. Be the best at any cost. I was always taught that it's the taking part that matters and that is the message that I intend to communicate to all the boys under me at this school."

"But it's not 'Sport for All', is it, sir?" It's not Sport for David and me. So it can't be 'Sport for All'. If it was 'Sport for All' then David and I could benefit and we could go to the County Schools' Trials. Instead, David and I spend all our time playing around with people that I could beat playing left handed and practising shots that I can do with my eyes shut. How is that 'Sport for All', SIR?"

"Your arrogance and insolence are insufferable, Melton."

"As indeed, with the utmost respect, are you, sir."

"I know that my redeemer liveth, and that he shall stand at the latter day upon the earth."

"What has that to do with playing tennis for Devon Schools, sir?"

"It means that there is redemption for us all, even for someone as insolent and arrogant as you, Melton...even for you. In the meantime, however, before redemption day arrives, I suggest a further spell in detention to teach you some manners, humility and most of all, some respect for your elders and, may I also say, your betters."

I spent an awful lot of time in detention that summer.

**

1983 was O-Level year and that offered me a chance to strike a blow back at the pompous, self-righteous one.

I was taking eleven O-Levels (as was David) and determined to honour my father's memory the best way I could by working as hard as possible, preparing meticulously for all exams − except, of course, theology.

When it came to the day of the theology exam, I took immense pleasure in ignoring all the questions in the examination paper and spending the whole 90 minutes writing out Job 19:25 as many times as possible.

"I know that my redeemer liveth, and that he shall stand at the latter day upon the earth."

**

With the O-Level exams over, it was time to start playing cricket in earnest for North Devon Cricket Club, whom David and I had joined on the invitation of John Tasker, who like ourselves lived in the north of the county.

Playing against quality players 10–20 years older than me and more than holding my own made me feel as though I was truly becoming a man and leaving boyhood behind.

John Tasker always used to collect David and me at Greasy Eddy's Café on the west side of Barnstaple to drive us to the game – and breakfast and cigarettes at Greasy Eddy's Café was simply a unique and quite splendid experience.

Around five cigarettes together with bacon, sausage, mushrooms, tomatoes, fried eggs and beans at Greasy Eddy's Café had become the compulsory pre-game ritual for David and me. Whilst this was hardly the ideal diet for young sportsmen, Greasy Eddy had become a cult hero for both of us – a true living legend.

Greasy Eddy was invariably unshaven with unkempt hair as greasy as the scrumptious food he cooked and always, and I mean always, with a cigarette dangling from his lips.

To David and me and many of his other customers, this complete scruff bag was THE funniest man on the planet. And, oh yes, how could I forget? Greasy Eddy was also without doubt the finest living farter known to mankind.

As he released his seismic offerings on an unsuspecting world with casual aplomb, one could have almost believed that an overpowered Harley Davidson was passing through the café – except for Greasy Eddy's strange words that followed every 'effort'.

"Terry Hennessey: 1-0."

**

The O-Level results came through in the post in August.

Both David and I had done very well, not least because of the high quality of teaching at Tiverton. David passed 11 O-Levels with six grade A-s whilst I got 10 O-Levels with seven A-s.

To my enormous delight and considerable personal pride, I achieved a failure U in theology for my unique examination 'answer'.

That night the six of us had a party to end all parties on the farm. All of us, even young Sarah, were drunk by the end of the celebrations.

As we finally made our way to bed at four in the morning, I wondered to myself if life could be any better than this. Sadly, the next day was to prove to be somewhat less pleasant.

After breakfast, as Graham and I went out to work in the fields as usual, Brian said that he wanted to chat with David.

I ran into David later in the day in the fields.

"My God, David, what's the matter with you? You look as though you've been sentenced to a year's private tuition with the 'good' Reverend."

"It's Dad!"

"Is he OK?"

"Oh, he's fine. It's what he wants me to do."

"What does he want you to do?"

"He wants me to go to fucking university, that's what. He's put lots of money aside."

"Seems reasonable enough to me," I replied.

"To you maybe but I don't fucking want to go. I want to stay here."

"Well, tell your Dad that!"

"He doesn't want to know. He said that Graham's already left school with only two O-Levels and can't realistically do anything else but work here. He's convinced that life on the farm will only get tougher and tougher over the next ten to fifteen years. He wants me to have a better life. I don't want a better life. This IS my life. HERE!"

**

I came across David again later that day in the old barn used to store hay – he was sat on his own and for one of the very few occasions in all the time that I've known David, he was in tears.

"Shit, are you OK?" I asked.

"I don't understand why Dad doesn't want me to work on the farm. Why does he want to ship me off to university?"

"Because you have the ability to go there, that's why."

"That's what Dad said. He said I'm the first person ever from our family with the brains to go to university. He told me that he would have failed as a father if I didn't make the best of myself in life and not become a humble farmer like him. How can he say humble farmer? Dad's the finest man I know."

"So what are you going to do?"

"I'm going to do what he wants. I love him too much to let him down. I want him to be proud of me."

"Think of all the time that you'll have to study Shakespeare," I suggested.

"I don't need a bloody degree to help me appreciate the works of Shakespeare! If I'd have known that this was going to happen then I'd have deliberately failed all my exams."

"You can't possibly mean that?"

"Yes, I fucking do. You deliberately failed theology."

"That was different."

There was a rare silence between us and then David lashed out at the barn wall with a force that was frightening. The barn rattled and a bale of hay fell on David's foot.

"Owww! My fucking foot!"

The mood lightened.

"I really need to show you how to do that. Thanks to the 'good' Reverend, I have kicking the shit out of walls down to a fine art," I replied.

David started to laugh despite his pain.

"I think that I've broken my foot."

"Have you hell, you wuss."

I was now laughing too.

**

David and I went back to school to study for our A-Levels. I chose to study French – which had always been my favourite subject. I adored the works of Molière and Hugo, but above all, I simply loved the lyrical nature of the language.

I also studied geography as I felt confident that I would do well despite the teacher, who though not a pain in the arse to rival the 'good' Reverend, having an annoying habit of saying that 'punctuality is the essence of life' on a far, far too regular basis.

I never personally saw the relevance of punctuality to studying geography and although, at 16 years of age, I had no idea yet what was the essence of life, I desperately hoped that it would be more than mere punctuality.

I ended up choosing English as my third A-Level. I didn't share either David's love of Shakespeare or his flair for the English language, but John Tasker was the English teacher.

**

Before attending my first lesson of the new term, I was summoned to see the Headmaster in his study. My only previous visit to his study had been when I was told about my father's death.

60

As I walked in, I noticed, as I sat down, that his study had a panoramic view of all the playing fields at Tiverton.

I smiled to myself.

The Headmaster was as immaculately dressed as ever and greeted me with his customary brightness.

"Ah, good morning, young Melton. Welcome to the Sixth Form at Tiverton."

"Thank you, sir."

"I want to talk to you about your O-Level theology. During my twenty-eight years at this school, nobody has ever achieved an unclassified grade in any examination that they have sat."

"I didn't know that, sir."

"This is a very sad day. What makes it all the more remarkable is that you achieved such praiseworthy grades in other subjects."

I shrugged my shoulders.

"Now we checked with the Examination Board to be sure that there was no mistake, and they informed us of your most unusual entry – one sentence from the Bible written again and again. Most bizarre, I must say," continued the Headmaster.

"Job 19:25. One hundred and eighty-two times, I believe, sir," I replied with some degree of pride.

The briefest of smiles crossed the Headmaster's face but it was soon replaced by a quizzical frown.

"But why do such a thing?"

"As a protest, sir!"

"A protest against what, young man?"

"Tiverton School promotes and fosters excellence in everything that it does – education, behaviour, sporting prowess at rugby and cricket – but in tennis, it does not. It promotes and fosters mediocrity. David Pritchett and I have not benefited in the slightest over the past four years from how tennis is run at this school. We're even banned from going to representative trials."

The Headmaster listened attentively before responding,

"Young Melton, I have no wish to comment on that. I believe that we hire the best teachers and my stance has always been to allow them to teach in the style and manner that they so wish. I have always done that and will continue to do that. That is my way – the Tiverton way."

"Yes sir."

"And the point is, even if what you say is correct, that two wrongs do not make a right. In mathematics, two negatives make a positive but in life they do not. I'm not sure that all the pupils who attend this school realise the immense privilege afforded to them. However, I always thought that you were one who did appreciate it. That's why your actions both surprised and disappointed me. It costs time, money and effort to enter any pupil for any examination paper and all that is expected in return is that pupils give their best. A public examination is not a platform for you to make a personal protest on how tennis is run at Tiverton School. To do so is an abuse of privilege, it is abuse of public money and it reflects badly on this school. Do you understand, young man?"

The Headmaster's tone was calm and considered throughout.

"Yes, I understand, sir and I sincerely apologise for any embarrassment caused to the school."

"Your apology is both appreciated and accepted. Now be on your way, young man. You have a challenging and, hopefully, enjoyable two years ahead of you. I wish you all the very best. And no more of this type of nonsense."

"Yes sir. Thank you, sir."

The First Time

I arrived at John Tasker's room for my first A-Level lesson to find my fellow four pupils who were studying English already there. As there were only a few of us, John wanted to hold the lessons in his private room at the school rather than a normal classroom.

Along with David, there was Gary Barker, Jeremy Partridge and Peter Hannen. Gary was a rugby player and never short of a word or fifty whilst Jeremy was a geek who managed to make even me look like Casanova.

Peter, on the other hand, was widely acknowledged as the most intelligent pupil in our year – 15 straight A-s at O-Level only began to capture his intelligence.

John's room was full of comfy chairs, sofas and interesting photographs from his life. It was a world away from the usual classroom. As I walked in, Gary Barker was holding court on the subject of the opposite sex.

"I went into town last night and cracked off with a dirty girl. Real local townie – not too bright, but very willing. We found some back alley," said Gary.

"And what happened?" asked Jeremy Partridge.

"I got my hands inside her knickers. Begging for it, she was."

"And did you give it to her then?" David enquired in a very offhand manner that made me smile.

"Of course, I did. A standy-uppy from behind – loved it, she did."

Without anyone apart from me noticing, John Tasker had already made his entrance and was listening to the conversation with a rueful smile on his face.

John coughed loudly.

His private room fell silent in embarrassment, and there was much uncomfortable shuffling in seats.

"Good morning. Welcome to two years exploring, discussing and debating the delights and beauty of the English language. It's probably best if I start by explaining how I see the next two years and my 'rules' for being part of this class. Rule One is Christian names only. We'll have none of this 'sir' nonsense. Some of you know this already. Rule

Two is that you're here either because you love English language and literature already or because you genuinely, and I mean genuinely, want to learn. If you're only here because you want an A-Level to gain admittance to university then I very strongly suggest you do another subject. I'd rather have one totally committed student who wants to learn than ten who only want to pass an exam. There's still time to change your mind, is that understood?"

"Yes, John," we replied in unison.

"The plan is that we will cover all the defined writers and books on the curriculum, but rather than study them one-by-one, I want us to explore the works as part of key themes: love, religion, life and death. Based on what I heard of your conversation upon entering the room it's maybe most appropriate that we begin with love. Before we start work on *Romeo and Juliet*, I'm interested in all of you giving me your favourite quote on love that captures how you feel about the subject. From what I heard upon entering the room, given your *eloquence* on the matter Gary, let's start with you but please remember that the theme is love and not sex – not mutually exclusive, of course, but very different nonetheless."

"Love is a many splendored thing," Barker offered.

John's eyes rolled in indignation and a frown filled his face.

"Gary, I realise, that at your age, hormones are positively rampant. I also understand that since neither Reverend Brownley, as Boarding Lodge Supervisor, nor any young girl's parents are going to give you easy access to an environment where physical lust can be expressed in a human, intimate and horizontal manner, it is perhaps inevitable that the primitive urges within you will naturally gravitate towards a vertical expression of the most bestial form."

There was much humour and laughter in the class.

"However, all that notwithstanding, I expect some conception and expression of love that extends beyond mere cliché – 'splendored' isn't even the correct word, for pity's sake. Seriously, Gary, I understand that there's plenty of room in Mr Higgins' geography classes. Please give it some thought. Anyway, moving on and preferably upward, hopefully Peter can do better."

"And most of all would I flee from the cruel madness of love, the honey of poison-flowers and all the measureless ill," said Peter.

"Excellent, Peter – it's always good to hear Tennyson. Perhaps though you do need to get out a little more – women are a joy in life, not a danger."

Peter smiled.

"David, next please," said John.

64

"We that are true lovers run into strange capers."

David's passion and empathy with the words were all too evident.

"Very good too, David, but over the next few weeks I'd like to hear you reference someone other than Shakespeare. Sir William may have been the finest writer to have lived, but he isn't the ONLY writer to have lived. How about you, Jeremy?"

"I can't think of anything, sir."

"It's John, not sir, Jeremy, Rule One as I said earlier. And as with Gary, please give Mr Higgins' geography classes some serious thought. And finally to Jonathan."

"Love is all you need," I offered.

"Mmm, clichéd but at least I sensed some sincerity. You receive the benefit of the doubt since I would class Mr Lennon as a poet. Although regarding the quote, I would say that food, warmth and shelter are essential needs in life also. We need love, but love is not all we need. As for your needs, Jonathan, you need to improve if you want to stay as part of this class. You wouldn't want to do theology with Reverend Brownley now, would you?"

John had a wicked grin. The whole class laughed loudly.

"Right, let's move on. Have any of you heard of Isaac Watts?" came John's next question.

There were lots of blank faces. Peter Hannen piped up,

"He was a late seventeenth century English hymn-writer, I believe."

"Very good Peter. I'm impressed – even by your very high standards."

"Why do you ask, John?" asked Peter.

"Because he wrote my favourite quote on love – it's 'I seek a love so amazing, so divine. One that demands my soul, my life, my all'."

"I think that you'll find that Watts was talking about God when he said those words. Are you talking about the love of God?"

"No, I'm talking about the love of a woman – the magic, the mystique, the feeling of complete intellectual, emotional, physical and sensual fulfilment."

"But surely, that isn't what Watts meant when he wrote the words."

"Does it matter, Peter? Surely words, like beauty, are in the eye of the beholder?"

The dialogue continued in the same wonderful, inspirational vein. I was transfixed by the interaction between John and Peter.

At the end of the lesson, John said,

"Right, guys, your first exercise of the term. 'Without language there would not be love'. I would like to see a four-page dissertation from all of you on the matter. To make things interesting, there will be an additional handicap for two of you. David, make references to at least three writers in your dissertation and no reference in the slightest to Shakespeare. Peter, on the other hand, you can only answer by arguing against the case."

The entire lesson had been like an epiphany for me. Part of me was intimidated and at times overawed, but part of me was captivated by the passionate and intellectual debate. I wanted to be able to contribute, if not on equal terms, but in a meaningful way.

It was a real awakening as to what life could offer. Over the next two years, I would fall in love with the works of Oscar Wilde and, in particular, D.H. Lawrence.

Reading *The Rainbow* didn't seem like studying or work: it was more an all-consuming passion.

**

One of the glories of growing up from being a boy and becoming a man is discovering the vices in life. For David, his vices had become cigarettes, women and alcohol. Sadly, I was limited to cigarettes and alcohol.

Despite my lack of experience, or maybe because of it, Brian felt that it was time that he had a talk with me. He invited me into the living room – an usual event in itself as we spent virtually all our time as a family in the enormous kitchen.

Brian was unusually stern of face as he said,

"Now, you know that we have cows and calves on this farm. And it's the cows that make the calves."

"I know."

"Do you know how the cows make the calves?"

"Yes, I think so."

"Humans are the same – and if a boy and a girl don't use protection then they make babies. It's essential to use protection. Always use protection, Jonathan. Do you understand?"

"Yes," I responded.

"Good lad. If you use protection then you won't go far wrong in life. Now go and clean out the cow shed."

My relief that the conversation was at its end was considerable.

Sadly, the reality was that I was about as likely to be in a position to 'use protection' as I was to be spending an evening having an enjoyable chat and a beer with the 'good' Reverend. To say that I was hopeless with women was an understatement of monumental proportions.

David, on the other hand, was the complete opposite. Girls loved him. Whenever he was with them, he always had a natural ease and charm. He always had the right Shakespearean quote for the moment – David simply loved and adored the works of Shakespeare and, boy, could he make that love and adoration work for him with the opposite sex.

In comparison, I was intense, tongue tied and downright awkward with women.

**

The old barn on the farm had always been used to store bales of hay and to milk the goat. David and I had also come to adopt it as our own private meeting place.

During one of our many discussions there, David tried to help me with my awkwardness with the fairer sex.

"Cool it, man. You're too heavy. As soon as you go up to women, it's as though you have 'desperate' tattooed on your forehead. Relax, they're only girls, not aliens from the planet Zob," he said.

"I do try. I've tried to quote Shakespeare like you, but it just doesn't work. It always comes out wrong."

"That's because you don't love Shakespeare. If you love the words then they work. No woman worth her salt can resist the majestic beauty of Shakespeare."

"If you say so."

"You need to start with the basics, J.P."

"How do you mean?"

"Start talking to Sarah more."

"David, she's twelve. And she's your sister for God's sake."

"I'm not saying shag her behind the cowshed, idiot. If you talk to her, it'll help. Trust me. It'll get you used to talking to girls."

I looked out of the barn at Sarah, who was across the yard as we were talking about her. She was sweet, warm and kind like her mother but I was unconvinced.

"Mmm…," I said.

"Look, trust me. Within a year, I'll get you laid. No question."

I smiled – half-believing, half-not.

**

I did make more of an effort to talk to Sarah and David was right, it did help.

In October, there was a disco in the large main room at the local village hall – it seemed very strange to be holding a disco there as most of the time it was populated by middle aged and elderly women selling cakes and Devon country produce.

As I walked into the disco with David, I was as nervous as a kitten and it took quite a few drinks before I began to relax. I asked one, then two, then three girls to dance, and all offers were politely declined – but I wasn't going to give up.

I asked a fourth girl. I think that her name was Susan, but I can't remember for sure.

To my surprise, she said, "Yes."

Now, without being cruel, Susan wasn't the slenderest of girls that I'd ever met, and the brace on her teeth did not augment her looks. But she was willing to dance with me and that was all that mattered that night.

We danced for ages and then as the evening drew to a close, the DJ played *True* by Spandau Ballet. I had my first slow dance and then, my first French kiss.

Susan's brace felt strange against my teeth but it was exciting and I could sense some significant activity down below in my trousers. My embarrassment on the matter was considerable.

At the end of the disco, Susan scribbled her number on a piece of paper and said,

"Call me!"

I walked home full of satisfaction and achievement. I definitely planned to call Susan.

David had also weaved his unique magic with the opposite sex. Her name was Katie. Unlike my liaison, Katie was extremely attractive – tall, thin, with very nice 'bumps' in all the right places and wonderful long, flowing red hair full of bounce and curl.

The following day, David and I had the essential de-brief of the previous night in the old barn.

"Interesting start to life with the opposite sex, J.P. – I said that I'd have you laid within a year and have you laid, I will. That brace she had on her teeth – quite extraordinary. What was it like?" asked David.

"Strange!" I replied.

"Yes…," David paused before continuing,

"…I heard a poor lad kissed her last year and somehow got his bottom lip caught in her brace. He ended up making a right mess of his lip – torn to shreds it was – completely disfigured the poor lad!"

I listened in horror.

"You weren't thinking of calling her, J.P., were you?"

"No, of course not!"

"Good job too. You have to believe in yourself more. Push yourself. Go out with someone because you genuinely want to – not because you think that they're the only woman who will get off with you."

"Katie was nice," I said.

"Yes, she is." David's eyes twinkled brightly, and his smile shone from ear to ear.

"Are you going to see her again?"

"I think I might just do that."

**

The following summer, one Saturday night after cricket, David said to me in the North Devon cricket pavilion,

"Let's hit town, J.P. when John drops us off in Barnstaple. I think that this is a night for some seriously dangerous living. Katie and I have someone that we want you to meet."

"Who?" I asked.

"A woman – you know, that strange species that accounts for fifty per cent of the world's population and with whom, shall we say, you have some communication issues."

"What communication issues?"

"Exactly! What communication do you ever have with women?" asked David.

"I talk to Katie."

"She's MY girlfriend, and it took you three months before you could say anything more than hello! You've not even so much as kissed a girl since your close encounter of the teeth brace kind."

I sighed.

"I told you, J.P., last year that I would get you laid in the year and get you laid I will."

**

David and I made our way to The Red Lion in Barnstaple – a sanctuary for underage drinkers, it felt more like a student common room than a regular pub.

After buying two pints, we sat down.

"So who is this woman then?" I asked, trying to be cool, but merely betraying in my voice a mixture of trepidation and excitement.

"Shelly. She's a friend of Katie's."

"Is she like Katie then?"

69

"No. Not at all."

"Oh."

"Yeh, I know you fancy Katie, J.P., but I'm cool about it."

"No, I don't."

"And my cock's a kipper, J.P."

I laughed, knowing I was both beaten and rumbled.

"Is it smoked?" I asked.

"Not smoked but smoking. It's one red hot tool, J.P., red hot," said David with great irony and a self-mocking tone.

**

Katie and Shelly arrived 15 minutes late. Punctuality was never the essence of Katie's life, but it was always good to see her. She had always been genuinely kind to me, sensitive to my shyness with women and, together with David, she helped the early conversation with Shelly.

Despite my nerves, I was certainly ready that night, in David's words, to do some 'dangerous' living and there's no doubt that Shelly was indeed 'dangerous' with her dyed blonde permed hair, short denim skirt, skimpy cropped top and visible black knickers every time she crossed and uncrossed her legs. Chewing gum aplenty, she came across as a young girl of easy virtue.

After around an hour or so of drinking my inhibitions and nerves had disappeared enough for David and Katie to feel that they could leave Shelly and me alone as they went to put some records on the pub jukebox.

"Why does Katie call you J.P.?" asked Shelly.

"Because they're my initials."

"What do they stand for?"

"Jonathan Paul."

"Oh, I've kissed a few Pauls before but never a Jonathan."

With that, Shelly kissed me. My initial reaction was that Shelly was attacking my very brains with her tongue. She then ran her fingers across my groin area.

"I always like see an immediate reaction in my men!" said Shelly with a wicked smile on her face.

This carried on for around the next thirty minutes. It was as though I'd been French kissing all my life. I felt as though Shelly was devouring me – not that I was complaining.

At around 10.15 p.m., Shelly asked me,

"Do you want to walk me home?"

"That would be nice," I replied.

"Go and get something for the walk home then!" Shelly demanded.

"What?" I asked.

"Some johnnies, stupid," whispered Shelly.

I dutifully disappeared to the gent's toilet and put my 50p in the machine.

As I left the pub, David shouted after me.

"Have fun, J.P. See you later. Oh yes, and remember what Dad says."

"What?"

"Always use protection!"

I gave David the two-fingered salute that his mocking deserved.

As Shelly and I walked hand-in-hand through the streets of Barnstaple, nerves again began to overtake me – thankful that I'd had enough to drink to have the Dutch courage to go through with whatever I was about to go through.

"Let's go this way," said Shelly dragging me towards the local park.

"Is this the way to your house? I thought you lived in the opposite direction," I responded.

"Are you always this stupid? Don't tell me that you've not been to the local park at night."

"No."

"Have you ever actually been with a girl before?" asked Shelly, clearly frustrated.

"Yes, of course I have."

"Come on then."

Once in the park, Shelly led me into some bushes which, judging by the number of used condoms lying around, was clearly a very popular spot for such activities. Part of me was revolted, but I'd passed the point of no return.

I tried to put the condom on but was making a singularly poor job of it.

"All you boys are the same. Give it here," as she snatched it off me.

With effortless dexterity and a little help from her mouth, Shelly had the condom on my penis in a matter of seconds. She then took her black knickers off, hitched her denim skirt up, lay down in the bushes, took hold of me and eased me inside of her.

I found the whole experience both bewildering and exciting. Within less than 10 seconds of entering Shelly I came, the significant quantities of alcohol doing little to dampen my all too obvious ardour.

"UHHHHHHHHHHHHHHH. Oh God, that was…wow. Wow!"

"Was that it?" she asked.

"I'm sorry. Should it last longer?" I asked.

"A *little* bit, yes."

"I'm really sorry. It's my first time."

"But you said earlier that it wasn't."

"I lied. I'm sorry."

"I'll kill that bloody Katie when I see her on Monday. She didn't tell me that you were a bloody virgin. I thought that you were a bit shy, that's all. I'm not a fucking local charity service for virgins to whet their whistle for the first time."

Shelly put her black knickers back on.

"I'm going home."

"I'll walk you if you want," I offered.

"Don't bother."

**

David started calling me 'Carl' one day as we worked around the farm. This went on for a couple of hours before I asked,

"Why do you keep calling me Carl?"

"Carl Lewis, the one hundred metres sprinter, of course."

"I don't understand."

"He's a sub-ten second man and so are you!"

David started laughing at his own joke.

I couldn't help but laugh too.

End of School

David and I were having our Saturday pre-cricket match ritual of a hearty breakfast-cum-lunch at the legendary Greasy Eddy's Café.

As always, Greasy Eddy was unkempt with the seemingly permanent cigarette dangling from his lips and his unique digestive system generating its usual remarkable level and intensity of by-products.

Another eruption to rival the most powerful Harley Davidson ensued. Even though David and I had heard it hundreds of times before, we both sniggered like the schoolboys we were.

"Terry Hennessey. 1-0," said Eddy.

"Why do always say that, Eddy?" I asked.

"It's a long story," he replied with a sigh.

"We've got thirty minutes before we need to leave for the game," encouraged David.

"When I was a lad, my Dad had the same skill in the bottom department that I have. A lifetime of beans, I guess. Anyway, we both loved our football, and we used to equate the volume of our efforts to goals. A little pipsqueak fart was a six yard tap in, whereas a real house rattler was a thirty yard volley into the top corner."

"And that's where Terry Hennessey comes in?" asked David.

"Aye, my Dad and I were watching *Goals on Sunday* one day and we both let fly simultaneously – real Richter scale stuff. And on telly, Terry Hennessey scored with this thirty yard scorcher, a real ripper, and all the commentator said was 'Terry Hennessey. 1-0.' My Dad and I fell about pissing ourselves laughing. He laughed a lot, my Dad. So we adopted it as our catchphrase. It's daft what you remember isn't it? I loved him; he was my hero – he had so much life and laughter to him, but one morning he left for work and never came back. The poor old sod dropped dead in the street from a heart attack. I'd give every penny that I own if I could have that morning again – if only to say goodbye to him. So every time I let one go and say the words, I think of him sat in his chair laughing. Some people think it's disrespectful, but I know the old bugger. I can see him in heaven laughing every time I say the words."

I looked at Eddy and there were tears in his eyes yet a smile on his face.

Silence fell over the Café momentarily.

"Is your mother still alive?" asked David.

"Maybe, maybe not – who knows? Certainly not me. Within six months of Dad dying, she'd taken up with some guy and married him. Six fucking months – she'd been married to one of the finest blokes to have ever walked this planet for eighteen years and the poor sod is barely cold in the ground and she's off with a poncey bloody insurance salesman. I was so disgusted that I left and joined the Merchant Navy. Never went back. Lost contact in the end."

David looked at me.

"Who gives a shit anyway?" Eddy added.

"Too fucking right, Eddy, too fucking right," I said.

"Enough of this stuff, lads. Three brews all around, eh," said Eddy.

"Definitely," David said.

I nodded in approval.

**

As 1984 became 1985, aside from the key issues of taking A-Levels and S-Levels, choosing which university to go to consumed David's and my time.

I'd always assumed that David and I would go to different universities. I was therefore taken aback when David and I were having one of our many discussions in the old barn and he asked,

"What university are you going to go to?"

"Whichever decent one will have me, I guess," I replied.

"Wherever you go is where I want to go."

"Nice idea, my friend, but it could prove a little difficult to manage."

David's body language was clearly, very unusually, agitated.

"We've got to sort it out, J.P. We HAVE to go to the same place. It's bad enough that I have to go to bloody university at all – without not knowing anyone when I get there."

"Don't be daft! I don't know anyone who makes friends as easily as you. Anyway, what about Katie, don't you want to go to the same university as her?"

"It would be cool, I guess. But at the end of the day, I know loads of people and I get on fine with them all, including Katie of course, but I've only one true friend…that's you, my dear old mucker."

In the final week of summer term, John Tasker proposed that the Pupils play the Teachers at tennis and, much to my delight, sought and obtained the support of the Headmaster.

Even more pleasing, I was drawn to play against the 'good' Reverend Brownley in the potentially deciding match after Paul Davenport, mediocre of talent and undeniably beloved by the 'good' Reverend, had played Peter Bailey, the physics teacher, and David had played John Tasker.

On the day of the challenge itself, after Paul Davenport had been beaten comfortably by Peter Bailey, John frittered away chance after chance to beat David leaving David to eventually emerge the victor. There was decidedly a sense of stage management about it all.

Now to say I was fired up for the match with the 'good' Reverend, rarely could a statement be so under. Nothing other than the complete humiliation of the man in his ridiculous white capacious shorts, black socks and dog collar would suffice.

After finishing my A-Level exams, I'd virtually lived on a tennis court, practicing every possible hour with David. My form was the best it had ever been, and I positively relished my final appearance on the Tiverton School tennis courts.

I served first and put in four big, booming first serves – including three straight aces. My return of serve was similarly thunderous, and it was the fourth game before I lost a point.

During the fifth game, the 'good' Reverend pulled up with an 'injury'.

I was frustrated beyond belief.

"Shame about my injury. I felt I was starting to get into my stride, and it was going to be a real tight contest," declared the pompous, pious old goat.

John laughed at the ridiculousness of the statement, as did David and I.

"What's so funny, Mr Tasker?" enquired the 'good' Reverend.

"If you'd have played fifty sets, you wouldn't have made it a tight contest! Why not give credit where credit is due? Jonathan's the best tennis player I've seen in over ten years at the school," replied John.

"Always the pupil's friend, eh, Mr Tasker – ability is of no value without discipline. Winning has no style or substance without humility."

John just smiled and said nothing.

Later that week Mr Parkerton, the Headmaster, approached me in the corridor one day.

I immediately wondered what I'd done wrong.

"There you are, young Melton. Do you have five minutes for a word in private?"

"Of course, sir," I replied with some slight trepidation as we entered a quiet and empty classroom at the end of one of the many school corridors.

There was seriousness as always to the Headmaster, but a kindness in his voice.

"I've been Headmaster of this school for over fifteen years. I've always believed that the role of the school is twofold. Firstly, we are here to optimise the potential of our students. Secondly, it is to help prepare students for the next stage in their lives – whatever that may be. In general, I feel that we succeed."

I was silent.

"However, young Melton, I do think that we failed you in some way."

"In what way is that?" I asked.

"I watched you play tennis the other day and although I'm more a rugby man, I couldn't help but notice what ability you have. I was not at all impressed by that racket throwing malarkey of yours a few years ago. I see all these young American and East European chappies up to those capers at Wimbledon; it's not British though, and it's most certainly not Tiverton School. We want Tiverton School to create winners, but also young men who, when they do lose, they do so with dignity. But, as I've said to you before – two wrongs do not make a right and I'm sure that Tiverton could have done more to harness and develop your clearly very considerable ability."

"I'm certainly very disappointed at some of the decisions that were taken," I replied.

"Ultimately, as Headmaster, I take the responsibility for any decisions that are taken."

"I didn't mean that as a personal criticism of you, sir."

"I would not have a problem if you did intend it as a personal criticism. In fact, I feel it would be warranted. Headmasters are as human as anyone and, as such, we make mistakes. Sadly, with regard to the development of your tennis, I accept that I made one such mistake. As such, I would like to apologise to you."

The Headmaster offered me his hand. I could feel emotion well up inside of me as I took his hand and shook it.

"Many thanks, sir."

"I hope university offers you the opportunity to develop your sporting skills better. Which one have you chosen?"

"Probably Sheffield, sir – dependent upon results."

"I don't imagine for a minute that will be a problem, young man."

There was a brief silence between us.

"I need to go now," said the Headmaster as he set about his way.

**

The exam results came out in August and both David and I obtained our three A-Levels – myself with two A-s and a C, whereas David obtained an A, a B and a C. I had expected an A in French, but was absolutely delighted at also attaining an A in English.

Typical of the man, John Tasker called personally to congratulate the two of us in achieving A-s. Inevitably, Peter Hannen made it three out of three in John's class.

To celebrate our success, Brian and Alison threw another party-to-remember for the family, Katie and me. Once again we all consumed a considerable amount of alcohol that night, none more than David, who was very sick.

Although David was generally funny and, on the surface at least, full of life throughout the evening, there was also a real sadness to him.

"Here's to a brilliant new adventure then," he said at one point, the dissonance between his words and the intonation all too evident.

And later, when no one was around, I saw him and he looked downright miserable.

The party at the farm that night was to mark the end of an era.

Katie went to Durham University whereas David and I went to Sheffield. I was to study French with Business Studies whilst David, of course, did his beloved English Literature.

University

To help integrate students into university life and their new surroundings there is an 'Intro Week' the week before the first term begins.

In many respects, Intro Week is a strange and surreal experience. For the vast majority of first year students, it is their first real time away from home.

Some students find this liberating whilst others can find it very intimidating – initially at least. Some are able to make new lasting friendships very easily whilst others find it very lonely being away from the loving care of their parents.

What struck me most of all during Intro Week was that, other than with David, virtually every conversation that I had with anyone was very superficial and rarely went any further than which school you'd been to, what A-Levels you'd done and what course you were studying.

It was like being at school but in a different uniform – jeans rather than school trousers – except, of course, at school, one doesn't have the Christian Union knocking at your door on a regular basis.

David was quickly well and truly into his stride with the opposite sex and bedded two different women during Intro Week alone.

Inevitably, it was very different for me. Although I was over six foot and, if I say so myself, I wasn't exactly ugly, I still struggled woefully with women.

"What about Katie?" I asked David the morning after one of his night befores.

"What about Katie? Life is for living."

"I could do with some living myself if I'm honest."

"Still the desperate man! Relax and they'll come flocking, bud, trust me."

"I'm just not comfortable. I don't understand women. I don't feel comfortable with them. Going to an all-male school didn't help."

"I don't understand women either. Complete bloody mystery. And I went to the same school as you, if you haven't forgotten. You need to start believing in yourself, J.P. – because if you don't believe in yourself then no woman is ever going to do so!"

**

At the 'sports bazaar' during Intro Week, David and I went to join both the cricket club and tennis club at the university. We were welcomed with open arms by the cricket club and invited immediately to winter nets.

However, the 'welcome' we received from the tennis club was somewhat less warm.

"Have you played any representative tennis?" we were asked.

"No," we responded in unison.

There was an immediate derisory and knowing glance between the two guys manning the tennis section desk.

"The teacher we had didn't approve of representative sport. I'm a reasonable enough player but J.P. here is genuinely good," said David.

"What school did you go to?" asked one of the guys.

"Tiverton," replied David.

David's response was met with laughter before the other person on the desk added his thoughts on the matter,

"I was at Exeter College. Tiverton were shit. We stuffed them. Look, guys, some of the sports clubs here cater both for players of the standard needed to play UAU competitive games and also for more recreational participants. But we can't – there simply aren't enough matches. We've got more than enough people with representative experience. You'd never get a game, sorry."

Not for the first time in my life, I walked away cursing the 'good' Reverend.

**

David and I were pretty much inseparable during the first few weeks in Sheffield. However, as the first term progressed I saw less of him – he stopped attending cricket nets after a few weeks as he spent more and more of his time with the Drama Society and the fellow students studying English Literature.

I began to wonder what all the fuss had been about that had made David so adamant that we needed to go to the same university.

However, it forced me to make the effort to meet other people and do different things. Sadly, I didn't bond with the fellow students doing French or Business Studies – but thankfully, during that first term, through the cricket club, I was to meet two of the most inspirational characters that I've ever met in my life in Simon Firth and Ian Bestall.

79

Ian and Simon were, like me, first year students. Both of them were highly intelligent with a very different perspective on life.

The first time that I visited Simon's room in his Hall of Residence only served to exemplify this. Whilst many students tried their best to customise their rooms as a 'demonstration of their individuality', none did this quite as dramatically or successfully as Simon.

On his door was a hand written sign saying 'Welcome to the Pleasure Dome'.

As I entered his room for the first time, I was staggered how, in the space of four weeks, Simon had somehow disposed of his Hall of Residence bed and replaced it with a park bench with the quotation above it:

'Guilt for being rich and guilt thinking that perhaps love and peace isn't enough and you have to go and get shot or something.'

The walls of his room were covered with silver foil and masses of foliage from the local park – it certainly made a change from the ubiquitous poster of the female tennis player showing her naked bottom that adorned many hall rooms at the time!

Most remarkably of all, Simon had built a small pond in the corner of his seventh floor room in which lived two frogs. If ever a room captured a person's spirit then that room certainly did Simon's.

"John Lennon," I said referring to the quote.

"Indeed, J.P. Very few people know that. I've never been a fan of The Beatles but some of his quotes are immense."

"It is a great quote and really quite poignant given what happened to him. Love the frogs as well, by the way."

"One's called Ethel and the other Merman."

I laughed.

I laughed a lot when with Simon.

**

It was Rag Week Pyjama Jump – an excuse for thousands of scantily clad students in female nightwear to have a thinly veiled drunken Roman orgy in the name of some charity or another.

The event started in the pubs near the University Halls of Residence and would end up, for those of sufficiently strong constitution to survive the journey that took in virtually every drinking establishment en route, in various nightclubs in the centre of town.

Well into the spirit of the evening in more ways than one, I strolled merrily along West Street, the main street going into town, which consisted mainly of public houses and Indian restaurants, in my 'splendid' blue nightie.

I came across a female student sat in a bookshop doorway looking very unhappy and depressed with life.

"Same nightie – I have to say that you look better in yours than I do in mine," I said with uncustomary alcohol-fuelled confidence.

There was no reply.

"Are you OK?" I added with some concern.

All the young woman did was cry and shake her head.

"Sorry, I always have this effect on women."

A brief smile flickered across the young woman's face.

"Seriously, if there is anything that I can do to help, just say," I added.

"If you could sit and talk with me for a while then I'd be very grateful," she replied.

"How can I refuse a damsel in distress?"

I sat down beside her.

"What's your name?" I asked.

"Helen. And yours?"

"Jonathan. What's the matter?"

"I miss Wigan."

"Each to their own, I guess."

Another brief smile flickered across Helen's face.

"Wigan is not the centre of the universe, that's for sure. What I mean is that I miss my parents and my boyfriend. I'm so desperately lonely and homesick. I hate this place."

"Have the Christian Union been around to see you?"

This time a smile turned to laughter before she replied,

"They most certainly have, wouldn't go away, in fact. But they couldn't help me as what I wanted was my parents and my boyfriend, not God. I thought that the Pyjama Jump would cheer me up but it's only made me more depressed and desperate to be back home!"

The two of us sat there talking in the shop doorway of the street for an hour – in our nighties on a cold November night watching hundreds of people wander past in their bed clothes.

It was a surreal moment.

"Where do you live?" I asked.

"Tapton Hall!"

"Same as me – I've never seen you."

81

"I hate the food almost as much as I hate Sheffield. My Mam cooks light healthy meals and all you get here is greasy stodge. I am so fed up. All I do is sit in my room, alone, night after night."

"Why don't I walk you back to the Hall?" I suggested.

"No, there's no way you want to be with an old misery guts like me. Go and have some fun. I'll be all right. It's bad enough one person being miserable on Pyjama Jump Night without making it two. Anyway I feel better after talking to you. Thanks!"

"No problem and don't be silly. Anyway, I've had enough to drink already. I absolutely insist on walking you back!!"

"I suppose if you insist, how can a damsel in distress refuse?"

"She can't."

Helen smiled, and we made our way back to the Hall of Residence passing several scantily clad revellers and over-indulgers heading in the opposite direction.

Once back at Tapton, I invited Helen to my room and made her some coffee. Helen sat on my bed, looking delightful with her shoulder length auburn hair.

"Your room's tidier than mine," said Helen.

"I hardly have any stuff, which helps. These rooms are really small," I replied.

"Can you give me a hug?" asked Helen.

I was only too willing to oblige.

After a while, hugging turned into kissing.

"Can you please just hold me if that's all right with you. I don't want sex, and I don't want to lead you on," she said.

Helen stayed with me for around an hour, holding each other and drinking coffee. I'd had sex before, but this was the first time that I'd been truly intimate with a woman – it was enchanting, the human warmth and affection as much as anything.

Helen's vulnerability genuinely touched me and, in a strange way, that helped me feel comfortable with her.

**

For the remaining weeks of term, I saw a great deal of Helen – I gave her someone to talk to about her loneliness and homesickness and in return she gave me a real confidence in dealing with women.

Come the penultimate day of term, I went out for a Christmas drink in the Halls of Residence bar at Tapton with Helen, dressed, as usual, in a black t-shirt and denim jeans.

82

"I've got a university place sorted out in Manchester that I can commute there every day from my home in Wigan. This is probably the last time we'll see each other," said Helen.

"I'm really happy for you," I replied.

"I shall miss you. You've been so kind to me."

After the two of us had had a few more drinks to celebrate her excellent news, we then had a few drinks more.

As the bar was closing, Helen gave me a Christmas card that said 'Thank You' on it. Helen then kissed me on the cheek and said,

"I've a present for you in my room."

"My God, I'm sorry. I've nothing for you. Typical hopeless male, I guess."

When back at her room, Helen told me,

"Lie down on the bed, close your eyes and be still."

To my complete surprise, Helen then proceeded to unzip my jeans and fellate me. I'd never had anyone do this to me before and it was a wonderful experience albeit, typical of me at the time, a very brief one.

Afterwards, Helen and I lay together for a while.

"I'm sorry, but you can't sleep with me. My parents are coming to collect me tomorrow and knowing Pops he'll most probably arrive at something daft like seven thirty a.m. I would like you to stay as I'll probably never see you again but I don't want to take the risk."

"We could stay in touch," I said.

"It won't work. My boyfriend's the jealous type. I'm not complaining. I like the fact that he's jealous."

Helen kissed me on the cheek and gave me a big hug.

"Have a good life. I hope you find someone special. She'll be a lucky woman."

"It's been an absolute pleasure for me. Not least the Christmas present," I replied.

Helen smiled.

"Every girl should have her secrets, you deserved it."

And with one final hug, I left Helen's room for the last time.

**

Back at Sheffield University after Christmas, other with than the cricket club and legendary reprobates such as Simon Firth and Ian Bestall, I spent a significant amount of time on my own.

I was more content. For the first time that I could remember, I felt that I didn't have anything to prove to myself or anyone else.

I started to spend my Saturday afternoons watching Sheffield Wednesday. I loved standing on the Kop at their Hillsborough ground with the local fans. The fans had such humour and resilience – and they often needed it.

I became hooked on watching Wednesday and even started going to some away games. What hooked me about football was the very strong sense of belonging to something, that and the passion – things that, at the time, I didn't have in my university life.

** **

Towards the end of term, David made a rare appearance at cricket nets.

Afterwards, together with Simon and Ian, we adjourned to our favourite student pub haunt, The York, in Broomhill.

"Hey J.P., I've organised an English Department social event for tomorrow lunchtime. All drinks are for free," announced David.

"Good for you!"

"Are you going to come?"

"Nah, I've got tickets to go and watch Wednesday play at West Ham United."

"What, you are such a 'sad' person! You're going all the way to bloody London. It's a four-hundred-mile plus round trip."

"Maybe I am 'sad' but I like watching Wednesday. Anyway, free drinks or no free drinks, apart from you, I don't know anyone who is doing English. I just can't be doing with making the effort to communicate with and get to know people I've never met," I replied.

"Still shy and sensitive, eh?"

"Look, David, shy and sensitive or not, I'm going to go and watch Wednesday play at West Ham. End of fucking story – all right!"

"Keep your hair on, J.P. Message clearly communicated. If you change your mind, you'll be more than welcome. Anyway, must go. Need to see a man about a dog!"

"Off in search of a shag at the Students' Union Disco, more like," interjected Simon.

"Dick show at the Disco," added Ian.

"You're only jealous, you lot. Some of us have it and some, sadly, do not," replied David.

"Have what? Standards? The Union dick show is not likely to be the place where I meet a woman. It's a false, unnatural environment. I know I'm sounding like a pompous windbag but meeting the woman of your life is where the mystery of life weaves its magic and Cupid's arrow leaves its everlasting mark. Don't the French have a phrase for it, J.P.? Let life do what it does or something like that?" asked Simon.

"Laissez la vie faire?" I offered.

"That's the one. If it's going to happen, it's going to happen. Love is a natural, spontaneous flower best cultivated in an environment where conversation can flourish. I'm afraid the delights of New Order's *Blue Monday* in the Octagon Building fail to meet my romantic vision of life. Public houses remain the natural home for the otherwise dying art of conversation – a last bastion in a changing world."

"Jeez, French, romantic visions, Cupid's arrows – no wonder you guys spend all your time with beer refreshment rather than horizontal refreshment. And on that note, I shall bid you fine gentlemen farewell," responded David.

Meeting Sophia

It was Saturday March 15th 1986.

Many years later, I can still remember that Saturday as though it was yesterday.

Despite quite a few beers with Simon and Ian the night before, I was up early to catch the Sheffield Wednesday supporters coach that was due to depart from near Wednesday's ground in Hillsborough at 9.30 a.m.

Before leaving my room in the Halls of Residence at Tapton Hall, in the classic manner of a Virgo, I went through the same ritual before every game, home or away – diligently checking that I had my tickets both for the supporters coach and the match itself.

A couple of local bus rides later, I was at the ground ten minutes before the supporters coach was due to leave. I gave the coach steward my coach ticket and before boarding the bus, to be absolutely sure, checked again that I had my match ticket with me.

Incredibly, I could not find the ticket anywhere. I couldn't believe it.

Stood next to the coach, I searched my pockets for a full five minutes before deciding reluctantly that there was little point in going on a four-hour plus journey to West Ham if I didn't have a ticket.

I made my way back to my room at the Halls of Residence.

Once there, I turned my room upside down in a mixture of anger and frustration – but still could find no sign of my ticket.

I made myself a cup of tea, calmed down and remembered David's invitation of the previous evening.

**

The Broomhill Tavern was a few yards down from my usual haunt, The York, and more upmarket than the normal student pub. As I walked into the bar, I was not a little relieved to see David all by himself.

"J.P.! I thought that you were going to London to watch the mighty Fowls lose."

"So did I, but somehow I lost my ticket. I got up early and went all the way to Hillsborough. I just can't fucking believe it," I replied.

"I do that shit all the time but you're so organised."

"Not this time."

"Anyway, time for a beer, me feels. As you can see, we are positively overwhelmed by attendees at this point in time. If no one else comes, we've a big budget that you and I can work through."

Over the next 10 to 15 minutes, people did start to arrive at the event, and my discomfort levels started to rise dramatically. Meeting new people was such a trauma for me and I again cursed under my breath to myself over losing the ticket.

David did his best to make me feel comfortable – taking the time to introduce me to all of the people as they arrived and trying as hard as possible to make me feel as welcome.

Somewhere in the region of 25 people must have turned up that day but the names of the people went in one ear and out of the other.

However, the drinks were free and after a couple of pints with the prospect of more to follow, I was floating around from the periphery of one conversation to another.

On the classic old premise that one drink is nice, two drinks are enough and three drinks are not half enough, I could feel myself, albeit by default, drifting into a major afternoon's drinking session courtesy of the English Department Social Society.

**

Halfway through my fourth pint, I was staring blankly out of the pub window.

I felt a tap on my shoulder and turned round to see it was David.

"Sophia, this is J.P. J.P., this is Sophia. Sorry, I need to pop for a waz. I'll be back in a tick."

My jaw dropped when I saw Sophia – she was without doubt the most unbelievable looking woman that I'd ever, ever seen. Quite simply, she absolutely took my breath away.

I was not the most eloquent with the female species anyway but Sophia, pretty and petite with a stunning figure and long, curly brunette hair would have left me momentarily speechless regardless.

Brunette heaven, I thought to myself.

Whilst all the women attending the Social event were in the regulation university uniform of jeans and t-shirts, Sophia was dressed in a black skirt above the knee with a red belt that matched the most magnificent high red stilettos.

It was as though Sophia came from a different planet. I had to speak to her. I didn't care if I made a fool of myself.

"Amazing shoes!" I said with most uncustomary confidence.

"I believe that shoes both red and vertiginous should be mandatory in every woman's wardrobe," she replied.

"I love the skirt as well. I'd forgotten what a woman's legs look like in this place."

"I woke up today feeling this desperate urge to express my femininity. I've had jeans on all week and needed a change."

"You look fabulous!"

"Well thank you, young sir."

At this point, David re-joined us.

"I feel better for that," said David.

"My life is enriched for that knowledge, David," said Sophia.

"Can I get you both some drinks?" I asked.

"Vodka and tonic," said Sophia in the most gorgeous feminine voice.

"Another beer, J.P.," added David.

As the barman poured the drinks, I kept staring at Sophia open jawed. Sophia caught me doing this and gave me a knowing smile. I thought about ordering another beer for myself, but decided given the situation that an orange juice was somewhat more appropriate.

To my astonishment, I had felt completely at ease with Sophia.

I clenched my fist and told myself that I had to keep going. I instinctively felt that this was the chance of a lifetime.

I wandered back with drinks in hand for David and Sophia.

"Don't you have someone else to talk to, David?" demanded Sophia.

"No!" said David.

"Well J.P. and I were having a very pleasant discussion on the importance of red stilettos in modern society before you interrupted us with your grand tales of toiletry events."

"All right, point taken," said David before wandering away in a huff.

I could scarcely believe either my ears or my luck.

"He's a love, David, but I see him all the time during the week; same for everyone else here. I wasn't going to come today, but the shoes red and vertiginous were simply begging to be worn," said Sophia.

"I love the word 'vertiginous'."

"Me too – it's like delectable. Some words are simply sumptuous."

"And what an apt alliteration!"

Sophia laughed, and as we talked, it was as though no one else was in the room. Maybe it was the drink – there again, maybe not. There was something about Sophia that put me at ease. Her confidence, natural humour and energy were contagious – and, boy oh boy, that breathtaking smile of hers.

It was a smile that could illuminate the world.

"Why does David call you J.P.?" asked Sophia.

"Jonathan Paul. He's called it me ever since we first met years ago."

"Jonathan's so much nicer than J.P."

"I've never really thought about it."

"Oh no, Jonathan's definitely nicer. It's much more you. Tell me, what course do you do?"

"French with Business Studies."

"I so love French. Say something to me. Make it lovely and romantic."

"Je voudrais passer toute ma vie avec vous."

Sophia's eyes sparkled as she clearly knew enough French to realise what I'd said.

"Mmm…yes, that is romantic but shouldn't it be toi and not vous if you want to spend the rest of your life with me. And voudrais is so unspeakably polite. For any man in my life, it needs to be veux."

"Mais bien sûr, mademoiselle. Je veux passer toute ma vie avec toi."

"I'm not sure about the rest of my life, but I am available for the afternoon if you're interested," replied Sophia.

"Shall we go then?"

"Can I finish my drink first?"

"No!" I replied with assertiveness that I didn't believe was in me.

"Can I at least get my coat! Where are we going in such a hurry?" she asked.

"No idea," I replied.

"I simply adore a man with a plan."

Sophia picked up her coat and followed me out of the pub.

I never even thanked David for the invite.

"Let's go down to the botanical gardens," I said.

"Fine by me," replied Sophia.

As the two of us walked around through the main Halls of Residence area and down towards the botanical gardens, I had the sudden realisation that it was spring – basking in the joy of the sun shining on trees that were beginning to bloom.

She tucked her arm inside mine as natural as anything.

Sophia exuded femininity from head to toe – slim but wonderfully curvaceous at the same time. Until she came into my life, I'd often questioned, almost laughed at the idea of love at first sight – this mythical concept of the thunderbolt to the heart.

I've never doubted it since that day in March 1986.

That afternoon, as Sophia and I talked effortlessly about anything and everything, I felt like a man having the dream of a lifetime. It was as though I'd known Sophia all my life. All my usual nervousness with women seemed to disappear into the ether.

I felt confident and at ease. It was as though I'd become a different man in her presence.

We sat together on a park bench, talking whilst watching the sunset come down over the botanical gardens.

"What do you want from life?" asked Sophia.

"When I was at school, my English teacher's favourite quote on love was 'I seek a love so amazing, so divine. One that demands my soul, my life, my all'. That really says it all about what I want in life."

"That's lovely, and aside from it being beautiful, it fills my head with ideas."

"Like what?" I asked.

"My immediate feelings are that a love that demands one's soul, one's life and one's all, is a love that takes a large degree of capitulation or relinquishing oneself to the power of that love."

"Absolutely!" I concurred.

"However if you go through life tentatively, shielding yourself from the things that might hurt you, then a love that is all-embracing will never be yours"

"Is that what you do?"

"Probably, thinking about it. But I think a lot of people do."

"Why? I just don't understand why you, or anybody for that matter, would want to do that."

"To put the feeling of love like that in someone else's hands is a very difficult thing to do, inasmuch as it requires one to be vulnerable and receptive, as love like that does not *happen* to anyone, one has to allow it in and bask in its glory. Most of all, a love like that is passionate – it's like paradise on the edge of the abyss. Love like that can be very complicated!"

I was silent.

"I think that I've touched a nerve there, haven't I?

I nodded and said,

"You certainly have. I've always loved the quotation. I now actually begin to understand why."

"Come on, you. Let's walk, I'm getting cold now," said Sophia.

We had no particular destination in mind. It didn't seem to matter.

"I'm normally not this confident – certainly not with women. You somehow bring out the best in me," I said as we walked.

"Just be spontaneous and carefree in life. Life is for living. Embrace life, love life. Close your eyes and let yourself go," replied Sophia.

Sophia closed her eyes, and despite the vertiginous red stilettos and skirt, she began to spin around and around, faster and faster and faster. With her eyes still closed, she started to lose balance, and as she stumbled, she fell into my arms.

"You could have hurt yourself," I told her.

"I knew that you'd catch me," she replied.

I kissed Sophia for the first time.

She smiled at me and said,

"You're nice, there's something different about you."

"Why?" I asked

"I'm fed up with men jumping on me. The sex can be incredible at times, but I've definitely accumulated some significant 'emotional rubbish' during my brief time here in Sheffield."

"What on earth is 'emotional rubbish'?"

"Oh, mostly totally unnecessary and overrated dates – I guess it's a phase I'm going through. It seems that before Christmas, I compulsively collected men."

I laughed.

"What are you doing with your collection then?" I asked.

"It's going through a clean-up process."

"A clean-up process?"

"The clean-up process involves selectively ignoring some of the lovers I've acquired whilst actively dismissing others. I'm hoping that eventually it will lead to a quieter life. Not too quiet mind! As part of my long term strategy, I still need to keep an eye out for that one man who dares."

"Dares what?"

"That's for me to know and for the man to find out," replied Sophia coyly but with the broadest grin on her face.

"You are a tease," I told her.

"Me, never," replied Sophia with the most innocent look.

I felt like an ice cube melting.

"Dares to ask you to the cinema tonight?" I asked

"What's on?"

"Not the slightest idea."

Sophia was silent. I was not to be deterred and asked,

"Does it matter?"

"No."

"Let's go then."

"Why not?" said Sophia.

For the briefest of moments, I closed my eyes and clenched my fist in celebration.

Sophia and I walked into town, stopping off at a McDonalds on the way since neither of us had had anything to eat at all that day. With a deadpan face and expression, Sophia commented and asked me,

"Thank you for bringing me to such an incredible place. Do you always take women to the best places?"

I laughed before responding,

"Twelve Chicken nuggets and a large packet of French fries – true romance indeed! Stick with me and you'll get nothing but the best. What more could a woman want?"

"To unwrap jewellery presents and arrange huge bunches of flowers to name but two."

"Does that happen often?" I asked.

"No, much to my chagrin."

Suitably sustained with food, we went to the biggest and most upmarket cinema in the centre of Sheffield, the Gaumont in City Square, and I bought Sophia an ice cream for dessert.

"No expense spared!" she joked.

Apart from *Prizzi's Honor* there wasn't much else on at the four different screens. As I gave Sophia the cinema ticket stubs as a memento, she smiled and said with mock affection,

"I will treasure them forever."

**

About half way through the film, I kissed Sophia. This time it was a long, deep, sensuous kiss.

We both smiled.

"I want to spend the whole night with you. I can think of nothing better than the first thing I will see tomorrow morning is your face," I said.

Sophia paused for what seemed like an eternity before saying,

"I'd like to wake up to you too. Do you want to leave immediately again or wait until the end of the film?"

"Let's go now."

"Your place or mine?" asked Sophia.

"Where is your place?"

"Halifax Hall."

"Your place – it's much nearer."

I immediately went to the gents toilets at the cinema to buy some condoms. I couldn't believe what was happening to me. I kept thinking that this was a dream and that I would wake up and, sadly, it would be all over.

With no time to waste, I suggested to Sophia that we take a taxi to Halifax Hall.

In the taxi, I told her,

"I've had sex before but I've never actually been to bed with a woman."

"So what?" asked Sophia.

"So be gentle with me!" I joked

Sophia laughed and kissed me on the cheek.

When we got to her room, she lit some candles, put the lights out and then undressed.

In the candlelight, Sophia looked more stunning than ever.

I undressed as well, somewhat awkwardly as my assertiveness of the day was starting to diminish. The effects of lunchtime drinking were long gone, and the reality was that this was the first time that I'd ever been with a woman stone cold sober.

"I'm nervous, really nervous," I said.

Sophia smiled at me and told me,

"Being vulnerable is not a bad thing, it's a good thing. Relax and let yourself go."

Sophia kissed me. She ran her tongue sensuously around my neck. It was as though every nerve ending in my body was on fire. I could feel the orgasm building up inside of me with Sophia's electrifying touch.

"Oh God, I'm going to come."

"Don't worry. It doesn't matter."

I felt her tongue tease my lips as she gave my penis the gentlest of caresses and I came immediately.

"Shit. I'm sorry," I said.

"As I told you, don't worry. It's nice for me to be with someone who is so excited. It's a compliment in a way."

Sophia's kind words immediately made me feel infinitely better and significantly less embarrassed by the brevity of my efforts.

"You enjoyed it. That's all that matters," she said.

"I've never felt anything like that. It was so soft and gentle."

"You're very gentle yourself. I like that. All you need is some practice, and I think that can be arranged somehow."

I looked into Sophia's brown eyes and said,

"I love your eyes, they're gorgeous."

"Why?" she asked.

"They're amazing and soulful. I feel that I could drown in them."

**

I stayed the whole night in Sophia's room. The two of us were very cramped in a small single bed, but I didn't care – it gave me more reason to be close to her and hold her in my arms.

In the middle of the night, we both woke up and started kissing again. Sophia's touch and sensuality was a joy to behold. I was more relaxed and comfortable. Sophia eased me on my back and got on top of me. She kissed me as she gently went up and down on me.

For the first time ever, I was enjoying making love. I don't know how long it lasted – maybe five minutes, maybe 10 minutes. The time wasn't important. I was simply blown away by the sheer intimacy of it all.

Part of me didn't want to come; I wanted this unbelievable sensual experience to go on all night. Sophia told me,

"I want you to come inside me."

I was exhilarated as her tongue and lips sensuously ran over my ear lobes. I sighed with the unadulterated bliss of it all. Sophia tightened the muscles inside of her.

I came in an instant as my entire body arched and spasmed in a sublime moment of ecstasy and release.

"As I said earlier, you need practice, that's all. It's nice for me to be the dominant one sometimes," said Sophia.

"Oh shit," I replied.

"What's the matter?"

"We didn't use a condom!"

"Oh."

There was a pause before Sophia continued,

"You're going to have to marry me then!"

I looked confused and bewildered, but was in no way intimidated or disturbed by the prospect.

Sophia laughed before saying,

"I'm on the pill, silly. I hate condoms. I like to feel a man come inside me. Did I have you worried there?"

"No," I replied.

"No, I don't think I did."

Sophia ran her fingers softly over my forehead before adding,

"You're nice. Lovely, sweet and gentle."

"So are you!"

"Not all the time. Late twentieth century woman in all her pomp! Men need sex, and so do I!"

Sophia laughed again. This time there was a filthy, deliciously dirty ring to her laughter.

**

When morning came and I opened my eyes, the first thing that I saw was Sophia's gorgeous face. I smiled the broadest of smiles and simply lay staring for ages at her sleeping peacefully.

Sophia finally did awaken.

"Do you want a cup of tea?" she asked.

"That would be nice."

Sophia looked at the electronic clock by her bed which said 9.36 a.m.

"Goodness, is that the time. I must hurry. Can you go and get the Sunday papers while I make the cups of tea? I'm afraid I need to throw you out after the tea."

"No problem. Why the hurry?"

"Because I want to go to church."

I looked at Sophia bewildered.

She laughed before saying,

"Yes, I know. The truth is that I am probably the most unlikely and most bafflingly paradoxical church-goer this side of the Vatican. But the facts are that I truly believe and that my life wouldn't be half as good if I didn't go."

"Are you winding me up?" I asked.

"Not at all, I love going to church."

"But all the God Squad are normally pious, po-faced and irritating."

"Because I go to church doesn't mean I am well-behaved. To call me pious or full of discipline or restraint couldn't be further from the truth. Now scram! Get those papers and quick! End of the road, turn right and the shop is at the bottom of the hill."

It was a glorious sunny morning – spring in the air, a hint of green in the trees and the birds were singing. I shouted aloud at the world, full of exuberance, "Hello Birds, Hello Trees!"

Upon buying the Sunday papers, I noticed that Sheffield Wednesday had lost 1-0 at West Ham. I was pretty unconcerned by that – to be honest I'd completely forgotten that they had been playing.

As I took out the money to pay for the papers, I found that inside my pocket was the ticket to the game.

Discovering Love

I left Sophia to be the most unlikely and bafflingly paradoxical church-goer this side of the Vatican and walked back to my Halls of Residence as though walking on air, a man on his own personal pink cloud.

Once back in my room, I made myself a cup of tea, put the radio on and stared out of my room window smoking cigarette after cigarette and reliving every glorious moment of the previous 24 hours.

It was time for lunch, but I didn't care. All I wanted was another slushy, romantic record to be played on the radio so that I could bathe in my new found joy whilst looking out of the window at the spring sunshine.

Shortly after 12.30 p.m. there was a knock at my door.

I opened it to find David, looking full of life, with the biggest smile on his face.

"Tell me that you did it, J.P.?"

"Did what?"

"Jeez, you and Sofe! I came around last night, and early this morning but you were nowhere to be found. So, did you?"

"Did I what?"

"Did you shag her?"

"David, can't you express such a sensitive and private matter in Shakespearean rather than vulgarian tones?"

"So, the boy's in love. Not that I blame you. Sofe's brilliant. I tried once or twice myself, but she always blew me out – said that she had enough stray dogs in her life without adopting another one. When are you going to see her next?" asked David.

"I've no idea."

"You do want to see her again, don't you?"

"My God, YES!"

"Jeez, J.P., you need some serious coaching. The woman is NOT going to come chasing after you."

"So what do I do?"

"Right, she'll be in the same lecture as me tomorrow at eleven a.m. – twelfth floor of the Arts Tower. Give her a bunch of flowers, arrange to see her again and let her go on her way. Keep it to a straight 'yes' or 'no' response. Got it?"

"I think so."

**

I bunked off lectures and went to Broomhill and spent £15 on flowers. I was an absolute bundle of nerves as I walked down the hill to the Arts Tower.

I kept telling myself to stay positive, stay cool. I arrived a full 10 minutes early. Despite the twelfth floor being a no-smoking area, I lit a cigarette to calm my nerves.

People started to come out of the lecture room. I saw Sophia walking and talking with a man. I prayed that this guy wasn't another one of her collection of men. A wave of adrenaline surged through my body together with a whole host of emotions running through my head – excitement, fear, lust, adoration.

I even had an erection. I took a deep breath and walked with purpose towards Sophia.

"I'll see you later," said Sophia to the man.

She gave me a welcoming smile. My nerves calmed – a little.

"Nice flowers!" she said.

"They're for David. I buy him flowers every Monday," I replied.

"Shame – I thought that they might be for me."

"Mayhap they are – but only if you meet me seven p.m. at the Broomhill Tavern tonight."

Sophia was silent for a moment. My heart seemed to skip a beat.

"Why not? They are very nice flowers, I suppose. But make it seven thirty p.m. And make sure you're carrying a copy of the *Daily Telegraph*."

"Why?" I asked.

"Otherwise I might not recognise you."

**

I arrived at the Broomhill Tavern 10 minutes early, ordered a beer and nervously lit a cigarette as I sat down on the comfy furnishings in the relatively empty bar area.

The minutes passed and no Sophia.

7.30 p.m. came and went – it was now past 7.40 p.m. I told myself to stay calm.

97

And then in she walked – looking a million dollars in a pair of black jeans that showed in great detail what a stunning lower body she had. In contrast, her top was baggy and pink but very feminine and the crucifix around her neck very prominent.

"Well, good evening, Miss Chatterley," I said.

"And a good evening to you, Mr Melton. No *Daily Telegraph,* though. You're lucky I recognised you."

"Yes, and for you no shoes red and vertiginous!"

"If I wear them too much, they lose their magical properties. Anyway don't you like my ankle boots? I love their heel – so sexy. I feel like a dominatrix when I put them on."

"They're delectable and sumptuous," I replied.

"I love those two words."

"You said. So do I. They're words that sound like the word they're describing. Like 'buzz'. What's the term for such words? Ona, ona….?"

"Onomatopoeia," said Sophia.

"That's the word. Are you an English student, mayhap?"

"Mayhap indeed – nice word, by the way, where does it come from?"

"I invented it," I said.

"I like it."

"I've always felt that 'possibly' was such a dull word whereas 'mayhap' is just much brighter. The 'May' gives it a springiness whilst the whole feel is 'may hap(pen)' which again is much more upbeat than possibly. It's also a little like 'mayhem' – there's a spirit of adventure to the word."

"Not to mention the sense of fortune and chance in the word 'hap'. I love etymology."

"Ety-what?"

"Etymology. It's the study of the history of words. Nice hair, by the way," replied Sophia.

"Well thank you."

"Not sure about the designer toilet roll on the chin, though."

My head dropped into my hands.

"Oh God, I forgot about that. Cut myself shaving."

"Come here you daft ha'p'orth."

Sophia gently removed the toilet paper from my chin and then sensuously wet her finger before softly wiping away any remaining residue.

"OK?" I asked.

"You'll live!"

I bought Sophia a drink and we talked.

After a while, we kissed sensuously. I loved her smell, her taste, her very touch.

"Any chance of some more of that practice you talked about?" I asked.

"Mayhap, mayhap not…I suppose you could come back to my room and see the flowers that you bought me, now that I've arranged them. Nothing more mind, I'm a prim and proper young lady."

We finished our drinks and set off for Halifax Hall, arm in arm.

**

As she'd said, Sophia had beautifully arranged the flowers in a very pretty vase. Once again, she lit some candles; we undressed and went to bed together.

Sophia set about a lesson in educating me in the sensitive parts of her body – her neck and ears, the backs of her legs, her sexy buttocks, her feet, her gorgeous breasts and, most of all, her clitoris.

She took my hand around her body.

As I played with her clitoris, I could sense her body getting more and more excited. Sophia kissed me, and as her tongue entered my mouth, I could feel myself come involuntarily. I was partly very embarrassed, but the other part of me didn't care. I just wanted to carry on touching her.

I could feel Sophia's muscles tensing.

"Are you all right?" I asked.

"Firmer, harder, faster – don't stop!"

I carried on as directed until Sophia sighed softly "yes". I opened my eyes to see the look of exhilaration on her face as she came.

It was around 10 p.m. on Monday 17th March 1986 that Sophia had her first orgasm in bed with me.

"That was lovely," said Sophia.

"I'm sorry. I came really quickly – again!"

"It doesn't worry me so it shouldn't worry you. You'll change in time. With hands like yours I'm in no rush."

"Je veux passer toute ma vie avec toi," I said.

"I have lectures tomorrow and then I'm busy for a couple of days. But you can see me Thursday night if you want," replied Sophia.

"I want!"

**

I knocked on Sophia's door, and she greeted me at the door in the same black dress and red shoes she'd worn the previous Saturday. With seductive lipstick and dazzling make-up, Sophia looked the most stunning that I had seen her yet.

We left her room to make the delightful early evening stroll to the pub, through leafy backstreets, past charming old Victorian houses.

"Oh, thou art fairer than the evening air,

Clad in the beauty of a thousand stars," I said.

Sophia looked at me quizzically.

"Don't say that you don't recognise the quotation?" I asked.

"Of course I recognise the quotation. I'm not sure whether it's Marlowe or Shakespeare."

"Who then? Your credibility as an English student depends on this!" I teased.

Sophia thought deeply for a minute before coming to her conclusion,

"Marlowe...then again it could be Shakespeare. No Marlowe, definitely Marlowe!"

"I'm impressed!"

"Phew, credibility retained! The shame of being outwitted on Seventeenth Century English Writers by a French Student and worse still, a French Student doing Business Studies would have been too great a shame to bear. It could easily have ended our relationship."

"Don't you like the quote then?" I asked.

"It was all right...no, it was more than that. It was nice. You seem to have more of a love of English literature than some of my fellow classmates. You've hidden layers and I like that. Keep it up, Melton!"

We arrived at the pub and sat down with our drinks.

I asked Sophia the same question that she'd asked me a few days earlier,

"What do you want from life?"

"To fulfil myself as a person," she replied.

"Not to be happy?"

"From everything that I've seen in my brief nineteen years on this planet, it should be enough in life to be content. I think that being happy is a statement used far too lightly. Happiness is not an everyday thing, it is a special day out, or a special smile from someone you care about, or a piece of good news never expected, or a massive downpour of rain on a summer's evening or even an incredible piece of writing that I'm reading for the first time. To be content every day should be more than enough for everyone, with lots of moments when true happiness is felt strewn in for good measure."

"But don't you want more?" I asked.

"How many people TRULY have that level of contentment and happiness? I don't think that it's a jaded view on life or not wanting enough from life, it's simply looking at happiness in a different way. I think that the word 'happy' has become an overused word nowadays. It should be a state of mind and feeling that is actually very special. Being happy should be something out of the ordinary, being content should be the norm and more than enough for anyone."

"And have you found that contentment, that happiness?"

"At times yes. At times no."

"Now for example?"

"Yes, I feel good now. I feel content sat here with you."

"And when you don't feel content, what do you do?"

"I tell myself that 'This too shall pass'."

"Does it work?"

"Together with going to church and adopting a positive attitude, yes. Things do go wrong in life, but you have to tell yourself that things will change, they always do. Whatever you feel, no matter how negatively, it will pass. Not tomorrow, not next week, maybe not even next year but it shall pass in the end as everything always does."

"Give me an example; I want to better understand what you mean."

"For ages I didn't have a good relationship with my mother. She couldn't relate to me at all. My two sisters are totally different to me – one's a secretary and the other's a hairdresser. Both left school at sixteen, and my mother felt that I should do the same. Nobody from our family has ever been to university and my mother always felt that going to university is what 'posh' people did – public schoolboys like you."

"I'm not a public schoolboy. I'm just a boy that went to public school."

"David always says that."

"David is right!"

"Any way I digress. There was a time in my life when my mother and I didn't get on at all. It was bad enough the irritating sibling rivalry with my sister Sandra but when it extended to my mother for a while, life at home was pretty awful. It felt as though my mother and sister were picking holes in literarily everything I did."

"Can't have been easy?"

"No, it wasn't. The Electra complex came to Roundhay, Leeds with a vengeance, I can tell you."

"As long as a woman can look ten years younger than her daughter, she is perfectly satisfied," I said.

101

"Dear old Oscar. No, it wasn't that – I almost wish it had been that because I think that I could have handled it better. It was simply down to the fact that I wanted to do something with my life and my mother deeply resented that. She was far more comfortable with my two sisters, Bev and Sandra, who were much more like her."

"How did it resolve itself then?" I asked.

"Dad was great as was my grandmother, my Mum's Mum, and between them they smoothed over the troubled water. I've always got on better with my Gran than with my mother. It has definitely improved with my mother though. I think that she is actually quite proud of me now. But it was genuinely tough for a while with home and school. I didn't feel I belonged anywhere."

"School as well?"

Sophia sighed before saying,

"At the school I went to, all the people I knew who were from a similar background to me left school early. They thought that I was a freak for wanting to go to uni. Any intelligent, good looking bloke that I met generally never got any further than what I looked like whilst all the female students in the sixth form thought I was this trollop because I had some fun with the guys. I never actually did anything with most of them, but there's always the male ego – the bluster and bravado of the adolescent male. As I say, I felt that I didn't belong anywhere and it made me sad. But I kept telling myself 'This soon will pass'. And it has. Since coming to Sheffield, my life is good now – particularly since I've stopped collecting men."

"But you've collected me."

"You're my Charity Project. And anyway, you're lovely. You're definitely growing on me!" teased Sophia.

"Charity Project?"

I pretended to sulk, crossing my arms and looking away from Sophia. She wrapped her tongue around my ear and gently ran her hand over my groin.

"You don't convince me, Melton. You're acting all hurt, but you're not. Give me a kiss!"

"No!"

Sophia continued to do unmentionably amazing things to my ear. I now had an erection that was virtually bursting out of my jeans.

"Show some decorum, woman! We're in a public house!!"

"I love it when you assert yourself."

"You're impossible, Sophia!"

"That's what my mother used to say to me. Shit, I'm seeing a man who's turning into my mother in less than a week. Shame, as I had plans for you tonight."

"What plans?"

"That's for me to know and for you to find out," said Sophia.

**

It was a beautiful clear night as we walked back to Sophia's room with a full moon and seemingly every star in the sky clearly visible. As we walked hand-in-hand, we stopped for a moonlit kiss under an old street lamp.

Once back in Sophia's room, I could see my flowers still in full bloom and well cared for. A smile crossed my face.

Sophia went into one of the drawers in her room and pulled out a blindfold and some handcuffs.

My eyes widened in complete astonishment.

"Right, you. It's my period, but I'm still feeling incredibly naughty. I've always wanted to do this, but it's never seemed quite right. I won't hurt you, but I've always had this fantasy since reading some of the Marquis de Sade stuff when I was younger. Are you willing to abandon yourself to my wanton desires?"

"God yes."

Sophia put the blindfold on and handcuffed me to her bedpost. She then set about teasing and tantalising me for what must have been the next hour or so. As usual it started with my ears and neck and lips. Then she played with my nipples until they hurt – soft and sensual mixed in turn with brutality.

After that she teased my stomach, I was ticklish but my hands were cuffed, and I was helpless to resist. Finally, she teased my penis for what seemed like an eternity whilst continuing to abuse my nipples.

I wanted to come, needed to come, and I was begging Sophia – where was a premature ejaculation when one needed one, I asked myself?

Sophia continued to tease and tantalise me until the ecstasy turned to pain.

"Please Sophia, PLEASE," I begged.

At last, Sophia took pity on me.

I ejaculated with a scream that could probably have been heard half a mile away.

"Did you enjoy that?" asked Sophia.

"It was unbelievable. Painful but in a nice way," I responded.

"I loved it. I've always wanted to do that but never felt the time was right with anyone until now. It's strange – we've only known each other a week, but I feel that I can say or do anything with you. You don't judge me. Apart from Dad and Gran, I feel as though everyone else that I've ever known in my life doesn't understand me and always ends up judging me or criticising me or both. You accept me for who I am and I find that so liberating."

Sophia uncuffed me, took my blindfold off and we spent our last night together before the Easter break.

She Loves Me, She Loves Me Not

I caught the train to Sheffield very early on the Sunday morning, eager to see Sophia again before the start of the summer term. David was to follow with Brian later in the day with most of my belongings.

I was excited beyond words and could barely sit still on the train and ended up prowling the carriages like a caged, chain-smoking lion.

When my train arrived at Sheffield Midland Station at 1.48 p.m., I could see Sophia already on the platform waiting for me. She just looked amazing with the red shoes replaced by equally vertiginous black boots.

In a black, skirt she was the absolute epitome of everything that is magnificent about the female species.

Before disembarking the train, I closed my eyes, clenched my fist, took an enormous deep breath to try to expel all the tension from my body and told myself firmly "Let's do this!"

I flung my arms around her and gave her a big affectionate kiss.

I sensed some affection coming back from Sophia.

"Did you miss me then?" asked Sophia.

"Now there's a rhetorical question if ever there was one, Miss Chatterley."

Sophia smiled and said,

"Let's get the bus down Eccleshall Road and walk up to my room through the botanical gardens."

"Sounds good to me!"

**

As we wandered through the gardens and passed the point where I had kissed Sophia for the first time, I glowed inside. We were talking effortlessly and easily as though we had never been apart.

When we finally arrived back in Sophia's room, now full of D.H. Lawrence memorabilia, we went to bed immediately.

I let myself go as Sophia had continually encouraged me to do so and gave my hands free rein to express themselves over the whole of her body. Her grip on me grew tighter and tighter until she let out a

105

glorious, deep sigh as her body spasmed and contracted in a moment of sensual and sexual release.

I sighed to myself in sheer and utter joy.

Sophia kissed my right hand and said,

"Your hands are incredible. Have you been practising on someone else over the holidays?"

"Mayhap," I said with a coy grin.

"I don't think so, Melton."

"Mayhap you're right, mayhap not."

"I'm going to have to work harder to keep you to myself then, aren't I?"

Sophia kissed and licked my nipples. I was already in a state of considerable arousal and excitement, but this took me to new levels. I was desperately trying to hang on – the last thing I needed was another case of premature ejaculation.

"Relax. You may think that you're going to come straight away, but you won't. Trust me," said Sophia.

Sophia's mouth moved from my nipples and as she started to kiss and nibble the tip of my penis, she teased both my nipples in turn with one hand whilst, with her other hand she started to gently stroke the ring piece of my bottom.

The feeling of exhilaration running through my veins and every nerve ending in my body was unbelievable.

As I was about to come, Sophia entered me with her finger. Wave upon wave of exquisite and intense pleasure flooded my body. I could feel myself yelling out with the unadulterated ecstasy of it all. My complete body spasmed, as I underwent what I can only imagine a physical exorcism would feel like.

I gradually came down from sexual Nirvana and started laughing out loud.

I opened my eyes to see the most wicked grin on Sophia's face as she said,

"That should keep you in check for a little while yet."

I noticed my left leg was still twitching involuntarily.

"God, where did you learn to do that?" I asked.

"Here and there, along the way. So are you going to lie there all day? I didn't come back early to lie in bed with you! It's a lovely spring day outside. Come on!"

"Nag, nag, bloody nag. Woman gives man best experience of his albeit limited life. Man happily still orbiting Planet Zob and all woman does is nag to go out. I'm lost for words."

Sophia smiled and gave me a kiss.

106

"Come on, get dressed you. It's a perfect day for a walk."

**

It was a glorious, sunny late spring day with the gentlest of breezes in the air. As we strolled, hand-in-hand, without a care in the world, through the delightfully undulating and leafy Endcliffe Vale Park, we got talking on all manner of English literature – Shakespeare, Byron, Wilde and others.

"With all the memorabilia in your room, is D.H. Lawrence your favourite author?" I asked Sophia.

"No question. The fact that my name is Chatterley adds to the whole magic of it all. It was the incredible and intense sexuality to his writing that attracted me. It fuelled my early teenage masturbatory habits, I guess."

"He's my favourite author too," I replied.

"No way!" exclaimed Sophia.

"'When I read Shakespeare I am struck with wonder that such trivial people should muse and thunder in such lovely language'. D.H.L. says in two lines everything that I feel about Shakespeare. And it seriously pisses off David, which is not without its merits from time to time."

"Yes, that quote would piss off David."

I laughed.

"I always wanted to go to Nottingham University because they have an international reputation for research into Lawrence," said Sophia.

"Why didn't you?" I asked.

"It was totally bizarre in retrospect. I tried three times to go for an interview there and three times I failed. The first time I was ill with food poisoning. The second time there was a train strike and for the third interview there was confusion over the date and I ended up turning up on the wrong day and nobody was available to interview me. In the end I decided that it was destiny – that there was a force beyond my control taking me somewhere else. Bringing me here to Sheffield, I guess. Do you believe in destiny?"

"If you'd have asked two months ago, I'd have said what a load of old baloney. However, the day we met at the Social do, I was going to watch a football game in London but I couldn't find the ticket in my pocket, so I didn't go. But then after I met you the ticket reappeared. Totally bizarre as you say."

"Incredible."

Sophia let go of my hand and started to skip on her own.

"So what is your favourite work of Lawrence's then?" she asked.

107

"*The Rainbow* – I just loved Ursula. She was my heroine…brave, strong and resourceful but at the same time really sensitive and oh, so very sexy. For the last year at school, Ursula was my girlfriend – in my head anyway. Sad really I guess, but I was in love with her or at least the idea of her. I wanted to leap into the pages of the book and be with her."

Sophia sat down on a park bench. I sat next to her as we surveyed the glorious expanse of green and blooming spring flowers around us.

"I loved Ursula too. Part of me wanted to be her – to live in those times, to experience what she went through. There's one passage from *The Rainbow* that is imprinted on my soul."

"What?" I asked full of excitement and enthusiasm.

Sophia threw her head back and closed her eyes.

"If I think too much, I can never remember. If I switch off and let it flow then it comes to me."

I was silent, waiting. After a few seconds, Sophia opened her eyes and began to speak,

"And then, in the blowing clouds, she saw a faint iridescence colouring in faint colours a portion of the hill. And forgetting startled, she looked for the hovering colour and saw a rainbow forming itself."

I was transfixed.

My spine was tingling, and I could feel the goose bumps covering every inch of my arms. I loved D.H. Lawrence and, in particular, the character of Ursula. And somehow Ursula was now being brought to life in front of my very eyes in the form of this stunning, gorgeous, wild, wilful, magnificent force of nature that seemed to be from another planet.

"More, more," I said.

Sophia smiled.

"Well, if you insist, sir."

"I DO insist!"

"Where was I?"

"…and saw a rainbow forming itself."

"Oh yes."

Sophia closed her eyes, and she started again, even more passionate and animated than before.

"In one place it gleamed fiercely, and, her heart anguished with hope, she sought the shadow of iris where the bow should be. Steadily the colour gathered, mysteriously, from nowhere, it took presence upon itself, there was a faint, vast rainbow. The arc bended and strengthened itself till it arched indomitable, making great architecture of light and colour and the space of heaven, its pedestals luminous in the corruption of new houses on the low hill, its arch the top of the heaven. And the rainbow stood on the earth. She knew that the sordid people who crept hard-scaled and separate on the face of the world's corruption were living still, that the rainbow was arched in their blood and would quiver to life in their spirit, that they would cast off their horny covering of disintegration, that new, clean, naked bodies would issue to a new germination, to a new growth, rising to the light and the wind and the clean rain of heaven."

I knew the words by heart myself and began to mouth along in sync with Sophia.

"She saw in the rainbow the earth's new architecture, the old, brittle corruption of houses and factories swept away, the world built up in a living fabric of Truth, fitting to the over-arching heaven."

Sophia opened her eyes briefly and then closed them again as she threw her head back in sheer unadulterated joy. When she finally opened her eyes again and looked into mine, I said,

"I love that so damn much. It always makes me think of Pandora's Box."

"Why?" asked Sophia.

"What is the last thing out of Pandora's Box?"

Sophia laughed, immediately understanding my thinking and said,

"Of course...it's Hope."

Sophia looked at me, and the pupils in her brown eyes dilated as they sparkled. I knew that Sophia liked me, but this was the first time that I had sensed something much, much more.

"Do you have a cigarette?" asked Sophia.

"I didn't know you smoked."

"Only when I'm exhilarated and need to wind down."

I gave Sophia one of my cigarettes and after lighting it she asked me,

"Do you know when *The Rainbow* was published?"

"I'm not sure exactly. Somewhere around 1915, maybe 1916 I think,"

"Yes, 1915. So many people are being needlessly killed and slaughtered in a pointless war, and he writes that; it flabbergasts me. The world is remarkable, for something terrible there is at the same time always something truly wondrous."

I kissed Sophia – deeply, passionately, overflowing with emotion.

**

109

We carried on walking for the rest of the afternoon and as we finally made our way back to her room, we took a minor detour en route to stop off at a fish and chip shop.

As we sat on the wall outside the fish and chip shop on that April evening eating our gastronomic delight of fried haddock, mushy peas and chips out of a newspaper, I could as easily have been in Paradise.

"I love being with you, I just love being around you. I feel a different person when I'm with you," I said.

"I love being with you too."

"Why?"

"Because I feel that you want to be with me and that's all. I don't sense any ulterior motive to our conversations – that you're not trying to fathom out whether I'm going to give-in this evening or not."

"Well actually I do hope that you are going to 'give-in this evening' as you put it. But when we're talking I'm only interested in what you have to say. Having sex with you is amazing. As you know, I'm really inexperienced, and I'm still learning – learning quickly I hope. But talking to you is just as amazing as when we're in bed together, if not more so. The stuff with D.H. Lawrence and *The Rainbow* was an unbelievable moment for me," I replied.

"I know. I can tell. I loved it too. It's so very tiresome when talking to men and realising that they are not listening to my views on the relative quality of mushy peas in Leeds versus Sheffield chip shops, but instead are wondering if I swallow or not."

I laughed and Sophia added,

"What I am trying to say is that it is great to enjoy company without having to adjust my own behaviour. I used to adjust my behaviour loads before Christmas to enable myself to pick up some stray dogs and then decide whether they would be put back on the street or if they were indeed the pedigree pet for life, not just a novelty."

"Am I a novelty?" I asked.

Sophia looked me straight in the eye and said,

"No!"

The broadest smile crossed my face.

"At least I don't think so! We'll have to wait and see, won't we?" she added.

The broad smile disappeared from my face.

"Don't look so glum. We've known each other for little more than a month. You don't even know my second name."

"Sophia, if the male ego was a penis then you'd give it the best ever blow job only to leave the next day!" I protested.

Sophia laughed before saying,

"Good spirit, Melton. I like spirit in a man. A little harsh but I can live with that. There's certainly some truth in what you're saying."

"OK, so what's true and what's not?" I asked.

"Very importantly, lying, or making things up for the sake of it, are a total waste of time in my opinion. I will not waste any energy on trying to make things better or easier when they are not. I do like a little artistic licence though, but never so much that I deviate from the truth."

"Fair enough, I agree that you are a fundamentally honest person. Nevertheless, I do feel that I'm dancing to your tune. I'm inexperienced and never ever had a proper girlfriend. This is all a big adventure for me. However, you seem in complete control which I suppose is to be expected. But all this, 'maybe I'm a novelty and maybe not' shit really does piss me off. You're using your female power, for want of a better phrase, to turn me into a plaything."

"You seem willing enough to be my plaything."

I laughed before saying,

"Yes and no. I just want to know whether you want to go out with me or not! That's all. I think it's a fair enough question."

"You're right, it is a fair question. I adopted this 'control' or 'power' behaviour, as you call it, a few years ago. It was a mechanism to deal with men. During my first encounter with a man, I was unceremoniously dumped, so my behaviour changed. By using the 'power' behaviour, as time went on, I was able to figure out the skills that I needed to bag the illusionary man of dreams. The 'power' behaviour though has now become second nature and seems hard to shift, which is fine, because if the truth be known, I quite enjoy watching men writhe and bend over backwards in their innate, intrinsic animal mating ritual."

I laughed as Sophia continued,

"So in that respect, your analysis of me is correct, I am wholly aware I am using my female power, but I enjoy it all the same. The problem arises when men confuse bodily lust with soulful love or, horror of horrors, they actually deem me suitable for a long-term relationship. I say horror, because most of them are so far out of their league and don't realise. I would eat most men for breakfast, and that's not even talking about the physical side of things."

"I've no doubt you would. But where does that leave me? Answer the bloody question! Do you want to go out with me or not? Am I your proper boyfriend?"

Sophia looked me firmly in the eye and said,

"Yes, I think that I want to go out with you."

"Yessssssssssssss!" I screamed.

"Maybe. Softly, softly – Mr Melton. Give me time, I need time."

"OK," I said.

Sophia gave me a gentle peck on the cheek. As we set off walking, she put her arm inside mine in the way that I had come to adore.

"What is your second name then?" I asked.

"Theresa. I hate it!"

**

Back in Sophia's room after three or four hours of walking, talking and eating together, I felt a strength and confidence building inside of me – that and a burning, yearning, hungry, insatiable sexual desire for her.

"I want you. I want you now," I said.

Sophia said nothing but gave me the horniest, filthiest yet knowing look. She took her clothes off, and I did likewise.

We kissed passionately. I was excited beyond words, and I could tell from the burning desire with which Sophia was kissing me that no foreplay was needed.

For the first time, I was dominant and eased inside of her. The sexual act which had seemed alien to me until that point now seemed the most natural thing in the world – no blindfolds, no handcuffs and, thankfully no premature ejaculation.

As Sophia and I continued to kiss and our groins rubbed together, a whole myriad of emotions and sublime sensations ran through my body. Finally, at long last, in an act of love, my penis finally was part of my body rather this uncontrollable organ with a mind and action of its own.

I came. It was unbelievable – love and lust mixed together in the most glorious, heady concoction.

"Do you have a cigarette?" Sophia asked me afterwards.

"I sure do!"

"Isn't it great?" asked Sophia.

"What?" I replied.

"To sit and talk for the sake of talking, not as some sort of diversion, or road to the bedroom. I love talking with you. I love listening to your opinions and views on life, literature and all things unfathomable."

"And me too. I would want to spend time with you even if we weren't having sex together."

Sophia gave me an affectionate kiss before saying,

"I know, and it's lovely. Most people don't like going too deeply, in their own lives or in their ponderings on more general, philosophical issues. Afraid of what they might unearth, perhaps?"

"Maybe," I replied.

"Mostly because of laziness, I think."

"But that's not the case with me. So PRECISELY what do I have to do to become your official boyfriend?" I asked.

"I want to be wooed! I want to be courted. I want to be seduced."

"I thought I'd already done that!"

"Melton, you have no idea about women. I want some romance."

"I bought you some flowers!"

"Yes, and I loved them. I want you to write to me. I am definitely the most avid reader I know. Any words are appreciated. I have lamented the fact that letters are seldom written these days, because there is nothing better than a sheet, or better still, a few sheets of handwritten paper to read."

"I'll write to you then if you want."

"But leave it a couple of weeks. I have loads to do. I know that first year exams don't mean that much, but I still want to do well. My degree is very important to me."

"Two weeks?" I exclaimed.

"Two weeks will pass in an instant. Anyway, I remember you telling me that you wanted to play cricket."

"I did but I'd rather be with you."

"Now listen to me. I need my own space and freedom. Don't hem me in," replied Sophia.

There was a silence. I smiled brightly and with mock dramatics said,

"Oh, woe is me. She loves me, she loves me not."

"Love is more complicated than that. It isn't a yes or a no. It's more 'Does he loves me a little, does he love me a lot, does he love me passionately or does he love me insanely? Or does he perhaps not love me at all?'"

"I just love you!"

Sophia smiled and replied,

"Yes, I believe that you do."

"How do you feel about me?" I asked.

"That's for me to know and for you to find out."

I was silent.

"It's for me to find out too. I love being with you, but this is all too quick. Give me time and space. I'm a little bit frightened at this point if the truth be told. I promise not to mess you around, but I do need some time. As I said earlier, I want to be wooed, I want to be courted. I want to be seduced. I want the magical tension that is there at the start of a relationship," said Sophia.

"OK. If you want to be wooed and courted, then that's what I'll do!"

"As I say, leave it a couple of weeks and then surprise me with a letter or a note on the Union Notice board. I need to find out whether I truly miss you or not."

Paradise on the Edge of the Abyss

Monday 5th May

Dearest Sophia,
"Roses are red, violets are blue,
It has to be said that I fancy you."

I feel that I have it in me to become the first ever Bard of Sheffield. As an English Literature student, I would welcome your feedback.

Best wishes,

Jonathan

8/5

Dear prospective Bard of Sheffield,
Assessment of your kind offering is as follows :

Flowers: B+ (I've never been given a Violet before!)
Poem : D-

Would constructively suggest that the writer raises his game significantly if he wishes to achieve objective of becoming first ever Bard of Sheffield.

Sophia

Thursday 8th May

Dearest Sophia,
I'm glad that you liked the flowers. Although harsh, I have to admit that the feedback on the prospective Bard of Sheffield's first ever poem in life was fair.

I was fed up with course work and went for a walk into Endcliffe Vale Park and sat on the same benches as when we talked about D.H. Lawrence's *The Rainbow* a few weeks ago. Inspired by the location and the memory, I have hopefully 'raised my game' as suggested with the following :

The Sun shines, there's a gentle breeze,
You're in my thoughts, always with such ease,
My heart flickers, then passion burns,
The body trembles, my flesh just yearns,
My poor senses, they do barely cope,
To see you again, I can but hope

Feedback on the above to the usual address greatly appreciated.

Jonathan

Monday 12th May

Clearly the poem left you so stunned by its brilliance that you cannot find the words to describe your feelings about it.

In the absence of feedback, as prospective first Bard of Sheffield, I feel it my duty to make additions to the English language where no suitable words currently exist.

With this in mind, I have been pondering on the following...if progression is going forward and going backwards is regression, does this mean that going sideways is just gression?

If so, is our courtship currently going through a 'Gressionary' period? Answers on a postcard to the usual address.

Jonathan

15/5

Jonathan,
Haven't had time to respond to you this week as I am genuinely struggling with Chaucer revision – not least because he bores me to the point of stupefaction.

I must concede that I agree with your note. I do feel that our Gressionary Period is nearing its end though. In not seeing you for a few weeks I knew it would be either out of sight, out of mind or absence makes the heart grow fonder. I have to say, and this may please you, it definitely seems a case of the latter.

By the way, if there was ever a word that deserved to get official recognition, it is 'gressionary'. Without it being a real word, it still captures the essence of what you are trying to convey by using it, how extraordinary. The prospective first Bard of Sheffield is showing good signs of progress and certainly adds more value to the life of this particular English Student than the dreaded Chaucer.

Sophia
(P.S. I did like the poem. Very sweet and touching)

Thursday 15th May

Dearest Sophia,
Many thanks for your letter. Can we meet – maybe just for lunch? I know that you're really committed to your exams but even you must eat.

Many thanks for letting me know. A refusal will not offend.

Friday 16th May

Sophia,
I noticed that you picked up my note but no answer. I therefore conclude that lunch is not an option.

If so then I am willing to don female wig and pantyhose in order to sneak into Halifax Hall to join you for evening meal tonight.

Please advise whether the above is possible and also what denier of pantyhose would be most appropriate for me.

Life is such a drag without you (boom boom).

Prospective First Bard of Sheffield

Tuesday 20th May

Dear Missing Person,
I'm sorry to be demanding, but honestly woman sometimes you just need taking in hand. I've always long suspected that the "T" initial in your name actually stands for Trouble.

Lower Refectory today 1.30 p.m. Be there!!

Jonathan

20/5

Trouble indeed!

I always like to see how far I can push the men in my life. Irrespective of the reason they are in my life for, men need to be taken to the edge of STC land, where the sheer cliffs mean a certain death for many that have hurled themselves there.

For others, more controlled, more brave and, most importantly, more understanding, the cliffs have meant a decision they have not regretted: the taking-in-hand of the recalcitrant Miss ST Chatterley.

And haven't you gone and done it! After only a few short weeks. My love, gratitude, respect and admiration will forever be yours, kind sir. Do not mock the ability of the outrageously gifted prospective first Bard of Sheffield on all matters female and flighty.

Thanks for the push. I am in dire need of those almost every day in one way or another. Sadly, the Lower Refectory at 1.30 p.m. is not possible. I will though concoct another note to you that should be forthcoming very soon, if the dreaded Chaucer allows me.

Sophia

Friday 23rd May

Sophia,
A very, very average (and rather old) Joke for you...
Two men are sat in a Public House.

First man: I've heard that Sophia Chatterley is going to join the Army?
Second man: What as?
First man: As a gunner.
Second man: A gunner?
First man: Well, she's always 'gunner' write notes to the Prospective First Bard of Sheffield, but never does!

HAHAHAHAHA!! Boom, boom!! (Original date of joke around which this adaptation is based is estimated something in the region of the year 1724).

Honestly some men are just so bloody ungrateful aren't they? You teach them about a woman's body, you show patience regarding their complete lack of sexual experience, you give them inspiration and fire their creativity to become the Prospective First Bard of Sheffield, in fact, you are downright gorgeous with them, and you send them the best letter that they have ever, ever received and what thanks do you get, eh?

None whatsoever, that's what!...not a sausage!!...just witter, witter, nag, nag about not sending the aforementioned Bard any letters!!!

Now who would possibly want Sophia's lot, eh?

By the way, purely as an aside to the above, I thought that I should casually mention in passing, not that it has relevance to anything in particular, that I absolutely and utterly adore you, Miss T for Trouble Chatterley.

Have a very good day!

Jonathan

23/5

Dearest Jonathan,
You are not being ungrateful. You deserve to get more from me, but Sophia is doing exams, her grandma is not well, and there has been an incident requiring a significant amount of time in the laundry room. The grandma situation is particularly concerning.

Did you know that to adore someone that they have to be receptive to it? Or at least, to obtain any benefit from it, it should be either received or even falteringly reciprocated. I say falteringly, because although bodily love has never been a problem for someone as tactile as me, something as abstract as an emotion is tricky territory.

But this Sophia has trained herself in the transference of tactility into intangible matter, and so has become adept at basking in such compliments. Thank you, my liege, for bestowing such kindness and confidence.

Now I shall wish you a nice afternoon and evening. I have another exam Monday morning but then there are no more exams for the next month. I shall leave you a note after the exam letting you know where we can meet. When we meet, I shall attempt to express my feelings towards you.

Sophia

Friday 23rd May

Regarding receptivity…well, I never ever took you to be a woman who can dish it out, but can't take it herself. Your last letter to me said quote unquote "My love, gratitude, respect and admiration will forever be yours, kind sir."

However, anything that comes back the other way creates discomfort? – I'm sorry but 'Houston, we have a problem here'. Either that or your original comments were either OTT (over the top) or lacked sincerity, and this is the root cause of the 'tricky territory'. I very much hope not.

Maybe you've had it all your own way for too long!

**

I decided that enough was enough – it was time to go to Halifax Hall to see Sophia and I bought a packet of cigarettes and a large cup of coffee for the bus journey.

After making my way through the corridors of the Hall of Residence and finally reaching her room, I banged on the door aggressively. Sophia opened it and upon seeing me, the biggest smile filled her face.

"Oh, it's you. Perfect timing, I was about to come and leave you a letter and then try and find you in the Students' Union."

I was silent but noticed that Sophia was all made up and dressed in a black skirt and boots.

I pushed her onto her bed and forced her skirt above her waist. I ripped her tights away with a mixture of my hands and teeth before easing her black knickers to one side.

I'd been through it a hundred times in my head during the previous few weeks. I just knew, fuelled by a heady mixture of passion and frustration, that if I let myself go – transferring all the touch and knowledge from my hands to my mouth, I could make Sophia come with my mouth.

All the coffee that had been drunk along with the numerous cigarettes that I'd smoked en route had left my mouth bone dry, which was exactly how I wanted it.

My mind emptied – for five minutes, maybe 10 minutes, the only thing that mattered was my tongue and her clitoris. It was like sheer white light in my head.

As Sophia became more and more aroused, she held my head tighter and tighter against her clitoris. I was almost suffocating, but I was a man possessed. The white light in my head grew brighter as the muscles in Sophia's legs began to twitch involuntarily.

I was totally at one with her as the muscles in her whole groin and stomach area tightened.

"Oh yesssss, that's it," she sighed as her vice like grip on my head slackened – the white light inside my head turning to a kaleidoscope of colours.

And then joy of joys, all this amazing warm liquid flowed out of Sophia. I drank it as though it was the very nectar of the gods.

I pulled myself up the bed. Sophia was laying there, clothes in a dishevelled state, her right hand around her neck in post-coital bliss. As she opened her gorgeous brown eyes, I could see her pupils dilating like crazy.

"So that's what orgasm tastes like, I've often wondered. Do all women do that?" I asked.

121

"Around one in thirty or perhaps one in forty, so I've been told. I started masturbating when I was around twelve or thirteen and, if the truth be told, it freaked me out a bit. I thought that I was losing bladder control every time I had an orgasm. But our family doctor was great. She knew immediately. I love it now I've got older. I can feel it building inside of me, and I feel so incredibly feminine, so damn sexy when I come. However, it does have some disadvantages. I am very, very wet and need to get these knickers off."

"Oh no you don't, young lady! Bend over."

"Yes, sir, if you insist."

I pushed her soaking wet black knickers to one side and entered Sophia from behind. She was very wet, and I slipped straight in. Sophia moaned a sigh of pleasure. The frustration from when I'd arrived at her room was now replaced by unadulterated animal lust.

I held Sophia firmly by the hips and could smell the sweet, musky odour of her orgasm. The smell was intoxicating, and like so many times when with Sophia, it was as though I was breathing the very elixir of life itself.

I could feel the orgasm well up inside of me and as my buttocks clenched and went into involuntary spasm, I ejaculated into Sophia with a mighty scream.

"Somebody needed that!" said Sophia with a laugh in her voice.

I felt an overwhelming sense of relief.

"Now if my liege can please give me my leave. I'll get cystitis if I don't get these wet knickers off," she added.

As Sophia undressed, I said,

"I've never actually noticed you do that before when you come."

"Most men don't. The sheets get a bit wet, that's all. Sometimes when I'm ovulating, it's like Niagara Falls which can be a bit inconvenient. But most of the time, it's a nice amount."

"When you came in my mouth it was just unbelievable – absolutely bloody amazing. My God, how I'd love to be there when you have a Niagara Falls moment!"

Now undressed, Sophia came over to me naked and put her arms around my neck.

"That was lovely, thank you. No, it was better than lovely, it was incredible – I've never had an orgasm with a man going down on me before. That was the problem the other day. I was so horny, almost climbing the walls in fact. I was going to come around and see you."

"You should have," I said

"The problem was I wasn't sure that I'd find you and that I'd end up wasting time with my exam coming up. So I got my vibrator out. It did the trick, but I had so many orgasms that the bed was soaking and I couldn't sleep in it. I ended up having to take the sheets to the laundry room and then sleep on the floor whilst they dried. Not exactly the ideal preparation for sitting an exam."

"How's your Gran?" I asked.

"Not well. I feel terrible. I'm sick with worry. As I've told you, I get on much better with her than I do with my mum. I do hope that she's going to be OK. Do you have grandparents still alive?"

"No, all of them died before I was born. There was a great grandma on Dad's side, but she died when I was very young. What's wrong with your Gran?"

"It seems to be a problem with her stomach."

The concern on Sophia's face was very clear. I didn't know what to say.

She forced a smile before asking,

"You've not come to be depressed by me. Tell me what that last letter you sent me was all about? You were so stern with me! Is it because you felt that I was leading you a merry dance, like I did my previous little collection of playthings?"

"Yes."

"Nothing could be further from the truth. And as for you suggesting my comments were OTT and insincere – I am positively bristling! You do have my love, gratitude, respect and admiration. Having love for someone and being in love are different things. I've already told you that lying, or making things up for the sake of it, is a total waste of time in my opinion."

"You have indeed."

"Truth is probably the most important thing in life to me. Apart from love, that is. I will not waste any energy on trying to make things better or easier when they are not. Is that understood?"

"Yes, ma'am!" I replied and saluted with my right hand.

There was a smile on Sophia's face that was broad and full of life to replace the forced smile of a few moments earlier.

"And neither have I had it my own way very often...or at least, not often enough!" she said.

I laughed.

Sophia looked out of her window as she continued,

"I am uncomfortable with genuine compliments and praise because I have taught myself a long time ago that these are rare, and though I am very good at digesting compliments that are only skin-deep, or are referring to my 'horizontal refreshment' skills, as David so funnily puts it, the Inside stays hidden and wrapped in a comfort blanket and only

123

gets to see the light of day when the owner of said Inside and attached body has totally convinced herself that it is safe to expose the ever so precious inner workings of herself."

"There's a sense of detachment as you talk about your inner workings."

"Better to be cynical and sarcastic than to get hurt on the inside has been the motto until a couple of months ago," said Sophia.

"That's sad," I replied.

"You're right. It needs dispelling. I'm working on it."

"Does that mean I'm your boyfriend?" I asked.

"Maybe…we Librans need patience."

"How much patience?"

Sophia sighed.

"Maybe tomorrow, maybe next week. You're pushing me again."

"OK, I'll go."

"I'll see you tomorrow. I know that I can be a pain. You need to give me time and space, that's all. I do like you. I like you a lot. What time tomorrow?"

"Three p.m.?"

"That's perfect. I'll see you then. Today was just incredible by the way. I adore you," said Sophia.

"Don't I need to be receptive to it?" I replied.

Sophia smiled.

"Touché, Melton. Smart and sexy – quite a combination!"

I left Sophia's room a different man.

**

Tuesday 27th May

My Dearest Sophia,
The Sex Goddess of my dreams has once again disappeared from my life. The Prospective First Bard of Sheffield can therefore draw a number of conclusions.

1.   Prospective First Bard of Sheffield has finally been consigned to ever increasing ranks of emotional rubbish. Strategy of actively ignoring my letters has been adopted.
2.   You are busy with further 'laundry related' incidents and don't have time for my nonsense.
3.   You are not well and want me to come and look after you.
4.   Something bad has happened in your life.

5.   D.H. Lawrence has returned from the dead and has swept you off your feet with a piece of work that even exceeds *The Rainbow* in terms of quality.

Or any mixture of the above, of course. Dependent on which one is correct, my response is as follows.

1.   Shit, fuck, bollocks.
2.   I really wanted to be present at the next 'Niagara Falls' event.
3.   I'm sorry, get well soon. I'll come around tomorrow night around 7 p.m. to check that you're OK.
4.   Yelps, if there is anything that I can do then please just let me know.
5.   Can I have a copy, please?

Most of all I hope that the answer is not number 4.

Thinking of you,
Love

Jonathan
xxxxx

**

There was a knock at my Halls of Residence room door.

I opened it to see Sophia there and suddenly realised that she had never been to my room before – that I had always visited her.

She was dressed in a plain white t-shirt, jeans and a pair of old training shoes. She looked absolutely exhausted and threw her arms around my neck. I held her instinctively, and she sobbed in my arms.

"What on earth is the matter?" I asked.

"It's my Gran. She died today."

"Oh my God, I'm sorry. I'm so sorry."

Sophia kept crying.

"Is there anything that I can do, my love?"

"Hold me for a minute. And then make me a nice cup of tea and give me a cigarette."

I did as Sophia requested and held her tight.

"I've only got coffee, I'm afraid."

"That's fine – as long as it's wet and warm."

125

As I made Sophia a cup of coffee, she stopped crying as she smoked her cigarette.

"If it's not a sensitive question, what did your Gran die of?" I asked.

"Stomach cancer – by all accounts she'd known for months that she had it, but she never told a soul. It was only in the last couple of days that she gave in to the pain. I can't understand why she never told me. We were so close."

Sophia started crying again. I held her and tried to console her with what words I could muster.

"Maybe dignity, maybe privacy, maybe it was because she loved you and didn't want you to know she was in pain."

"But I never had chance to say goodbye to her in person. Why did she do that? Why? Why? Why? I don't understand."

Sophia was now sobbing again.

"You know what D.H. Lawrence said, don't you?"

"What?" asked Sophia snivelling.

"The dead don't die. They look on and help."

Sophia forced her first smile since coming into my room.

"You will come to the funeral with me, won't you?" asked Sophia.

"But I don't know any of your family," I responded.

"That doesn't matter. I want you there! I want you there! You're my rock."

"OK, I'll be there."

"Thank you, thank you so much. Now come to bed with me. I don't want sex. Please just hold me."

Ring of Faith

I met Sophia's parents, Terry and Christine, for the first time at her grandmother's funeral. Both were in the late forties of average height and build with their hair at an intermediate stage of greyness.

I was very nervous about the meeting, but both of them were honest, unpretentious and down-to-earth people. They made me feel welcome immediately.

"We're glad that you could make it today, Jonathan. Sophia's told us so much about you," said Terry.

A big smile crossed my face.

"I'm honoured that Sophia invited me. Please accept my sincere condolences."

"Thank you," replied Terry and Christine in unison.

Sophia cried throughout the funeral service.

I tried my very best to comfort her.

**

After the service, we went back to Terry and Christine's house, a very nice large and detached property on the outskirts of Leeds in Roundhay, undeniably one of the more affluent and pleasant areas of the city. The garden was beautifully and lovingly maintained.

"Nice house," I commented to Sophia as we walked up the front drive together.

"My parents were left some significant money in a family Will shortly before I was born and they invested it all in this house. I've always loved it – it was home to me even though I felt an outsider if that makes sense."

"Yes, it does."

"That's why I loved my Gran so much. Dad's great but Gran was the one person who seemed to understand me and what I wanted to do with my life."

Once inside the house, Sophia's two older sisters, Bev and Sandra, came over to join us. Like Sophia, both were pretty brunettes but, as

127

Sophia had remarked, they had a totally different aura about them. They both bore a similarity to their mother, Christine, which Sophia did not.

One of them was clearly pregnant. Sophia had never mentioned the fact.

"Hello, I'm Bev...."

"I'm Sandra."

Cheerfulness exuded from the two of them.

"Is it true that you're from public school?" asked Bev.

Before I could answer, Sandra added,

"I'm pregnant."

"I'd have thought that was perfectly evident to Jonathan," replied Sophia.

"Yes, I am from public school but hopefully I'm quite normal really."

"I'm not sure you're normal if you go out with my sister," said Sandra.

"Charming as ever, Sandra, dear sister."

"I work in the central post office and Sandra's a hairdresser, we're both on our own today because our husbands couldn't get time off work," continued Bev.

Terry came over to join us. He was clearly experienced in dealing with an all-female environment.

"Are my daughters annoying you, Jonathan?"

"Not at all," I replied.

"He's from public school, Dad," said Bev.

"It doesn't matter where he's from. Being hard-working and honest is what matters in life," replied Terry.

"And love," added Sophia.

Sandra sighed.

"I'd like to think that I'm both honest and hard-working," I said.

"Come on Melton, it's time to go. I've work to do tomorrow and we need to get back to Sheffield," said Sophia.

"We all have to work tomorrow, Sophia. Some of us have to do it for a living," replied Sandra.

"Now then, Sandra!" said Terry.

"Let's go!" said Sophia.

"OK!" I replied.

There followed much family hugging, except between Sandra and Sophia.

Terry shook my hand and said,

"We hope to see you again, Jonathan."

"I hope so too."

Sophia and I walked silently to the bus stop, located on the edge of Roundhay Park. Once there, a safe distance away from the house, Sophia let out a shriek of frustration.

"That bloody sister of mine. She's always the same."

"Not exactly best of pals are you?"

"She never forgave me for having her spending money cut when my parents were saving up for me to go to university. She wanted a new pair of shoes for some dance or another, and she had to buy a cheaper pair. Dad wouldn't let her buy the ones she wanted on credit, and she's never forgotten it. How bloody childish! That was over four years ago."

"Bev's nice," I said.

"Bev's lovely. I never know what to say to her, but I love her to pieces. If the whole world was like her then it would be a much better place to live in."

**

We caught the bus to the centre of town and then walked to Leeds Central station to take the train back to Sheffield.

Once on the train, Sophia gave me a big hug and a delicate affectionate peck on the cheek before saying,

"Many thanks for today. You were great."

"Your father treated me like your boyfriend. Am I?"

"Maybe," replied Sophia.

I hung my head with a weary sigh.

"You are, I suppose. I genuinely like you and that scares me. But there is something I need to get off my chest first. During our five weeks apart whilst you were wooing me, I had sex with someone else."

I put my head in my hands.

"Who?" I demanded.

"Nobody you know. Nobody I know even."

"What?"

"There was a disco at Halifax Hall. I couldn't sleep, so I wandered down for a dance to try to tire myself out. There was this incredible dancer there, and one thing led to another. I'm sorry. Now you're officially my boyfriend there is no way that this will happen again. I'm not like that. If I'm committed to someone then I'm committed to someone – full stop, no debate."

I said nothing. The pain inside of me was immense. It was as though someone had stuck a knife in my chest and twisted it. I felt sick and was struggling for breath.

"Listen to me. It will not happen again. I was a free agent when it happened. Now I'm not. For me, there is a big, big difference," added Sophia.

I ran my hands through my hair.

"Say something, please," said Sophia.

"There's nothing to say," I replied.

I could feel tears welling up inside of me. There was no way that I was going to let Sophia see me cry.

"Look I just want to be on my own. I'll come and see you tomorrow in your room," I said.

"What time?" asked Sophia.

"Three thirty p.m. is as good as any."

"I'll be there waiting for you."

I stood up and walked to another carriage on the train. I couldn't get away soon enough from Sophia. The tears were welling up inside of me and I started to say,

"Nobody, just nobody nor nothing is ever going to make me cry again."

After repeating the mantra ten, maybe 15 times, the need to cry subsided.

My emotions of devastation were being swiftly replaced by anger.

**

It was Thursday, over-25's night at Barry Noble's Roxy Nightclub – THE 'singles' event in Sheffield. The club was situated in the centre of town and absolutely enormous inside. Despite being less than twenty years of age, I had no problems gaining admittance.

Once inside the club, I was hit by the seething mass of humanity there – men and women alike. I attacked the dance floor with a never-before seen sense of purpose, looking for any woman remotely interested in my advances.

I saw an attractive blonde woman, probably in her late thirties and wearing a purple dress that left little to the imagination. I danced with her for maybe half an hour and we grew ever more flirtatious with every song. The DJ then played a slow song.

"Would you like to dance?" I asked.

"I thought that's what we'd been doing."

"You know what I mean!"

"Yes I do and yes I would like to dance."

We embraced together and danced.

"What's your name?"

"Jonathan. And yours?"

"Karen."

I kissed her passionately. I moved to Karen's neck and ran my tongue towards her ears. She sighed.

"I want you," I said.

"My place or yours?" she asked.

"Mine's about three quarters of an hour in a taxi. Where's yours?"

"Only about half an hour away – but it's a small shitty university room."

"We'll do mine then. Let me get my coat and bag."

**

On the way to her house, Karen and I made out in the back of the taxi. I was burning with pure animal passion. I had my hands up her purple dress only to be disappointed at the pair of tights that were in my way. I ran my hand seductively over her groin. It was pure lust.

"We'll be there soon. I'm not giving a show to the taxi driver," said Karen.

I controlled myself.

When we arrived at her flat, I paid the taxi driver and we walked to her front door hand-in-hand. Once inside, Karen said,

"It's not much, I know – a shitty old council flat but it's home, I guess."

I was not interested in a tour and like a caged animal let loose, pulled Karen towards me.

"Let me go to the bathroom," she said.

"No."

"Yes."

"No."

I pushed her playfully onto her settee, took off her shoes and then pulled her tights and knickers down with my hands.

"Hells bells, you're like a man possessed. At least let me take my dress off."

"No."

I undid the zip on my trousers and entered her. I thrust as hard as possible and let vent all my anger of the day on her in the sexual act. With our tongues entwined, I came.

"Sorry," I said.

"No need for sorry. Nobody's wanted me that much in fifteen years. It was bloody marvellous. NOW can I go to the bathroom?"

"Sorry!"

131

"Stop saying sorry. Go and find us a bottle of wine from the fridge. The glasses are over there."

Karen returned from the bathroom in a white cotton dressing gown and sat beside me.

"I have to say that I needed that! Do you want a cigarette?" she asked.

"You bet!"

Karen handed me a cigarette and lit it before lighting her own.

"I don't know what possessed you tonight, but I was glad to be on the receiving end of it. I've not had sex for five weeks since my husband left. Tonight's been the first chance I've had to get a baby sitter sorted and everything."

"I'm sorry your husband left. My girlfriend shagged someone else," I replied.

"Goodbye to bad rubbish as far as my husband is concerned. His new floosy is welcome to him. Tell me about your girlfriend. Do you love her?"

"God yes, I love her, I really do. She's the first proper girlfriend that I've ever had, and she's the only one that I'd ever want. I love her, and I just don't understand why she did what she did."

"Sometimes there is no understanding. How old are you both?"

"Nineteen."

"Being nineteen and in love can be a bit scary for a girl."

"Scary?" I asked.

"Yes, scary – particularly if it's your first time in love. I did it myself – panicked at that age and had a one night stand. You look back and think how stupid you were, but you did it all the same."

"What happened?"

"I never told my boyfriend, and he never found out. I've always regretted not being honest with him. I was going to tell him once we were married, but he was killed in a motorcycle accident a week before our wedding. I still think about him every day – probably the only time in my life that I was truly happy. I ended up marrying some useless oaf who made my life a misery for nearly twenty years."

Karen puffed on her cigarette and sighed before saying,

"If you love her and she loves you then you have to forgive her. Love is difficult to find in life. I'm not sure that I'll ever find it again. There again, one needs to stay positive."

I said nothing, there was nothing to say.

"Do you want me to call you a taxi?" asked Karen.

"Yes please."

We chatted aimlessly for 15 minutes until the taxi arrived. As I left, she said,

"If you love her, do everything that you can to make it work. Love is truly precious."

I kissed Karen on the cheek and made my way into the night air.

**

I went to Sophia's room with a strange mixture of confidence and guilt. I knocked on her door, and she immediately flung her arms around my neck.

"It's good to see you. I hardly slept last night," said Sophia.

"It's good to see you too."

"So?"

"Of course I want to be with you. I love you," I replied.

We kissed. The amazing feeling when Sophia kissed me was simply unsurpassable. It was as though her tongue reached every part of my body.

We lay on the bed together, embracing whilst Sophia played with my fingers sensuously. Our bodies seemed to fit together naturally. Whilst making love with her was simply sensational, holding her in my arms was, if anything, even better.

"I need to go to the toilet," said Sophia.

Sophia returned and gave me a tender loving kiss and embrace.

"Did you have sex with someone last night?" she asked.

"Next question," I responded.

Sophia looked at me.

"OK, OK."

Sophia pulled back from me to listen.

"Yes, I did have sex with someone last night."

Sophia now sat upright with arms folded. Her body language was bristling with indignation and anger.

"I understand," she said.

"I don't want your fucking understanding. I want your love."

"And you think you're not going to get my love by having sex with someone else," said Sophia with a raised voice.

"So it's OK for you to do it but not for me."

"That's not the point."

"So exactly what is the point?" I asked.

Both our voices were now raised.

133

"The point is that we weren't going out together when I had sex with someone else. You committed to woo and court me, so it was your responsibility to stay faithful."

"What?"

"You heard!"

"Does this mean that you are now not going to be my girlfriend?"

"Very possibly!"

"That's not bloody fair!" I shouted.

"Look, if I commit to a relationship then I am totally committed. No question at all," said Sophia.

"So you weren't committed before?"

"No. But then as soon as I do commit, you go off and have sex with someone else."

"I'm sorry, it will never happen again. You broke my heart when you told me what you'd done. You have no idea of how much you hurt me. You surely know that I love you with a passion and a commitment – the like of which you are never going to get from someone else."

Sophia smiled and said,

"The nature of the woman defines how she is loved."

"What?" I asked.

"I said the nature of the woman defines how she is loved. I need to be loved with passion and commitment."

"Does that mean that you forgive me then?"

"I don't know."

"I'm going. I just can't deal with this," I said.

"Perhaps it's better. I need time to think. I'll leave you a note maybe in a couple of days or so."

**

The next day I arranged to see my bank manager and arranged a loan for £300.

I went into town. After a couple of hours looking around various jewellers, I was finally able to find a gold and sapphire ring with the sapphire flanked by two small diamonds for £295.

Once I'd bought the ring, I caught the bus to Sophia's halls of residence. I was very nervous as the bus made its way out of the centre of town and into the leafy suburbs where Halifax Hall was located.

I took a deep breath as I knocked on Sophia's door. I was relieved to see her answer.

"Oh, it's you!"

"I've bought you this."

I handed Sophia the ring, and she smiled.

"I've bought it you to show how much I love you. I had to borrow the money, but that doesn't matter. What matters is that I think that you and I can be absolutely amazing together. You can't begin to imagine how much I love you. You wanted Paradise on the edge of the abyss, and that's where you've taken me."

"It was your decision to go there. I didn't force you," she replied.

"Look, it's up to you what you do with the ring. If you want it as an engagement ring then that's fine by me since I'd marry you tomorrow. However, anywhere on your left hand will do for me. Just wear it on your left hand and be in the lower refectory at three p.m. tomorrow if you want to be my girlfriend. If you're not there or you turn up not wearing the ring on your left hand then I'll understand. I'll not bother you anymore."

Sophia was silent.

"I'm really tired and fed up of the games. I love you with a passion and commitment that no one will match, but you need to decide whether you want that or not," I added.

"You're right, I do."

"Do what?" I asked.

"Need to decide."

"See you tomorrow then?"

"Perhaps."

**

I was in the Student's Union lower refectory cafeteria 10 minutes early. The counting of minutes turned into the counting of seconds. I watched my watch hand go round with fellow students happily eating, drinking and talking around me.

Three p.m. arrived, and Sophia walked in, dressed in a pink cardigan, black jeans and sandals. I had no idea from her body language as to what her decision was.

I smiled at her, and she smiled back.

Sophia's hands were in her pocket. She sat down opposite me and put both hands on the table.

The ring was on the left hand, on the largest finger adjacent to her wedding finger. She smiled again at me.

I immediately clenched my fist and then put both hands over my nose.

I cried unashamedly. My hands now covered my eyes as the tears started to flow.

135

I felt Sophia holding my hands and then she kissed them.

"I want to be with you, Melton, you daft romantic sod."

I pulled my hands from my face, wiped my eyes, took a deep, deep breath and told Sophia,

"And I want to be with you. I love you so much. Fresh start?"

"Fresh start!"

"As boyfriend and girlfriend?"

"Yes, as boyfriend and girlfriend."

"You've made me happy beyond my wildest dreams," I said with tears still in my eyes.

"And you make me so happy too. Do you want to come back to my room?"

"Do I ever?"

**

We made slow, gentle but very passionate love.

It was heavenly – soft, sensual yet so erotic at the same time. We both had orgasms of unadulterated ecstasy as we each came in turn with abandon.

"No more Paradise by the abyss. Just simple Paradise," I said.

"That's how it should be. The good thing though is that we were totally honest with each other. The truth is as important to me as love," said Sophia.

"But the truth is rarely pure, and never simple."

"You love Wilde, don't you?"

"Yes, I do love dear Oscar but he's also right in what he says."

"Maybe," said Sophia.

It was starting to go dark, and Sophia got out of bed to light some candles in the room.

"I love it when you light candles," I said.

"Yes, they are very romantic. I've always liked them. They somehow make a moment special."

Sophia put the radio on.

"Why on earth do you want the radio on?" I asked.

"We'll only have it on for around half an hour."

So we lay there holding each other and listening to the radio. Then at around 9.45 p.m., there came a voice on the radio that said,

"And the next request is from Sophia Chatterley for her boyfriend, Jonathan. Sophia wants to say that she thinks the world of you. Sophia picked the following record as it reminds her of the first time the two of you met."

136

The radio DJ then played *The First Time Ever I Saw Your Face* by Roberta Flack. The lyrics to the song are etched onto my soul:

'And the first time ever I lay with you
I felt your heart so close to mine
And I knew our joy would fill the earth
And last till the end of time, my love.'

As the music played and I hung on every word, a whole host of thoughts and memories flooded through my mind. I thought of when I saw Sophia for the first time that Saturday lunchtime in the pub at the English Department social event and how she just took my breath away. I thought of the first time I kissed Sophia later that same afternoon and of her first orgasm with her in my arms.

But most of all, I thought of how much I loved her.

All the madness of the past few weeks was forgotten in an instant.

At the end of the record, Sophia looked me in the eyes and said,

"I love you."

"You've never said that to me before."

"I know, and it's true. I genuinely do love you."

"Still scared?" I asked.

"No, I'm happy!"

"Not just content."

"No happy – genuinely happy. Now shut up and hold me!"

Love Blossoms

Sophia and I met up with David in the Students' Union lower refectory cafeteria.

David looked fit and healthy and full of life. After exchanging pleasantries, Sophia came directly to the point as she asked David,

"Jonathan and I want to live together next year but we can't afford anywhere on our own. What do you think?

I smiled.

"I'm not surprised you can't afford it with the ring that J.P.'s bought you. You mad reckless romantic fool you."

"But it is so incredibly delightful!" replied Sophia.

The smile on my face grew broader still.

"Look at him. He's like the cat that got all the cream!" said David.

"I may just be a little happy with life at the moment."

"A *little* happy? He cried you know, David."

"Sophia!" I exclaimed.

"Twice!" she added.

"He always was an old softie," joked David as he gave my right cheek a little pinch.

"Can we get back to the matter at hand, please, lady and gentleman? We're here to discuss housing for next year not how I feel about Miss Chatterley. OK!"

David and Sophia looked at each other and laughed.

"OK!" I repeated.

"Is he always this assertive these days?" asked David.

"He tries. I humour him every now and again," replied Sophia.

"Look – what are we going to do about next year?" I again asked.

"Keep your hair on. Leave it with me. I know a few people," said David.

**

I played a great deal of cricket that summer, forcing my way into the University First Team side on a regular basis as did David, Simon and Ian.

To add a strange and surreal humour to every game of cricket he played for the university, Simon had created his own ritual by exposing his genitalia on the field of play at some point.

However, Simon's unique activities aside, it wasn't a particularly successful season for the team but it was a very good one personally – probably my best for three or four years.

By the end of the term, some of the players were approaching me to see whether I wanted to be first team captain for the following year.

I went to see Simon one day to talk about it and as we sat on the park bench in his halls of residence room as his frogs, Ethel and Merman played in the pond in his room, he said,

"J.P., you know that I want you to be captain next year, but I do have one major concern."

"What's that, my friend?"

"I need assurances that you will allow my todger to roam free on the field of play next year."

"Your todger has already become legendary. If anything, I am more likely not to pick you if you stop doing it."

Simon smiled.

"However I do draw the line at you bringing your frogs to any game," I added.

Simon looked bewildered at my comment and simply replied,

"Why on earth would my frogs want to come and watch Sheffield University play cricket, frogs don't like cricket!"

There was little that I could offer in response to such inspired logic.

At that point, the sun appeared from behind the clouds and reflected off the silver foil that was behind the fresh and lovingly assembled foliage on his room walls.

Whereas before I had looked upon Simon's room with incredulity, park bench and all, I now sat in wonderment at the beauty of what he had created.

I was duly elected as captain of cricket.

**

The end of the summer term and university year itself came all too quickly and, sadly, Sophia and I decided it wasn't practical to stay in Sheffield over the summer. We had an emotional parting as she went back home to Leeds and myself to Devon. I worked on the farm whilst Sophia took a summer job in a local supermarket.

To break the summer up I spent a few days at Sophia's parents' house in the delightful Roundhay area of Leeds. When I arrived at

Leeds railway station, Sophia was there to meet. She gave me the biggest hug imaginable on the train platform together with a kiss that seemed to last forever.

"I've missed you," I said.

"I've missed you more," said Sophia.

"How are you?" I asked.

"Apart from my accursed sister, I'm fine. Thank goodness she doesn't live with my parents anymore; that's all I can say."

"How are your Mum and Dad regarding us sharing a room next term?"

"They are both cool and relaxed over the matter – but don't expect to be sharing a room with me whilst you're here. If you want any fun, it will need to be an outdoory!"

"Sounds interesting!"

"Not for me. I've too many bad memories of bus stop fumblings. The park is kind of all right, but I remember once being interrupted by a very enthusiastic canine who totally quelled what little real passion was going on. I'm afraid it's going to be limited to some hugs and stolen kisses during your time here. I'm sure that you will survive."

**

Sophia also came down for a week to the farm that summer and Brian and Alison loved her from the first minute they met her. Sophia was also the first and probably only woman I've ever known that caught Graham's attention.

"She's gorgeous!" he said one day after Sophia had left the room.

"You see, there is more to life than tractors and combine harvesters, dear brother," joked David.

**

Like Sophia's parents, Brian and Alison wouldn't let Sophia and I sleep together and so Sophia shared Sarah's room.

On her first morning there, Sophia came to join me in the old barn as I was milking a goat by hand.

"Lucky goat!" teased Sophia.

"Are you at all envious?" I asked.

"Maybe," she replied with a wicked smile on her face.

"I can see to you next if you want!"

"That's why I'm wearing a dress and no knickers," said Sophia as she lifted up her pink dress to display a complete absence of foundation garments.

Suddenly the task at hand with the goat had no interest whatsoever for me. I walked over to Sophia and ravaged her, pushing her against the barn wall as she threw her arms around my neck and wrapped her legs around my back.

I took her. It was joyous, unbridled animal lust. She weaved a spell of sensuous magic on my neck, and I came in a glorious moment.

Sophia adjusted her hair and her clothing and, almost in an instant, looked as prim and proper as it could be possible to look.

"All I need to do now is find some panties and then I'll look for the local church. You can't beat a quickie before Sunday Morning Service," she said.

I laughed.

"I leave you to finish the goat off. I'll see you later, lover!"

**

Whilst Sophia was there, we went walking together every night around the farm and its surroundings.

"It's so beautiful here, isn't it? Look at that sunset – it's spectacular," said Sophia.

"I've always loved this time of day on the farm, the colours as the sun sets over the fields are just wondrous. I can't describe how happy I am that you're here to share this with me," I replied.

"They're lovely, aren't they, Brian and Alison?"

"The best – the very best."

"You never talk about your real parents," probed Sophia.

"Nothing to say really – my mother and father split up when I was young. Dad had custody but died in a road accident. My mother had abandoned us for some muscle bound gym instructor. Good riddance to bad rubbish as far as I'm concerned!"

"Don't you have any contact with her at all?" she asked.

"None at all – I have no desire to see her again."

There was a long silence between us.

"Are you happy?" I asked.

"Yes I am – very happy in fact."

"Not just content?"

"No, not just content – I've found out that happiness can be an everyday thing. I'm only sorry that I gave you such a hard time during our courtship."

There was a bittersweet mixture of elation and regret in Sophia's voice.

"I was a bit manic myself if I'm honest," I replied.

"I needed to be sure, that's all. Sure that any man in my life would have the courage, persistence and sheer determination to win my heart."

"Am I the only person that you've loved?" I asked.

"Truly loved – yes. Before I became the most paradoxical oversexed, romantic, churchgoer this side of the Vatican, I was a simple sixteen year old romantic churchgoer. I was young, naïve and believed in one true love in life. Ironic when one considers how many men I've had sex with in the past two or three years. But there was a day when I believed that I would only make love with one man and that would be it."

"So what happened?"

"More a case of who happened. His name was Anthony Gillespie. 'Tone' as I used to call him," said Sophia.

"Tone?"

"I know, dreadful now thinking about it. Anyway I was seriously smitten but I wouldn't have sex with him until I was convinced that he loved me. Sure enough, he convinced me – if the truth be told, I wanted to be convinced. We ended up having sex at his parents' house when they were away one weekend. I was totally lost in love!"

"Totally?!"

"Or so I thought at the time. Then about three weeks later, I found him in the pub with another girl. All his mates were with him, and they laughed at me. I'll never forget it. His mates laughing at me bit deep, very deep. I cried and cried for days. I went to church, thought positively and told myself 'This too shall pass'."

"Did it?"

"Slowly, bit by bit. I decided to seduce each one of his mates one by one. The more that they had laughed at me, the more I mis-used my female power – real Paradise on the edge of the abyss stuff. Sex was my weapon, and I used it with force. And always, but always, I kept something, the key part of me, to myself. I promised myself that no-one, not ever, ever would do that to me again."

"I remember you said to me that your Inside stays hidden and would only get to see the light of day when you had convinced yourself that it was safe to expose your inner workings. You felt that it was better to be cynical and sarcastic than to get hurt."

Sophia smiled ruefully before saying,

"It's true. It's me. Or at least it was me. I remember you telling me that it was sad. And you were right – it was sad. You broke through my defences – my very own pedigree pet for life. You make me feel that I belong. You make me feel secure. You put what happened to me as a sixteen year old girl into perspective. You make me happy. I never imagined that I could be this happy. Content yes, but happy no."

"You are much less shocking and brutal than when we first met."

"I'm not becoming boring, am I?" asked Sophia.

"My God, no – I was just wondering."

"I don't feel the need or desire to be shocking and brutal anymore. I feel happy and secure. I finally feel that I belong."

"The belonging thing, I feel the same – amazing, isn't it? Brian and Alison were simply wonderful and caring foster parents, but I've never felt that I really belonged either. Not at home, not at school, not at university, well not until I met you. With David, sometimes, yes – but that's about it."

"Two stray souls who find their soul mate! It appeals to my sense of romance," said Sophia.

She had the broadest smile on her face.

**

As promised, David had found a house for Sophia and me to share with himself and three other students.

Although the building was rundown and showed little, if any sign of investment by the landlord, it had clearly once been a most grandiose house, impressive high ceilings and all.

We were all paying rent from the beginning of September so Sophia and I decided to move in as soon as the house was available to us. Our prospective housemates were not arriving until the start of term, and we had the full run of the house.

Sophia and I loved the extra space that we had when nobody else was around in the big house; it was a four weeks to savour.

We had both saved some significant money from working over the summer and as soon as we were back in Sheffield, Sophia suggested that we go out for a particularly nice Italian meal at the 'poshest' restaurant that we knew – an out and out treat considering how relatively little money we had.

Sophia was taking a bath as I did my best to look smart in the only suit that I had. As she came back to our room wrapped in a towel she told me firmly,

"Go and sit downstairs and wait for me."

"But can't I stay? I like to watch you get dressed," I moaned.

"No, no and thrice no!" Sophia smiled and kissed me on the nose before adding,

"I want you to go away. I want it to be a surprise. Now scram, Melton!"

I trudged down the stairs of our 'new' house reluctantly.

Although Sophia and I had now been 'boyfriend and girlfriend' for nearly three months, this was different – we were now 'officially' living together and going to 'posh' restaurants together.

I could feel the excitement, anticipation and expectation running through my body as I heard her footsteps coming down the stairs.

When she came into view, my eyes lit up. Sophia looked absolutely bloody amazing in a new black, strapless dress.

"Not bad for fifteen pounds in the summer sale, eh?" she asked.

"You look a million dollars never mind fifteen pounds," I replied.

I searched for the right words to say, and from the depth of my heart and soul, I found something that did justice to my feelings for her,

"She walks in beauty, like the night,
Of cloudless climes and starry skies
And all that's best of dark and bright
Meet in her aspect and her eyes."

"I so love Byron!" said Sophia.

"Oh, did he write something like that as well? What a remarkable coincidence! Who'd have thought that Byron would have written the very same thing – surely proof, if any were needed, of the ability of the prospective First Bard of Sheffield."

"You daft sod."

"You just look unbelievable. A timeless moment to yearn for more," I said

Sophia pushed me playfully.

"Now I did write that!" I added.

Sophia looked me in the eyes and then whispered "You're lovely," before giving me the softest, most sensual of kisses.

What followed in the restaurant was a quite divine romantic evening of seductive glances, happily looking into each other's eyes as we moved our heads from side to side in our own private mating ritual.

Once back into the house, we made love in wanton abandon on the corner of the staircase.

<u>Madness, Mayhem</u>

All six members of our student house were in their second year at university, and we got on very well together, initially at least. During the autumn term, all six of us would have Sunday lunch together in the big old kitchen – warm, charming, friendly events where the cheap wine and conversation flowed.

Everything in the house was peace, harmony and light.

**

As Christmas grew nearer, it started to snow. I wrote Sophia a poem and left it on the Students' Union notice board.

My gorgeous woman,

Roses are red,
Violets are blue,
If snowflakes were love,
I'd send a blizzard to you.

All my love,

The prospective First Bard of Sheffield
xxxxxxxxxxxx (forever)

Dear First Bard of Sheffield,

It pleases me to see that my liege has made a long overdue return to writing poems for me – once again around the theme of roses and violets.

Despite its simplistic nature, it is a work of great import to this particular reader.

As such, in my heart at least, you are no longer 'prospective' and

---

should now take your rightful position as First Bard of Sheffield with appropriate pride.

Suggest you meet me here at the notice board tonight at 7 p.m.

Let's pretend we're meeting for the first time.

Love,

Sophia
xxxxxxx

I left the house separately from Sophia and arrived on time at 7 p.m. at the Union Notice Board only to be kept waiting, as usual, by her for a good 10 to 15 minutes. It was a quiet time in the Union building and I smoked a cigarette to help pass the time.

I was full of excitement.

When Sophia finally arrived, just as she had done in September before term had started, she looked absolutely sensational.

During the autumn term, with cold weather and lectures, Sophia had understandably tended to dress in a safe and comfortable manner. However, it was time for the magnificent vertiginous red shoes to make a comeback together with the most sumptuous red dress that I'd never seen before.

The way that Sophia was dressed that night was anything but safe and comfortable. It was positively dripping with danger.

"You look amazing," I said.

Sophia gave me the most filthy, horny glance imaginable and then kissed me, her tongue softly caressing my lips.

"Pleasure's a sin and sometimes sin's a pleasure," I added.

"You seem to have an obsession with Byron whenever I wear a new dress, Melton!"

"I thought that we weren't supposed to know each other."

"Oh yes, sorry! But I wouldn't dress like this for a stranger."

She took my hand and pressed it against her upper thigh. I could feel her suspender belt beneath her dress.

"Sexy red underwear – to match the dress and shoes," she said.

I sighed.

"Even though I'm in love, it doesn't mean I still can't be a femme fatale from time to time."

Sophia licked her lips seductively.

I smiled and said,

"My God, woman – you're going to need a serious confessional the next time that you go to church. Not with her the mere passing of time, but of timeless moments to yearn for more."

"That's nice – two lines now. You might have a decent poem written by the new millennium," joked Sophia.

"That's all the thanks I get!" I replied.

"You're lovely. I'm very lucky. I've been in love before, but I actually love you."

I looked quizzically at Sophia.

"Do you understand what I mean?" she asked.

"A bit, maybe," I responded.

"Men, goodness me – I sometimes wonder whether they understand love at all."

Sophia gave me an affectionate kiss on the cheek and put her arm inside mine.

**

David returned from the Christmas break troubled and brooding, and as the New Year progressed, he became positively disruptive and single-handedly turned the peace and harmony that had previously existed in the house into one of chaos and confrontation.

The two other women in the house, Catherine and Tanya, were very good friends – well, at least they were when we started sharing the house together. They both knew David via the Drama Society.

David being David it was perhaps to be expected when five weeks into the first term, David and Tanya were sharing one of the rooms in the house together.

I knew David well enough that the complete absence of any mention of Tanya's name during Sophia's and my brief visit to the farm at Christmas spelt trouble.

And once all six of us were back in the house for the second term it was pretty evident, to me anyway, that David had returned somewhat less enamoured of Tanya than he had been before the Christmas break.

Their relationship clearly wasn't going to last, but it was still a little surprising when by the third week of the second term, David started having sex with Catherine.

The situation lasted for around five weeks and clearly wasn't sustainable – something had to break. Catherine and Tanya were increasingly at each other's throats, and everything came to a head one traumatic evening.

147

Sophia and I were sat around the kitchen table drinking coffee and Catherine, along with Tanya, was sat on the settee close by. Very matter of factly, Catherine casually dropped into conversation,

"You do of course know that David is having sex with us both, don't you, Tanya?"

Tanya stormed out in tears.

I went to find David, who was in his usual haunt, The Pomona Pub, a short walk down the road from our house. He was constantly there – far more than in either Catherine or Tanya's room and, most definitely, the lecture room had ceased to play any part in his social agenda.

As I walked into The Pomona, David was working his way through yet another pint, oblivious to the drama that was taking place in the house.

"Catherine's just told Tanya about the two of you," I said.

"Bloody typical," was the grumpy response.

"What are you going to do?"

"I'm going to finish my pint and then have another one - maybe two. I'll let them get it out of their system whilst I have a few jars. Fancy a beer, J.P.?"

"No, I'm fine," I replied.

I returned to the house wearily and, upon my return, Catherine immediately asked me,

"Is he in The Pomona as usual?"

"Yes."

"If Mohammed won't come to the mountain then the mountain will have to go to Mohammed," she said.

So, Catherine, Sophia, and I, also joined by a still tearful Tanya, traipsed down the road to find David.

"Shit," said David when he saw us all arrive in the pub.

"So which one of us are you going to go out with David? You have to choose," demanded Catherine.

"I can't believe that you've both done this to me, tell me it's not true," moaned Tanya.

David was silent.

"Come on, an answer!" demanded Catherine.

"Yes, an answer," said Tanya.

David pondered for a further 10 or 15 seconds before uttering the immortal line,

"Couldn't we have a threesome?"

"You arrogant, stupid wanker," said Catherine.

148

"I can't believe that I've spent the last four months of my life with such a selfish and self-absorbed bastard as you, Pritchett!" shouted Tanya.

David merely lit a cigarette and said,

"The nature of women defines how they are loved and by whom."

**

Originally both Simon and Ian had started the academic year in the Halls of Residence at Sorby Hall but changed their mind when there was a night raid by other students, full of Christmas alcohol, on 'Simon's park', which was his room there.

Simon recounted the tale of the raid on his room at length as we sat on the cricket pavilion balcony at the University Westminster Road ground one sunny day in May.

"The Philistines made a random SAS-type attack on my room. There were four of them – dressed all in black and wearing balaclava helmets," explained Simon.

"Weren't you frightened?" I asked.

"Not a bit, my only concern was for Ethel and Merman! But I was helpless against such overwhelming odds!"

"What happened?"

"The silver foil and foliage went out of the window first and then they sprayed my garden bench with luminescent paint. All of which I could live with, but what they did to Ethel and Merman was nothing less than an act of diabolical barbarism."

"What did they do?" I asked.

I heard Ian sniggering away in the background.

"You unfeeling bounder, Bestall. As three of them held me down, the barbarous philistines blew up both frogs with a straw until they were the size of balloons and then threw them out of my window on the seventh floor," said Simon.

"What happened to them?"

"They both died. At least I was able to find them and give them a decent burial in Endcliffe Vale Park. I couldn't stay in Sorby Hall after that."

"Well, let's face it, Sorby always has been a little strange that way," I replied.

By now the entire cricket pavilion balcony was either in fits of laughter or stunned silence.

**

Once out of Sorby Hall, Simon and Ian had formed, with three other likeminded males the '505 Club' – 505 being the number of the house that they shared together.

By the summer term, David, now 'officially' fed up with women, when not in the local pub or playing cricket, would spend most of his time there with Simon and Ian. Events at the house became legendary around the university – the only way I can begin to describe it is as a more intellectual version of *Animal House*.

After finishing my second year exams, I went with David to see the '505 Club' for myself.

There was a sheep's head in the middle of the kitchen table.

"My God, what's that?" I asked.

"Ah, the sheep's head – it was the last week of last term and everyone in the house had spent their grant," said Ian

"A mixture of foolish living and frog welfare support," added Simon.

"The banks wouldn't lend us any more money to extend our already extended overdrafts," complained Ian.

"Miserable, capitalist bastards – we literally had nothing to eat. We faced the prospect of a week without food."

"Thankfully Dan in the house had done some serious Territorial Army Survival training and Pete still had enough petrol in his clapped-out old car to get us to the moors and back."

"So the five of us led by Dan went and killed a sheep – a daring plan to fight back against capitalism and growing supermarket supremacy. A radical marketing and supply chain strategy revision to remove the middle men from the food chain," outlined Simon.

"What did you do with it?" I asked.

"Pete's dad is a butcher and he knew exactly what to do. The meat was a tad on the aged side but with a bit of creativity we had enough food for the five of us for a week," replied Simon.

"Mutton stew, mutton soup, mutton curry, mutton à la banane. You name it, we did it," said Ian proudly.

"The recipe for mutton à la banane was a little questionable but the mutton curry was undeniably a culinary highlight of the academic year," added Simon.

"Do you miss Ethel and Merman?" I asked Simon.

"Of course, every day, but life goes on. Life is for the living. I now have two new frogs, James and Stewart."

"He even built a pond in the back courtyard for them. That's where most of his grant went!" interjected Ian.

"That and compensation to the landlord for the unauthorised renovation of his property. We were able to settle out of court. The important thing is that the pond can remain while the frogs and I are here," finished Simon.

**

With individuals such as Simon, Ian and David in the team, once the exams had finished, somewhat inevitably the after-match cricket club drinking sessions became somewhat heavy.

After one session, the four of us were working our way through Sheffield city centre on our way home around one o'clock in the morning.

David, being unable to walk upright by that point in proceedings, decided his only course of action was to swim home and he performed a unique 'doggie paddle' on the pavement.

This highly amused a passing policeman – initially at least.

"Very good, sir – excellent street swimming technique but could you please stand up and walk home in an upright rather than horizontal manner," said the officer.

David ignored the officer's pleas to return home in conventional mode. After another five minutes of the policeman's persuasion falling on deaf ears, his amusement on the matter had come to a close.

"Sir, I think that you need to spend a night in our cells."

"We'll sort him out," said Ian.

"Yes indeed, fine officer of the law. You can be assured that we three fine upstanding citizens of the student community will look after our own in a suitably appropriate manner," added Simon.

"That's what worries me," retorted the policeman.

"Seriously, I'm supposedly in charge of this lot as captain of the team. Plus I share a house with our legendary land swimmer. I'll sort him out. Pritchett, get to your feet. Your father will not be impressed if his son ends up in clink for the night. Understood?" I said.

David said nothing but struggled to his feet and walked upright long enough for the policeman to disappear in search of other mid-town mayhem. It was very clear very soon though that David was unable to walk much further so we flagged down a taxi.

The drama didn't end there as David then proceeded to decorate the inside of the taxi with the 'fruits' of his evening's drinking. The driver immediately stopped the taxi and ejected the four of us – demanding £25 to cover all his cleaning costs.

The three of us who were still sober, relatively at least, felt it better to pay than risk a further encounter with the police. Having emptied the contents of our pockets, we agreed with the taxi driver that £21.74 would be acceptable compensation.

The night duly ended with Simon, Ian and I taking turns to carry David home.

It was no surprise to anyone that when the results for the summer examinations were announced, David found himself on the pass/fail borderline.

...and Romance

The bar staff in The Pomona pub knew David by name and started to pour his pint of beer as soon as he walked through the door.

Sophia and I ordered our drinks as well and we sat down together.

"So what are we going to do next year?" asked Sophia.

"To be honest, David, as much as we'd like, Sophia and I can't afford a house on our own," I said.

"Cards on the table, I'm up for anything except another year in Halls of Residence. Being in a room on my own would drive me scattier than I am already. I'd spend all my time in the pub," added David.

"I thought that you did that already," retorted Sophia.

"The three of us could live together!" I said.

"That would be brilliant. The two of you are the only two real friends that I have in the world. You're the only thing that I can actually rely on in this fucking place."

Sophia and I looked at each other – not knowing what to say. David let out a deep sign and continued,

"I'm letting everyone down – my parents, even all the bloody women that I've blown out, bless 'em. Look guys, I so need your help. I don't want to be with anyone but the two of you."

"All of which is very understandable but there needs to be some ground rules if this is going to work," said Sophia.

"Ground rules?" asked David.

"Yes, ground rules. Jonathan may be willing to live with a womanising drunken vagrant, but I'm not!"

"I'm not that much of a vagrant," protested David.

"Yes, you are," I said.

"Right, three house ground rules, Mr Pritchett. Firstly, you can have sex with no more than one woman in the house in any term. Secondly, drinking is limited to a weekend only activity. Thirdly, you cook at least two meals a week for the three of us," said Sophia.

"Agreed! I cook a mean breakfast," replied David.

"Promise?" asked Sophia.

"As a gentleman, my word is my bond."

"That's what worries me, you are no gentleman," replied Sophia.

The next day the three of us went and found a nice small house a few hundred yards around the corner from where we were already living on Eccleshall Road.

It had a nice big lounge and kitchen along with a cosy double room for Sophia and me and a small modest single room for David.

**

Once summer term had finished, Sophia and I decided to stay together in Sheffield. Although we had saved some money, we certainly didn't have enough money to last the summer, so we both found temporary jobs.

Sophia worked in an office of a small local company doing some filing and similar simple and at times very tedious administrative tasks, whilst I humped beer barrels around the Wards Brewery.

We'd both arrive home about 6 p.m., and if it was a warm summer's evening, the two of us would walk up the road to either the botanical gardens or Endcliffe Vale Park and wander around hand-in-hand, occasionally stopping to feed the ducks and swans.

Whenever we went to Endcliffe Vale Park, if possible, we always sat at the same park bench where Sophia had magnificently recounted from *The Rainbow*.

We had come to very much view it as our own private bench. As we looked out over the park and its trees and flowers one evening, the sun was setting.

"I've not hear anything from the Bard of Sheffield this year. Has he retired?" asked Sophia.

"Absolutely not!"

"Let's hear some of his work then."

I sat and thought for a couple of minutes.

"You don't have anything do you?" teased Sophia.

"Patience, woman!"

After a couple more minutes I said,

"The sun is setting, I stare into space,
If I close my eyes, I still see your face,
You are so damn sexy as night draws in,
I think of you, my thoughts drenched in sin,
The neon lights now start to shine so bright,
And all I can do is think of what I might."

"Not bad. Not bad at all. A little bit too pretty for my liking though. I want more raw passion."

154

"There's no satisfying some people with my poetic labours. Give me a couple more minutes."

I sat there, but nothing came.

After about five minutes, Sophia said,

"It's getting cold. Stop thinking Melton; we'll be here all blooming night. I'll tell you what – because I'm in heels and a skirt tonight give me a few minutes start and see if you can catch me."

With that Sophia set off running as best she could in heels. I gave her about three minutes start and set off after her. I caught up with her in the woods that were on the edge of the park. The closer I got to her, the more Sophia started to laugh.

She hid behind a large tree out of view, and when I finally caught up with her, she gave me the most gloriously deep, sensual French kiss.

"I hoped that you'd catch me up here. It's deserted at this time of day," she said.

"I want you. I want to love you, I want to hold you, I want to talk with you, I want to protect you. All at the same time – all the time," I said.

"That's more like it – more raw passion. You want me ALL the time?"

"Yes!" I said.

"Now?"

"Yes!"

"So what are you waiting for?"

I put my hand up Sophia's skirt and brushed my hands over her groin.

"This is no time for foreplay, Melton. Take me."

Not being one to argue with the love of my life, I did just that. Once I'd come, Sophia laughed and said,

"I'm so happy."

"Me too."

**

At weekends, local buses were very low cost and one of the great things about Sheffield is that many a beautiful place in Derbyshire is only a relatively short bus ride away.

There were so many wonderful memories that summer of glorious weekend days that we spent together in Bakewell and Chatsworth – walking in the countryside, alongside rivers and in sumptuous gardens full of the joys of an English summer.

155

We also did some new things that we'd not done before together. It was clear that from spending time with Sophia that, aside from her love of literature, she loved singing, dancing and going to church. These were key parts of her life and things she wanted to share with me.

So we started dancing to music together every day. I felt uncomfortable and un-coordinated at first. But Sophia kept encouraging and, bit by bit, my confidence grew.

Within a few weeks, I was moving at least moderately well and, as the summer progressed, we often danced the night away together alone in the house.

The next challenge was singing. Sophia had a very nice voice. However, my voice was comparable to that of a tone deaf foghorn. Inhibition, discomfort and a crippling lack of confidence didn't help either.

"It doesn't matter if you can't sing, it's about expressing yourself and enjoying it," Sophia said repeatedly.

"But my voice is terrible, and yours is so good," was my familiar retort.

"Goodness me, Melton, you're so anal at times. Let yourself go and stop thinking so much!"

**

Sophia found out that The Bear pub in the centre of Sheffield ran Karaoke nights every Thursday and she dragged me into town.

The pub was very crowded and everyone seemed to be having a good time. Unlike me, they seemed not to have a care in the world whether they could actually sing.

"Right you, it's our turn," said Sophia full of excitement.

I felt sick with nerves.

"OK, what are we singing?" I asked.

"*Can't take my Eyes off You*. I play it all the time around the house."

"Tell me about it!"

"You should know all the lyrics then. Don't look at the screen. It doesn't matter if you get the words right or wrong. All you need to do is sing it with all your heart and dance with all your soul."

"But what if people laugh?"

"Trust me, they won't. You'll be fine, we'll be great. Ready then?"

I breathed in as much air as I could and then forced it out.

Sophia started singing the song as though the words were for me and that no one else was in the pub. As she danced provocatively, I was drawn in and started dancing with her.

Without thinking about it, the song naturally turned into a duet between the two of us. To my considerable surprise, I began to genuinely enjoy myself.

When we finished, and to my eternal amazement, Sophia and I were given a standing ovation by the 'audience' in the pub and an encore was demanded. The biggest smile crossed my face.

Sophia kissed and hugged me before saying,

"I told you that you could do it. Remember this. It's not what you do; it's the energy and passion that you do it with!"

I laughed with unbridled joy before doing the encore that received the same rapturous applause.

Needless to say, Sophia and I could barely control ourselves when we got home as yet another sublime night of passion ensued.

**

"Why don't you come to church with me on Sunday?" asked Sophia.

"Not a fucking prayer if you excuse the pun."

"Why are you so hostile towards the Church?"

"I've only ever prayed once in my life. It was when my mother left and my prayers were not answered. And then my Dad died."

"Sometimes terrible things happen for a reason. If that hadn't happened then we might not have met. Sometimes painful experiences take us down a different route in life or take us to a better place. Maybe they can even bring some sort of redemption," said Sophia.

"Don't talk to me about redemption. We had a teacher at school that always talked about redemption and all the tiresome old twat did was make my life a misery."

Sophia was silent. She pondered for a while before saying,

"I love you whether you come to church with me or not!"

"I love you too, my love," I replied.

**

With the twelve months' rental on the big house at its end, it was with some considerable regret when Sophia and I had to move out at the end of August into the smaller property around the corner.

There was less than 600 yards between the two houses, and in order to save money Sophia and I did everything by hand. Despite there being

157

only the contents of a single room, it still took us virtually all day and we were absolutely exhausted.

When we'd finished, Sophia was definitely upset and emotional.

"We'll still be as happy in our new house, won't we? Despite all of David's shenanigans in this place, I've never been happier," she said.

"Of course we will. Why shouldn't we be?"

"I don't want anything to change, that's all. I'll miss that old double bed."

"What you need is cheering up!"

"And how are you going to do that Melton?" asked Sophia.

She licked her lips seductively.

"No, not that."

Sophia looked disappointed.

"Well, yes, of course that, but I wasn't actually thinking about that. I've saved some money up this summer and was thinking anyway about a short a break."

"Where?" asked Sophia.

"Inter Railing to Paris. I reckon that if we find cheap accommodation we can stay for a few days."

"Paris! I've never been to Paris! I'm so excited!"

"Neither have I. In fact I've never been abroad. I'll need a temporary passport."

**

We found a nice, clean, but cheap hotel on the edge of the city at Malakoff.

Using a mixture of the Metro and our young and willing feet to see the city in all its glories, we wandered around Paris hand-in-hand – in love and full of life's joys.

We visited The Left Bank, Notre Dame, the Champs-Élysées and the touristy Eiffel Tower in our three day stay. The two of us ate cheaply in street side cafes, watching the vibrant city fly by us as we lived in a divine world of our own.

On our final night there, we decided to watch the sunset over the city from the Sacré-Cœur church.

We caught a bus to the gardens at the bottom of the hill of the Basilica and looked at the climb up to the beautiful and iconic white Sacré-Cœur church above us – the highest point in the city.

We had three choices – a leisurely stroll up to the Church through the gardens, a lazy ride with all the tourists in the funicular or we could take the direct, more physically demanding route up the hundreds of steps by foot.

"So what do we do?" I asked.

"It has to be the steps."

"OK!"

"Let's make it a race. I like showing how physically stronger and fitter I am than you," said Sophia.

"Like hell you are, Mademoiselle Chatterley."

"Want a bet then, Melton?"

"Name your price!" I replied.

"The loser pays for dinner for two tonight."

"Fine by me."

Sophia and I set off and by half way I was winning the race but I was exhausted and Sophia strolled past me to win comfortably. I laughed, head bowed as I reached the top.

Waiting for me, Sophia was also laughing long and hard.

"It's not how you start the race, it's how you finish it. A meal for two at a nice three-star restaurant off the Champs-Élysées will do me perfectly."

"And how much is that going to cost?" I asked.

"Oh, at least £200 I'd guess."

"That's ten times my budget!!" I replied aghast – still struggling for breath and excuses.

Sophia laughed and said,

"Only joking! The usual street side cafés are fine by me. Being with you is what matters!"

Once I'd pulled myself together physically and stopped coughing, we made our way to the steps in front of the church.

The view of the city at sunset was breathtaking with the contrast between the setting sun on the rooftops and the neon lights in the relative darkness of shadowy back streets.

And all the while, as we stood there, African drummers were beating on the steps to bid farewell to the sun for another day.

I was blown away by the romanticism of it all and looked at Sophia adoringly.

She gave me a gentle kiss and then removed the ring that I'd given her the previous summer from her finger.

"It's about time this ring found its proper home," she said.

She moved the ring onto her wedding finger.

"Does that mean what I think it means?" my voice trembling with excitement.

"And what do you think it means?" asked Sophia.

"That you want to marry me?"

"Would you like that?"

As the final strands of sun were setting on the city, I looked into Sophia's alluring brown eyes for what seemed like minutes but was probably only seconds before replying,

"I love you more than you could ever begin to imagine. Of course, I want to marry you."

"I know it's usually the man that asks, but as a late twentieth century woman I thought that I'd seize the moment. Nothing would make me happier than to be your wife. I love you. I feel that we belong together."

Sophia kissed me gently on the lips. The two of us both smiled at the same time and then held each other tight.

"It's impossible to feel better than I do just now," I said.

"All downhill from here, then, isn't it?" joked Sophia.

The Final Year

I took out another bank loan for £1,000 to buy Sophia a truly magnificent diamond engagement ring as moving the 'other' ring from one finger to the other simply wasn't enough for me.

It was a lot of money for me at the time, but it just didn't matter when I saw the joy in her eyes as I gave her the ring.

**

At the beginning of October, David joined us in the house ready for the final year's work and exams. In accordance with the house rules, he cut his drinking right down along with his previously rampant womanising.

And yes, though not as good as Greasy Eddy – there again what could be? – David did cook an excellent breakfast. He even took responsibility, bless him, for keeping the house clean and washing the dishes. And a thoroughly admirable job he did too.

To recognise his efforts, Sophia bought David a 'pinny', which he wore with enormous pride. In return, Sophia did David's washing and ironing – including, most valiantly, his undies.

The final university year together was a wonderful one. The three of us were extremely close, inseparable at times, and I increasingly realised that in the same way that I viewed David as the brother that I'd never had, so did Sophia.

With his commitment to his English degree and house cleaning duties, David was far less active with the Drama Society in his final year. He did, however, commit to do one play, a production of Shakespeare's *Twelfth Night*.

Quite appropriately, David was cast as Feste.

Come the second term, Sophia and I trekked to see the show on its first night. In comparison with David's previous acting efforts, which, quite frankly, had been average at best, his performance as Feste was absolutely awesome.

If ever there was an acting part written for anyone then it was Feste for David. Both David and Feste had the exterior of the 'sage fool' – capable of great humour and an ability to mock the pretentious.

161

However, beneath the surface, deep inside both David and Feste lay a breaking heart.

David lived the life of Feste every day and knew the character inside out. Watching him on stage, it was almost as though David was playing himself.

Sophia and I went to the after show party to celebrate David's performance and we met Stefanie Barton, whom David had started seeing.

Stefanie was dressed from head-to-toe in designer clothes. Her shoes probably cost more than my student grant for the term, and she was adorned with a lavish matching diamond necklace and bracelet.

"Stef, come and meet Sofe and J.P.," said David.

Stefanie walked over as though she was gracing us with a Royal presence. I didn't know whether to bow or curtsey.

"Nice to meet you," said Sophia.

Stefanie ignored her.

"I love your necklace and bracelet," added Sophia.

"Yes, it's white gold. I can't believe how people in this dreadful place think they're silver. White gold has such class. Platinum is so tacky and dear oh dear, plain gold is so plain, so bourgeois," replied Stefanie.

Stefanie was clearly looking at Sophia's engagement ring as she said the words.

"What course are you doing?" I asked.

"Ah, Intro Week talk again. David, are we going soon?" asked Stefanie.

"If you want," said David

As the two of them left together, Sophia said,

"I hope she doesn't come round and stay at our house. David's only allowed one woman in our house per term, and I'd like to think that he'd make better use of his limited rations."

**

Despite our reservations, Stefanie established herself as a most unwelcome and moderately regular evening guest at our student house.

"You have such incredible clothes, Stephanie," said Sophia.

"I hate jeans; they're so proletariat, so mundane."

Both Sophia and I were wearing jeans.

"Is that your car outside?" I asked.

"Yes, sadly," replied Stephanie.

"Why sadly? It's a Porsche. I'd love a Porsche."

"I suppose you would, wouldn't you? I wanted an Aston Martin. All my friends have Porsches. I can't believe Pater at times – positively frugal with his money with me. Mater doesn't want for anything and yet I have to drive around in a Porsche."

"He's a good man your father," said David.

"Yes, I suppose he is. He's generous with his employees, too generous if you ask me – unfortunately his generosity doesn't extend to me, his only daughter."

"Jeez, Stef. You have a luxury apartment, £10,000 a month allowance – and the rest. You went to Roedean, you go on phenomenal holidays, what more do you want?" asked David.

"An Aston Martin, that's all."

**

"You don't like her, do you?" asked David one night as the three of us were eating dinner in our living room.

"Who?" I asked.

"Stef."

"She's a bit of a snob," I said.

"In my beloved sister Sandra's words, she's a pretentious cow. I'm usually not one to quote my sister but in this case it seems somehow apt," added Sophia.

"She's says I'm her bit of rough," said David.

I laughed.

"And her old man's great – brilliant bloke and seriously loaded. Stef says that I'm the only man she's ever taken to meet him who he actually liked. Deep down, she's quite insecure and desperately seeks her father's approval. And a man like me always needs a contingency plan in life."

Sophia and I looked at each other appalled.

"Hey guys, not everyone can live in Love Haven, 14 Fluffy Cloud, Nirvanaville, Utopia like you two. Probably more's the pity – but some of us have to just get on with our life and make the best of it," said David.

Sophia laughed and replied,

"And it's a *pink* fluffy cloud, not any old common or garden fluffy cloud."

**

The following week, Stephanie was back again – much to the irritation of both Sophia and me. We decided in advance to ignore her as much as possible.

"Where do the two of you plan to go on honeymoon?" asked Stefanie after around five minutes of silence.

"It's not something we've really given much thought to at this point. We need to get good degrees first," I replied.

"You should go to Antibes," said Stefanie.

"Where?" asked Sophia.

"Oh, you've not been to Antibes? How can one survive having not been to Antibes? There again, I don't suppose that you have the money, do you? More likely to be a weekend away in a B&B in Scarborough, I suppose. And the islands off that coastline are simply sensational. Not exactly the Isle of Wight! I went there last year with mater and pater. The Côte d'Azur is like paradise – provided one goes to the right places, of course. Simply marvellous!"

"I've never been to Scarborough!" I said.

Sophia smiled, but my understated humour went over Stefanie's head.

"Me neither," said David.

"We went to Paris last September," interjected Sophia.

"Oh lord, Paris is so passé – full of tourists with no money, style or sophistication. Simply wretched, it is. The hotel on the Cap d'Antibes, now that is proper style. And as for Saint-Paul-de-Vence, simply heaven. I don't suppose any of you have been there either."

"I always liked Devon, where we lived," said David.

"Me too, great years on the farm!" I added.

"What – with all those yokels who can't even speak the Queen's English? I doubt if there's a decent restaurant in the county. And the smell of manure everywhere. Quite dreadful, I imagine."

"Is your father called Dick, by the way?" asked Sophia.

Cue much schoolboy sniggering on the settee from yours truly and, yes, David as well.

"Dick Barton. *Haha.* Nobody's ever made that witticism before to me. His name is Ron actually, and he's a very successful businessman. Something you couldn't begin to understand! I definitely should be going now," replied Stefanie.

After Stefanie had left, I turned to Sophia and said,

"Well, at least she gave us an idea of where we can go on our honeymoon."

"Everyone has some redeeming features, I suppose. I'm not sure they have B&Bs on the Côte d'Azur though."

"Leave it with me, my love. I might just have a solution."

"I simply adore a man with a plan," said Sophia smiling.

Later, I rang Brian and asked him what if any money was left in my father's trust fund and found to my considerable delight that around £13,500 was left.

From talking to a number of travel agents, I worked out that for little more than £3,000 Sophia and I would be able to spend nine days on honeymoon in the South of France.

**

The second term in the final year at university is job interview time. Rather like Intro Week, it's a process that has its own unique charade. One job interview is pretty much like another – same questions, same answers.

I'm sure that the vast majority of interviewers find the process equally uninspiring as they wade through a mass of intelligent but inexperienced students – many of whom are arrogant enough to think that they already know everything about life that they need to know.

Having gone through the process, Sophia and I both received a number of job offers and, since we had no plans for a long distance marriage, the best situation would be if Sophia took a job with an advertising agency in London and I worked for a newly formed hi-tech company in Swindon.

The ideal place for us to live was Reading – back to the place where I'd spent the first seven years of my life.

The two of us accepted our respective offers. The only pre-condition was that we both obtained at least a lower second for our degrees

**

It was nearly the end of the second term, and the three of us had precious little money left from our student grant. We sat around our living room one Sunday afternoon pondering on life's rich and varied tapestry.

"We not been honoured by the presence of the daughter of Dick in the last week," said Sophia.

"We broke up. She told me to get lost," replied David.

"Why?" I asked.

"Well she wanted me to go skiing with her parents at Easter. And I wanted to go to the farm. I spend little enough time there anyway. And I can't even bloody ski. Stef said it would be fun for me to learn, but I want to see Mum and Dad. C'est la vie, I guess. The truth is that I miss her father more than I miss her. Great sex though, and it was a hell of a good contingency plan."

So David, his contingency plan in tatters, also had to find a job. He received an excellent offer from an engineering firm in Oxford and a truly awful offer from a company in Aberdeen.

The job in Oxford had two pre-conditions to his employment – namely that David obtained at least a lower second in his degree and also that he had a clean driving licence.

Since David had ended the second year on the pass/fail borderline and seeing as he'd hardly ever driven a car much less passed his test, these were pretty daunting pre-conditions for him.

Ever the optimist though, with a smile on his face and a swagger in his step, David immediately booked for his driving test.

"Ten lessons are all that I'll need," he said.

"But you've barely driven before," I replied.

"I did. I drove back in the summer of 1984."

"One lesson, wasn't it?"

"No, I'm sure it was two," replied David.

"Well, that makes ALL the difference!"

David invited Sophia and me out for the afternoon with him and his driving instructor for his final lesson before his test the following day. Although hardly the world's greatest driver myself, even I could tell that David's driving was only pretty mediocre at best and truly shocking at worst.

However, to the bewilderment of all concerned, most notably his own driving instructor, David passed his driving test.

One job offer pre-condition down, one to go.

**

By the end of May, the three of us had finished all our exams and all that remained was a two-week gap to wait for the results. The English Department results came out first, and we all rushed to the Department to find out what degrees Sophia and David had obtained.

To our collective delight, David had obtained an upper second Special Honours Degree, which meant that he had performed out of his skin in his final year whilst Sophia had got a First – I was so very, very proud of her.

Two days later, I was to find that I had obtained an upper second Special Honours Degree.

How the three of us partied that night! After several hours' drinking and smoking, Sophia included, we were all most definitely less than sober.

As we worked our way through the fifth and last bottle of red wine at around three o'clock in the morning, the atmosphere became more than a little poignant as all three of us realised that it was the end of an adventure and nothing would ever quite be the same again.

With genuine, albeit alcohol-fuelled, sentiment, David said,

"I want to thank you both for your brilliant support over the last eight months. You're the best friends a man could have. I'll never forget what you've done. Fabulous food, J.P. And Sofe, my beloved, it's the only time my skidders have been clean in three years here!"

Sophia and I laughed as David continued,

"Whatever happens in the future we should always look back to this time the three of us have spent together in this decaying, ramshackle house in Sheffield as a very special time in our lives."

"I'll drink to that," said Sophia somewhat worse for wear.

"You know, people spend too much time regretting the past and not enough time celebrating it," added David.

He then raised his glass and said,

"A toast – celebrate the past, don't regret it."

"Celebrate the past, don't regret it," we said in unison.

**

The rest of June and early July was a time for Sophia and I to finalise our stag and hen party arrangements and, of course, the wedding itself as we took enormous joy in buying each other wedding rings.

Sophia planned to have a hen party back home in Leeds with her sisters, mother and some old school friends whilst for me it was a week-long cricket tour with Sheffield University to Devon together with Ian, Simon and David.

We played some good cricket against some good sides that week, but the cricket was the minor activity. It was about young guys having fun and I don't think that I've ever laughed as much as I did during those five days.

"Gentlemen, this evening we will undertake the noble and little known art of faggot racing," announced Simon in his role of Tour MC.

Everyone in the tour party, except Ian, looked suitably bewildered and at a complete loss.

"Judging by the blank faces and vacant expressions, I can only assume that we have a group of virgin faggot racers. Possibly even a group of virgins. Nevertheless, my fine associates, to those unaccustomed to this fine and remarkable sport, the basis of faggot racing involves stripping naked and, subsequent to the removal of all garments, most importantly those of a foundation nature, a rolled up newspaper is then inserted between the cheeks of one's bottom and then set alight."

Everyone burst out laughing.

"The winner of the race is the person who can run the furthest with the alight newspaper before feeling the necessity to remove said newspaper from between the cheeks. Any questions?"

Silence descended on our group.

"Then, my fine associates let the revelry begin."

So all fourteen of us on the tour, some reluctantly, went to the beach in Torquay and stripped stark naked at around midnight. There was a massive expanse of sand for our race as the tide was out.

Thankfully, apart from ourselves, the beach was deserted. We all prepared to light our appropriately placed newspapers.

"Any pre-race tips?" I asked Simon.

"You've got the *Daily Telegraph* and not *The Times*, haven't you?" replied Simon.

"Yes, but why?" I enquired.

"Everyone knows *The Times* burns far too easily and quickly."

Despite using the recommended *Daily Telegraph*, unseasoned faggot racing practitioners such as myself were quickly left by the wayside as we felt the heat of the flames on our bare bottom cheeks.

This left twelve of us naked on Torquay beach to watch and cheer Simon and Ian battle it out valiantly to the last. Finally a yelping Simon gave up the noble battle as the burning on his buttocks became too much to bear.

Aware of Simon falling by the wayside and as the race's valiant victor, Ian continued running, triumphant and ablaze into the sea – the cool water offering some much needed respite and relief after the burning flames.

As creators of such a remarkable event, it almost goes without saying that both Ian and Simon had obtained First Class Special Honours Degrees.

The next day, on the final morning of the tour, as I went from the hotel room that I was sharing with David to have a bath, I was physically robbed of my towel by Ian and then locked out of the room by David.

As long as I live, I shall never forget the look on the receptionist's face as I wandered into the reception area stark naked to ask apologetically,

"I hope you can help me, please. You don't possibly have both a spare towel and a spare pair of keys to my room?"

An elderly couple in the reception area looked on in bewilderment as the receptionist went searching for a towel.

"Nice morning, isn't it?" I said.

There was no reply.

The Marriage and Honeymoon

I arrived back at our student house, desperate to see Sophia. We had the time of our lives on the tour and laughed until it hurt, but I missed my woman and couldn't wait to be with her again.

As I walked through the door, I found Sophia in the kitchen wearing a delightful short pink summer dress and her beloved pink sandals.

"Hello, you," she said.

"Hia gorgeous!"

"Missed me?"

"Yes and no."

"No?" asked Sophia.

"We had so much fun. Firth and Bestall were phenomenal value."

"What kind of fun?"

"Just guys having fun – you're not jealous are you?"

"No, I'm not jealous. Curious, that's all," she replied with an air of nonchalance.

"Mmm…"

"Did any women try and seduce you?"

"You see, you are jealous!"

"Well, did they?"

"As it happens, no. And you know all too well I wouldn't be interested anyway."

"You wouldn't? And why is that?" she asked.

Sophia sidled up to me in her inimitable sexy style.

"Because I love you, that's why," I replied.

"How much do you love me?"

Sophia started to nibble my neck.

"This much!"

I put her hand on my groin whilst simultaneously putting my hand up her flimsy pink summer dress to feel the warmness of her groin through her knickers.

"What colour are they?" I asked.

"White, of course – all virginal for your return."

I unzipped the fly of my jeans, pushed her undies to one side and entered her.

"Somebody's eager," she said.

"Do you want me to stop?"

"You've started so you might as well finish."

We made love with Sophia pushed against the kitchen table. With her arms around my neck, her legs wrapped around my back and our tongues entwined, I came in an instant.

"Missed me?" asked Sophia again.

"Maybe yes more than no, if I'm honest!"

"That's more like it. Now that you've spent your excess passion, do you want to go upstairs so that we can make love properly?"

"Now that is a silly question. No, I'd rather go shopping for food and veg!" I replied.

"I've done that already!" said Sophia.

"That being the case, how can I resist?"

As we lay in bed together, Sophia said,

"I was speaking to Brian this week about the wedding."

"Yes?"

"He talked to your mother."

"So what?" I asked.

"And she'd like to come to the wedding."

I exploded with rage and shouted,

"Well, I'd like to have a million pounds, never have to work and just be able to laze around with you. Sadly, that's very unlikely to happen but it's a damn sight fucking more likely than that bitch being allowed to our wedding."

"Goodness, what's got into you?"

"What do you mean, what's got into me? How can you ask that? She abandoned me and my Dad. It destroyed him and damn near destroyed me. I'd rather not get married at all than her be there."

I could see the tears well up in Sophia's eyes as she said,

"I thought that you loved me."

"I do, but fuck off, no way!" my voice remained raised.

"I've never seen you like this. I wonder if I know you. I want to marry you, and then you say something like that."

I could now see the tears streaming from Sophia's eyes.

"I'm sorry, my love. I love you; of course I want to marry you. I just hate the woman," I said.

Tears continued to stream from her eyes. I held her tight and said,

"Look at me. You are the most precious thing in my life. You are the best thing to have ever, ever happened to me. Marrying you will be THE highlight of my life – that's why I don't want my mother there. I want it to be our day, and if my mother's there, it will just spoil it for me," I said.

Sophia stopped crying. She kissed me.

"I understand. I do. I'm sorry for raising the issue. I thought that it might be a good time to forgive and forget. Promise that you won't shout at me again if I say something?"

"I promise."

"Brian said that your mother is so sad at what happened between you and her. She doesn't expect you to speak to her. She wants to be there, that's all."

"Sorry, no way. Don't make me do this."

"I won't. I worry about you though. You never talk about your parents or your childhood. It's like all this anger, hurt and pain is hidden away inside of you. I worry that if one day I hurt you like that, you'll hate me too."

"You'll never hurt me!" I said.

"Not deliberately anyway. I love you. Because you don't talk to me about your childhood, it's like part of you is closed off to me."

"There's nothing to say, really. Look, I'm sorry I shouted at you. I don't want to argue with you. Can't we just change the subject? I thought we came up here to make love – not to have an argument!"

"I've got a headache!" said Sophia.

"I thought they came after we were married, not before."

Sophia finally gave me the slightest of smiles.

"Friends?" I asked.

"Hopefully we're more than friends."

**

Sophia went back to Leeds the week before the wedding – we felt this would make our wedding day and night even more special.

Sophia wanted to sort everything out and make sure that everything was in place personally – her wedding dress, her hair, her underwear, the two bridesmaid's dresses for her sisters, Sandra and Bev, the flowers, etc., etc. – the list went on and on.

In comparison, in the house on my own, my only concerns were my suit and, in particular, my speech. A couple of days before the wedding, I called Sophia on the phone.

"The First Bard of Sheffield wants to write you a poem especially for the day," I said.

"That's lovely. His output continues to be too limited for my liking – but don't make it part of the speech. Save it for afterwards when we're together. I love the fact that the only person who sees your poems is me," she replied.

"But without a poem, what am I going to say?"

"You'll be fine. Don't worry about your speech!"

"But I do worry – I want it to be just right for you."

"Remember what I said to you when we first met?" she asked.

"You said lots to me when we first met. Most of it was shocking – the wild, wilful, late twentieth century woman in all her pomp."

Sophia laughed and said,

"I'm a softie underneath."

"I know that now but boy were you a challenge back then."

"Me, never! Anyway, Melton, you're changing the subject. Don't worry about your speech. Don't even write anything beforehand, David won't. Remember what I always say – be spontaneous, be carefree. Live life. Life is for living. Embrace life, love life. Let yourself go. Remember the karaoke evening?"

I laughed and said,

"How can I forget?"

"Exactly. So just be yourself and everyone will love the speech."

"OK!"

**

After a week on my own, I only too pleased when Friday evening came around and I could meet up with David, Brian, Alison and the rest of the family at a Leeds hotel.

David and I wandered into the city centre for my last drinks as a single man. Being a Friday evening in summer, pretty much every pub was full to bursting point but finally we were able to find a quiet little corner and sat down.

"We've come a long way together," said David.

"We have indeed!"

"From Devon to Sheffield and soon to Oxford and Reading – it's great Oxford and Reading being only about thirty miles apart."

"We'd stay in touch anyway. I can't ever imagine us not having some contact – particularly as Sophia adores you."

"She adores me?" asked David.

"Of course she does. You're like the brother she's never had – same for me."

David smiled and said,

"Look, J.P., don't take this the wrong way but I never thought that I would ever envy you anything but I'll envy you tomorrow. You truly

173

are one of the luckiest men alive. Beneath the abrasive surface, Sofe is one of the nicest, kindest women I've met."

"She's kind of sexy too," I added.

"Can't think why she wants to marry you!" said David.

I smiled and replied,

"Me neither!"

**

Saturday 23rd July 1988 was a glorious sunny day.

David and I made our way to the St Augustine's Roman Catholic Church and we sat outside for a while enjoying the fresh summer air and soaking up the atmosphere.

I wanted to try to take everything in – to imprint it on my mind and never forget it.

As people started to arrive, David and I made our way to the front of the church to wait for Sophia. It wasn't the most beautiful church in the world, but it didn't matter one iota. There were no more than forty people there – Sophia and I had limited it to our close friends and relatives.

I saw Ian and Simon arrive – charm and sophistication personified, impeccably dressed and unrecognisable from the faggot racing heroes of the cricket tour of two weeks earlier.

Then after what seemed like an age waiting, Sophia and her father, Terry, arrived at the church.

I'd not seen her wedding dress before the day and Sophia looked absolutely bloody magnificent – the gorgeous flowing white dress, her hair, her make-up, her shoes and everything about her was just sheer and utter perfection.

But even more than how she looked, I smiled with pride as the warm glow of love radiated from her.

As Sophia walked down the aisle with Terry, it could have been St Paul's Cathedral or Westminster Abbey as far as I was concerned. Although we'd been together for over two years, I still couldn't quite believe that I was marrying such an amazing woman.

Best of all though, I was marrying my best friend.

After the wedding service and the exchange of vows, I kissed Sophia with a real passion and smiled at the fact that this stunning woman was now my wife.

We signed the register and made our way to the hotel for the wedding breakfast. Terry had found a charming hotel on the edge of Leeds heading out towards the moors of Ilkley.

As Sophia and I ate our food we were aware of the tremendous fun and laughter that was being had on the table shared by Ian and Simon, along with John Tasker and his wife.

Then it was time for the speeches. Terry was a little emotional in his speech as the love for his youngest daughter shone through – at times he even struggled to get the words out.

I felt for him.

It was then time for the David show.

"Good afternoon Leeds. Ravishing ladies, immaculate men, it is my enormous pleasure to be best man, master of ceremonies, chief cook, bottle washer, valet and man servant to not only my best friend J.P., but also my second best friend, his wife, Sofe. There is little that can be said of the bride other than the fact that she is, apart from my dear old mum, the finest woman I know – and more than moderate totty, it must be said."

The first of several laughs came from the audience.

"For J.P., there is much to say. Fresh from a naked appearance in a Devon hotel reception, he has scrubbed up well for the day. The incident involving the sheep on Bodmin Moor is sadly still under investigation by local constabulary, but such is Sofe's dedication that she has said that she will stand by him after the inevitable prosecution."

Some people laughed whilst some looked bewildered. David continued unabated,

"What surprises me though is that considering J.P.'s limited skills with ladies, he should end up with such a notable catch. In his youth, we used to call him Carl."

I cringed with embarrassment as David paused.

Ian called out, "Why Carl?"

"Because he was always sub-ten second man in his lovemaking with women!"

Sophia burst out laughing and, inevitably, the audience followed in raucous laughter. I could have died. I wanted the floor to swallow me up. Sophia gave me a playful kiss on the cheek, which at least made me feel a little better.

"Anyway, whilst I could regale you with many wondrous tales of the groom's inadequacies, enough is enough. As I said earlier, he is my true friend and I shall never forget what both he and Sofe have done for me in the last year. I had a tough time at university for a while and they both helped me through it. I wish them all the luck in the world, but I don't think that they'll need it for a moment – I've never known two such well-matched people. I was going to quote Shakespeare today but know how much both of them don't have the passion for him that I do.

175

So I'll leave it to Elizabeth Barrett Browning, who simply said 'Love is best'. And it is – as are both of my friends."

David turned to Sophia and me.

"I love you both. Sofe, J.P., to a glorious past and a brilliant future."

There was warm and considerable applause from the audience.

"Ladies, gentlemen, please raise your glasses, I give you the bride and groom."

"The bride and groom," said the audience as they drank their champagne.

"And now, ladies and gentlemen, it is the man of the day himself, Mr J.P. Melton."

David's speech had made me a little emotional. Now I was just plain scared – I'd never spoken in front of people before. As I stood up, Sophia said,

"You can do this, I know you can. Remember – let yourself go!"

"Good afternoon…" I paused looking for inspiration.

"…I'd firstly like to thank Terry and Christine for today and finding such a fabulous location. And a big thank you to Sophia's sisters, Sandra and Bev, who were both radiant bridesmaids. I'd also like to take this opportunity to very much thank Brian, Alison, Graham and Sarah for giving me a family life and home that most people related by blood are not fortunate enough to have, never mind someone adopted."

I stopped whilst everyone applauded.

"And David, well, your speech could have been kinder to me. However, I guess that's what wedding speeches by the best man are all about – a chance for the world to laugh at the idiosyncrasies and mishaps of the bridegroom."

I turned to David and said,

"You're a truly great friend – the best. Thank you."

David raised his glass to me before I continued,

"Obviously, I'd like to thank everyone who has made the effort to come here from far flung places, my very good friends from university, Ian and Simon and perhaps most of all, John. Not only is he missing his first match for North Devon Cricket Club in five years, but also because he was such an inspiration to me at school. In fact, seeing John reminds me. To me, the only thing that really matters in life is to love and be loved. John's favourite quote is 'I seek a love so amazing, so divine. One that demands my life, my soul, my all.' Well, I sought a love so amazing, so divine and, to my eternal delight, I found that love. To my eternal fortune, I've found someone who fills my life, my soul, my all, and today, truly beyond my wildest dreams, I'm so very lucky to be marrying that person. I love you, Sophia Melton."

It was as though the whole room sighed. As I looked out over the room, I could see nothing but smiles.

"Since Sophia and I have a plane to catch, I will leave it there. I have pressing matters with my wife that I need to attend to."

There was much laughter.

"So ladies and gentlemen, the bride!"

"The bride", toasted everyone and applauded raucously.

As I sat after my speech, Sophia said to me,

"I knew you could do it. Let yourself go! You are incredible when you stop thinking and just do it."

I whispered in Sophia's ear,

"Je veux passer toute ma vie avec toi."

Sophia smiled as she replied,

"Moi aussi."

After the reception and what seemed like hundreds of photographs, it was a quick change of clothes for the two of us followed by a hurried drive in Brian's old pickup truck to Manchester airport to catch the early evening flight to the South of France.

After the excitement of the day, we fell asleep in each other's arms on the plane.

**

We arrived in Nice at around 7pm in the evening to the sight of pouring rain – no, more than that, an absolute deluge of rain. However, the hotel for our honeymoon was simply superb, all marble floors, fragrant fresh flowers and delightful soft furnishings.

Once ensconced in our hotel room, inevitably the first thing that Sophia and I had to do was consummate the marriage – something that I'm pleased to say that we did with a ruthless efficiency – thankfully with no sub-ten-second performance.

After we'd made love, Sophia asked me,

"Did you write a poem for me then?"

"Mayhap!" I replied.

"Mayhap yes, me thinks."

"Do you want to hear it then?" I asked.

"You know I want to hear it. I'm the First Bard of Sheffield's biggest fan!"

"You're the First Bard of Sheffield's only fan!"

Sophia laughed.

I reached for the piece of paper in my pocket.

"OK then...here goes...

There is, betwixt a smile that I aspire to
That sweet aspect that shows me faith
No more to life than that my woman has
No matter what has gone or been before
Her smile is for happiness."

"That's lovely," said Sophia with the biggest smile on her face.

"When you smile, my life does light up. I just wanted to write something that tells you the past before we fell in love does not matter one iota," I replied.

"There are parts of the poem I'm sure I recognise though."

"You're right, the first line is very much Shakespeare as is a bit of the second line."

"Shakespeare?"

"Yes!"

"Henry VIII?" asked Sophia.

"I'm seriously impressed."

"A very fortuitous guess, if the truth be told. I love the poem. I'm so very lucky – marrying the very first Bard of Sheffield."

Sophia kissed me and said,

"I need to get ready now!"

"Get ready?" I asked bewildered.

"Yes!"

"And go out in this? It's absolutely pouring down!"

"Come on, Melton – it's our wedding night, and rain is so romantic."

**

Around 9.30 p.m., we braved the elements to go for something to eat. It was still raining extremely hard and neither of us had an umbrella, but Sophia didn't care and nor did I.

We walked to the sea front in Nice, which is the Promenade des Anglais. Looking out towards the Mediterranean, we stopped in the soaking, pouring rain for an embrace and kiss – it felt like the first time with Sophia, adrenaline pumped through my veins as the rain ran down my face.

After the kiss that seemed to last forever, I opened my eyes and looked around to see a very depressed looking man in the rain walking his dog.

"I bet he didn't expect to come across two young lovers kissing on a night like this!" said Sophia.

"I'm not sure I expected to be kissing outside on a night like this. But, my God, you're right! Kissing in the heavy rain is just unbelievable."

I made eye contact with the man as he passed by and he smiled.

After walking down Promenade des Anglais for a while, Sophia and I took a left turn towards the delightful, albeit very touristic Old Market in Nice, an area full of restaurants. We chose a suitable place to eat and wandered in soaking wet.

The mass of restaurant tables outside in the open air were covered to protect them from the pouring rain. Most of the tables inside were empty, as very few people, local residents and tourists alike, had decided to brave the elements that night.

We both looked like drenched rats, but the first thing that I asked the waiter to do was to take a photo of us.

I kept that photo of the rain-drenched two of us in my wallet for many years to come as a reminder of that adrenaline-filled, inspirational kiss on our honeymoon night.

**

The next day was like a different world as the pouring rain had been replaced by glorious sunshine. We walked from our hotel to Nice station and boarded the train to Cannes and once there, took a boat to Îles de Lérins.

As we travelled over the Mediterranean Sea in the midday sun, Sophia looked truly stunning with the wind in her flowing brunette hair. Again I had to take a photograph that I would always keep with me as a memento of another glorious moment.

Once on the Îles de Lérins, we visited both the monastery and the famous castle on the edge of the island – a place with many legends surrounding it. The almost awesome tranquillity and serenity of those islands made me truly think that Sophia and I were in heaven itself.

That night, we went back to the hotel and we made love on the balcony outside our room. That's not strictly true – in fact, we shagged on the balcony. There's no doubt that there's something wonderfully illicit about having sex in the warm open summer air, the noise of a vibrant city all around you.

I felt truly alive and the world alive with me. As with the kiss on the sea front a day earlier, there was a fantastic surge of energy through my veins when I finally came inside Sophia.

**

179

The next few days we travelled around the region. As much as I enjoyed the pouring rain with Sophia, I was grateful that the weather was kind to us for the majority of our honeymoon.

We visited Monte Carlo, where we spent a magical day touring the area around the Casino Gardens and jewellery stores. The Casino itself at Monte Carlo is truly remarkable, and after a tour of the extravagant building, we wandered down Avenue de Monte Carlo to look at the expensive shops.

All the famous names were there – Prada, Hermes, Valentino and Gucci.

"I want to buy you something," I said.

"Look at the prices!" replied Sophia.

"There must be something."

After a great deal of time and searching, we were able though to find a small and relatively inexpensive purse in Gucci, which Sophia simply adored. It was all I could afford, but Sophia acted as though I'd spent a million dollars on her.

"It's the first present that you've ever bought me as your wife. I'll treasure it forever."

I smiled.

"You don't think we married too soon, do you?" she asked.

"Absolutely not! If you're in love, you're in love. It doesn't matter how old you are, does it? You don't regret it already do you?"

"No, of course I don't regret, silly. We're both twenty-one and that's how old my sisters were when they were married but it seems, I don't know…maybe it's because nobody else I knew at uni was getting married."

"Maybe they weren't in love?" I replied.

"Maybe – I do love you but…"

Sophia's words trailed off before I said,

"But what? It was you that asked me, remember?"

"Yes, I know and I'm glad that I did. And our wedding day was incredible. And I thought your speech was better than David's. Ignore me; I don't know why I asked the question anyway. I'm so happy that we're together. It's as though I belong to you – that we belong to each other. I never thought I could be this happy."

"My love, if there is one thing that I do know, it is that we are great together!"

An Unexpected Addition

With a combined income of little more than £25,000, the two of us could only afford the mortgage for a very small one bedroomed flat. Thankfully we found a suitable flat that was unoccupied at the time, and we were able to move in immediately once the solicitors had sorted out all the necessary paperwork.

We were both suitably smug and proud when we became the official owners. Sophia and I both put in an enormous effort to make our 'cupboard' feel like a real home.

We had very little cash to spare, but it was remarkable how decent we had the place looking. Watching Sophia paint the skirting boards was a delight in itself as specks of the gloss paint were regularly embedded in her brunette hair – much to my amusement and her chagrin.

At the end of each day, we'd open a cheap bottle of wine and celebrate our efforts for the day before making love in our new pristine double bed.

Our sex life at this point was simply sensational – affectionate, sensual, downright sexy, playful, adventurous, occasionally very naughty, always, always fun and with Sophia being Sophia, often very wet indeed!

The bank holiday weekend before we were both due to start work, Sophia and I made the 25 mile journey to Windsor to walk by the Thames and then down the Long Walk, which stretches from the castle there.

It was a wondrous, gloriously sunny day as we flicked water and threw grass at each other during the day and then had a pillow fight at home before making love.

**

Driving into London was a trauma in itself so taking the train into London was the easiest way for Sophia to get to work. I would drop Sophia off in Reading and then drive around 40 miles to Swindon in the clapped out old Astra that we bought with a bank loan for £2,000.

We soon settled into a good, albeit tiring, routine from Monday through to Friday. We had the same ground rules as at university with her washing and ironing and me cooking.

Our lives were typical of many graduates in their first year of work – both of us had fairly low ranking jobs, Sophia at an advertising agency script writers' and me as inside sales for a hi-tech company involved in computer components.

It was a matter of proving ourselves before we could progress.

We would spend some time at weekends in Oxford with David, but he didn't have enough space in his flat for the two of us to stay over. Plus he was entering another dark period in his life. After an inspired final year at university, he was back drinking and womanising in earnest. And judging by the state of his flat, David had mislaid all the cleaning skills that he'd shown the previous year.

He was increasingly unhappy every time we met him. With the demands of work, I wanted to spend some 'quality time' when not at work and David's vision of 'quality time' whenever we went to see him seemed to involve drinking half a dozen pints in a pub and 'chatting up' any woman under 50 years of age.

After several drinks one night and David's singularly and spectacularly unsuccessful 'dialogue' that decidedly offended a poor unsuspecting middle aged woman, Sophia and I returned briefly to David's flat before the drive home to Reading.

His flat resembled a war zone – dishes and pans were unwashed and clothes strewn everywhere. David looked very sad as he rhetorically asked the two of us,

"Why on earth do I have to live this life, why can't I be back at home working on the farm?"

"Why don't you talk to your father? I'm sure he'd listen," suggested Sophia.

"It would break his heart, that's why!" replied David.

He then proceeded to drink his second bottle of red wine in less than 25 minutes after leaving the pub.

**

Over the Christmas period, Sophia was continuously sick for two whole days with food poisoning from something that she'd eaten at a Motorway Service Station on our long journey back from Devon.

Doctors were called out on emergency, and gradually Sophia started to feel better after receiving medication. She was severely dehydrated

182

and lost almost three pounds in weight during her illness. We went back to work in the New Year feeling as though we'd not had a proper break.

Although she missed three days at work, Sophia made a full recovery and we thought nothing more of the incident over the subsequent couple of weeks.

However, toward the end of the month, Sophia said to me one morning over breakfast,

"Being on the pill, my period is usually like clockwork. I'm seven days late now."

"I noticed that too"

"When I was ill over the New Year period, I never thought about it at the time but I was told to use alternative forms of contraceptive if ever I had sickness or diarrhoea."

"Do you think you're pregnant?" I asked.

"Perhaps. We'll see."

Sophia bought a home pregnancy kit and the test showed positive.

To be completely sure one way or another, we took the day off work and visited our local General Practice on January 29, where the matter was confirmed.

Sophia looked shell-shocked when the doctor told her.

In complete contrast, I was euphoric. I could not have been happier. Just being married to Sophia was a privilege in itself but to be a father as well – oh, joy of joys! – I pondered to myself.

On the drive home, Sophia was far more reserved and practical.

"Can we afford to have a baby?" she asked.

"Of course we can!" I responded.

"I so want to have children with you but I'm finally starting to make some real progress in my job. I'd have preferred to wait at least five years, if not longer, before becoming a Mum. I'm only twenty-two. I know my sisters were both pregnant at my age, but this isn't what I want. I'm sorry. I can see how happy you are about it. Don't be angry with me!"

"You are being perfectly reasonable so how can I be angry with you? Ultimately it's your body and ultimately your decision!" I replied.

"It's our decision – not just mine!"

"Yes, it is and, you're right, I do want us to have this baby. But it's not my body or my career. Look, I love you and I'll still love you and support you whatever decision you make. Why don't you give yourself some time and make the decision that you want to make. You're more important to me than any child!"

**

After much silence and pondering, Sophia asked me a couple of days later,

"You so want this baby, don't you?"

"Yes you know I do, but it's YOUR decision," I replied.

"No, it's OUR decision!"

"Yes and no. As I've told you, it's your body and your career. We've time and opportunity to have a child later if we want."

"But what if the abortion goes wrong though? What if this is our only chance? I may be the most paradoxical church-goer this side of the Vatican, and I may not have been to church in the past few months but I do still believe in God, and abortion is wrong. It is a human life growing bit by bit inside of me. That matters to me more than money, more than my career."

"Is that what you really feel?" I asked.

"Yes, whatever I feel about its impact on my life and my career, I can't have an abortion. It's contrary to everything that I have ever truly believed in."

"Sophia, my love, I really want the two of us to be parents. We can make it work. We'll find the money if I have to work every hour God sends. And your career will be back on track in no time. We can do this!"

"I love you. With you by my side, I feel that we can do anything," she said.

"I love you too, and you have no idea how happy you've made me!"

Sophia smiled before replying,

"So not exactly yes and no then, is it?"

**

Once the decision had been made, Sophia was as committed to having the baby as it was possible to be – she stopped drinking immediately and everything she ate and did had our baby's health in mind.

Morning sickness took its hold but to her enormous credit, despite the long commute on a crowded train and my frequent advice to take it easier, Sophia never missed a day of work.

We both worked even harder and ran our flat on a very tight budget to save every possible penny for the birth of our baby – sadly the Friday evening flowers had to go but, if anything, the siege mentality brought the two of us closer still.

We hardly ever went out and I think I read more in those nine months than I'd ever done at university. Sometimes we would just lie in each other's arms on the settee watching television. It didn't matter what was on – the two of us were truly happy.

And once the morning sickness had passed, Sophia's being pregnant didn't affect our sex lives – and, boy, did I find the growing bump inside of her unbelievably sexy.

After 14 weeks and with growing confidence that no problems would occur in the pregnancy, we decided to share our news with the world.

Sophia's parents were delighted; as for Brian and Alison, yet to be grandparents themselves, I doubt if they could have been happier if it had been their own flesh and blood.

**

At four months, Sophia had a scan, and we were told that the baby was healthy – much to our great delight.

"Do you want to know the sex of your baby?" asked the young male Doctor.

"What do you think?" Sophia asked me.

"I want to know. I want to think about a name," I replied in very excited tones.

"I'd like to know too," she said.

"It will be a baby girl," said the Doctor.

When I looked at the scan which showed our little daughter alive and moving inside of my beloved Sophia I felt such pride and delight that I was going to be the father of a little baby girl.

**

The two of us spent hours pondering over a name. After much discussion, we decided to each list our favourite five.

"Sophie, Katrina, Melissa, Oriana and Sandra," suggested Sophia.

"Sandra?!"

"Only joking," laughed Sophia before continuing,

"I could only think of four."

"Well, my five are Beatrice, Imogen, Ursula of course, Melissa and Viola."

"Looks like Melissa then," said Sophia.

"That's fine by me. And the second name?" I asked.

"Sophie after my grandmother?"

"Sounds great to me!"

At the end of May, due to a number of members of staff leaving where I worked, not uncommon at that time for companies along the 'M4 corridor' of Reading, Newbury and Swindon, I was given a major promotion plus a company car.

Two weeks later, Sophia was told that she also would be given more responsibility and a significant salary increase should she choose to return to work after giving birth.

We both felt that life was coming together and beginning to work for us. Sophia was particularly pleased as she felt that we would now be able to afford a good nanny.

With me now having a company car, we were able to sell our own car, and both of us felt that we had enough available cash to do something special in early June as that would be the last chance for Sophia to travel anywhere by plane whilst pregnant.

By scouring various travel agents for the best possible deal, we found a very cheap holiday that would allow us to spend a few days in Sitges to the south of Barcelona.

After spending so much time in the tight confines of a small one bedroomed flat, we were excited beyond words about the holiday.

**

We stepped off the plane at Barcelona airport. The heat washed over us and left us soaked with sweat.

Sophia was 23 weeks pregnant, and the weather was far too hot for her. The only way we could enjoy our small break was to adopt a Spanish type siesta, sleeping in the afternoons and then having fun together in the cooler evenings.

On the last night there, we went 'skinny dipping' in the Mediterranean Sea in the cooler air of the midnight moonlight. After our naked swim together Sophia allowed herself a very rare mouthful or two of alcohol as the two of us sat drinking Cava on the beach.

With no one around at around three o'clock in the morning, we made love to the sound of incoming waves.

After making love, Sophia and I sat around talking and working our way gently through the bottle of Cava. Before we knew it, the sun was rising on the horizon and an awesome blend of oranges, yellow and blues welcomed the new day.

That dawn was as though I was breathing the very elixir of life. I felt so goddamn alive, so intoxicatingly happy, so totally fulfilled and in love.

As the sun rose in the blue Mediterranean sky, Sophia turned to me and said,

"Promise me that we'll always be together and that it will always be like this."

"Of course it will – why on earth shouldn't it be?" I asked.

"Maybe having Melissa will change our lives for the worse. Maybe you won't love me anymore; it happens you know," Sophia continued.

"Sophia, my love, if anything, baby Melissa will make our lives better still. And don't be daft, I'll always love you."

Sophia smiled at my response but was insistent in her demand in a very playful and affectionate way as she said,

"I want you to *promise* you will always love me."

As Sophia made her demand out of the corner of my eye, I saw a pebble on the beach in the shape of a heart.

I went over and picked up the pebble and gave it to Sophia whilst crouched on my knee in the form of a classic marriage proposal.

"This heart shaped pebble is a token of my commitment to the promise that the two of us will always be together and that I will always love you."

"You old romantic softie, you," replied Sophia.

"That's all the thanks I get!"

"I'm only teasing. It's lovely. I love you so much, you daft sod!"

**

After our short holiday, every penny that we could save, we did. An occasional drink in the summer sun outside the local pub on a Sunday became the major social event in our lives. However, sustained by the literature of Lawrence, Wilde and Byron together with our love for each other, time passed quickly.

Our sole indulgence between Sitges and the birth of Melissa was to celebrate our first wedding anniversary in July. We decided that we would dine at the Ritz in London in the sumptuous surroundings of the delightfully elegant and ornate dining room there.

Every mouthful of food and sip of wine was savoured and if not quite the exhilaration of sex on the beach in Sitges, it was certainly a magnificent way to celebrate our first wedding anniversary.

On the train journey home, we huddled together on the train seat like the young lovers we still were.

As the train home left London, I said to Sophia,

"I love you more than words can say."

"When I was around seventeen, I used to idly dream of being this happy. But felt that it could only be a fairy tale – like a creation of writers to offer a brief escape from the mundanities of life. I sometimes have to pinch myself, I feel so happy!" replied Sophia.

At that point, baby Melissa gave a kick inside Sophia. Both Sophia and I smiled.

"And that's enough from you, young lady", we both said simultaneously.

We laughed and then kissed.

**

We made our plans for after the birth.

Assuming that Melissa was born to schedule, Sophia decided that she would return to work mid-November pending a successful post natal examination.

So we set about finding a suitable nanny but sadly we were only able to find two potential candidates – Jessica, in her twenties and Sally, in her fifties.

"For me, it's got to be Jessica. Sally's so stern," said Sophia.

"Sally will be very efficient though, and she's far more flexible. I'm not comfortable with Jessica's terms. All this minimum forty hours a week and maximum forty-eight hours a week stuff and, worse still, if we're more than five minutes late home, she feels that constitutes half an hour," I replied.

"But she's so warm and kind. I feel like a naughty schoolgirl with Sally."

"That's because you are still a naughty schoolgirl at times."

"But only with you, Melton."

There was silence.

"Come on you, decide," demanded Sophia.

"Sally!"

"Not the answer I wanted, you! Look, we're not going to ever need less than forty hours a week and we can't really afford more than forty-eight anyway. It will be good discipline. My boss is cool about it. I can get in early and leave early – work seven a.m. to three p.m. If you leave home at nine a.m., you'll be in work by ten a.m. and you can then work as long as you want because I'll be back by five. You've said your boss is comfortable with that. And then if you need to be away a couple of nights a week on business, we've got an extra eight hours."

"You make it seem really straightforward," I replied.

"Life can be if you want it to be. So are we decided, husband dearest?"

"If you say so."

"You know it makes sense," said Sophia.

**

In the early hours of September 28th, Sophia went into labour, and I drove her to Reading General Hospital – the same place coincidentally that I had been born.

During the journey Sophia was in considerable pain but I was like an excited little boy. I was almost incredulous when I thought about the scarcely believable reality of becoming a father.

However, after around five and a half hours at the hospital, there was little sign of further progress. Sophia was clearly in absolute agony despite an epidural and gas to help with her pain.

I tried to help her every bit of the way with what I'd learnt at pre-natal classes and never left her side – but the reality is that there's very little most men can do in such a situation.

My little boy excitement of earlier had now turned into a sense of helplessness in not being able to ease the pain of the woman I loved.

My heart sank further when the doctor asked to see me outside.

"Don't be long," said Sophia.

"I'll be back as soon as I can. Don't go anywhere!" I replied trying to make light of the situation.

I could tell by the doctor's body language that the situation was not good. He explained to me,

"There is a problem. Your wife's blood pressure is now dangerously low, and I am concerned that she may go into hypovolemic shock. You can see that she's exhausted, which doesn't help. She may lose the baby but to being direct, I'm more concerned about her if she doesn't give birth soon."

"What can be done?" I asked, desperately trying to stay calm as my insides churned.

"We'll do our best. The nurses will keep her warm, and they're going to fit her with an intravenous line to try and get some fluids back into her. The best thing is to keep her calm and focused. The next push is critical."

I could feel my hands shaking as I felt sick to the pit of my stomach. It felt as though a heavy weight was pressing on my chest.

"Please give me a minute and I'll be back in there! I want our baby, but she pales into insignificance compared with my wife. If you have to terminate the pregnancy to save her then just do it! OK?"

"We'll do everything we can," replied the doctor.

I went to the toilet and looked at my reflection in the mirror – I could feel terror and panic running through my veins. Part of me wanted to cry, part of me even considered praying but I told myself that that had done no good before in my life so why would now be any different.

I took a deep breath and told myself to be positive.

As I re-entered the room, Sophia was still in immense pain and looked absolutely drained. She was covered in blankets, and an IV line was feeding into her arm. The concern of all the nurses in the room was all too evident.

It was time to push again.

"Come on you. I don't have all night. I'm tired and hungry!" I said.

"I'm not having a ball either! I'm tired and I want to go home," replied Sophia.

"Well just bloody get on with it then woman, for God's sake"

"Men, goodness me – all the sensitivity of the average garden gnome."

I could see the annoyance in Sophia's face as she said the words. Thankfully that annoyance, coupled with her frustration, translated into extra effort as she made the next push.

Melissa's head appeared. My heart leapt with unrestrained joy. Sophia pushed again, clearly straining every possible sinew.

Finally at 8.46pm Melissa, sweet Melissa was born. Her first cries in the world were a delight to behold, but I was more concerned about Sophia.

"Is she OK?" I asked the doctor.

"I'm sure she'll be fine. She's beginning to stabilise."

I started to cry with a mixture of unadulterated relief and happiness. I put my head on the bed next to Sophia's hand, and she lovingly stroked my hair.

"Is sir happy now?" she asked in mock indignation.

I continued to cry as Sophia gently caressed me.

The maternity nurse gave Melissa to Sophia to hold and I sat up next to the two of them in bed and held them both tight, tears of relief and joy still streaming down my face.

I was now the father of a beautiful baby girl and, more importantly, still the husband of a stunning, gorgeous wife.

"I love you so much, and I'm so damn fucking proud of you. And you, you little woman, Melissa, are just downright bloody amazing," I said.

Sophia smiled brightly whilst Melissa gurgled.

I stayed for ages with them before the maternity nurse finally asked me to leave to enable Sophia to get some much needed rest.

I walked into the night air relieved, deliriously happy and as proud as punch. I sat on a wall outside the hospital feeling the happiest man alive.

I clenched my fist and threw my head back as I took the deepest breath imaginable.

My life felt complete – totally complete.

As Sophia had said, it felt like a fairy tale.

Melissa

The next six weeks were close to idyllic – though the three of us were crammed together in a small one bedroomed flat it didn't seem to matter.

But for the need to earn money I'd have happily stayed at home playing with baby Melissa all day – I just loved to hold my tiny baby in my arms and rock her to sleep. Sure there was the crying, the sleepless nights and the seemingly endless production of dirty nappies but Melissa was my daughter, my own flesh and blood and I loved her.

And Sophia, in addition to being my lover, wife and best friend, she was now the mother of my beloved daughter.

"We could survive on just my salary if needed," I said.

Sophia puffed her cheeks at the idea before responding,

"Yes, we could but why should we? I don't want to scrimp and save all my life – like my sisters are doing. That's why I went to university. It's so claustrophobic in this small flat. I need to go out occasionally. I'm fulfilled as a Mum, I truly am – but I need to be fulfilled as a woman too. I know that you'd play with Melissa all day but for me, it's not stimulating to do it *all* the time"

"I want you to be fulfilled in every way."

"I suppose you could stay at home, and I go to work – very late twentieth century woman with her house husband," suggested Sophia.

"Now there's an idea!" I replied.

"Are you SERIOUS?" asked Sophia in bewildered tones.

"Yes and no…well no, I suppose not. There again, I do kind of like the idea. The problem is, of course, that I have a better job than you!"

"Not for long, mister, not for long!" came back Sophia.

"It's just that once you've paid your train fare to go to work, and then paid Jessica, there's going to be very little money left out of your salary at the end of the month."

"But money's not the issue. I thought we'd agreed that. What we agreed was that it was important for me as a woman to be fulfilled and working. Right?" asked Sophia.

"You're right. It is what we agreed."

"And anyway you, if the six week post natal examination tomorrow gives me the all clear, your wife will be looking to be fulfilled in other ways. They say some women lose their libido after giving birth, but I'm not one of them."

**

The next night I arrived home to find Sophia waiting for me dressed only in black underwear, seamed black stockings and suspenders and the most magnificent vertiginous black heels.

"Wow," I said.

"Does sir like?"

"Sir indeed does. I can't believe that you gave birth only six weeks ago. You look amazing."

"All down to a sensible diet and lots of pull-ups. The doctor is similarly impressed with how my nether regions have healed too. Good as new, he said. Giving birth at only twenty-two has some benefits, it seems."

I looked at Sophia with a mixture of love, lust, wonderment and adoration.

"Are you just going to stand there, Melton, or am I going to see some action? I've catered to your needs, hand and mouth, oil and cream over the last five weeks and now it's your turn!"

I pushed Sophia onto the bed and pulled her underwear to one side.

Although we'd not had sex for a couple of months, my mouth knew her clitoris so well and I instinctively knew what to do. Very quickly, Sophia's leg muscles contracted and her back arched.

"Oooooooh, YES!" she cried as she came in my mouth.

I'd forgotten that her orgasm tasted like the very nectar of the gods.

"Are you ready?" I asked.

"Ready for what?" replied Sophia.

"Ready for me to take you?"

"You, sir, can wait. You've waited for a couple of months so you can wait a little while longer yet. Now find that vibrator and kiss and caress me while I have some fun!"

I did as I was told, and it was unbelievable – the unadulterated joy of watching the woman I loved sexually fulfilled and satisfied. I kissed, caressed, stroked and played with every part of Sophia's body as orgasm followed orgasm – another 'Niagara Falls' experience as the bed sheets were drenched.

"Make love to me whilst I have a play!" demanded Sophia.

I entered Sophia from the side, and she kept playing with the vibrator. I gently pushed in and out as it was the first time we'd made love after she'd given birth. Sophia was very wet, and the sensation of the vibrator was giving me immense pleasure – never mind her.

Sophia let out a deep sigh, and I could feel her come all over me. I was so excited by the sheer sublime sensual magnificence of her wet orgasm that I came immediately.

"Boy, I'm back!" said Sophia.

I laughed a deliciously filthy laugh.

**

Sophia returned to work, only doing short four hour days to begin with.

As nice as the nanny Jessica was, she was a real 'clock watcher'. Nevertheless, even when Sophia started to work her full quota of hours, it did seem to be working with Jessica as Sophia had planned. Sophia would start early and finish early, and I'd start late and finish late.

Melissa seemed full of life and clearly liked Jessica. Everything in the garden seemed rosy.

**

The week before Christmas was fraught – far from winding down before the festive season both of us were very busy at work, and I needed to be away on business on the Wednesday and Thursday evenings.

Furthermore, the week started badly as Sophia was a few minutes late home on both the Monday and Tuesday, clocking up an hour of Jessica's time in the process.

The Wednesday morning was another ordinary grey, cold winter's day with a touch of frost in the air.

I was giving Melissa a loving hug. She was warm, smiling, kicking and full of life as Sophia and I talked before she went to catch the 5.30 a.m. train to London.

"Wouldn't it be great if it was a white Christmas this year?" I said.

"It would be a nightmare getting to Leeds and Devon, but yes, I agree with you. If snowflakes were love, you'd send a blizzard to me!"

"You remembered what I wrote to you!"

"Of course I do. Whatever happened to the first Bard of Sheffield?" asked Sophia.

"He fell in love, got married and had children!"

"Aah, happens to us all, I guess. Literature's loss is my gain, I suppose. What time are you back on Friday?"

"Around seven thirty p.m. I told you twice last night!" I responded.

"Sorry, I'm still a bit of a nappy brain. I'll write it down, so I don't forget..."

Sophia mumbled to herself as she wrote,

"Only thirty-one hours of Jessica's time left this week. Leave work early every day to be home by five p.m. for when she leaves."

"Right, I need to go, give me a kiss then," I said.

I gave Sophia the biggest French kiss imaginable.

"Down, tiger. Not in front of the baby! We can do all of that palaver on Friday night," joked Sophia.

"But we always do it front of the baby!"

"The poor thing will probably be mentally scarred for life."

"Right, see you Friday. I'll call you later. And you'll be back at five p.m. every day, right?" I said to reinforce the situation.

"Don't worry. Stop nagging – you're like a mithering old woman sometimes. I've written it down. Now drive carefully. It's a lot of driving at this time of year. I don't want any traumas for Christmas. I want us to be able to relax and see our families and open all of Melissa's presents together."

"Who's nagging now?" I replied.

**

The next day evening, I called Sophia from my hotel to find her in a most agitated state.

"I've had the most enormous row with Jessica," she said.

"Why? Anything wrong with Melissa?"

My voice was full of anxiety.

"No, Melissa's fine, lovely as always. I was held up again today at work and now Jessica's saying that with twelve and a half hours yesterday and thirteen and a half hours today, she's done 42 hours for the week and will only work six hours tomorrow."

"Can't you take the day off?"

"I've worked so hard on this project, and it's such a career maker, I only need to go in for a couple of hours for the meeting itself. If Jessica would do the basic eight hours then it's fine. But she refuses flatly! Bitch! We need to talk over Christmas what we're going to do about her."

"So what are you going to do?" I asked.

"Jessica has a friend. She's not a registered nanny, but Jessica says she's a natural with children. She's willing to do nine till five tomorrow, and that's perfect for me. My meeting at work is at noon and it'll be over by one thirty at the latest. I'll be home by three thirty!"

"Are you sure?"

"It's only the once, and I will definitely be back by three thirty. It's not ideal, but I'm sure it will be all right."

I said nothing.

"Anyway, enough of all this stress – I'm stood here in your favourite black panties, is there anything sir would like me to do?" asked Sophia.

"We had phone sex last night!" I replied.

"So we can't have it two nights running?"

"Keep the black panties for me tomorrow night."

"Spoilsport!" replied Sophia.

**

It was Friday December 22nd 1989.

Whilst driving home and listening to Christmas records on the car radio, I kept thinking how good Christmas was going to be. I stopped at a Motorway Service Station and bought Sophia some flowers.

Flowers in hand, I fully expected to see Sophia's face as soon as I stepped through the door of our home in Reading at around seven o'clock.

However, I found the place in total darkness.

"All right, I know you're there. Very funny!" I shouted.

There was no sign of Sophia.

"Come on, this is beyond a joke. I've had a long day!"

I put the living room lights on and saw a note that had been left on the table.

Dear Sophia,
Sorry! Waited until after 5.45 but I have to go.

Melissa seems fine.

A very Merry Christmas and a Happy New Year to you all.

Alison x

196

I made my way to the bedroom and put the light on. I saw my beloved Melissa lying on her stomach in her cot and smiled to myself.

As I moved towards her, Melissa was silent and motionless. I initially thought that Melissa was just sleeping but then, as I picked her up in my arms the true horror of the situation dawned upon me.

Melissa was totally bereft of any life – no movement, no breath, no nothing. I felt as though time was standing still.

I couldn't speak. I couldn't feel.

I had to consciously tell myself that I needed to continue to breathe.

I shook Melissa hard hoping that she'd scream and burst into life but she didn't. I felt that my dreams were evaporating in front of my very eyes.

I took Melissa through into our small living room and sat there in stunned silence, holding my beloved baby.

I lost all track of time.

**

I heard Sophia's voice as she came through the door to the flat.

"I'm sorry. You wouldn't believe it! Meeting started an hour late, meeting went on an hour longer than expected, crash on the underground network in London and then to cap it all, my train from London broke down, and I was left sat there for over two hours. I hope that you had a better day!"

I didn't answer.

"What's the matter, lover?" she asked upon entering the living room.

"It's Melissa – she's dead"

"WHAT?" Sophia screamed.

"It's Melissa – she's dead!" I repeated.

"She can't be. Let me see."

Sophia came to sit with me and as soon as she saw and held Melissa for herself, she burst into a flood of tears.

"NO. PLEASE NO!" she screamed.

Sophia sobbed uncontrollably, almost hysterically, for ages.

"It's all my fault. If I had been on time, this wouldn't have happened. I can never forgive myself. NO. Please, please, please NO. This is so fucking unfair. NO. Please NO. NO, NO, FUCKING NO!"

I just sat there in silence as Sophia continued to cry hysterically.

**

Sophia called for an ambulance.

We made our way to the hospital, the same hospital where Melissa had been born less than three months earlier – the magical fairy tale of that day had become pure and simple devastation.

Sophia and I talked with the doctor; well at least Sophia did as I stood there, in silent distress and total resignation.

"There will need to be an autopsy on your baby. My immediate assessment is that is we have a case here of sudden infant death syndrome," said the doctor.

"Cot death?" asked Sophia.

"As I say, that is only my immediate assessment. There needs to be a full autopsy and post-mortem investigation carried out by a suitable experienced paediatric pathologist."

"How long will that take?"

"It will probably be done early in the New Year. This time of year is awful. Have you contacted the police?"

"The police?" asked Sophia

"Yes, it's a formality but they need to be informed."

After the doctor had finished talking to us and set about his other duties, I finally spoke,

"I need to go to the toilet."

"I'll wait here," replied Sophia.

All I wanted to be was on my own. I walked outside the hospital and sat on a wall. It was the same wall that I'd sat on in such joy and happiness after Melissa was born less than three months earlier.

It was pouring with rain, but that was of little concern to me. I put my head in my hands. I wanted to cry but I couldn't – the pain just wouldn't come out.

**

We asked that Sophia's parents, Terry and Christine, as well as Brian, Alison and David stay away.

Sophia did all the phoning around, invariably sobbing as she spoke, whilst I sat in our living room silently.

**

Two members of the police arrived, and we sat together in our small living room, a pile of unopened presents for Melissa still in the corner of the room.

The policewoman began the discussion,

"So Mrs Melton, you left your daughter with Alison Broadbent on the Friday."

"Yes, but she left before I arrived home. I was late. Hasn't she broken some law or another by leaving Melissa alone?" asked Sophia.

"Did you have a formal nanny contract with her?"

"No, she wasn't actually the nanny. She was only babysitting Melissa for the day."

"The first thing to be clear about is that if SIDS is confirmed as the cause of death then there would unlikely be any police action anyway. However, there is some Health and Safety legislation under which a nanny could possibly be prosecuted. But if she wasn't the actual nanny, I'm not sure anything can be done. I would be highly critical of Ms Alison Broadbent – but that's only my personal perspective."

"I see," said Sophia with resignation in her voice.

**

The New Year, new decade, started with another hospital visit – this time to see the paediatric pathologist after the autopsy. He was a kindly man, balding and in his mid to late fifties.

Sophia and I sat down together in his office.

"Can I offer you both a cup of tea?" he asked.

"No, thanks," replied Sophia.

I shook my head.

"I'll come straight to the matter at hand. The autopsy can provide no explanation for your daughter's death. Therefore, my diagnosis is one of sudden infant death syndrome," said the pathologist.

Sophia and I were silent.

"Sadly SIDS is remarkably common. The suffering it causes for parents is terrible. You have my deepest sympathies."

"It's so hard to come to terms with," said Sophia.

"I know it's difficult but you need to focus on the two of you now. Do you have any other children?" asked the pathologist.

"No," said Sophia.

"You'll need to support each other, that is for sure. If you need counselling then please don't hesitate to contact us. Some people think that there's some sort of stigma over counselling, but it does help. I suggest you take this sheet. It provides all the details."

"Thank you. You've been very kind," replied Sophia.

**

199

Five days later, on January 8th, we had baby Melissa's funeral.

It was a dark, damp, cold January day as they lowered Melissa's tiny coffin into the ground. I felt as though I was in Hell itself as the cold wind bit through me.

As Sophia and I stood separately at Melissa's graveside, thoughts of my father's funeral flooded back into my mind.

The only other thing that I could think of was that they had buried my beloved baby without her even having been christened.

It is said that when a heart breaks, it screams out in pain – it may not be possible to hear the plaintive cry, but the silence is deafening.

The only sound that day was the deafening silence between Sophia and me.

Where It All Went Wrong

Sophia and I were sat in our living room. We didn't want the television or radio on or any music playing.

I was staring blankly at the four walls, not bearing to look at the photograph of Melissa on the table in front of me.

"How do you feel?" asked Sophia.

"How do you think I feel?"

"I don't know. That's why I asked!"

I was silent.

"Goodness me, it's like talking to a brick wall," she said.

I remained silent.

"I feel as awful as you do, but life goes on."

"How do you know how I feel?" I asked.

"That's the whole point; I don't know how you feel unless you talk to me. This is bloody awful enough without us not talking and me feeling that you blame me for what happened."

I was still silent.

"You do blame me, don't you?" asked Sophia.

"I just can't believe it's happened," I replied.

"I can't either. I feel like crying every single minute of the day, but I keep telling myself to be positive and that this too shall pass. I love you – whatever has happened, whatever has changed, no matter how terrible, there is one thing that I hang onto and that is that I love you."

I was silent again.

Sophia came and sat on my knee.

"Do you still love me?" she asked.

"Yes!" I replied.

"That's a good start. Look, we're young, healthy and have our lives in front of us. We saved some money, and we both have good jobs and career prospects. We have to look on the bright side. I'm totally devastated at what happened, beyond words, but I keep telling myself that it could have been you. That would have been too much to bear."

**

201

"Why don't we move apartment? Maybe we should move to a better house in a nicer area and put what has happened behind us," I suggested to Sophia.

"Now that is a good idea. Maybe a new house in a new place will bring us better luck," she replied.

"Houses and places don't bring bad luck"

"This one has though – hasn't it?" replied Sophia.

**

We sold our flat in Reading and made a massive profit on the sale – but there was no joy to be had in our gain – and moved to a very nice two bedroomed flat in the charming area of Finchampstead not far from Wokingham on March 28th 1990.

As we left our flat in Reading, Sophia talked positively of a fresh start and a new beginning. She also felt that it was about time that the most paradoxical church-goer this side of the Vatican adopted a new church.

I hoped that she was right about a new beginning, but as much as I was pleased to leave Reading, I was unconvinced.

In the three months since the New Year, our sex life had radically changed – whilst previously it had been very regular, vibrant and full of love, affection and passion it had become very functional and very, very occasional.

The problems were solely on my side. I started to feel uncomfortable making love to Sophia, that somehow it wasn't right that I should be doing something enjoyable after Melissa's death.

**

Sophia seemingly always wanted to talk about what happened with Melissa, whereas I didn't want to talk about it at all. I didn't actually want to talk about anything.

I began to dread her raising the issue of our baby Melissa dying.

Sophia would cry over what happened – although perhaps she was also crying over the fact that our relationship was beginning to unravel and disintegrate.

I couldn't bear to hear her cry, but it hurt too much to console her – I feared that if I did then I too would start crying, but unlike Sophia I'd never be able to stop.

Whereas at the time of Melissa's death, I'd fretted over my inability to cry – now the thought of crying frightened me and I found myself

202

continually returning to my school-day's mantra, 'Nobody, just nobody nor nothing is ever going to make me cry again.'

**

Sophia cried less and less as time went by and she seemed to be becoming stronger by the day. Regular Sunday visits to the church were helping her, and I really envied Sophia her faith in God.

She returned from church one Sunday to find me, as usual, sat in complete silence on my own.

"Cup of tea?" she asked.

"No."

"What have you been up to whilst I was at church?"

"Nothing."

"Sweetheart, you really need to talk about it," said Sophia.

"Talk about what?" I asked.

"About Melissa, for goodness' sake, what else do you think?"

"Why do I need to talk? There's nothing to say."

"Because I'm worried about you."

The concern in Sophia was all too evident.

"I'm all right, leave me alone."

"You're not all right. I know you, Melton. To have gone through what happened is bad enough. But the biggest tragedy is you and me. This whole thing is tearing us apart. Some days, I wish that Melissa had never been born – that, without her, we'd still be like we were six months ago."

"Do you really feel that way about Melissa?" I asked.

"I certainly don't want to. She lived less than three months, but she was my first child, and I loved her – no matter how short her life was. I don't want to regret her being part of my life. But you make me feel like that. You're my lover, my best friend and my husband. I want you back in my life. Please, for me."

I was silent.

"How do you feel about counselling?" asked Sophia.

"I don't need counselling – you're over reacting. Just give me time and space," I retorted with a sigh.

**

I worked longer and longer hours at work, and the increasingly limited time that I spent with Sophia was further compounded by my decision to start playing cricket again that summer.

Unlike during my days at university, Sophia started to come and watch me play.

The irony is that, when I started playing again, I didn't enjoy it; it was a case of anything to get me out of the flat and to be in my own little world.

As the summer progressed, things continued to steadily decline. Sophia was doing her very best to be supportive and sympathetic, but she was receiving little or no help from me.

**

On our second wedding anniversary, I arrived home from work, and as I walked into the living room Sophia was lying seductively on our settee in sexy black underwear.

I was quite shocked and said nothing.

Sophia jumped up and came over to me.

"Happy anniversary," she said handing me a big card and a small present.

I closed my eyes in horror.

"Shit, Sophia, I'm sorry, I forgot."

I could see the anger and hurt in Sophia's eyes.

"No, you're not sorry. You're wrapped up in your own world of self-pity. You need help, you need counselling. For goodness' sake, one counselling session is all I ask. Instead, I have to deal with interminable self-pity and disinterest towards me. I'm your wife."

There was a rare anger in Sophia's voice.

"I'll pull out of it, I will. I promise. But I don't need help. The last thing I need is to have to talk to a total stranger about all of this," I protested.

I threw my head back in frustration and then held my head in my hands, partly in anguish, partly in disbelief at the situation.

Sophia put her arms around my neck. She kissed me gently and tenderly.

"I know how hard this has hit you. I wish you'd talk to me, that's all. I love you, but I can't help you through this if you won't talk to me," she said.

I sighed in exasperation.

"No card, no present – now I'm not going to let you off without giving me something. This is my best black underwear and sheerest pair of stockings, and I want some serious attention from you, Melton. The bedroom! Now!"

A rare smile crossed my face.

"Yes, miss – at your command!" I replied.

After some of the most sumptuous foreplay imaginable, Sophia got on top of me. I wanted to come inside of her. I pushed my groin upwards against hers.

"No," she said.

I pushed again against her.

"No. Let me!" insisted Sophia.

I let her make love to me gently. I was submissive and could feel the orgasm slowly and sensuously building inside of me. As we built together, I was exhilarated by the sublime ecstasy of the moment as wave of pleasure followed wave of pleasure – her tongue tantalising very pore, every inch of my mouth, neck and nipples.

I could feel Sophia's muscles start to tighten again. She screamed and bit my neck fiercely. Pleasure and pain – it was simply exquisite.

I could feel her come as her warm liquid flowed all over me. She tightened her stomach muscles again, and my whole body spasmed as she bit my neck as I came inside of her.

"I needed that. I'm a woman with needs!" said Sophia.

"That was just amazing!" I replied.

"The only person stopping that being a regular event is you, Mr Melton. Anyway, are you going to lie there or actually make an effort and open your card and present?"

In a beautiful small box was the heart-shaped pebble that I'd given Sophia on the beach in Sitges.

I opened the card and read it.

I want someone who brings a love so amazing, so divine into my life – a love that demands my soul, my life, my all. A man who gives me heart-shaped pebbles and promises to always love me.

The position is sadly vacant at present, but nothing would make me happier than if the recipient of this card wishes to re-apply.

All my love, your wife

Sophia

xxxxxx

"I'm sorry, my love," I said.

"It's all right. I know how difficult it's been for you because I know how difficult it's been for me. But please tell me how you feel – that way we can help each other."

"I can't put it into words. It's just an emptiness that consumes me."

**

September 28th was Melissa's birthday. I was driving Sophia to the station to catch her train into London for work.

"I'm leaving work early today. Will you come with me to Melissa's grave?" asked Sophia.

"No, you go. I'll maybe come with you next time," I replied.

"You always say that and you never do. It's her birthday."

"I've got stuff to do. I'm really snowed under at the moment. Next time, eh?"

Sophia sighed.

As we arrived at Wokingham station, I wished Sophia a good day at work.

She got out of the car without so much as a goodbye.

**

A few weeks later, Sophia and I were having breakfast together.

Sophia broke the silence.

"Why don't we go out tonight? Nothing special – have a drink somewhere or go for a pizza?"

"I've arranged to meet David."

"Can I come, it'll be nice? He's my friend too! You seem to be spending more time with him than me."

"I don't spend more time with him."

"So can I come or not?"

"Not really."

"Why?" she asked.

"It's a guys' night out, that's why."

"I don't like the sound of that! Why is it that you always end up sleeping over? Would you rather be with him?"

"No, it's nothing like that. Just David and I and some of his mates having a drink, that's all! It wouldn't work – one woman with ten guys."

"Now I do like the sound of that!"

"You know what I mean."

"Yes, I do but sometimes it's a bit miserable in this flat on my own as I don't know anyone around here. All my friends and work colleagues, David apart, who seems to have become your sole preserve, are in London."

"Why don't you stay over with them then?" I suggested.

"Because I want to be with you, that's why. It's a shame that you clearly don't feel the same way."

I was silent.

**

The Beatles' back catalogue came out on CD. I bought all the old albums, *Revolver* and *Abbey Road*, which I'd listened to as a child, along with a pair of headphones to listen to them on.

I disappeared into my private world with the intention of shutting everyone and everything out.

It didn't work, and rather than get better with time, the pain of the memory of holding dead Melissa in my arms increasingly haunted my dreams and most waking hours.

Although Sophia and I had moved, my mind was increasingly locked in the small bedroom of our flat in Reading.

And if not there, then I was thinking about my father – compounded by the fact that I was now listening all the time to the same music as I had done in the house in Taplow.

**

As November became December, Sophia and I were arguing over everything and nothing – we argued over major issues such as the fact that I never talked to her, that I was never at our flat and that I was always working as well as more 'trivial' issues such as me no longer buying her flowers.

I collected Sophia one evening at the station and on the drive home, Sophia said,

"I was asked out again today."

"Who by this time?" I asked.

"Dan Sutter again! I think that he's got the hots for me."

I ignored Sophia.

We arrived home and sat down together after making a cup of tea.

"I'm totally fed up with this," said Sophia.

"Fed up with what, for God's sake? I just don't know what you want," was my frustrated response.

207

"I want the man that I married back in my life."

"I'm the same loyal, faithful, honest man that I've always been."

"That isn't what I mean, and you know it."

"Yes I know. I know it's my fault. Everything is my fault."

"I'm not saying that," responded Sophia.

"Yes, you are."

"No, I'm not!"

"Well what are you saying, woman?"

"I'm saying I want more from life. I want a husband that I see and do things with. My goodness, we've not even had a proper holiday this year. It's always either cricket or work or something. I'm so fed up!"

"I just don't know what's the matter with you – we've a nice flat and we both have flourishing careers. I thought that's what you wanted. Instead, all you do is complain. Nag, nag, nag – all the time."

"Sod our careers, Jonathan. I'd go back to a tedious summer job and a rented student house tomorrow if it meant that you gave me your time and, goodness me, some genuine affection. I need to feel that you actually want to be with me. I feel like an outcast in my own home. I'd live in a cardboard box if I could have the love back that you once gave me – if we talked together as we used to talk."

"I've had enough of this melodramatic shit. I'm going to see David," I said as I stormed out of the flat.

**

On the car drive to Oxford, I thought of how our argument was almost a 'word for word' re-enactment of my mother and father arguing all those years before.

A shudder ran down my back.

I arrived at David's flat and knocked at his door.

"Oh, it's you again," said David.

"Nice welcome!" I replied.

"You'd better come in, I suppose."

We sat down amongst the debris of David's life.

"What are you doing here?" asked David.

"I've come for a drink!"

"I'm not going for a drink with you."

"Why on earth not?" I asked.

"You should be at home with Sofe and not out drinking yet AGAIN with me and my boozy mates. You are married to one of the most wonderful women on the planet. Yet, to my complete incredulity, you never want to spend time with her. Are you stupid or something?"

208

"No!"

"Well, if you're not stupid then you are a wanker. No, that's not true. You're a fucking stupid, self-centred, self-pitying selfish wanker."

I was speechless.

"Bud, dear, dear bud if you have any sense at all, you should go back home this very minute and leave the drinking to sad bastards like me who have no decent woman in their life," concluded David.

**

I arrived back home exhausted. Sophia was already in bed, reading some work.

As I came through the door of the bedroom, she jumped out of bed and put her arms around my neck.

"I'm glad that you decided to come home. I'm sorry for earlier."

"No need to be sorry. It's me that should be sorry."

"Do you want to make love? I'm feeling very naughty!" said Sophia.

"Sorry, my love, I'm absolutely dog tired. Can we save it until tomorrow?"

"If you want?"

"Tomorrow, I promise."

"It's the company Christmas party tomorrow. But I don't need to go. If the truth be told, I don't even want to go with it being the anniversary of Melissa's death."

"No, you go. It'll do you good. We'll have a great time over Christmas. It's about time that I treated my wife to some good old fashioned romance," I replied.

**

I took Sophia to Wokingham station to catch her train for her Christmas party shortly after lunch. It was a cold, damp, overcast day.

As she was about to get out of the car, Sophia said,

"I'm so not in the mood for a Christmas party."

"You'll enjoy when you get there. And, starting tomorrow, we're going to have a fabulous time together," I replied.

"It's always tomorrow with you!" she replied.

Once Sophia boarded her train, inspired by David's words of wisdom and much needed reality check, I immediately started work on my plans for the weekend.

Undeniably, Melissa's death had been an absolute tragedy but, as Sophia herself had said, it was long overdue to start looking on the bright side of life.

It was long, long overdue that I showed Sophia how much I loved her and to bring the love she deserved back to her life – a love so amazing and divine as it had been before with her. I was determined that we'd get back to those wondrous, glorious days.

I booked a plush hotel for the weekend and bought a huge bouquet of flowers as I made my way into London to surprise her. I even found some theatre tickets for Christmas Eve.

It was finally time to move on.

**

Sophia's company's Christmas party was being held in their own offices, and I arrived there, around 7.30 p.m., flowers in hand, to a scene of much merriment, mayhem and laughter – party poppers, empty champagne and wine bottles strewn everywhere, people embracing et al.

I remember feeling good. People around seemed happy, full of festive joy, and once again I felt happy too.

I asked the first person that I came across at the party,

"Do you know where Sophia Melton is?"

"Probably upstairs in the marketing department, mate!" came the slurred reply.

"Where's that exactly?"

"Next floor up – turn left when you get out of the lift. Nice flowers, by the way!"

"Thanks!"

When I reached the next floor, it was pretty deserted. I looked around and in the various offices to see if I could find anyone. Amongst the party debris, I finally found someone alone drinking the last remnants of a bottle of wine in a small office on their own.

"Have you seen Sophia Melton anywhere?" I asked.

"I saw her around twenty minutes ago with Dan Sutter. Maybe try his office?"

"Where is that?"

"Ugh. Too much alcohol. Let me think. End of the corridor. Turn right and then it's either second or third door on the left."

"Cheers! Happy Christmas."

"And to you also!"

As I walked down the corridor to Sutter's office, I positively revelled at the thought of a long weekend with Sophia, followed by a love and joyous sex filled Christmas.

I smiled at the prospect of seeing our relatives again – of trips to Leeds and, of course, back to the farm in Devon. I even pondered on the possibility of a white Christmas; if snowflakes were love and all that.

Sutter's office door was closed but not locked.

I opened the door and saw Sophia on her back on the desk, tights and knickers around her ankles having sex with someone whom I could only presume was Dan Sutter.

Sophia immediately made eye contact with me and instinctively pulled away from the person she was having sex with.

I turned away and ran for the door. Sophia shouted after me,

"Jonathan. Come back. For goodness' sake, come back. Please come back."

I reached the emergency stairs and ran as fast as I could.

I don't think that anyone would have caught up with me that night. Once outside the office block, I kept running and running.

After five or 10 minutes of running at full pelt, out of breath and no longer knowing where I was, I stopped to throw the flowers in the nearest bin.

The Passing of Time

I wandered the streets of London for hours. I had no idea where to go or what to do. In the end, I took the last train to Sheffield and booked into a cheap hotel near to the university campus.

Although very tired, I couldn't sleep. I'd not eaten for hours, but I wasn't hungry either. I thought about going out to find somewhere to have a drink, but I knew that if I started to drink then I'd probably never stop. And anyway, the last thing I wanted was to be surrounded by people full of Christmas spirit.

I'd hardly smoked since leaving university, but I bought a packet of twenty cigarettes at the hotel reception and then smoked them, one after the other, through the night – sat in my room staring into space.

I looked at the wedding ring on my finger and pondered long and hard on whether or not to throw it away. Instead, I took the ring off my left hand and put it on the corresponding finger of my right hand.

I finally fell asleep exhausted, numb from any pain or feeling.

**

I was woken by the cleaning maid knocking on my door at around 11.30 a.m. with a gruff, broad Sheffield accent and her abrasive tones,

"You need to vacate the room immediately!"

"OK, sorry. I'll be out of the room in less than ten minutes."

"Make it five or you'll be charged for another night!"

"Frankly, I don't give a monkey's toss whether you charge me for another night!"

"No need to adopt that tone with me."

"Oh, just fuck off," I whispered.

I vacated the room unwashed and unshaven and walked into the city centre, buying more cigarettes en route.

I wandered into a relatively deserted old and somewhat dilapidated café on the edge of the city centre and sat there trying to compose my thoughts and pull myself together.

But it was no use – the image of Sophia's infidelity on an office desk still consumed my mind, my every thought.

After three hours or thereabouts in the café and around ten cups of coffee, I decided to stay in Sheffield. I bought some cheap clothes, essential toiletries and a local newspaper to look for a flat that I could rent for a few weeks.

By eight in the evening, I had found a modestly furnished and somewhat dirty bedsit. I went to the bank cash till and paid cash for five weeks' rent in advance.

**

I called David from a public payphone.

"Hello!"

I recognised Brian's voice.

"Is David there?" I asked.

"Yes, I'll get him. Happy Christmas, by the way, Jonathan."

"You too."

David came to the phone.

"Jeez, J.P. Thank Christ. Are you all right? I've not been able to stop worrying about you. I've even stopped drinking!"

"I'm OK," I replied.

"Sophia told me what happened. She's beside herself. She's so sorry. Most of all, she's seriously worried about you, as am I. Where are you?"

"I'm just getting my thoughts together as to what I'm going to do."

"Come down to the farm. Mum and Dad would love to see you. It'll do you good!"

"Thanks, but I'll be fine! I'll be in touch."

"Sooner rather than later I hope," said David full of warmth.

"I'll see you around, my friend."

**

On the first working day of the New Year, I took a train to Wokingham station to collect my company car. As I collected the car from the station car park, I recollected how optimistic I'd been as to the future for Sophia and me when I'd originally left it there.

I phoned the apartment to check whether Sophia was there and, relieved to find that there was no answer, went there to collect some belongings – a few clothes and, most of all, the cup that my father had presented to me in our home garden after our tennis match together.

I saw that there was a letter there addressed to me from Sophia.

I opened it.

213

My dearest husband,
I'm so, so very sorry!

I could write pages but have too much to say to you.

We need to talk! PLEASE!

All my love,

Your wife Sophia
xxxxxxx

I tore the letter up and threw it in the bin. I left my keys to the apartment on the work surface in the kitchen, took my modest belongings and drove to Swindon.

I was met by my manager, Phil, in reception.

Phil had always been good to me and had helped me to develop my career. He shook my hand warmly and we went to a small drop-in room close to the reception area and sat down together.

"I was saddened to receive your letter of resignation, Jonathan. I felt that you had a positive future here," he told me.

"Yes, I'm sorry too but I need a change, Phil."

"What are you going to do?"

"No idea."

"Seems like you have a definite career plan in place!"

I smiled.

"Are you sure about this?" he asked.

"Yes!" I replied.

**

I looked through three or four pages of the paper without anything sparking my imagination and then I saw it – an advert for air stewards with language skills such as French and German. I loved speaking French and had had little chance to use my language skills since leaving university. I also thought that it would be an opportunity to see far away exotic places that I'd never been to. I'd only ever been abroad three times in my life – all with Sophia.

In reality, it was the nearest thing that I could find to joining the French Foreign Legion that didn't involve anything as traumatic or dangerous as using a gun.

I sent my job application in immediately, and by the following week I'd been interviewed. I was offered a job conditional on me successfully passing the training course, which I subsequently fairly sailed through.

I moved from Sheffield to the Coventry area, as most of my flights would be going from Birmingham airport, and as a stop gap I sub-rented a very sparse and unfurnished one bedroomed flat. At least it was a step upwards from the dirty and grotty 'bedsit' that I'd been living in.

**

The first few months in my new job drifted by as I lost any real awareness of time. It's strange how some days seem like a lifetime, and at other times, months can pass in what seems little more than a matter of days.

As it turned out, I didn't particularly like working as an air steward – I wasn't using my French very often, and though I did visit some exotic locations, I rarely ventured away from my hotel room mini-bar and very soon, every hotel room began to look the same.

Despite this, on my days off from work I couldn't wait to get back to work as at least it gave me something to do.

I had no awareness of the world around me. What had supposedly been a temporary move into the flat in Coventry whilst I found something better became a permanent move by default.

I had no television and no radio. As furniture, I had only purchased a single bed to sleep in and, somewhat bizarrely, a deckchair that I had bought cheap in a local second-hand shop to sit on. There were no pictures on the wall, and the only contents of my kitchen were a microwave, a knife, a fork, a spoon, a cup and some washing up liquid.

The only luxury that I allowed myself was a crappy old second hand CD player, which I'd bought from a work colleague, and the complete Beatles back catalogue on CD. Other than The Beatles, the only other CD I owned was Sinéad O'Connor's version of *Nothing Compares to U*.

After all, Sophia had left me and not the other way around – or at least that's what I kept telling myself.

I no longer had a car and was going to work on a pushbike, bike clips and all. In fact, the only thing to show any record that I existed at all was a bank account, and even that was only kept on reluctantly – if I could have been paid 'cash in hand' by the airline then I would have been.

215

As I sat in my deckchair listening to *Revolver*, *Abbey Road* or Sinéad O'Connor, wading through bottle after bottle of wine and packet after packet of cigarettes, my theory was that if I didn't exist then I wouldn't feel pain.

**

It was a truly glorious late summer's evening and my first French speaking flight had taken me to Nice. I walked down to the sea front passing young suntanned skateboarders having fun en route.

I sat smoking on the bench, watching the sun go down over the Mediterranean Sea. I thought about my honeymoon there with Sophia and allowed myself a rare smile.

I took out from my wallet the photo taken of us on our first honeymoon night as Sophia and I ventured out in the pouring rain and sat for ages looking at the photograph. I even briefly considered contacting Sophia to 'talk' as she had put in her note, but the vision of her having sex on an office desk came back into my head.

Anger and pain filled my veins.

Night was setting in as I wandered back to the hotel and I decided to settle in at the bar there for another night's extended drinking.

As I sat there working my way through my second bottle of red wine, one of the air hostesses whom I worked with, Carole, joined me.

She was wearing an expensive jade green dress showing off her excellent figure. With her brunette hair tied back she looked wonderfully attractive and full of life – very different to the calm, cool professional she was in her airline uniform.

"You look really great tonight, Carole. I just love that dress," I said.

Carole smiled a warm, friendly smile.

"Thank you, Jonathan."

"Are you going anywhere special?" I asked.

"I met this charming French guy last time I was here. We agreed to go out together, and I've just spent an hour in a café waiting for him. I tried to call him, but there was no reply."

"More bloody fool him, that's what I say!"

Carol laughed and said,

"Too bloody right!"

"I apologise in advance if I don't make for good company but would you care to join me for a consolation drink?" I asked pointing to the remaining half bottle of red.

"Why not indeed? I certainly don't have a better offer and the escalator's broken," replied Carole.

"I know. That's why I'm sat here."

"And the first flight tomorrow's cancelled."

"Nobody told me," I said.

Carole sat down, and I poured her a glass of red wine, followed by around 30 seconds of awkward silence between us.

"I do like that dress," I said eventually.

"You've already said that."

"Have I? Well, it is a nice dress. You can't really say too many good things about a dress like that. It's jade green, and it's very nice – very nice indeed."

"Why did someone of your background become an air steward?" she asked.

"How do you mean?"

"Public schoolboy, university-educated."

"I've never really thought about it that way," I replied.

"It staggers me, you know. Here I am saving every penny I can so that I can study law at university. I look back on my life with nothing but regret. I messed around at school, married young. A right bastard he was to boot, I regretted it as early as the honeymoon night. Thank Christ we never had any children. I'm nearly thirty now but still believe that I can do something with my life."

I was silent.

"Have you ever been married?" asked Carole.

"Yes."

"How many times?"

"Just the once."

"What happened, if you don't mind my asking?"

"Shit is what happened. She left me. That's all there is to it."

There was another awkward silence between us before Carole suggested,

"Hey, rather than sit here together and get ratted, why don't we go out for something to eat?"

I blew my cheeks out to indicate a total lack of interest before saying,

"Nowhere will be open – it's getting on for ten o'clock."

"Complete nonsense, man. This is Nice. This is Southern Europe. This isn't downtown Accrington on a wet winter's Sunday evening."

"Well when you put it that way."

"Come on, lazy. I'll buy."

"OK, if you insist, ma'am, then who am I to resist?"

217

Carole and I walked to a local restaurant in the heat and black air of a glorious summer's night. The conversation actually began to flow, and I started to feel more at ease.

"You know that you're a source of discussion and fascination to many of us at work – in particular to my friend Wendy," said Carole.

"I can't imagine why."

"Wendy thinks that you're a drugs trafficker."

I laughed and asked,

"And what do you think?"

"I said that you were gay. Most of the guys are after all. Tell me, are you gay?" asked Carole, pouting.

"No, I'm not gay, and I'm not a drugs trafficker either. My God, don't you and Wendy have anything better to talk about?"

"Only some of the time."

Our easy conversation and banter continued and as the night wore on, for the first time that year, a woman was gradually and slowly sexually arousing me. I began to actually feel human again, as distinct from the walking dead.

Suddenly and quite unexpectedly, Carole exclaimed,

"Oh shit, it's him."

"Who?" I asked somewhat taken aback.

"Him that stood me up. Come and sit next to me. I want to make him jealous."

I was very pleased to oblige and moved closer to Carole.

"Now kiss me," Carole demanded.

I gave her a gentle kiss on the lips.

"For Christ's sake, man, I'm not your bloody grandmother. I said give me a kiss."

This time my mouth opened and I felt Carole's sensuous tongue inside my head.

"Now that's more like it," said Carole with a broad smile on her face.

My right hand was around Carole's waist, and she pushed it down towards her thigh. I could feel the outline of her suspenders beneath the fabric of her jade green dress.

"Tights for work, stockings for fun, that's what I say!" stated Carole.

"I couldn't agree more with that as a woman's foundation garment strategy. I've always thought that there should be some law against tights," I replied.

"I think that you should pay the bill, Jonny, and we should go back to the hotel. You don't mind me calling you Jonny, do you Jonny?"

218

"I've been called Melton, Melts, J.P., Jonathan and worse besides in my life. I've no problem with Jonny, but I do have a problem with paying the bill. You said that you'd pay – remember?"

"So I did, you cheapskate. Any chance of going halves?"

"Why not? But I'll have to pay you back later. There's not a cent in my pocket."

"At least that settles the argument of your room or mine. We're going to your room so you can pay me immediately. Don't think you're sneaking out of paying for your share of the meal, you penny-pinching rogue."

"Madam, I am a man of honour. How dare you suggest such a thing?"

The two of us left the restaurant and headed back to the hotel. As Carole and I wandered back in the Nice evening air, arm-in-arm, for the briefest of moments I almost felt normal again.

The climb up 10 flights of stairs to get to my hotel room only served to further bond the two of us in shared cigarette-induced shortness of breath and exhaustion.

My hotel room was modest, and there was nowhere to sit apart from on the bed. Before I had a chance to offer Carole a drink from the mini-bar, she ran her tongue gently against my neck.

"That's bloody wonderful," I mumbled.

Carole unbuttoned my shirt and ran her skilled tongue over my nipples. I eased Carole onto her back and then hitched up her jade green dress to reveal the sight of her lacy stocking tops and green knickers that matched her dress.

As I went to kneel on the floor, Carole asked,

"Do you like my undies then Jonny?"

I nodded in appreciation before pushing her legs apart and pulling her lace green knickers to one side to go down on her.

For the first time in months, I felt energised by life. I was absorbed in Carole's groin – the excitement in me growing as her stomach and leg muscles tightened and twitched as she approached orgasm. When Carole finally came, she had an enormous pelvic contraction and let out a piercing scream.

I looked up at her and laughed, and she laughed back.

"I don't suppose you have any condoms, do you Jonny?"

"No, sadly – nor any idea where we can find any."

"Not to worry. I've an idea," suggested Carole with a wicked grin on her face.

We undressed each other. Once naked Carole reached into her handbag and pulled out some hand cream.

219

"Lie back and relax, Jonny."

Doing as I was told, Carole smeared the hand cream all over my genitals and slowly, softly and gently brought me to a climax. There was no love there, but there was sensuality in abundance.

As I was about to come, Carole anally penetrated me with one of her fingers, intensifying what was already a most pleasurable experience. I screamed uncontrollably as I ejaculated. Carole carried on masturbating me regardless, and the pleasure was now turning to pain.

"Stop, Please…STOP," I pleaded.

"Good, was it?" asked Carole.

"I think that I needed that more than you can ever possibly imagine."

"Just as well, you still owe me 110 francs for the meal."

As I passed Carol the money. I saw one of the photos of Sophia in my wallet and had a feeling of vindication, revenge almost – that being with Carole was at last some small payback for the sense of betrayal and being cheated upon.

**

I awoke late the next morning with my usual hangover from the previous night's drinking, but I also awoke with a smile on my face for the first time in ages.

Carole went back to her room to change for work and the next time I saw her, it was very much business as usual. The jade green dressed sex siren of the night had metamorphosed into the smartly dressed professional air steward of the day.

As we left the hotel on the bus for the airport, I sat with Carole.

"Tights again?" I asked.

"But of course, my dear."

"I enjoyed last night."

"So did I, Jonny. I can't wait to get home and tell Wendy. She'll be so jealous. She's got a real thing about you."

"I've never noticed. Can I see you again?" I asked.

"Not until Tuesday."

"Ideal. I'll be back from a long haul trip to the States around Tuesday lunchtime, and I've got the next day off."

"Your place or mine, Jonny dearest?"

"Well mine's a complete tip, a bit like the war torn areas of Beirut if I'm honest."

"Somehow dear that doesn't surprise me. Come around to my flat around seven thirty in the evening. I'll leave the details in your pigeonhole."

Rock Bottom

December 22nd was the anniversary both of Melissa's death and Sophia's infidelity. I didn't know what to do. For weeks, I was dreading the day. Should I work or should I take the day off as a holiday? Should I look to spend time with Carole?

I finally decided to take a day's holiday on my own. Inevitably within an hour of waking up on the 22nd I wished that I'd gone to work.

I started drinking with a vengeance.

The more I drank the more morbid I became, and the more morbid I became, the more I drank. My last memory of the day is staggering mid-afternoon, cigarette in hand, around a mile to the local supermarket to buy two more bottles of wine.

I didn't re-join planet Earth until around half way through the next day when I awoke fully clothed laying upside down on my bed. I got up to the sight of empty wine bottles and cigarette packets strewn around my small flat.

My mouth was dry, I felt sick, and my head felt as though someone had taken a hammer to it.

I was due at work in a little over two hours for a transatlantic flight to San Francisco and needed to clean myself up quickly and take a taxi to work. I only made just about made it on time as the taxi had to stop by the roadside as I was sick on the pavement.

It wasn't until the Boxing Day evening of the 26th that I realised that Christmas Day had passed without me noticing and it wasn't until New Year's Eve that I could even face having a drink again.

As the world around me was celebrating New Year and enjoying life, I longed for a return to my boring routine existence at work punctuated by excellent, emotionally detached sex with Carole.

**

Carole and I were lying in bed together at her flat one night, sharing a cigarette.

"You do know, you and me, Jonny dear, we ain't a long term thing," said Carole.

"I know that. In a year's time you'll be at university and knowing you, you'll be going out with the top law student in your year."

Carole laughed and said,

"That's one of the three things that I like about you, Jonny dear. You know me so well, but you never judge me."

"What are the other two?"

"You don't want anything from me. Every man that I've ever slept with wanted something from me but you don't."

"Apart from the sex, that is," I said.

"And that's the third thing I like about you. You are rather good, you know."

"I was taught well."

"You loved her, didn't you?" asked Carole.

"She left me. That's all there is to say."

There was a silence between us before Carole said,

"Jonny dear, I have a confession to make."

"You're a transsexual!" I replied.

"No, stupid. You remember that night in Nice when I said I'd been stood up."

"How can I forget?"

"I wasn't stood up. It was you that I was after all along. Do you think I'm a terrible evil woman, Jonny dear?" she asked.

"No, Carole, manipulative, selfish, self-centred, single-minded and decidedly wanton. But evil and terrible, most definitely not."

"I'm not *that* wanton. I'm just a woman with needs from time-to-time," she said.

Carole took my hand and pushed it down to her warm and moist groin.

It seemed the most natural thing in the world.

**

The spring and summer of 1992 came and went until, around mid-August, Carole bounded up to me at work overflowing with excitement.

"They've arrived – my A-Level exam results. I can't open the envelope. You do it for me, Jonny," she pleaded.

"What if they're not what you need?"

"Open the bloody envelope, man. Do as you're told for once."

I opened the envelope.

"Geography – A, History – A and German – B," I said.

Carole jumped in the air and screamed with delight for what seemed like a full minute, maybe more.

"I've done it! I've bloody well done it! Newcastle uni here I come. No more shitty dinners, no more shitty hotels, no more shitty customers and, yes, no more shitty job."

"I'm very pleased for you, I really am."

"Give me a hug, Jonny."

I put my arms around Carole's waist as she held me around my neck so tight that I was struggling for breath. As she finally drew away from me, I could see tears flowing down her cheek.

Wiping away the tears, Carole laughed and said,

"I've not cried in years. I'm sorry. I'm so happy I could explode."

**

For the next six weeks, Carole and I were inseparable and she continually picked my brain on university life, what she should wear, what she should do, what she shouldn't do, etc., etc.

It was nice. I actually felt needed; that I could actually add some value in what was for me otherwise a humdrum and, worse still, increasingly futile existence.

Before I knew it, it was time for Carole to leave for Newcastle. I took her out to a good restaurant for a final meal, and when we got back to her flat, we were both very full and neither of us fancied sex.

We went to bed together, and Carole fell asleep. However, I couldn't sleep at all and eventually got up to have a cigarette. As I sat there smoking and thinking, Carole awoke and got out of bed to come and put her arms around me.

"A penny for your thoughts, Jonny."

"If you're going to university, you're going to need every penny that you can get your hands on. You definitely don't want to be wasting it on the nonsense in my head," I replied.

"Come back to bed. I'm as horny as hell," she said.

For the first time, I began to realise that I would miss Carole.

**

I helped Carole take her numerous suitcases to Birmingham New Street train station. We made the journey by bus together almost in complete silence. She bought her ticket, and I helped her load all her belongings on the train.

Once everything was safely in the luggage racks, Carole said to me,

"I don't do Goodbyes, Jonny."

"Neither do I."

224

"Just take this and go."

Carole handed me a carefully wrapped present. I started to open it.

"Not here, my dear. Open it later. I need to be on my own. Get my thoughts together."

Carole gave me a gentle kiss on my cheek and sent me on my way with a pat on the bum. I hung around the end of the platform until the train left. Trains and their goodbye windows, I thought to myself.

I wandered aimlessly outside the station and opened Carole's present. Inside was the jade green dress that she had worn on our first night together along with a hand-written message.

Dearest Jonny,

Something to remember me by. From what you've said I don't think that I'll need this where I'm going.

I've enjoyed the times we've spent together and in particular the past few weeks but feel that we shouldn't stay in contact. You were exactly what I needed at that point in my life. Someone for hassle-free fun, to meet my womanly needs, someone who would let me get on with my studying in peace.

Many thanks for everything, but now it's time for me to move on. I hope that you understand that.

As a final thought, someone once said to me of you that there was no future with a man who lived so much in the past. My advice is to say that there is no future _**for**_ a man who lives so much in the past.

Please don't hate me for my cowardice in writing this letter rather than saying these things face-to-face and I do sincerely hope that you come to terms with whatever is eating away inside of you.

May the future bring everything for you that you would wish for yourself.

Take care,
Love and best wishes,

Carole x

**

As the weeks passed that autumn in 1992, I became increasingly melancholy and reclusive. With the colour that Carole brought no longer in my life, my grey existence was becoming blacker by the week.

My alcohol and cigarette intake significantly increased again, and I was increasingly haunted by my father's face every time I looked in the bathroom mirror.

I became convinced more than ever that my father had indeed committed suicide.

I also thought more and more about my mother's words to my father during the tennis match fracas at Tiverton School, "He's your son when it suits you, isn't he, Robert? But only when it suits you."

What had my mother meant? I wondered. Was my father not my biological father?

With all these thoughts of my father and my mother floating around my head on a near permanent basis, plus my seemingly endless pain over Sophia and Melissa, my mental state declined apace as autumn became winter.

**

Late November during an overnight stop in Paris en route to Chicago, I was feeling more maudlin and depressed than usual and, after a few drinks and then a few drinks more, I dragged myself to the bottom of the hill in front of the Sacré-Cœur church.

I looked up at the beautiful white floodlit church and sighed.

The funicular that ran up the hill had stopped running by that hour leaving me to shuffle, with crouched and rounded shoulders, up the numerous steps – a stark contrast to Sophia and me in love, energetically running up the same steps those years before.

Once in front of the church, the place where Sophia had proposed to me, I looked over the dazzling panoramic view of Paris by night. Cigarette in hand, I took out my wallet from my coat pocket and pulled out my two photographs of Sophia.

"Why oh why oh why?" I said to myself again and again.

There's no doubt that I missed Sophia so. It wasn't just the love, the fabulous conversation and the amazing sex; it was the fact that Sophia had been the best friend that I'd ever had in life.

I thought again of the last time I'd seen Sophia – of her having sex over a desk at an office Christmas party with bloody Dan Sutter. I still couldn't even begin to forgive her. For all the mutual understanding, joy, happiness and love that had once existed between us, all I continued to feel was anger, pain, betrayed and cheated.

I shuffled my way back to the Metro station. On the journey to my hotel the Metro train was crowded with theatre goers and after getting off the train, I decided to have one more drink in a bar before going to bed for the night.

As I went to pay for my drink, I suddenly realised that my wallet was no longer in my pocket. After frantically searching my body and clothing, I worked out that a thief must have taken my wallet on the crowded Metro. I didn't care about the money that was in the wallet – not that there was much in there anyway.

However I'd lost the photos of Sophia that were in my wallet – the honeymoon pictures of the two of us on the rainy night in Nice, and Sophia, with the wind in her hair on the boat from Cannes to Îles de Lérins – mementos of much happier times.

The barman took pity on me and my lack of money and gave me the drink free of charge. I thanked him graciously and left, making my way back to the hotel disconsolate.

On the way back I passed through the 'red light' district in Paris and as I walked, one of the women propositioned me.

I can't remember her exact words but the intention was clear. The woman then told me that she had a friend and that would make it more fun, if that was what I wanted. I remembered that I had £500 in cash in my room. I reasoned to myself that I couldn't possibly feel any worse than I did already.

I had the woman call her 'friend' over. After some negotiation, the two women agreed that they would accept pounds sterling rather than French francs to come back with me to my hotel room.

For many men, three in a bed, with two women and one man, is the 'ultimate male fantasy' but the reality was that the events of the night were sordid and squalid rather than in any way sexy or sensual.

It was as though what was happening was happening to someone else and not to me. I felt like a degraded animal rather than a human being, but I still ended up spending the full £500 just to have the two women stay a few hours longer.

Whatever feelings I had over the whole episode, I didn't want the women to go. I didn't particularly like either of the women, and I certainly wasn't enjoying what the three of us were doing – but I'd have done anything or paid anything not to be on my own that night.

By three o'clock in the morning all my £500 was gone, and it was time for the women to go. Each woman thanked me in turn and asked me for a kiss on the cheek. After what had gone on, I was struck by the absurdity of such an act of gentility.

Within five minutes of their departure, I couldn't remember their names.

I went to the bathroom and looked in the mirror. I felt the full burden of my failed existence. I went and lay on the bed and curled into a ball.

I could feel emotion welling up inside of me and I said,

"Nobody, just nobody nor nothing, anything is ever going to make me cry again. Nobody, just nobody nor nothing, anything……"

The words trailed off, the mantra didn't work and I started crying.

I laid there and wept as my suppressed emotions finally came out; the floodgates well and truly opened.

I thought about my mother and how she left me as a child. I thought about my sweet baby Melissa, dead in my arms – why did she have to die the way that she did?

I thought of my father and my guilt of not wanting to be with him when he needed me most. I thought of how I could have been there for him but I hadn't been; that instead I'd wanted to spend my time on the Pritchett farm in Devon rather than be with him.

I wondered whether I'd done this because he wasn't my father and that deep down I'd always known that.

Above everything though, I thought about Sophia. The magnificent, gorgeous, stunning Sophia whom I'd loved so very, very much. I thought of how I missed her, how I longed for her – her touch, her gorgeous brown eyes, her hair, her smell, her friendship, her love.

I read once that love is the essence of life, and when love is killed, the heart dies.

**

I'd sit in my deckchair in my grim flat in Coventry surrounded by empty wine bottles and cigarette packets, often crying.

I felt worthless as a man. I desperately needed help but I didn't do anything as I felt that I wouldn't be able to talk to anyone. I didn't want people, particularly dear and close friends like David, to see what I'd become.

I felt alone and isolated in my misery. I had suppressed grief too much and for too long and it had most definitely come back to haunt me.

**

I was on a return flight from Switzerland to Birmingham airport. It was only a small thirty-seater plane and the journey was becoming decidedly bumpy. Not surprisingly, many of the passengers were becoming increasingly nervous.

I was head steward on the flight, and the captain of the plane indicated that he wanted to speak with me in the cockpit.

When I walked into the cockpit, the captain, normally unflappable, was showing definite signs of strain. The back of his white shirt was soaked in perspiration down his back, and his brow was most decidedly furrowed.

"I don't believe air traffic control, there's a massive thunderstorm and hailstorm ahead, and they've only just told me. It would have been good to know that around ten or fifteen minutes ago. They've told me that it's likely to get worse before it gets better. Do your best with the passengers. It's going to be quite a ride," he told me.

He then announced over the public address system,

"Captain here. I'm sorry that the ride is proving a little bit bumpier than usual. We're going through a thunderstorm so please adopt the emergency brace position until I advise otherwise."

The next few minutes were like a roller coaster ride. It was absolute pandemonium. People were being sick all over the plane. Others were deep in prayer. Some were hysterically crying. All my fellow steward and I could do was our best to comfort everyone and help them stay as calm as possible.

The only thought that crossed my mind was whether this would finally be the night when I would be put out of my misery; the night when I would finally find some peace.

However, the plane finally did somehow make its way through the storm.

The captain announced over the intercom,

"Captain here, we seem to have made our way safely through the storm. Please feel free now to sit back and relax. Please accept my apologies for any inconvenience and I hope that you enjoy the rest of your flight."

Spontaneous applause broke out amongst all the passengers, intermingled with some cheering.

The captain called me again to the cockpit.

"Good job, Jonathan. You stayed wonderfully calm. That helped me, and I'm sure it helped the passengers. I'll certainly be letting the powers-that-be know about this."

I smiled ruefully to myself – little did he have any idea of what was actually going through my mind.

**

Christmas was approaching, and I was dreading another 'celebration' period on my own, not least the memories of December 22nd and the double helping of death and infidelity. After the previous year's drunken oblivion, I had no idea what I was going to do or where I was going to go.

My mind-set sunk further into the abyss. Cycling to work one day, I deliberately turned right 'blind' into oncoming traffic. I closed my eyes and braced myself for the end. Purely by chance, nothing was coming my way.

So I did my two flights for the day and then changed to go home. I was somewhat taken aback to find an unsigned note in my locker.

"The Lord helps those who help themselves."

It reminded me of 'Auntie' Annie and a rare genuine smile crossed my face. However, I neither cared nor wondered who had sent the note and simply made my way back to my war torn zone of an apartment.

**

As I sat in my Coventry flat alone working my way through my second bottle of wine for the evening, I thought again of my father. I could almost sense what went through his mind the night he died. I imagined him closing his eyes and bracing himself for the end.

I thought of Oscar Wilde and his famous words from *The Ballad of Reading Gaol*, seeing my flat in the same way that he saw the jail,

'It is only what is good in Man
That wastes and withers there
Pale Anguish keeps the heavy gate
And the warder is Despair'

Suddenly there was a knock at my flat door. Nobody ever came around to see me. Hardly anyone even knew where I lived.

There was another knock.

"Fucking hell," I muttered.

A third knock quickly followed.

"OK, OK, I'm coming!" I shouted.

When I finally opened the door, there was David Pritchett stood there with the broadest of grins on his face, looking infinitely better than the last time that I'd seen him.

"Jeez, J.P., you look bloody awful. You look as though you've aged ten years."

"You sure know how to do wonders for a man's self-confidence."

"You've no idea what a difficult man you've been to track down. It was almost as though you'd disappeared off the face of the planet."

"That was the intention," I replied.

"Are you going to invite me in then, you miserable old scrote? I've got a proposal to make for you. I call it my Master Plan."

I smiled.

I thought how wonderful it was to see my friend again.

The Master Plan

David and I went to the nearest pub, only a short walk away from my flat. Although pleasant enough, I'd never been there as I'd always drunk alone in my deckchair at home.

We ordered a couple of pints, found a quiet corner of the bar and sat down.

"So how's life been treating you?" asked David.

"It's great being an air steward. It's given me the opportunity to see some interesting places in lots of different parts of the world. I'm now head steward on some flights. Yeh, life's really good."

David gave me a look, one that clearly conveyed incredulity, and after a short silence he responded,

"Mmm…I've seen your flat, very impressive – definitely the flat of someone whose life is in good order. Seeing as you've got your life so sorted then I don't expect that you would be in the slightest bit interested in my job offer?"

"OK, cut the sarcasm, Pritchett. Just go ahead and make the offer. I *might* be interested."

"Since we last spoke, when was it? Jeez, probably nearly two years ago. Anyway, in the meantime, I've become Commercial Director at a smallish, but very successful and profitable company in Sheffield. Engineering lubricants and chemicals – not sexy I know, but it's a brilliant product range and still very much unexploited. There are some great export opportunities, particularly in France. The problem is that no one at the company has the right language skills, or even the right attitude for that matter, to make it happen. There's not a doubt in my mind that you're the right person for the job, J.P. I need someone I can trust. The salary will be highly competitive, and we'll give relocation support to assist your moving from Coventry to Sheffield. In fact, there's only one drawback to the job offer."

"What's that?" I asked.

"You'll have to work for me!"

I laughed.

David added, with a wicked smile on his face,

"I reckon that we could both deal with that though."

"The problem is that I've some existing commitments. You know how things are. Can I have a few days to think it over? If you leave me a contact telephone number then I'll give you a call with my answer in the next two to three days."

I could almost smell the bullshit as I said the words.

"Hopefully it won't be a repeat of the last time that you said you'd give me a call," said David.

"Look, I promise I'll call you."

"Brilliant! I look forward to it. You're the man I want for the job."

"But please tell me, just how, in the space of around two years, have you gone from being a drinking, womanising waster into being Sales Director of a thriving small company?" I asked.

David smiled, and then protested, very much 'tongue in cheek',

"I was never that much of a waster."

"Not half!"

"It all started early last year. There was a Drama Society reunion at Sheffield University. There was nothing much going on in my life at the time bar, of course, the key decision of which pub to drink in for the evening. As such, I thought why not? Anyway, to cut a long story short, at the reunion, I met Stef again. Do you remember Stef?"

"Stefanie Barton? How can I forget her?"

"Yes, anyway, Stef and I 'bonded' immediately."

"Bonded?"

"We were shagging before the reunion even finished. Afterwards, we decided to continue seeing each other and, lo and behold, it turned into something of a whirlwind romance and two months later we got married!"

I was silent.

"I know that you and Sofe never liked Stef but she's all right. In fact, she's more than all right otherwise I wouldn't have married her."

"Really?" I asked.

"Yes! And stop looking at me like that, J.P. I tried to track you down to be the best man at my wedding. In fact, I've spent most of the past eighteen months trying to find you. I ended up hiring a private investigation agency to track you down."

"I really am sorry that I missed your wedding."

"Such is life. It didn't matter anyway because I found someone else to be best man and, as it happens, he did a much better job than you'd have done anyway."

"Anyone I know?" I asked.

"Yes, Graham. He gave a speech full of sparkling wit and hilarious stories."

"The same Graham that is your brother?"

"Yes! And why not?"

We both laughed.

"Only joking! He was bloody awful. He lost the wedding rings and could barely string three words together in his speech. Stef was fuming – incandescent in her rage, in fact!" said David.

I smiled and asked,

"Is Graham still single?"

"He's found love."

"Never!"

· "Yes, it's the new combine harvester they have on the farm. I can see it now – do you Graham Edward Pritchett take this Series 3000 Combine Harvester to be your lawful wedded soul mate, to have and to drive, to love and to clean, through good harvests and bad…"

I laughed and said,

"You are rotten to your brother."

"I love him, he knows that. I like taking the piss out of him, that's all. Deep down, I'm still a bit envious of him. He got to stay on the farm, after all. But I'm making the best of what I've got and really can't complain with where I've ended up. Anyway, where was I?"

"Your wedding day."

"Oh yes, so Stef and I went on honeymoon, an overpriced jobbie in the West Indies, seriously OTT, not my cup of tea at all, but Stef loved it of course. Then when we got back Stef's Dad, Ron, offered me the job as Sales Director at his company, Barton's."

"I can't believe it! I remember that being your contingency plan at uni."

"It was indeed! Now, for a man in a shitty dead end job in Oxford, it was not exactly the most difficult decision of my life."

"I can imagine."

"And I haven't looked back since. I'm actually quite good at the job, much to my surprise. Sales have increased enormously this year and, all-in-all, I'm feeling on top of the world."

"You certainly look well on it," I commented.

"I reckon that if you accept my job offer then the two of us will have the times of our lives. It won't be an easy ride. You'll have to work very hard, but I've no concerns on that score as you've never been afraid of hard graft. My motto at the company is work hard, play hard."

"Interesting!"

"We will be the Two Musketeers – truly one for each other and each other for one," said David.

"Not exactly Dumas!" I replied.

234

"It's better than 'one for both and both for one'."

"More dumb ass than Dumas if you ask me."

"Speak for yourself, J.P."

It was clichéd, corny even, but a big broad smile crossed my face. David's company along with the alcohol was making me giddy with excitement rather than melancholy at life's woes and misfortunes.

I realised how much I'd missed his friendship and what a stupid proud fool I'd been in not contacting him.

"Another pint or are you driving?" I asked.

"I am driving, and I will have another pint. And being serious for a minute, I'm making a lot of changes at the company and the problem is that there are some old dinosaurs there being difficult about things. I need someone working for me that I can trust. Barton's is a wonderful little company, and with a few changes that I've got in mind, we'll become more successful still. The way I see it is that, over the next five or six years, Stef and I can have a couple of kids and then Ron will retire with his grandkids and leave me in charge of the business. I call it 'My Master Plan'."

We both drank our fifth pint of the night to celebrate his glorious vision. Sadly though the evening had to come to an end and as David left to return to Sheffield in his car, I shook his hand and said,

"Thank you. It was great to see you again."

"No thanks needed, J.P. Give me a call, right?"

"You have my word."

**

The next day, the first thing that I did was to call the airline and give my notice. I could start working for David after the festive period and phoned him with my decision. He was delighted, as was I, and then he asked me,

"What are you doing for Christmas?"

"I don't have anything planned."

"Why don't you come and join Stef and me for the Christmas vacation period at our house in Fulwood? It's a big house, and there's a great guest bedroom that you can have for as long as it takes you to sort yourself out with somewhere to live in the Sheffield area."

I was silent.

"Mum and Dad will both be there for Christmas."

"Well if that's the case then I'd be delighted to join you all for Christmas. As for what I do after that, it's another discussion for another day," I replied.

"Fair enough, but brilliant that you're coming for Christmas. Everyone will be so pleased to see you again. I'll send you directions and a map in the post."

**

Despite the quality and clarity of David's map, upon arriving at my destination in the very upmarket area of Sheffield that is Fulwood, I was convinced that it was the wrong address as it was no ordinary house; it was a veritable mansion with massive gardens and imposing front gateway to boot.

I checked the address and the map for a good few minutes and decided that I must be at the right place. I made my way through the gateway and knocked at the front door, suitcase in hand.

Such was the size of the house I half expected a pompous butler to answer, and was somewhat relieved when David came to the door with a beaming smile on his face.

"Come in, J.P. Merry Christmas. Welcome to our humble abode."

"Merry Christmas to you too."

I handed him a bottle of quality wine.

"Cheers!"

David took me through the enormous, expensively decorated and furnished entrance hall into a yet bigger lounge area to meet Stefanie. The whole house exuded style, class and money – an awful lot of money.

Stefanie, just as she'd been when I'd met her years before, was dressed from head to toe in the best possible designer clothes.

I was very nervous and somewhat on edge.

"So you must be Jonathan," she said.

"J.P. brought us some wine!" said David.

Stefanie said nothing and gave the bottle a withering look.

What followed was fifteen minutes of nervous and very stilted conversation in the very plush surroundings of the lounge. Even though David and I had known each other for years, it was remarkable the effect that Stefanie had, not only on me, but on the both of us.

Thankfully Brian and Alison arrived – just as I was beginning to yearn for the solitude and loneliness of my Coventry flat.

It was simply wonderful to see them both again and to my delight the two of them had hardly changed at all since I'd last seen them – Brian as big and full of life as ever and Alison as warm and kind as I remembered her, both with smiles to light up the evening.

As soon as they came into the lounge, Brian shook me warmly by the hand whilst Alison gave me an enormous hug.

"My, you've changed, Jonathan," said Brian.

"You've lost so much weight!" added Alison.

Brian and Alison's comments had me glancing towards a mirror full of paranoia. I had to admit that I was not exactly a 'good advert' for the 'Cigarettes and Alcohol' diet that I'd been on for much of the previous two years.

"How are Graham and Sarah?" I asked.

"Graham is still the same old Graham. He's gradually taking over the day-to-day running of the farm."

"Is he still more interested in tractors than women?"

Alison laughed heartily before replying,

"It certainly seems that way. Sarah's going steady, though, with a nice young man from an adjoining farm."

"She's twenty-three-years-old now. It's about time she was married," added Brian.

Alison gave Brian a dig in the ribs.

"You can't hurry love, my dear."

Alison then turned to me and said,

"I was very sorry to hear that Sophia and you have split up."

"I was sorry too."

"Is this the same Sophia that ruined my wedding day by getting drunk and crying?" asked Stefanie.

"She was upset, Stef!" responded David.

"As you keep telling me, darling. You've told me again and again that Graham was nervous, and Sophia was upset. The facts are that, between them, the two of them ruined my wedding day!"

"You should complain, Stefanie. She ruined my life!" I blurted out.

Everyone looked at me stunned. There was a period of awkward silence in the room – almost as though everyone, Stefanie included, was waiting for me to say more.

"How long are you in Sheffield for?" I asked Brian and Alison to break the silence.

"Only for a couple of days, sadly!" said Alison.

"What are your parents doing for the Christmas vacation, Stefanie?" asked Brian, trying his best to make polite conversation.

"They've gone skiing in Switzerland. I wanted to go with them along with David, but he forced me to stay here because you were coming, didn't you darling?" she replied.

"Always joking, aren't you, dear?" said David.

237

Meet the Family

David persuaded me to move in temporarily with him and Stefanie, and between Christmas and New Year, we rented a van to collect my belongings from Coventry; such that they were. My Beatles CDs, my clapped out old second hand CD player and my one truly valued possession – the cup from my tennis game with my father in the back garden in Taplow.

I left the jade green dress in the wardrobe. Carole had moved on, and it was now time for me to do the same.

Once back in Sheffield, David took me to collect my new company car; a shiny new metallic blue Vauxhall Cavalier. After being given the car keys, I spent the next two hours driving around the city playing with the various electronic gadgets.

Later that day, Stefanie's parents returned from their Christmas skiing jaunt, complete with excellent suntans from their time on the piste.

They came over to join us at David and Stephanie's house.

"This is Ron Barton, Managing Director and Owner of the Company. Ron, this is Jonathan Melton," introduced David.

"I'm pleased to meet you, Ron," I said.

"Mr Barton to you, laddie. Welcome to my company."

In his early to mid-fifties and although not massive in physical stature, there was an aura about Ron Barton that exuded power and genuine authority. I respected him from the moment that I first met him.

Sadly, I was not able to extend the same respect to Stefanie's mother. Her name was Elizabeth, and she bore all the hallmarks of a woman with far too much money and far too little style and class – speaking in a ludicrously phoney upper-class accent and dressing in expensive designer clothes that were all at least a size, if not two sizes, too small.

Like Stefanie, Elizabeth was very dismissive and patronising. However, for all Stefanie's failings, she had some wit – albeit mostly scathing – together with education, style and taste. Elizabeth all too evidently had none of these attributes.

During drinks, I was informed that there would be a New Year's party at the Barton parents' mansion and, as a new employee to the company I was duly invited.

"I think all employees should be made to attend, Ronald dear. They don't know how lucky they are in a city like this to have a job as good as Barton's or to be invited to a house like ours on New Year's Eve," said Elizabeth.

"Quite right, Mater. People these days have no gratitude. They expect something for nothing," added Stefanie.

"Just like you then, Stefanie," quipped Ron Barton.

I virtually choked on my drink and struggled desperately to contain my laughter. Stefanie was initially lost for words but quickly came back fighting,

"I did some very worthwhile things for Barton's last year, Pater."

"You did indeed. I've never doubted the quality of your work, only the quantity!"

"I put in my hours," protested Stefanie.

"I'm sure you do. It's a shame though that you're never in the office for all of us to see how committed you are," replied Ron.

I caught David's eye and we both smiled at each other.

"Enough of this talk about work at Christmas, Pater, it's boring me. Tell me, Mater, was the skiing as marvellous as always this year in Gstaad?"

**

I arrived at the Barton parents' mansion and, having met Elizabeth Barton, it was everything that I expected. The house was very big and very expensive and the internal decoration had clearly cost a fortune. However, costing a fortune and good taste don't always go hand in hand.

The bathroom alone was a unique experience with walls of lush purple velvet, a gold plated Greek statue in the middle of the room and a massive corner bath with Ron and Elizabeth's name engraved on massive customised marble tiles around it.

Music by the James Last Orchestra blared out of four speakers in the room as soon as the lights were switched on. I smiled to myself in bewilderment.

Upon leaving the bathroom, I overheard Stefanie talking with her mother.

"I can't believe how some employees have the temerity not to attend tonight. How do young people expect their careers to progress if they don't make an effort?" asked Stefanie.

"I know but you know your father. Far too kind he is," her mother responded.

I was the only person at the party who was single and unattached and found it a very dysfunctional, almost disorientating event. Thankfully, David was very helpful and took the time to introduce me to everyone.

"Bill Carrington, Ernie Badger, sales managers for Yorkshire and Lancashire, this is Jonathan Melton. He'll be responsible for our efforts to penetrate the French market."

"Hi," I said.

"Happy New Year, David. Looking forward to another great year after the outstanding 1992 we had," said Bill Carrington.

"1992 was truly superb considering that every economic report tells us that we're in the middle of a recession. I think that next year will be even better for us," replied David.

"It's certainly going to be different. You're the man to take us forward. We're all right behind you. Total commitment to the cause," replied Bill.

"Aye, right behind you," added Ernie.

**

I was shy and uncomfortable in the 'alien' surroundings and spent large portions of the evening on my own. To pass the time, I played a game with myself of spotting which people there at the party were Barton employees and which people were their respective spouses and, to my amusement, I was generally right.

For all Mr Barton's considerable attributes, his company was clearly a typically north of England sexist environment with men holding all the senior positions and women in secretarial/administrative roles. The only exception to this was of course Stefanie, who was in the esteemed position of purchasing director!

Virtually all of the men spent the evening 'scoring points' off each other to try to change their position in the 'food chain' and improve their status in the company.

I couldn't help but be amused how many men were hanging on David's every word and had to remind myself that this was indeed the same David that I'd known and loved for all those years – that glorious human mass (or should that be mess) of drinking and womanising fame.

I took to listening in on conversations.

"I should have had his job as Sales Director," said Bill.

"You should that," replied Ernie.

"Fucking student – I've forgotten more about this business than he bloody knows. Twenty years I've given to this company. We may have grown eight per cent last year, but all the bloody growth was in Scotland. Here today, gone tomorrow that business, you mark my words."

"Here today, gone tomorrow, Bill. You're right."

"And this bloody France market nonsense now. But, worst of all, fucking electronic mail. I've been doing business for twenty years without so called e-mail. A load of old codswallop if you ask me. Old Man Barton and I go back years, and he's not going to care a bloody jot if I use electronic mail or not!"

"He'll be stopping the chocolate Hobnobs next," added Ernie.

"He's a bloody idiot. Says we can grow fifteen per cent next year. I tell you, sales are more likely to go down fifteen per cent. We'll sell bugger all in France and nobody but him will be using electronic mail. He's a twat, nothing but a fucking student twat."

"Fucking student twat. Aye Bill."

It was time to join the discussion, I decided.

"Got your garlic and bread and beret ready then?" Bill asked me.

"I don't think business in France is like that," I replied.

"That right? I'll tell you something, young man, if you sell as much as £10,000 in the first six months next year, I'll buy you a beer and that's not something I do often."

"1987 was the last time you bought me a beer, Bill," added Ernie.

"We are a Yorkshire company, and we do business in Yorkshire. It's what we do," said Bill.

"And Lancashire, Bill."

"Needs must, Ernie."

**

My people-watching and listening switched from the men to the women. It was a similar story of back biting.

"Have you seen Cheryl in that dress? Size sixteen in a size ten dress. Mutton dressed up as lamb if ever I've seen it," said one woman.

"Pass the mint sauce," replied her 'friend'.

"Sorry?"

"Pass the mint sauce."

"Oh yes, very good. Mint sauce, lamb, mutton – I'll remember that one."

Little more than five minutes later, Cheryl joined them.

"Cheryl darling, you look fabulous in the dress – takes years off you. My, you've lost so much weight. You must tell me your secret."

**

David came over to talk to me,

"How you doing, J.P.?"

"OK, sort of. It's not really my kind of event. I'm just passing the time people-watching and listening."

"I tell you, there are so many people at this fucking company who are smarm, smarm, smarm to my face and then slag me off behind my back. The only people that I trust are you and Ron."

"Bill Carrington and Ernie Badger have really got it in for you. Particularly Bill," I replied.

"Tell me about it – bloody dinosaurs the pair of them. They think it's still 1978. And, Jeez, talk about provincial. Bill seems to think that business in Scotland is some strange exotic piece of export business that's going to come and go. I tell you, there needs to be changes here. It's you and me against the world with Ron's help."

"The Two Musketeers?"

"Too bloody right – to thy own self be true in this place. See you later, bud. I need to go and be smarmed again! I'll leave you to your people-watching."

**

Aided by the free bar, midnight soon arrived and as the chimes of Big Ben were heard on the truly enormous television in the main lounge, virtually everyone joined arms for a chorus of *Auld Lang Syne*.

I wanted to be alone with my thoughts and went outside for some evening air. One of the women at the party had well and truly overdone it at the free bar and was being sick outside.

"Are you OK?" I asked.

"Yes, but my husband will kill me; he only joined the company in August. Christ, I hate this kind of do. They do my head in."

I was silent.

"Shit, what am I saying? You're nobody, are you?" asked the woman.

242

I smiled and said,

"No, don't worry. I'm new myself and certainly nobody important."

"Thank Christ for that!"

"I just came out for some fresh air. I'll see you later maybe," I said.

I sat on a wall on the edge of the extensive floodlit garden.

My thoughts were of Sophia. I kept telling myself that I had to move on, that I had to stop looking back – that my life with Sophia was in the past and that my New Year's Resolution should be 'to find a new love, a new life'.

I tried to convince myself that if I said the Resolution enough to myself then I'd start believing it.

**

After two weeks in the job, David asked me if I wanted a drink after work. We went to the Bulls Head pub in the Ranmoor area of Sheffield; an upmarket pub often frequented by couples engaging in an extramarital tryst.

David and I bought ourselves some drinks and engaged in some idle banter around work for around five minutes.

And then, in walked Sophia.

The whole range of emotions and thoughts passed through me when I saw her – not least that I hadn't washed my hair that day and that the clothes I had on were old and scruffy.

In contrast, Sophia looked absolutely magnificent – brunette of hair and stunning of figure, immaculately dressed in a sumptuous black dress.

She smiled as soon as she saw me and seeing her smile; my heart lit up and seemed to skip a beat. It was like the first time that I ever met her, I had to remind myself to breathe, and my stomach was positively churning with nerves and excitement.

I had no idea whatsoever what to say to her. Even something as simple as Hello was beyond me.

Then, the image of the last time I'd seen Sophia came into my head. The image of her having sex on an office desk with Dan bloody Sutter.

My nerves and excitement disappeared and the all-too-familiar feelings of anger, pain, and being betrayed and cheated upon filled my every vein.

I walked straight out of the pub without saying a word or even looking at either Sophia or David. I jumped into my car and, before either of them could follow me out of the pub, I sped away and found a remote location to park.

I sat in my car, chain-smoking.

**

I arrived back to David and Stefanie's house in Fulwood. By coincidence, David arrived at the same time.

He stepped out of his car and walked towards me.

"I'm sorry, J.P. – that was a bad idea. I should have talked to you first."

"Too bloody right you should!" I replied.

"She still loves you, Lord knows why, but she does. She was utterly devastated at my wedding. She didn't know where you were or what you were doing. She was at her wit's end over you. She only wished that you could have been there. Why don't you sit down and talk to her? Nothing more, just talk."

"Talk about what? She fucking left me! What's there to talk about?"

"She didn't leave you. You can tell yourself that, you can tell the world that, but it isn't true. You left her!"

"She fucked some bloke on an office desk!"

"J.P., I love you as a brother but sometimes you can be a complete wanker; a nail-on 24 carat idiot. Sofe is so very, very sorry for what had happened. She still loves you. She's still your wife. I repeat. STILL YOUR WIFE. At least just talk to her. What you and Sofe had was unique. I don't understand how you can just totally give up on that without at least some effort."

"I love you too; you're the brother that I never had. But just stay out of my life with Sophia."

"You have no life with Sofe for me to be involved in," said David.

"Don't be fucking pedantic. You know what I mean."

"Yeh, I know. Consider me officially out of your life with Sofe then. But she's one of my best friends and I don't want that to change."

"Whatever!"

"Still mates though, right?" asked David.

"You and I will always be mates," I said.

"The Two Musketeers, eh?"

"Absolutely, still one for each other and each other for one. But let's never argue again over Sophia, eh?"

"Agreed," said David.

**

I found myself a very pleasant two bedroomed apartment in Hathersage, a delightful little Derbyshire village not far from Sheffield. It seemed a world away from the 'war zone' of my flat in Coventry, deckchair et al.

I joined the local village cricket team and with David's help, also became a member of the prestigious Hallamshire Tennis Club. I even started watching Sheffield Wednesday again since, in 1992 and 1993, they had probably the best team that they'd had during my lifetime.

My life had structure and, with the job going very well, some value.

But I still missed Sophia desperately.

**

July 23rd was the fifth anniversary of Sophia's and my wedding.

Compulsively driven, I went back to St Augustine's Roman Catholic Church in Leeds where we were married.

I parked in the street outside and made my way inside the front door. The church itself had hardly changed at all, still relatively austere by the standard of the Roman Catholic Church; but it hadn't mattered on our wedding day, and it didn't matter as I walked in again.

As I wandered around the church my mind was full of all the good things about the day five years previous – the way Sophia looked, the sunshine and the speeches – the sheer unadulterated optimism of the day.

I smiled to myself, thinking of better days as I wallowed in a sea of positive nostalgia.

I went to the side of the church and imagined myself watching the two of us getting married.

Then, to my amazement, I saw Sophia walk through the doors. She was dressed casually in a pink top, black jeans and ankle boots and looking as gorgeous as ever.

I panicked and immediately hid on the floor amongst the pews in order to avoid being seen. I noticed a piece of chewing gum stuck underneath the pews as I lay on the church floor, and focused on that to help me stay calm.

Thankfully Sophia didn't notice me, and she sat silently in the church for around five or 10 minutes.

Eventually, she left.

After I was completely sure that she had gone, I picked myself up off the floor and wandered outside the church. I leant against an outside wall at the back of the church and lit a cigarette.

As I stood there smoking, I couldn't believe that my life had reached such a point where I was now hiding from my estranged wife under the pews on a church floor.

Cracks Appearing

The success of Barton's continued throughout 1993 and 1994, and it seemed that David could do no wrong. Business was growing at nearly 20% per year and, unsurprisingly, both Messrs Carrington and Badger had left the company by mutual consent.

It was an exciting environment to be working in – very good products, sales were increasing every month, and in David I had an excellent and dynamic boss.

During those two years, there was plenty of laughter around the company; usually involving David and Old Man Barton. David was truly in his element, confident with his success, always supported by Old Man Barton and full of charisma in every internal and external meeting.

And boy, oh boy, could we party in that period. Everyone at the company eagerly and expectantly anticipated the quarterly sales meeting. The meetings were a celebration of the outstanding results and invariably followed by drinking, partying and clubbing late into the Sheffield night.

The fact that alcohol could be a celebration rather than an anaesthetic was very different from my days in Coventry.

**

David booked a local hotel on the edge of Sheffield to celebrate another record sales quarter for the company, and everybody there was full of life as the drink flowed into the night.

David came over to talk to me in the hotel bar, clearly the 'worse for wear' from an evening's general indulgence.

"There must be something more than this, J.P.," David ranted at me.

"How do you mean?" I asked.

"What do we build, what do we grow?" he asked me.

"We grow the business for Barton's, of course."

"What do we actually give back to society or to the planet?"

I was silent.

"I'd love to have children but Stef doesn't want them because she feels that children would compromise her lifestyle. You see, I love Shakespeare, whereas Stef now says that Shakespeare is passé. You tell me, how can the sodding woman say the greatest bloody writer in history is passé?" he asked.

I was merely in the role of listener as he continued,

"We don't see enough of each other outside of work, J.P. *Romeo and Juliet* is showing at the Crucible. We should go and see it together. It'll be like old times. I'll sort out tickets tomorrow and we can go next Friday if you're free."

"I've nothing better to do, why not?"

**

I enjoyed *Romeo and Juliet*. The line 'Dry Sorrow Drinks Our Blood' as Romeo's last words to his Juliet struck a very strong chord within me.

In fact, David and I both enjoyed the evening enormously and going to the theatre became a regular event in our lives. It certainly added some much needed variety to my life; something to nourish my soul.

Going to the theatre made me realise that I'd lost touch with the beauty and sheer majesty that language can have. I finally understood why David himself had been so passionate about Shakespeare for so many years.

Indoctrinated with the delights of the true Bard, David and I must have seen around a play a month over the next 12 months; some in Sheffield, some in London, some even in Shakespeare's home of Stratford.

**

"What are your plans for Christmas?" David asked me in the November during a weekend in Stratford when we went to see *Twelfth Night* together.

"Some much needed rest and relaxation in sunny Hathersage," I responded.

"You should come down to the farm, J.P. Mum and Dad would be so pleased to see you and to be blunt I could do with your moral support. Stef is going skiing in Gstaad with Ron and Elizabeth but then she's coming down to the farm on the 27th. I'd feel a lot better about the prospect of her being there if you were around."

248

On Christmas Eve, I made the long journey down to Devon with David. It was my first visit back to the farm in some six years. How the memories flooded back when I stepped out of David's car.

As I stood there on that cold night, I just wished that I could turn back the clock six years and do so many things oh so differently.

Brian and Alison, as warm and kind as always, were there to welcome me and Christmas Day proved to be a wonderful day with only the presence of Sarah's by now fiancé, Alan, to remind me that it was in fact 1994 and that time had moved on.

Sarah, now a delightful and attractively well-built young woman, and Alan were due to be married in the March of the following year.

There was much talk of wedding plans over that Christmas vacation and the wedding talk extended long into Boxing Day.

I decided to take a walk around the farm to get some fresh air into my lungs late in the day. After some 10 or 15 minutes, I wandered into the old barn where David and I always used to meet.

I remembered that Sophia and I had made love there in the summer of 1986. The old barn was the same as ever and the memory of the moment with her as I milked the goat came back to me vividly and seemingly filled all my senses.

I could smell her, feel her hair brushing against my face and her arms wrapped around my neck.

I stared out of the window in the barn. It was a crystal clear winter's night and I began to speak the following words to myself without consciously thinking:

"I look up to the heavens and the stars in the sky above
I wonder where you are now, my Sophia, my love
My life without you is empty and my soul hungers for your touch
Just to see your eyes would be plenty because I miss you so much."

David appeared behind me in the barn.
"Don't give up the day job, J.P."
I laughed and said,
"I agree, hardly Shakespeare in his pomp. It was just what was going through my mind,"
"She still loves you, you know."
"How is she?" I asked.
"She misses you. Call her, for Christ's sake. Nothing too heavy; take it slowly."

"I can't."

"Why on earth not?" asked David.

"I just can't."

"I've never seen two people more suited to each other than you and Sofe were. I wish Stef and I had even half of what you two had."

I was silent.

"Talking of which, Stef called. She's staying in Gstaad and not coming to the farm."

"Not a big surprise," I said.

"No, I guess not but still disappointing; disappointing beyond words in fact. She promised me faithfully. Mum and Dad are so upset."

"I'm sorry."

"Jeez, J.P., look at us – the thoroughly modern married man. You with a wife you never speak to and me with a wife who never speaks to my parents."

"But we are the Two Musketeers!" I said.

"Dumb Asses as you said, more like. Come on, let's go inside and try and cheer up Mum and Dad."

As I walked into the room, gloom had clearly descended onto the Pritchett household as the disappointment and feelings of rejection were clearly visible in Brian and Alison's eyes.

As the day went on, I could visibly see the anger growing inside of Brian and eventually he had to say something,

"That bloody woman has always thought that we weren't good enough for her."

"That bloody woman, as you call her, is our David's wife," Alison interjected.

"That's as maybe, but she still thinks that we're not bloody good enough for her high and mighty ways," Brian continued.

David was silent.

**

On New Year's Eve David and I made our way back to Sheffield and the annual jamboree at Old Man Barton's house.

David said little in the car.

Arriving at the house cum mansion, I saw that even more money had been 'invested' on the internal decorations and there were several remarkable new 'creations' to experience – the safari theme bedroom with its zebra skin wall covering and the latest bathroom creation where the bath was made to look like the Trevi fountain in Rome, the sink like the Sydney Opera House and the toilet like St. Paul's Cathedral.

Quite what Elizabeth Barton had against St. Paul's Cathedral or possibly the Church in general, I never had the courage to ask. Either way, lifting the dome off St Paul's Cathedral to 'take a pee' is something that I'm unlikely to forget.

David's mood darkened during the course of the party.

Everyone could sense it from his body language. Unlike the previous two years, where people were hanging on his every word, now they did their very best to avoid him as his sole consideration for the evening was in consuming as much alcohol as possible.

As the midnight hour approached, David, very drunk by that point, came over to me and said,

"You know, J.P., in all the sodding time that Stef and I have been together, she's only visited Mum and Dad on the farm once, and that was before we were married. I'll tell you, bud, I'll get even with her for the way that she's behaved towards Mum and Dad. You mark my words; I'll fucking make her pay."

**

In the early part of 1995, it was Sarah's wedding. David attended all alone, making excuses that Stefanie was ill with a very bad dose of flu.

At the reception held in a local hotel, David and I were sat together at the wedding breakfast, the only people there, aside from Graham, without partners.

"I fancy starting to play cricket again. What's the standard at Hathersage like? Do you think I'd get a game?" asked David.

"We are desperately short of quality bowlers. Given two or three matches to get your old rhythm and match fitness back, and I'm sure that you will be more than good enough for the standard that we play at."

"Brilliant!"

"I thought you went horse riding at weekends?" I asked.

"All Stef's friends at the riding club are a bunch of pretentious tossers. To be blunt J.P., I'd rather spend my spare time with some real people."

**

As the summer went on, David never seemed to have a drink out of his hand. He moved from drinking in his social time to also drinking in work time and lengthy lunchtime sessions in the pub became the norm.

251

Sales continued to climb, and this only served to convince everyone that everything was all right.

**

David had asked me to take over responsibility for a company, J. Norton & Sons in Bristol. It was a lost cause; Barton's had never done any business with J. Norton & Sons and, to be honest, we were never likely to do so.

However, it was the biggest piece of UK business for our major competitors and, as such Old Man Barton strongly felt that we should make a twice-yearly visit to retain contact.

The only available appointment at Norton's was a 9 a.m. meeting on a Friday morning, and a stopover in a Bristol hotel the night before was essential to ensure a timely arrival. Hearing that I was staying overnight and sensing an opportunity for another drinking session, David invited himself along to the meeting.

We arrived at the Bristol hotel at around 7.15 p.m. on the Thursday evening, and before even bothering to check in, David headed straight to the bar. When I joined him at around eight o'clock, he had already polished off a bottle of wine on his own.

Many further bottles of wine continued to flow freely, mostly in David's direction, throughout dinner at the hotel. After dinner, David finally checked in before demanding that the two of us 'hit' the bar in earnest.

At around midnight, some people who were with us at the bar decided to move on to the nightclub next door to the hotel and although the people were complete strangers, David felt that we should join them.

Since he would clearly have gone on his own to the nightclub in order that he could carry on drinking, I took the decision to accompany him.

Once in the nightclub, bar a brief excursion on the dance floor where David's dancing efforts resembled that of a 'Rhinoceros on Speed', he drank whisky non-stop until closing time at around two in the morning.

"I'm hungry!" announced David.

"We ate a big meal only a few hours ago," I protested.

"Come on, J.P., I fancy an Indian."

"It's two in the bloody morning, David!"

"So?"

"We've a customer meeting in only seven hours' time and the two of us should really be going to bed rather than on a mystery tour of Bristol. "

"I'll go on my own then you miserable scrote," he said in slurred tones.

I went with him.

I love Indian food. However, Indian restaurants still open after two o'clock in the morning are often not the most wonderful cuisine experiences on earth and our taxi driver that night recommended an absolute horror of a place.

We should perhaps have guessed from the name of the restaurant, which was the very appropriately named 'Ashoka'.

In fact, the food at the 'Ashoka' was even worse than shocking – it was truly, truly abysmal and I could feel my stomach rebelling almost immediately. Why I ate the food, I don't know, but I did.

After finishing the 'meal', washed down inevitably with three pints of lager by David, the two of us took a taxi back to the hotel.

En route, a man that we'd never seen either before or since dropped his trousers and 'mooned' at us in the street. The sight of a hairy bare male bottom at nearly four in the morning was undeniably a bizarre conclusion to proceedings as a closed bar and no room service at the hotel finally brought an end to David's drinking.

**

I was awoken by my alarm at around 7.30 a.m. and, despite only drinking mineral water since around 10.30 the previous night, I still felt rough after only around three hours' sleep.

The precarious state of my health was not helped by a visit to the toilet where the true horror of the Indian meal that I'd eaten a few hours earlier kicked in. I felt as though the whole world was passing through my backside and, worse still, the whole world was molten lava.

Toilet traumas completed, I made it to the hotel reception for the agreed time of 8.30 a.m. to meet up with David. He was there waiting for me and, quite remarkably, he looked very good; an absolute picture of health in fact.

The journey from the hotel to our business meeting location was only around twenty minutes, and we arrived at our meeting at J. Norton & Sons about five minutes early. We walked into the reception area which was grand but clearly lacking in any significant investment in the previous 20 years.

As we sat together, waiting for our contact, Theo Wilson, to meet us, David spoke up,

"Please accept my sincere and most profound apologies."

I looked at David in bewilderment, as did the young female receptionist.

"For what?" I asked.

David farted very loudly.

"Terry Hennessey, 1-0.," he said.

"Greasy Eddy, God bless him!" I added.

The young receptionist sniggered. I couldn't help myself and started to laugh as well. David's apology in advance of the 'event' had only served to make the matter even more amusing, and within a few seconds the three of us were laughing uncontrollably. David's constitution was human after all.

To add to the general hilarity, David added,

"I've got a real tortoise head. Can you please tell me where the facilities are?"

After close to a minute trying to stop laughing, the receptionist replied,

"Down the corridor, first door on the left."

David beat a hasty retreat, leaving an appalling smell, two laughing people and a wilting rubber plant in his wake.

Our contact, Theo Wilson, in his late forties and dressed as always in the same cheap brown suit, came to the reception area a couple of minutes later and, leaving the 'infected area', I did my best to stop sniggering and went over to meet and shake hands with him.

"Sorry for being a few minutes late," apologised Theo.

"Don't worry. No problem. My manager is washing his hands at the moment," I replied.

I was secretly relieved as I pondered what on earth would Theo have thought if he'd arrived a few minutes earlier.

"I need to use the Gents myself," said Theo.

Feeling somewhat dehydrated from the previous night's exertions, I needed a glass of water, and I was only too pleased to follow him.

Upon entering the men's lavatory, the two of us were confronted by a truly awful smell. However, far more remarkable than the smell, Theo and I were faced with the sight of David hopping from cubicle-to-cubicle with his trousers and underpants around his ankles.

I was speechless and didn't know what to say or do, never mind where to look.

David however, as quick as a flash, hopped up to Theo Wilson, looked Theo straight in the eye as he shook him firmly by the hand –

trousers and underpants around his ankles throughout – and asked in a very forthright manner,

"I'm very pleased to meet you, Mr Wilson, but what sort of a place is J. Norton & Sons when they don't even have paper in the gentlemen's toilets?"

"I'm very sorry. I can't apologise enough. I'll have the matter looked into," replied Theo.

The sight of seeing a man apologise to another man who is standing with his trousers and underpants around his ankles is one that will live with me forever.

After such an introduction by David, our meeting with Theo Wilson didn't last long. It was my responsibility to take the lead in the meeting but I was still totally bewildered by the event in the toilets and I barely said a word. Theo Wilson hardly had anything to say in the meeting either.

The meeting was over in less than 15 minutes, mostly consisting of stunned silence, and David and I shook hands with Theo Wilson before departing the building.

It has to be added, though, that Barton's did receive their one and only order from J. Norton & Sons that day.

It was an excellent order too – around £22,000 in total.

The Cracks Widen

The first weekend of September in 1995, a young lad called Steve Dalton turned up at Hathersage Cricket Club looking for a game on Sunday afternoons. He was starting at Sheffield University in the October and was new to the area. He had also been signed up to play semi-professional football locally on a Saturday and he wanted to play some cricket on a Sunday.

Steve's skills on a cricket field were clearly comparable to his football ability, and he scored hundreds in both of the remaining games. For someone very gifted, Steve was genuinely modest and a thoroughly nice lad.

I immediately liked him.

At the end of the season, Hathersage Cricket Club held its Annual General Meeting, and I was voted in as captain for the following season.

I may not have viewed being captain of Hathersage as great an honour as when I'd become captain of Sheffield University years earlier, but it was a privilege nonetheless.

I didn't expect Steve to be playing with us again the following season as he was clearly at least two levels in ability above our standard. However, he was adamant that he would be back to play for Hathersage.

**

At the end of the month, David and I again went out to the theatre. We started drinking early at around six, and after the theatre we went to a seedy Sheffield club to continue into the early hours.

David, after demolishing the best part of two bottles of whisky during the course of the evening, reached a point where he seemed unable to converse in a remotely comprehensible manner. Somewhat drunk myself, I staggered out of the club and into a passing taxi.

I thought little of David and how he would make his journey home.

As I struggled through the next day at work with the 'headache from hell' and dehydration from the previous night's excesses, I was taken aback to hear David tell me,

"I met a woman on my way home."

"You could barely string three words together when I left the club, never mind make coherent conversation with a woman that you'd never met before."

"She's called Sue. She's a nurse at Weston Park."

As if I wasn't surprised enough already, David added,

"I'm going to see her again this weekend, I've told Stef that you and I are going away to Stratford together to see a Shakespeare play. So if anyone asks, you know to say."

"OK!"

**

One early December Friday, I arrived home late from a business trip in the South of France to find an excited David waiting for me on my Hathersage apartment doorstep.

"How long have you been here?" I asked.

"Around twenty minutes but I wanted to see you in person. I've received a letter regarding a reunion dinner for all those involved in the Sheffield University Cricket Club during the 1980s. The letter's dated two months ago and must have got mislaid in the post. The dinner's tomorrow night at the Hallam Towers Hotel in Sheffield. The organisers asked if I knew where you were, so I decided to relay the information in person. Are you up for it, J.P.?"

"Not half. You bet!"

**

I was genuinely excited to attend the reunion dinner.

In the seven years that had passed since leaving university, I was fascinated by the changes that had taken place in some people's lives.

For some the intervening years had not been kind and they were in humdrum jobs or, worse still, unemployed – but for others, the seven years had been one long adventure of either tours around the world or working for noble and honourable causes in faraway places.

And for some, there was money and success.

Above everything though, it was simply wonderful to see Ian Bestall and Simon Firth again.

"J.P., the legendary J.P. The best cricket captain ever!" was Simon's inspirational greeting to me.

"How the hell are you, Simon?" I asked

"Simply spiffing, my old fruit. Working as an architect in Dubai. What a place —.it's an architect's dream. Total creative freedom with the money to back it up. Getting married next year. You and Pritchett have just got to come."

"Did you meet her in a pub as you always said?" I asked.

"Nearly. In a wine bar. Bestall's best man of course!"

Ian Bestall wandered over to join us.

"J.P. Captain, my captain!"

"It's good to see you, Ian."

"Guess what the lucky old bastard is doing?" asked Simon.

"Loitering with intent?" I responded.

"As good as! Writing for bloody television, he is. Could barely write his name at uni and now he's being paid to write romantic drivel for TV. Can't believe it!" replied Simon.

"Still got the frogs?" I asked.

"Undeniably – ten of them now. My fiancée Judith, fabulous woman, is even more obsessed with frogs than I am. She's acquired over a thousand pieces of frog memorabilia!"

"And do the genitals still get a regular airing?"

"Of course, but sadly not on a cricket field. I play in Sharjah and Abu Dhabi, and the locals are very sensitive to the old todger making an appearance on the field of play."

"Do you remember the cricket tour?" I asked them both.

"Never forget it!" said Simon.

"Great days!" I replied.

"Simply the best! It's great doing what I'm doing but I'd give everything to be starting uni again. Best years of your life!" added Ian.

**

Throughout my time at Barton's, Stefanie had been a director of the company with overall responsibility for all purchasing activity. Old Man Barton clearly had hoped that Stefanie would take an active interest in the business but, as he commented on a number of occasions, her presence at work was never more than fleeting.

It's easy to say in hindsight that Stefanie as purchasing director was a disaster waiting to happen. It wasn't that she lacked ability or flair; far from it, and she actually did some very effective things in her role which benefited the company significantly.

The problem was that she could never sustain sufficient interest in the job for any length of time. There was always some other passing fad or fancy to take her attention away, whether it was horse riding, skiing, tennis, even theatre for a while before she considered it passé.

One of Stefanie's 'purchasing tricks' was to buy a year's stock for a given raw material in one bulk purchase, invariably at a very significantly reduced price. This strategy often created some problems, not least for the poor individuals in the company's warehouse who would find themselves without any space as yet another large shipment of raw materials came through the door.

However, more by good luck than judgment and supported by Old Man Barton's money, these large bulk purchases often worked very much in the company's favour as many of the materials in question subsequently either became in very short supply or alternatively underwent a significant increase in price.

Inevitably though, her luck had to come to an end.

**

Julie, who was office manager at Barton's, called me over into her small office as I was walking by.

Julie was attractive with her auburn hair always in a bun for work and very efficient and professional, but she certainly loved to gossip and was always the person most in the know regarding everyone's personal affairs.

"Hey, J.P., come and listen to this?" she said.

"Listen to what?" I asked.

"There's going to be a major shindig in the main conference room between the Old Man, David and Stefanie. I switched the intercom on to listen in! The meeting's about to start – I've got an extra pair of headphones if you want."

"I'm not sure we should be eavesdropping."

"Please yourself!"

"Oh, go on then," I said.

I sat down on the one other chair in Julie's office, and we both waited expectantly.

A couple of minutes later, the meeting started.

"Right then. What's going on here?" asked a voice I recognised as Old Man Barton.

"Very simple, Ron. Stef was sent two e-mails and a memo stating that we would no longer require DBTCH as a raw material due to environmental legislation on the product, and she's gone and

259

committed to a year's supply on the product," said a voice that was clearly David.

"Nobody told me, and it was a not to be missed price deal," protested a third voice, Stefanie.

"I repeat, you were sent two e-mails and a memo on the matter, Stef! And of course, it was a not to be missed price deal. They can't fucking sell the product anywhere else. So instead of having to pay a fortune to dispose of their remaining inventory, Barton's been stupid enough to buy it off them. It defies belief!"

"You know I never read e-mail, and I never saw the memo," repeated Stefanie.

"That's because you're never bloody here. And you are the only person in this company who doesn't read their e-mail. The only one!" reinforced David.

"What's wrong with talking to me?"

"As I say, you're never bloody here!"

"You could have told me at home. We live together."

"You're the one who won't talk about work at home."

"Enough. I'm not interested in who's to blame and who did or didn't do what. I'll deal with that at a later point. I want to know what we're going to do about it," interjected Old Man Barton.

"Can't we use the material anywhere else?" asked Stefanie.

"If you'd read the memo or e-mails you would know that environmental legislation comes into place on 1st January next year effectively outlawing the use of the material," replied David.

"Environmentalists, what do they know?" said Stefanie.

"Brilliant, Stefanie Pritchett decides that the environmental legislation is inappropriate, so everything's fine, there's nothing to worry about," countered David.

"Enough I said. This isn't helping," said Old Man Barton.

"I did speak to Sam Rodgers, our attorney, and he said that the contract is binding," replied David.

"Sam's a good guy, but I double checked with an old legal pal, and he said the same. Whether we take the material or not, we are committed to paying £627,000. Christ, Stefanie, that's more profit than we make in two months!"

"We could refuse to take the material and see if they take legal action," suggested Stefanie.

"Of course, they're going to bloody take legal action. What planet are you on? It's a binding contract and they've got a watertight case. In twenty-seven years running this company, nobody has ever taken legal action against me, and it's not going to start now. And who would pay the legal costs anyway, Stefanie? You? I don't think so. No, it would come out of my pocket just as the £627,000 is going to come out of my pocket."

The anger and frustration in Old Man Barton's voice was clear to hear.

"We definitely don't want the material as we'll only have to pay a lot of money to dispose of it," said David.

"Agreed. Some sense at last. Right, Stefanie, this is what you're going to do. I will write a post-dated cheque for 1st January 1996. I don't want the bonuses for this year to be affected. Employees of this company have worked hard, and they should not lose out because of one person's monumental cock-up. The cheque for the full sum is on the condition that not a kilo of material is delivered. Can you make sure that's what happens?"

"Yes," replied Stefanie.

"Are you sure? David can handle it if you want?" asked Old Man Barton.

"I'll do it!" she reinforced.

"You'd bloody better!"

**

The following Monday, exactly a week before Christmas, an announcement was made at the company that David's role as commercial director would be extended to include purchasing. It was also stated that although Stefanie would retain her position as a director of the company, it would be in a non-executive position.

Stefanie was not present at the announcement to the employees, and she was never to be seen on the company site again.

**

Christmas saw David go alone to see Brian and Alison on the farm. He asked if I wanted to go with him but I'd been travelling a great deal on business in December, and wanted to stay at home.

I was expecting a quiet Christmas alone with my wine and cigarettes but to my considerable surprise I had a call from Steve Dalton two days before Christmas.

"Can you please put me up for a week over the holiday period?" he asked.

"Sure," I replied.

261

"You're a star. I've got a football game on Boxing Day, and it's too far to travel from my family home in Norfolk. And too expensive! My match fee will barely cover the train fare."

"You're really welcome but won't the Halls of Residence be open and more convenient for you?"

"Sure, but I'll have to pay. And anyway, they are pretty dismal places to be in when hardly anyone's around."

"Which Hall are you in?"

"Ranmoor."

"Hell, Ranmoor Hall is actually pretty dismal even when everyone is there!"

Steve laughed.

Although I didn't know him that well, the time with Steve proved to be most enjoyable. With someone for company, I made an effort on Christmas Day and cooked a traditional lunch – turkey, stuffing and all the trimmings followed by a homemade Christmas pudding and rum sauce.

On Boxing Day, I went with Steve to watch him play football. Based on what I'd seen of him on a cricket field, I expected him to be an outstanding football player – but I was taken aback at just how good he was.

To all the 100 or so spectators at the game it was very obvious that Steve had all the ability required to make it as a professional footballer – he was big, strong, excellent in the air, deceptively quick and with an absolute thunderbolt of a shot with his right foot.

**

It was time again for the traditional New Year's party at Old Man Barton's house.

"Can you take Sue to the party and 'pass her off' as your own girlfriend?" asked David upon returning from the farm.

"Are you mad? This is just plain crazy."

"Please, J.P. For me."

"OK, for you, I'll do it."

So on the night, I took a taxi and picked up Sue from her hospital flat on the way to the Barton mansion. It was the first time that I'd met Sue, and I was immediately struck by how she was the absolute antithesis of Stefanie.

Whereas Stefanie was all size 8 designer suits, posturing and flowing auburn hair; Sue was probably size 14, mousy haired and not a little demure.

"I can't thank you enough for tonight. I want to spend New Year with David," said Sue.

"I'm pleased to be able to help. How did you meet David?" I asked.

An enormous smile filled Sue's face as she said,

"I found him by the roadside – literally. There I was, finishing my shift at the hospital at around two in the morning and as I left, I saw this strange man asleep by the side of the road."

"I was with him earlier that night. We were somewhat the worse for wear. I left him on his own, and he must have decided to walk home," I replied.

"Worse for wear doesn't even begin to describe his state. He was so drunk that he stopped for a sleep on the grass verge. He told me that he quite often did that."

I laughed and replied,

"I can vouch for that. I've seen him roll into work a few times covered in grass and foliage."

"The problem that night is that it was pouring with rain. If I hadn't woken him up and taken him home, who knows what would have happened to him!"

"Indestructible is our David!"

She laughed before saying,

"I know he's married, crazy at times and clearly drinks too much, but he's deep down such a wonderful man. I so love being with him."

"I've known David for more than fifteen years. He has his frailties but I absolutely agree with you. He is a wonderful man, and you're certainly having a good effect on him. Since meeting you, he's drinking a lot, lot less. There again, I don't think it's humanly possible to drink more than he was doing before he met you!"

"More than anything I want to make him happy. If I can somehow ease what's gnawing away inside of him," she said.

Sue and I arrived at the party and to my embarrassment, and also no doubt to Sue's embarrassment as well, David introduced Sue to everyone there as my girlfriend.

**

Once home from the party, I poured myself my first drink of the New Year. Seeing Sue and David together for the first time that evening and the obvious bond between them made me realise once again what was missing in my life.

I made a firm New Year's resolution to myself for the coming year of 1996. I told myself that I should make a genuine effort to find myself a new girlfriend, someone amazing to share my life with.

Inevitably Sophia came to mind as I made my resolution.

I had genuinely been trying my best to move on. However, the reality was that every time I thought of her, my efforts were failing over and over again.

**

For three and a half months everything in my life remained the same.

I grew increasingly grumpy and tetchy with each passing week. Mundanity and lethargy are natural bedfellows of loneliness, and I was absolutely, utterly fed up of being alone.

I began drinking alone again and was seriously putting on weight.

And then on April 17th I met Maolíosa, amidst Dublin's seemingly eternal rain, in a hotel bar. I could scarcely believe it; I'd genuinely enjoyed being with a woman again.

The unique and remarkable mystique of the Emerald Isle was about to weave its magic upon my life.

The remarkable annus mirabilis of my life had begun.

In the words of the song lyric, 'just when you least expect it, just what you least expect'.

A New Flatmate

The next morning I took breakfast with a spring in my step and then bought an umbrella from the hotel shop, the fourth to add to my growing collection at home, before going to my business meeting.

After conducting my business for the day in Dublin, I made my way back to the UK.

The crossing took around three hours, and since I planned to spend the night in Anglesey before driving back to my home in Sheffield the next day, I had many a drink on the ferry. The lonely drinking session in a crowded bar was a stark contrast to the delights of the previous evening with Maolíosa.

After close to two bottles of red wine, I arrived in Anglesey somewhat less than sober and made my way, by taxi, to the hotel where I'd left my car.

I sat in the hotel bar alone continuing my solitary drinking session. The events of my time with Maolíosa now seemed a lifetime away, like some strange and magical dream.

I finally decided that it was time to have 'one for the road'. The barman was as ashen faced and grumpy as he had been all night.

"Another red wine, please," I said.

"Sorry, sir, the bar's closed."

"But you didn't call last orders," I complained in slightly slurred tones.

"This isn't a public house, sir. This is a hotel and the bar always closes at midnight. If we serve drinks after that, we could lose our licence."

"I only want one more drink. There's no one else here, for God's sake."

"There's no need to raise your voice, sir. I'm just doing my job. I think you should go to bed, sir," replied the barman.

"Christ, why do people have to be so bloody miserable," I cussed to myself as I made my way to my hotel room.

If ever there was a case of 'pot calling the kettle black' after my moaning and attitude with the poor Dublin taxi driver less than 36 hours earlier then I was that pot.

As I lay on my bed, fully clothed and drunk, the events of the previous evening played again in my mind.

Maolíosa's face kept coming back at me again and again – her smile, her eyes, her hair, her gentle manner. As I lay there, 50% awake, 50% asleep but 100% drunk, I started feeling more positive, as though maybe at last there was a possibility of a brighter future, that maybe my meeting with Maolíosa wouldn't be a one-off moment in my life and that maybe I would get to see her again the next time that I visited Dublin.

"Maybe, maybe, maybe," I slurred to myself, laughing.

**

I awoke and jumped out of bed and repeated my New Year resolution to find an amazing woman to share my life. As I said the words, this time there was a genuine belief.

As I made and drank a cup of tea in my room, I thought again of Maolíosa. A broad smile crossed my face. I thought to myself about the folly of infatuation with a woman I had known for only a few hours and that all logic told me that I was hardly likely to see again.

However, I was convinced that I would see her again, as she had been herself.

I rang David.

"Can I take the day off work?" I asked.

"Sure, no problem. Doing anything?"

"Starting the first day of the rest of my life!"

"Long overdue, bud. Best of luck!" he replied.

I walked for hours on the beach. It was a cold, breezy April day and bar a few hardy people taking their dogs for a walk, I was alone with my thoughts. After much pondering, I decided upon a simple two-step plan.

Firstly, I had to stop drinking on my own.

Secondly, I needed to regain my fitness as I was turning into a 'fat bar steward' – breakfasts like the one I'd eaten that morning needed to become a thing of the past.

"Fitness of body, fitness of mind," I told myself.

The two-step plan wasn't anything ground-breaking or radical. There was no thunder in the sky or dramatic music playing in the background to coincide with the creation of my own 'Master Plan'; there was just a splendid golden Labrador dog on the beach enthusiastically chasing a stick thrown by its owner.

I smiled to myself as the dog proudly returned the stick to its owner.

"There's so much that is good in the world. Why do we have to make our lives so complicated?" I muttered, unheard to the world.

**

The following weekend was the start of the cricket season – fusty old cricket pavilions from the winter break, freshly cut grass et al.

During the tea interval of the first game, Steve, David and I were sat talking as we ate our egg sandwiches. I'd only batted for just over an hour, but I was exhausted.

"My God, I need to get fit again," I said.

"I couldn't agree more. Having watched you play, it would significantly improve your cricket as I'm always struck by 'great hands, awful feet' when you bat. You'd be a much better player if you were fit," replied Steve.

"Never mind his cricket, this guy used to be the best tennis player I've ever known. These days he potters around the club like some middle aged git. You could be the best player at the Hallamshire!" piped up David.

"There's no way I'm better than Richard Sadler!"

"Maybe, maybe not; the point is that you could definitely be the second best player there instead of being barely in the top ten."

"I hate being in Halls of Residence. My room is like a soulless, rabbit warren. I want to live in a proper house or flat," complained Steve.

"It's a fair way out of town but I've a spare room. We got on really well at Christmas together, and I'd really welcome the company," I replied.

"That would be so cool. I'll give you in rent what I would otherwise have spent on accommodation at the Halls of Residence."

"Whatever. The money's not important to me. If I had more money, I wouldn't know what to do with it anyway. And, I'm seriously pissed off with living on my own. It's driving me scatty."

"I couldn't sponge rent free. No way!"

"Honestly, having someone share the flat will help with my fitness. I'll eat more healthily and drink less alcohol."

"You are genuinely serious about getting fit, aren't you?" asked Steve.

"Absolutely!"

"Right then, here's the deal. I've done some work as a fitness instructor in the past and genuinely know what I'm doing. So, instead of rent, I'll become your personal fitness coach."

"Now that IS an idea!" I said.

Steve laughed before adding,

"I tell you, I'm a tough taskmaster. I will not hesitate to seriously kick your overweight fat lardy arse if you're slacking."

**

At the beginning of May, there was another of the Barton's quarterly sales 'get-togethers'.

The 'get-togethers' had always been more about an excuse to party than a serious business meeting. However company results had started to decline, and the meetings moved from being something that had been celebratory and fun into something altogether darker in nature.

The results review session began at 10 o'clock in the morning, and it was clear that David was already drunk as he launched into a tirade on all and sundry over the declining profits of Barton's.

His hostility continued for most of the meeting and the evening session was little better as it became little more than an excuse for David to continue his drinking marathon. Anyone who had the affront to go home early merely became the subject of David's caustic derision and abuse.

Some stayed as long as possible, mixing mineral water with their alcohol where possible. Others, after the hostility of the day, had ceased to care what David thought of them and simply left regardless of the further abuse that came their way.

No one escaped David's wrath and, one of the Two Musketeers or not, I suffered with everyone else.

"Get yourself another drink, J.P.!" he told me.

"I'm OK. I'm working bloody hard to get fit and have no desire to drink shedloads of alcohol," I replied.

"It's a bloody sales meeting, and I'm your boss. Now get a bloody drink!"

"You may be my boss but getting pissed is not in my contract."

"I'm not surprised all the women in the office think you're a poof. Come to think of it, you probably are a pillow biter – sharing a flat with your teenage toy boy," ranted David.

"Manager or no manager, fuck off David. I'm going home. Sack me tomorrow if you want."

"Fuck off yourself, you cunt! You are sacked!"

The next day David had no recollection of the conversation.

**

In June, Steve and I were sat around the table in a pub celebrating Steve's birthday with David and Sue.

"How old are you?" David asked Steve.

"Seventeen."

"And you're at university already?"

"I had leukaemia as a child and couldn't go to school for ages. My Dad knew an ex-university professor, a fantastic guy, and he became my private tutor. He was a superb teacher, and I ended up doing my O-Levels two years early. My parents were cool with me coming to Sheffield even though I was only sixteen. They felt that I was mature enough and ready for it. Age is only a number as Dad says – it's who you are that matters, not how old you are. Some guys are playing top level sport at sixteen or seventeen so why not uni?"

"David, if you think this guy can bat you should see him play football," I interjected.

"I've been invited to pre-season training with Sheffield Wednesday," dropped Steve casually into conversation.

"My ambition always was to have been a professional sportsman. Sadly, I wasn't good enough," I replied.

"My ambition is to be happy, that's all. That and to meet the woman of my dreams. Haven't you ever been truly in love?" asked Steve.

I was silent.

"Of course he has, and he still is. The irony is that the woman concerned still loves him," David interjected.

"You sly old fox you," said Steve.

"And they're still married!" added David.

"But I've never met her," commented Steve.

"Whether she still loves me or not, Sophia's my past. What I need is a future," I said.

"Your problem J.P. is that you spend your life regretting the past rather than celebrating it," said David.

"Bah, celebrate the past, don't regret it. Utter bloody poppycock more like, if you ask me. My Dad topped himself, my mother abandoned me, my baby died from cot death and I caught my *loving* wife being poked by someone else on an office desk. What's there to celebrate in all that bloody crap?" I ranted.

"Your other problem is that you take life far too seriously," said David as he lifted his cheek before raucously breaking wind.

Sue laughed as she gave David a playful slap and said,

"David, you're incorrigible!"

269

"Your problem, J.P., is that you're always looking for a love so amazing, so divine, so bloody perfect. What you need is a woman that you feel comfortable breaking wind in front of."

"He certainly knows how to romantically sweep a woman off her feet, doesn't he?" said Sue with the biggest smile on her face.

"My Mum always says to me that what's gone and what's past help should be past grief," interjected Steve.

"*Winter's Tale*," said David.

"I don't care where it's from, the fact is that it's true," retorted Steve.

**

Later that evening, back home, Steve and I talked for some two to three hours into the early hours of the morning.

"My family broke up and separated when I was young. I'd gladly give my own right leg for my family to be reunited."

"I thought your Mum and Dad were happy?" I asked.

"They are. It's that things are, how shall I say, complicated."

**

I was delighted when Steve, at the end of June, wanted to stay for the summer vacation and take a temporary job before pre-season training with Sheffield Wednesday.

"Hey, we should go and see Oasis play at Knebworth in August. 125,000 people! It will be fantastic," suggested Steve one night.

"I'm too old for shit like that," I protested.

"Nonsense, since when is thirty too old?!"

Steve was right, I was 30 not 60. He mentioned the concert to David and Sue, and they also were very keen to attend. To add to the amusement, Steve set me a target of finding a woman to take to Knebworth with me.

I immediately thought of Maolíosa.

**

I'd started playing tennis again in the early summer of 1993 and having not played for some eight years, I felt that my best days had gone. But I was enjoying playing again nonetheless.

However, inspired by Steve's fitness regime and some savage beatings at his hands on a squash court, I had energy and drive back in my tennis game. I genuinely felt that I could do extremely well in the club's annual tournament, and to my considerable delight, that's exactly what happened.

After my semi-final victory, my opponent Paul Naylor gave me his unqualified support,

"Well played, Jonathan. You've really got your game together this year. I only hope that you can beat that arrogant, womanising prick in the final!"

The 'arrogant, womanising prick' was of course none other than Richard Sadler. Richard, in his mid-thirties, was the Club Professional, played for Yorkshire and had won the Annual Tournament for 10 of the previous 11 years.

His father, Ted, was President of the club and tennis ran in their blood.

Despite being a truly excellent player, Richard was perhaps better known for his lothario activities as a number of female members had succumbed to his 'charms' in his role as coach and Club Professional – amongst them, at one point, Paul Naylor's wife Barbara.

**

Normally tennis matches at the club were only for the benefit of the players themselves, but many people turned up to watch the final, even Stefanie. I'd never played in front of a crowd as large as a 100 or more people.

Without my playing particularly badly, the first two sets came and went in what seemed like no time at all and I found myself 6-4, 6-2 down to Richard. The longer the match went on, the more negative and defensive I was becoming.

My sole objective was to avoid humiliation in the third and what I felt was to be sure to the last set. Thankfully, Richard had lost his killer instinct of the first two sets and, despite numerous break points against me, I held on to lead 4-3.

At that point, quite unexpectedly, a light shower caused a temporary break in play.

Richard, understandably confident in his position, went to loiter around the clubhouse chatting up women, Stefanie included, with his usual easy style. Steve, meanwhile, came up to me with David at his side, his face as black as thunder.

"You, changing rooms, now!" he demanded.

I followed him sheepishly.

Once in the changing rooms, Steve asked of me,

"How do you think it's going?"

"Pretty awful, to be honest. The guy's a class act. Credit where credit's due, he can really play."

"He can play, granted. But fuck me, you'd think that you were playing Sampras, Backer, McEnroe and Borg all rolled into one the way you're approaching the game," roared Steve.

"Edberg, too – I always liked Edberg me," piped up David.

"For fuck's sake, you're showing the guy way, way too much respect. Where's your fight? Where's your belief? Where's your killer instinct?" asked Steve.

"One shouldn't forget Conners or Agassi for that matter," added David.

"David, bugger off if you're not going to be helpful. It seems that I'm the only one here who actually cares if Jonathan wins this match. You're either of the same mind or go and have a drink at the bar. Understood?"

The anger in Steve's eyes as he said the words was all too evident.

"Understood!" replied David.

Silence descended on the changing room.

Eventually David offered,

"I've only once seen J.P. on court with killer instinct."

"When?" asked Steve.

"At school, he hated the tennis teacher and when he had the chance to play him, he completely demolished him. Like a man possessed, he was."

"Do you remember?" asked Steve of me.

"Of course I do. I hated the pompous, pious old git. He ruined my tennis career single-handedly."

"And how did you feel when you were playing him?"

"I just wanted to win every point. Every point he won was like a personal insult. It was like a hatred for him that I channelled into positive energy."

"White Line Fever!" said Steve.

"What?" I asked.

"White Line Fever. What you've described is like my mental state before I play any game; even if it's only squash with you. That's why I always stuff you. That's what you need today! There's no way this match is over if you have the right attitude. Sadler will be in the bar now chatting up women, muscles getting stiffer by the minute. One good game against his serve when you go back out and the set is yours. And then once we're into the fourth set anything can happen. Attack him more, get to the bloody net behind your first serve, for fuck's sake.

272

You've become far too defensive. The guy doesn't have the stomach or the fitness for five sets. If you take him that far, you'll win."

"White Line Fever?" I asked again.

"White Line Fever!" repeated Steve.

**

The shower passed within 10 or 15 minutes, the court was cleared, and play resumed.

"White Line Fever," I muttered under my breath as Richard served to me.

Steve was proven right; Richard had stiffened up during the break and played a very sloppy service game. With new found aggression and belief, I attacked and broke his serve with remarkable ease considering what had gone before.

Serving for the set was a different matter. Richard had loosened up and made me fight for every point. However, following Steve's guidance, I kept attacking and kept following up my first serve at the net.

Despite two break points, I held on to win the set. Belief flooded through my veins.

Clearly jolted into life, Richard started the fourth set with a vengeance but I was so fired up that I refused to give an inch with a mixture of belief, grim determination and the best tennis of my life. White Line Fever had well and truly taken its hold on me, and the match went to a fourth set tie-breaker.

The tie-break stayed with serve until 3-3 at which point two consecutive lucky net cords followed moments later by two excellent first serves enabled me to take the fourth set.

As my serve flew past Richard on set point, I punched the air with passion, excitement and a real belief.

As I sat in my chair, I caught Steve's eye in the crowd. He clenched his fist at me, and I smiled back. I could sense that the momentum was well and truly with me.

It proved to be. Richard Sadler gave his best but, as Steve had said, he did not have the fitness. At 5-4 and 40-15 in my favour, a strong first serve was followed by a rock solid backhand volley that left Richard motionless on the baseline.

I had won. I looked at the heavens in disbelief before looking over at Steve. He was jumping up and down frantic with excitement. It was as though he had won himself.

I was suddenly aware that the already sizeable crowd had grown still further during the course of the afternoon and that everyone was applauding.

Richard came to the net to shake my hand and said,

"Well played, Jonathan, you deserved that. It's about time this tournament had a decent Final."

"Many thanks. Well played yourself," I replied.

I collapsed in my chair and threw my towel over my head. I could feel tears roll down my face. This was only a small tournament, but I didn't care. After all the frustrations with my tennis at school and very briefly at university, finally, I'd actually achieved something to reflect the ability that I had on a tennis court.

**

Afterwards in the bar, I was drained but delighted.

I sat with Steve and David as many people came over to offer their congratulations, including, much to my surprise, Stefanie.

Richard Sadler came over to join us, and the four of us continued chatting until around 11 o'clock when Stefanie came back over to talk to David.

"Are you coming or not or are you going to sit there drinking all evening as per the usual?" she asked.

"I'm going to sit here drinking as usual."

"As you like, I won't wait up. Use the spare room to avoid waking me."

"As you like, as usual dearest!"

"Well played again Jonathan. See you Richard!" was Stefanie's parting response.

Richard left around midnight, and by two in the morning only the three of us were left in the bar. Steve and I finally decided enough was enough and, being very, very drunk, that it was time to go home and sleep after the day of glory.

David, who had been out-drinking us all night by about three to one, saw sense for once against driving home and declared,

"I'm going to kip here in the bar for the night. J.P., consider tomorrow as a holiday. I'm taking the day off, and so should you. That's an order."

He laid himself horizontal on the snooker table and was snoring away in an instant.

**

Once back at our flat, Steve and I had a cup of tea before going to bed.

"Bloody fantastic, today. I was so proud," said Steve.

"It's all thanks to you. None of today would have happened without your help."

"I've been wanting to talk to you about something."

"What?" I asked.

There was a drunken silence between us. I saw the two cups together, the one from the previous day along with the one that my father presented me years ago in the back garden at Taplow.

"You know what really upset me about winning though?" I said.

"What?" asked Steve.

"My Dad would have loved it, he really would. And my fucking mother abandoned us both. And you know what?"

"What?"

"With that statement I'm going to bed. See you tomorrow. Can I be excused from morning training for once?"

"Course you can! I'm training with Wednesday now, remember?"

Maolíosa's Psychologist's Couch

It was July 24th.

On the ferry over to Dublin, I was nervous. Over the course of the three-hour early evening ferry journey, I reran the hours I had spent with Maolíosa in April.

When I arrived in Dún Laoghaire, it was raining *again*. It wasn't pouring down: just the permanent greyness that I had come to associate with the city of Dublin.

For all my excitement at possibly seeing Maolíosa again, there was always something about Dublin on a rainy day that gnawed at me.

It was definitely not a time for negative thoughts, however, and I made my way as quickly as possible to the Midlothian Hotel. Once there, before I went to my room or even checked in for that matter, I headed straight for the bar to look for her.

She was there; in the red, purple and green bar uniform it was the unmistakable Maolíosa, slender of frame, pretty of face and glorious of long blonde hair.

As soon as she saw me, she said,

"My, Jonathan, you've lost some weight, to be sure."

"Fitness regime! How are you, Maolíosa?"

"I'm grand!"

"Has it been busy here over summer?" I asked.

"No idea, it's the first time I've worked here since that night we met."

"What absolutely remarkable coincidence and good luck."

"Maybe," Maolíosa replied with a smile on her face.

The clock in the entrance hall of the hotel chimed eight times for eight o'clock.

"What are you doing tomorrow afternoon? I expect that my day's business will be finished by around one, or maybe two o'clock at the latest," I asked.

"I'll be seeing you, of course," replied Maolíosa.

The broadest of broad smiles crossed my face.

"When do you want to meet up?" I asked.

"Around half past two in the foyer here would be grand."

I checked in and took my suitcase up to my hotel room and once the room door was closed behind me, I jumped around like an over excited five-year-old.

**

The business meeting the next day dragged interminably but I made sure that I was in the hotel foyer at the Midlothian Hotel slightly before half past two.

As the clock in the entrance hall chimed once for the half hour, Maolíosa walked through the door, casually dressed in a white t-shirt and jeans with a light blue cardigan tied around her neck.

"Hello Irish woman," I said to her, trying my upmost to stay cool and calm.

"Hello English man," Maolíosa replied.

"You look fabulous. If nothing else, it's a pleasure to see you not in that *unique* bar uniform."

"For me too."

Outside, instead of the usual rain and greyness that I'd come to associate with Dublin, the sun was shining and the temperature was in the seventies – truly a glorious summer's day.

"Will you show me around Dublin?" I asked.

"I'd be delighted but you're not exactly suitably dressed as the 'Maolíosa Literature Tour of Dublin' is a walking tour. Plus I want to go dancing first!" replied Maolíosa, looking at my smartish attire and shoes.

"Dancing? I had better change."

I had some jeans and trainers in my suitcase, and I quickly nipped to the gentlemen's toilets adjacent to the hotel foyer to change.

"Dancing?" I asked again upon my return.

"Yes, I know. It's a very touristy thing to do, but they have afternoon dance parties at Gogerty's. Let's go. If we walk quickly, we can get to Temple Bar in ten or fifteen minutes. I'll take you the scenic way in."

**

As we passed through Merchant's Arch onto the narrow cobbled streets of Temple Bar, it was like being taken back in time.

"It's a little like the left bank in Paris," I said.

"I've never been myself but, yes, I've heard that too," replied Maolíosa.

And then in front of us there was a vibrantly coloured hotel and bar that immediately brought a smile to my face – almost as though the building had been transported from the Mediterranean to the centre of Dublin.

"Welcome to the bar named after Oliver St John Gogerty. Poet, author and otolaryngologist, amongst other things, but most of all in my heart, the inspiration for Buck Mulligan," said Maolíosa.

"Otolaryngologist?" I asked.

"Treatment of disorders of the head and neck."

"Well you learn something every day!"

Once inside Gogerty's, it was like I had entered a different world. It was very warm and welcoming. Irish music was playing and the strangest thing is that I immediately wanted to dance. As the music played, there were tutors showing and teaching some of the basic moves of Irish dance.

To my considerable surprise, it seemed the most natural thing in the world to me and two hours passed in what seemed the space of ten minutes.

I loved the music and, boy, did I love to dance. Irrespective of whether it was céilí or set, it was a simply magical experience.

I just let myself go and expressed myself.

**

"I enjoyed that enormously," I said to Maolíosa as we walked out of Gogerty's into the sunlit street.

"Touristy, I know, but it was fun, wasn't it? And I never thought I'd see an English man dance like that!"

"I felt great. Wow! So where's next?"

"Some basic Irish history," she replied.

We walked across the River Liffey over the O'Connell Bridge.

"Is it me or is this bridge an optical illusion?" I asked.

Maolíosa laughed before replying,

"No, it's not an optical illusion – the bridge IS as wide as it is long. It's the only one in Europe that's like that, I think."

Once over the river, we found ourselves at the General Post Office, a truly impressive Georgian building with sumptuously enriched entablature.

"This is one of THE symbols of Irish nationalism. It was the headquarters for the leaders of the 1916 Easter uprising. Despite all it stands for in terms of Irish freedom, we still had to pay the bloody English ground rent until around ten years ago," said Maolíosa.

"I'm bloody English," I replied.

"Yes, but you're nice!"

"We have always found the Irish odd. They refuse to be English," I quoted.

"Ah, feckin' Winston Churchill. Now he was bloody English."

"What's the statue?" I asked.

"Cú Chulainn!"

"Who?"

Maolíosa sighed.

"Dear me, first a Winston Churchill quote and now he doesn't who is Cú Chulainn is! This is clearly going to be a long day. He's an Irish mythological hero, who amongst various other feats, single-handedly defended Ulster against the armies of Queen Medb. Even an English philistine like you must have heard of Achilles?"

"Yes!" I replied bristling with indignation.

"Cú Chulainn was definitely comparable, if that helps put it into context. That's why people decided to put his statue here in commemoration of the 1916 uprising."

"Oh," I said.

Maolíosa started to walk again and I followed her.

"Now since this is 'Maolíosa's Literature Tour', who are your favourite three writers? And if you say Shakespeare then I'm going home now!"

"Well I really do love Shakespeare..."

Maolíosa sighed again and shook her head.

"And it depends," I said.

"Depends on what?"

"Whether you mean all writers or just English language writers."

"Why do I get the impression that everything with you is so complicated?"

"I'm sorry but I really do love Molière and Hugo. Particularly Molière, his best comedies of manners, like *Tartuffe*, is up there with anyone, in my opinion! Shakespeare, Wilde, you name it!" I protested.

"Fair enough, I've heard that too. But this is my literature tour! So English language only, please!"

"OK, OK, if that's the case then Wilde, D.H.L. and Byron."

"Not without merit. At least there is one Irishman in there, I suppose."

"So who are yours?" I asked.

"You'll have to guess!"

"With the reference to Buck Mulligan earlier, I'd say James Joyce is one."

279

"Ta daa," replied Maolíosa.

And there almost my magic, in front of me was a statue of the man himself, leaning on a walking stick and staring upwards at the sky.

"James Augusta Aloysius Joyce. I love this statue, it's always how I imagined him to be," said Maolíosa.

I smiled.

"I love his work even if he went to the wrong university in Dublin. And he was a terrible drinker," she added.

"The Irish love drinking, don't they?"

"Yes, you would almost think it was the national sport, but I sometimes think it's the national curse. If you go out at night it should be to have a good time, and maybe have a few drinks along the way. But for too many people in this country, the idea of a good time is to drink and nothing else."

"Wonderful writer though Joyce."

"Once upon a time and a very good time it was there a moocow coming down along the road and this moocow that was down along the road met a nicens little boy named baby tuckoo," quoted Maolíosa.

"*A Portrait of the Artist as a Young Man.*"

"I'm impressed or, at least, moderately so. Maybe today's not going to be that bad, after all. Would you like a nice walk in the park?"

"Lead on!" I said.

"We'll go the long way round. I'll take you over my favourite bridge."

As we walked along the edge of the River Liffey in the glorious July sunshine I held Maolíosa's hand and felt, for the first time in eons, really enjoying life.

After a while, we reached a picturesque cast iron, pedestrian bridge.

"This is where we cross; the Ha'penny Bridge," said Maolíosa.

"It's superb!"

"Other than the fact it was made in England, I think this bridge is utter perfection."

I smiled and asked,

"Why do they call it that?"

"That always used to be the toll charge for using it," replied Maolíosa.

Once over the bridge and south of the river again, we kept on walking and walking through glorious leafy streets full of elegant and lavish Georgian architecture until we arrived at St Stephen's Green. It was delightful there in the late afternoon sun.

"This city is such a different place in the sun. I've always thought of Dublin as such a grey, depressing place when I've been here before," I said.

"You sound like feckin' Roddy Doyle, he said Dublin was a dreary little dump. It's one of the reasons I love James Joyce, he wrote that when he died, Dublin would be written in his heart. It's how I feel."

As Maolíosa and I stood there, hand-in-hand, in St Stephen's Green, looking at the ducks swimming in the pond, I almost went to kiss her – but I thought better of it.

"Tell me about your parents?" asked Maolíosa.

"My Dad's dead. I don't know about my mother. The fact that I haven't heard anything makes me think that she's probably still alive, somewhere. Don't know, don't care."

"You don't know where your mother is? That's terrible, Jonathan!"

"She left my father and me when I was young. Dad never got over it. He probably committed suicide, in fact," I replied.

"You poor thing! Haven't you ever thought about contacting your mother?"

"No!"

"Why not?"

"I don't want to! There's no point anyway."

"I sense a lot of anger in you," she said.

"You sound like a psychologist," I replied.

"I studied it at Trinners."

"I thought that you studied literature?"

"No, literature was my passion. Psychology was my vocation. And don't change the subject. As I said, I sense a lot of anger in you. You call your father Dad but you always refer to your mother as mother."

I shrugged my shoulders.

"You must have felt very hurt when your mother left?" probed Maolíosa.

"Probably, it was a long time ago," I replied.

"What did you think about her?"

"Difficult to say, I can't remember."

"I don't believe you. You are telling me fibs. With something as emotional and traumatic as that, you must be able to remember how you felt about your mother."

"OK, you're right. I do remember."

"Then tell me!" demanded Maolíosa.

"I felt that she was a home breaker, abandoner, and creator of doom, despair and despondency."

"At least an honest answer this time, some progress I guess. And how did you feel about your father's death?"

"Being honest?"

"I see no value at all in being anything else," replied Maolíosa.

"I felt guilty. I preferred to be at my friend's farm and abandoned my Dad in a way."

"He's the one who committed suicide."

"It was an open verdict."

"Do you want to know what a psychologist thinks?"

"No, but I'm sure that you're going to tell me anyway!" I replied.

"Not if you don't want," said Maolíosa.

"Just tell me!"

"I think that you're subconsciously living with ghosts from your past. You had a very rough time of it no doubt – particularly your mother's departure, which has left you with feelings of guilt, abandonment and rejection."

"Abandonment and rejection, yes. But guilt over my mother? No way!" I protested.

"Mmm…"

"OK, there is something that has always bugged me. I heard my mother say to Dad once that 'He's your son but only when it suits you.' I can't put it into words but I often had the feeling that when they argued, and boy did they argue, the argument was over me sometimes."

"Why don't you talk to your mother? You need to know the truth. It will help you. It will help with all that anger inside of you. Trust me, I'm a doctor."

"Can we please just change the subject?" I asked with a weary voice.

"If you want?"

"I want!"

"You have a wedding ring, but you wear it on your right rather than left hand, why is that?" asked Maolíosa.

"My God, it's like being on a psychiatrist's couch!"

Maolíosa smiled and said,

"It seems a simple enough question to me and certainly not one that would normally in any way demand a psychiatrist's couch."

"If you really want to know, she left me."

"And children?"

"We had a baby girl. By coincidence, her name was Melissa. Anyway, she died and then my wife left me. Do we really need to be talking about this?"

"I think we do. So your wife left you?"

"She had sex with someone else."

"That's not the same thing!"

I was silent.

"Did you ever talk to your wife about how you felt over the death of your baby?" asked Maolíosa.

I sighed and then drifted off into my own thoughts.

"Well did you? Silence generally means yes but in this case, I think your silence means no," continued Maolíosa.

"Maybe it was because the pain was totally overwhelming and I just couldn't articulate my feelings."

"You don't have to be articulate. But you do need to express your emotions. Perhaps it would have helped if you had talked to your wife about the fact that you couldn't articulate how you felt. Maybe if you had done that then things would have been different between you and her."

"You weren't there, how do you know?"

"Do you want to know what I think?" she asked.

"I've a feeling that you're going to tell me anyway!"

"You felt so angry and so hurt about your baby's death that you ended up hurting the closest person to you in your life. Perhaps you wanted to hurt your wife? That you somehow blamed her for what had happened?"

"No way. No way whatsoever."

Maolíosa looked at me disbelievingly.

"OK, OK, even assuming what you say is true, maybe in part, it still doesn't justify what she did," I argued.

"We all make mistakes. Some mistakes are bigger than others, nothing more. It's a pretty big mistake not to speak to someone, who loves you dearly, about the things that most matter to you and to them. You have to forgive your mother and your wife if you want to move on in your life. If you don't, you'll always be stuck in the past, full of bitterness and inner suffering. There's no gain in life without pain! Do you know what Vergangenheitsbewältigung is?"

"Not a bloody clue!"

"It literally means coming to terms with the past. Germans often refer to it when talking about World War Two. They firmly believed that dealing with the past is the only way to move forward. If you don't overcome the past then you will always feel alienated."

"Are you saying that I'm obsessed with my past?" I asked.

"Maybe, maybe not but what I do see is someone who has never actually come to terms with what happened to him. Whether it is your childhood, the loss of your daughter or your marriage, until you do this it will always be a struggle to move forward in your life. Instead, you'll only spend your time and emotional energy looking backwards. From the time I've spent with you, you seem someone so obsessed with shutting out the past that you can't focus on the future."

"Have you finished now?"

"Yes, there endeth the psychological profile on Jonathan Melton. If only for the time being! You deserve a break."

I laughed.

"In plain layman's language, you should lighten up and not take yourself and life too seriously."

"You sound just like my friend David; he said pretty much exactly the same to me a few weeks ago."

"It's never too late to change, you know."

"What's gone and what's past help should be past grief," I said.

"Feckin' Shakespeare! But do the words actually mean anything to you?" asked Maolíosa.

"Sort of, I do accept that my ex-wife is still an issue of grief for me. Maybe even my mother, if I'm honest."

"It could also mean that they are not past help, you know! You should talk to them before deciding they're past help."

I laughed before saying,

"My friend David's always saying that as well; certainly with respect to my ex-wife."

"Haven't you considered that he might actually be right?"

"Bloody hell, enough, woman! I've really had enough of talking about my life and problems. I need some respite from all this bloomin' psychological counselling. I thought you'd just said I deserved a break from it all."

"Fair enough, let's walk to Trinners," said Maolíosa.

A Night in Dublin

Maolíosa and I passed through the hallowed gateway of Trinity College and its elegant courtyards and greens. As we reached the Old Library building, she asked me,

"You've guessed one of my favourite writers earlier. How about the other two?"

"Yeats?"

"Not a bad guess. When I was a teenage girl, I did love his poems. 'Tread softly because you tread on my dreams' and other beautiful stuff like that. But there are two writers I love more."

"Wilde?" I suggested.

"Oscar Fingal O'Flahertie Wills Wilde indeed."

"It is only what is good in Man, that wastes and withers there…"

"…Pale Anguish keeps the heavy gate, and the warder is despair. Now why does it not surprise me that you choose *Reading Gaol* when he wrote so much that had such wonderful biting wit?" interrupted Maolíosa with a sigh in her voice.

"Sorry!" I replied.

"Come on then, name the final, and actually my favourite, writer?"

"I'm guessing he's Irish."

"Yes."

"Please not Bram Stoker."

"Feck, no."

"Jonathan Swift?"

"No."

"Give me a clue!"

"He has one major thing in common with Oscar."

"He was gay?"

Maolíosa sighed again before giving me a clue,

"Both of them were born in Dublin, and they both died in the same city."

"Well, Wilde died in Paris."

"That he did," she replied.

My brain started to turn, raking its way through my memory banks.

"We don't have all day," said Maolíosa.

"I'm thinking."

"Is it painful, thinking? It looks painful."

"Samuel Beckett?" I offered.

"We are all born mad. Some remain so," quoted Maolíosa.

"*Waiting for Godot.*"

"It's my favourite piece of work ever. It was like an epiphany in my life when I read *Waiting for Godot*."

"Nothing happens, nobody comes, nobody goes, it's awful!" I quoted.

"Are all your quotes depressing ones?" asked Maolíosa.

"Mostly!"

Maolíosa smiled before saying,

"If we can put your depressing quotes aside for the time being then here we are – Trinity College, Dublin. Trinners – erstwhile educational home to Samuel Barclay Beckett, Oscar Fingal O'Flahertie Wills Wilde and, not forgetting, yours truly. It's one of the finest universities in the world. My first day here was the proudest in my life."

"Wow, what a place this is," I said.

Maolíosa smiled a rueful smile before replying,

"Come on, English man; let's walk back to College Green."

**

Once on the Green, with it being out of university term time, it was relatively quiet and peaceful. As we sat down together in the early evening sun, we seemed to be in a different world; impossible to believe that the centre of Dublin was a relatively short walk away.

"I used to sit here and dream of being a writer," said Maolíosa.

"Have you fulfilled your dreams?"

"I did write for the university newspaper plus a couple of short stories, that's all. One of the short stories was even published in a magazine."

Maolíosa looked sad as she said the words.

"It's something," I said.

"I wanted to do so much with my life," replied Maolíosa.

"You still can."

"If only…"

We were both silent for the first time since leaving Gogerty's.

"Let's go and see Oscar. This place is making me sad," said Maolíosa.

"I thought he died about a hundred years ago."

"His statue, silly. It's in Merrion Square not far from here."

As we walked hand-in-hand past Georgian door after Georgian door of sweeping terraces of houses, I asked Maolíosa,

"So we've talked about all things Jonathan Paul Melton. What about you?"

"So what about me?"

I looked at her in utter frustration.

"I've given you a hard time and the truth is not easy at times, I appreciate. But you've been *reasonably* honest with me and I suppose you deserve a response in fairness," said Maolíosa.

"Good!"

"My family were all from Dublin. It was my parents, Aoife, my sister and me."

"Were you happy?"

"Blissfully so – my Ma and Da never spent a night apart in the thirteen years that they were married."

"Were married?"

"Yes, sadly, my Ma died of cancer when I was twelve. My Da, Aoife and I were very close and we helped each other after the loss. But her death left such a massive hole in all our lives. Particularly Da, he never so much as went out with another woman after Ma died."

"That's sad."

"He always spoke of being reunited with Ma one day. I think that helped to carry him through the pain and the loss. His conviction and belief on the matter was always complete. He openly used to say to people that it was his destiny both in life and death to be with his beloved wife. That she was his one true love and soul mate."

"You use the past tense when speaking about your father, is he dead?" I asked.

"And here we are. The statue of Oscar Fingal O'Flahertie Wills Wilde," said Maolíosa.

"It's astonishing."

"Granite, green nephrite jade, white jadeite and thulite."

"Just superb," I said.

"Some come on then, English man, let's have some Oscar and nothing from *Reading Gaol* if you please!" demanded Maolíosa.

"Children begin by loving their parents; after a time they judge them; rarely, if ever, do they forgive them."

"What did I say earlier about lightening up and not taking yourself and your life too seriously?"

"I don't know; I've forgotten already!" I replied.

"Ignorance is like a delicate exotic fruit, touch it and the bloom is gone," quoted Maolíosa.

"Ah, *The Importance of Being Earnest*. Many people think that it's Oscar's best work, but I always preferred *Reading Gaol*."

"What am I going to do with you?" asked Maolíosa as she pushed me playfully.

I smiled and asked her,

"Do you like Oasis?"

"A strange question but I do in fact. Why do you ask?"

"Would you like to see them on the Saturday at Knebworth then?"

"You have tickets?"

"My flatmate does!"

"I'd love to but there is a precondition to me coming over."

"What?"

"Come dancing with me tonight."

"I've a meeting in the office back in Sheffield tomorrow afternoon," I said sadly.

"An important one?" asked Maolíosa.

"No, not really."

I saw a public phone booth on the corner of Merrion Square.

"Just give me five minutes," I said.

I ran to the phone booth and called David; thankfully he was still at work.

"David Pritchett."

"Hi, it's J.P."

"J.P.!"

"Do you really need me tomorrow as I'd love to take the day off?"

"Jeez, J.P., that's *two* days holiday you've taken this year. Are you all right?" replied David mockingly.

"Never been better! Well not in a long time anyway."

After calling David, I then rang the Midlothian Hotel to extend my stay by another night before running back to Maolíosa like an excited schoolboy.

"Sorted," I said.

She flung her arms around my neck. As my head moved towards hers, she smiled. I kissed her gently. I kissed her on the nose affectionately and then kissed her again, this time more passionately.

"You're a married man," said Maolíosa.

"Separated!" I replied.

"I suppose I can make an exception to my moral code on this occasion. Only this once mind."

We kissed again.

"So, you, what are we doing for food before dancing?" asked Maolíosa.

"I don't know."

"I'll pay for dinner if you can spell my sister's name correctly. If you're wrong, you pay. Fair bet?"

"Not really, seeing as I was going to buy dinner anyway. "

"See if you can anyway."

"A-I-O-F-E," I offered.

There was no great confidence in my guess.

Maolíosa smiled and said,

"Not a bad effort but it's A-O-I-F-E. I know the best place in town for Dublin mussels, and I now think it's right that you pay as you'd have lost the bet anyway."

So through the tree-lined avenues of Dublin, we set off walking hand-in-hand for the restaurant.

"I can't believe how green this city is," I said.

"What do you expect for the Irish capital, English man? Of course, it's going to be green!"

**

Maolíosa and I crossed over the River Liffey again, this time over Grattan Bridge with its cast iron ornate lamp standards. I felt as though I was walking on air. I was having fun in my life again.

We arrived at the Winding Stair bookshop.

"I love this place. I always used to come here as a girl," said Maolíosa.

"It's a bookshop. I thought we were going to a restaurant. I'm hungry!"

"It's a restaurant too, dozy. And it serves *proper* Irish food."

We went upstairs and were lucky enough to get a table by the window. I looked out over the River Liffey as the sun was beginning to set. I smiled to myself.

And, as promised by Maolíosa, the mussels were truly superb.

"I can't believe a woman like you is still single," I said as we ate.

"After Ma died, I ended up looking after Da and sis, even when I was at university. Ma did it with her own father. It was the natural thing for me to do at the time. Aoife led a carefree existence with boyfriends aplenty. Meanwhile, dear old Cinders here never had so much as a boyfriend, never mind a lover!"

My jaw dropped to the ground. My immediate reaction was to think that she was joking, but it was evident that she wasn't.

"Didn't that make you resentful?" I asked.

"Resentful?"

"Resentful that your sister led the good life while you looked after the family?"

Maolíosa thought for a few seconds and said,

"I was happy that Aoife had fun. I wasn't in any way envious of her. I missed Ma dreadfully, and all I wanted to do in life was to look after Da."

"How do you feel about your life now?" I asked.

"I only believe in three things. Destiny, Chance and, of course, Love. Destiny is kind and destiny can be cruel. Chance is as chance is – completely random. Love is the only thing that makes sense of it all. All we can do as individuals is to be accountable for our actions. Once you accept the life process then it becomes easier to make decisions. Everyone's past has both difficulties and triumphs, and once you accept this then you can approach the future with real optimism and belief."

"Are you my friend David's long lost cousin or something? He's always saying 'celebrate the past, don't regret it'."

"I look forward to meeting your friend. It's certainly a positive attitude to life. You also need to learn from the past though."

"You didn't really answer the question though!" I said.

"What question?"

"How you feel about your life now? What you said is what you think about life in general rather than specifically about you feel about your own life."

"Aren't they the same thing?" replied Maolíosa.

"No, and you know they're not!"

"A woman needs her secrets."

We both laughed.

I looked at her, absolutely enchanted with her radiance.

"Come on, tell me, laughter is no answer. I'm not leaving this restaurant until you answer me. How do you feel about your life now?" I demanded.

Maolíosa laughed again before saying,

"It's time to go dancing."

"I don't care."

Maolíosa was silent.

"OK, if you won't answer the question, then at least tell me what gives you enjoyment in life."

"I always enjoyed being a matchmaker. I had a knack of bringing people together."

"You speak as though your life has ended."

Maolíosa smiled before saying,

"Maybe it's that a new one is beginning."

I smiled as well and said,

"It's certainly about time that you started thinking about yourself rather than others."

"Maybe…"

There was a poignancy in her voice.

I was silent.

"No more talk, it's dancing time, get the bill paid and let's get a move on," she said.

"I can't work you out – sometimes you're really carefree and then other times you're very serious and analytical."

**

We walked back over Grattan Bridge towards Temple Bar. The river was floodlit in different colours and looked quite breathtaking. The lamps on the bridge now shone bright in the evening air as Maolíosa and I stopped under one of them.

We kissed in a gloriously romantic moment.

Once back again in Temple Bar, although a Thursday night, it was as though the weekend had already started. Dublin was alive with the laughter and the banter and the 'craic'. This was the Dublin that everyone had told me about. The atmosphere was truly magical, and its unadulterated sense of celebration highly contagious.

As we approached the club where we were headed, I could hear the music playing and wanted to start dancing in the street. Once inside, I was absolutely lost in the occasion as Maolíosa and I danced the night away.

For those hours, I felt free and liberated from my past; that everything that had gone before didn't matter anymore. All I cared about was the music, dancing and, of course, the wonderful Maolíosa.

I was living life, loving life.

**

It was three in the morning and the bar was closing. Maolíosa and I set off walking back towards my hotel, hand-in-hand.

As we walked through the cobbled streets, despite the late hour, Temple Bar was still alive with people, and positively bristling with highly contagious, cosmopolitan energy.

"The way that you dance I'd almost think that you have a drop of the Irish in your blood," said Maolíosa.

291

"I don't know about that. All I know is before yesterday I had hardly ever danced but once I hear the music, it's as though it touches something in my soul. I can't thank you enough for today, for the 'Maolíosa Tour', for a magical night in Dublin, for everything. I can't remember when I enjoyed myself so much."

"So now you have some positive thoughts around my name *and* the city of Dublin?"

"Well I do like Dublin more, that's for sure – except when it's raining, of course."

"I always think about you when it rains," replied Maolíosa.

I smiled inside. I wanted to say something to Maolíosa that captured how I felt. I closed my eyes and the words flowed,

"In life some lovers come and some lovers go
At times their memories melt like April snow
But when passion's burns and feelings hurt remain
A friend's words will so often softly ease the pain
And in such moments a precious bond is formed
And of greater import one's faith in life restored."

"Who wrote that?" asked Maolíosa.

"I did, just now. I was going to quote from Shakespeare's Sonnet 44 but could only remember the line 'for nimble thought can jump both land and sea'."

"Feckin' Shakespeare, and it's 'sea and land'."

"Feckin' Shakespeare indeed."

"Nobody's ever written anything about me before," she said.

"That's their loss and my gain."

Maolíosa smiled.

"I'm going to miss you," I said.

"You'll see me in a couple of weeks' time. I'll get a message to you at the hotel with my flight details for the Oasis concert."

"I really hope so."

"Beneath all that simmering anger and pain and guilt, you're rather a nice guy; all things being relative of course."

"The backhanded compliments are always the best."

Maolíosa laughed and pushed me playfully before saying,

"Anyway, this is where I turn left and you go right."

"Come back with me to the hotel."

"No, I'm going this way. If I don't, I'll turn into a pumpkin…or something."

"Goodnight kiss?" I asked.

Maolíosa kissed me gently and sensuously.

"Look, I must go and go NOW! See you soon, English man!" she said.

"See you soon, Irish woman!"

And with that, she made her way into the distance. I carried on towards my hotel and danced a jig of delight in the street. In my mind, I was Gene Kelly in *Singing in the Rain,* but with the Irish music of the night as my soundtrack.

Back in my room, I hugged my pillow as I went to sleep, dreaming of Dublin, its dance, its music and Maolíosa.

**

The next thing I knew was the housekeeper knocking at my door.

"I'm sorry, sir but you need to check out in ten minutes. The hotel is fully booked tonight, and we need your room."

"Sorry, I'll be out immediately," I replied.

I hastily gathered my belongings together and went to check out.

I was thrilled to find that Maolíosa had left a message for me as promised.

English Man,
Arriving 12.30 p.m. Stansted Airport on the 10th.

See you soon,

Maolíosa xx

The Weekend in Knebworth

It's a sad thing to admit but up to that weekend in Knebworth I'd never been to a music concert in my life, not even at university when there were always bands aplenty playing the Students' Union.

I was very excited, and it wasn't just the thought of seeing Maolíosa again.

David and Sue met up with Steve and I at our flat around nine o'clock in the morning. David looked fresh and bright, and Sue had a big smile on her face; although I did think to myself that she'd put on a fair bit of weight recently.

With me driving we all set off in my car; there was no way I was going to entrust the driving to David even with Sue around.

Inevitably our journey was to the unfortunate sound of David's flatulence along with the altogether more enjoyable Oasis albums *Definitely Maybe* and *(What's the Story) Morning Glory?* and various B-sides to their singles all playing at full blast with the four of us singing along at the top of our voices.

It was a joyous and celebratory journey although I did curse that I'd forgotten my camera as I very much wanted some photos as mementos of the day.

**

As we drove up to the arrivals door outside Stansted Airport, I saw Maolíosa stood outside, the breeze in her blonde hair and looking simply wonderful in the same jeans and white t-shirt she'd worn for our day around Dublin.

I felt nervous, very nervous.

I left the car in the pick-up zone, went over to Maolíosa and kissed her on the cheek.

"It's good to see you, Irish woman," I said.

"You too, English man," she replied.

Once back at the car, I made the introductions,

"Maolíosa, this is David, Sue and Steve. And this, guys, is Maolíosa. So how are we going to do this?"

"I can squeeze in the back in the middle," suggested Maolíosa.

"You're a brave girl. The bottom of this man I'm with hasn't been the best journey companion. I hope he behaves now you're here," said Sue.

Although it was very cramped with the five of us squeezed into my car, none of us seemed to care as we made our way singing to sunny Knebworth.

Even David's bottom behaved.

**

It seemed that the whole world was at the concert venue, not just a mere 125,000 people. After taking an eternity to park and make our way through hoards of security, the five of us found a nice patch of grass – seemingly miles from the stage but with an excellent view of all the large monitor screens.

Despite the fact that the PA system wasn't ideal, it was still a very enjoyable event with some great other bands on that day before Oasis came on; The Chemical Brothers, Ocean Colour Scene, Manic Street Preachers, The Prodigy and, perhaps best of all for me, The Bootleg Beatles.

With such a line up and the five of us getting on very well together, the time flew by. After the Manic Street Preachers finished their set, it was my turn to fetch the drinks and join the extremely long queue at the drinks tent.

"I'll come and help you," offered Maolíosa.

As we walked together, Maolíosa said,

"I'm sorry for being brutal with you at times when we were walking around Dublin, but I can see that there are so many things eating away at you so."

"Don't worry about it. There's no need to apologise as a lot of what you said was true. It's long overdue that somebody actually told me a few 'home truths'. You're right; I have been obsessed with the past. You're right; I am still full of anger. You're right; I haven't come to terms with what happened with my mother, my father, my daughter and, most of all, my wife. My problem is that I don't know what to do about it."

"As I've said before, you should just talk with your wife and mother."

"That's not going to happen."

"You're so stubborn. I feel that it's an argument I can't win. Let's approach it a different way then. What you actually want from life?" asked Maolíosa.

"There was a quote from my old English teacher at school. 'I seek a love so amazing, so divine. One that demands my life, my soul, my all.' I always felt that if I found that then everything else would fall into place. And for a while it did."

"That's a very romantic vision of life."

"You're right, it is."

"The problem I have is that such a romantic vision of life seems to be very conflicting with your refusal to express any true emotions to your wife about your past together – and your mother too whilst we're on the subject. It's almost paradoxical, I'd say, almost to the point of being deluded."

"Deluded?"

"Yes, deluded. Such an aspiration in life merely symbolises your desire for escapism, to avoid genuinely confronting yourself, your past and your hopes for the future. There is a sense of being in love with being in love, rather than real love. Which is what you obviously had with your wife," said Maolíosa.

"I always feel as though I'm on a psychiatrist's couch with you. Weren't you apologising a few minutes ago for being brutal with me?"

"And weren't you telling me that it was about time somebody told you some home truths?" retorted Maolíosa.

I sighed with frustration.

"I don't want to go on at you but until you come to terms with the past, you can't approach the future with any optimism. All you have is this escapist romantic vision rather than real emotions around genuine issues. It will always keep coming back to the same thing. You need to talk to both your wife and your mother. Until you accept what happened, or better still, forgive both your wife and mother, then you will never move on and forward in life."

I sighed in frustration again before saying,

"We're just going around in circles here."

"Redemption comes from forgiveness. Trust me, I'm a doctor," said Maolíosa.

**

Afternoon became evening and finally the Gallagher brothers were on stage singing their anthems that seemed to capture everything around being young and British in the 1990s.

296

There's something almost spiritual about more than 100,000 people in a field all singing the same song, and it was a wonderful sense of shared celebration for everyone there. It's all about belonging, I guess, as Sophia often said.

As Noel Gallagher sang *Don't Look Back in Anger*, Maolíosa leaned over and kissed me on the cheek and whispered in my ear,

"He's talking to you."

I smiled at her.

As the show neared its conclusion, Steve wandered over to have a word with me. The five of us had three rooms booked at a nearby Travelodge, and it had always been assumed that David and Sue would share one room, Steve and I another room with Maolíosa having the final room.

"I've met this fantastic woman! Can you help me out by sharing a room with Maolíosa for the night?" asked Steve.

I was absolutely delighted as I had no idea how to broach the issue with Maolíosa that I wanted to spend the night with her. It had seemed the most natural thing in the world to ask her back to my room after we'd been dancing together in Dublin, but this was different.

And anyway, she'd refused my previous offer!

As Oasis were working their way through an encore, I spoke to her,

"Steve's met a woman, and they want to be together for the night. I'm sorry about this, but we'll have to share a room. I can sleep on the settee or in the bath."

"Don't worry. We'll sort it out when we arrive at the hotel."

"Sounds good to me!"

**

Maolíosa and I bid our goodnights to David and Sue and Steve and his new found friend, and closed the hotel room door behind us.

I held Maolíosa by the waist, and she instinctively put her arms around my neck.

"I want to sleep with you tonight but understand if you don't feel the same way," I said.

"I can't think of anything I'd like to do more," she replied.

I smiled from ear-to-ear.

Maolíosa smiled at me back and kissed me gently on the lips.

We undressed separately and then dived under the duvet before either of us could see each other naked. I switched the lights off but with the curtains left open there was still sufficient light coming into the room from outside.

297

For ages, the two of us held each other, kissing.

Bit by bit, we became more relaxed and comfortable with each other. I moved to the more sensitive areas of Maolíosa's body – her neck, her ears, her bottom, the backs of her legs, her feet, the bend in her arms, her breasts.

I went down on her, gently and slowly at first, gradually building up as I tried my very best to gauge how her body responded to my touch. I wanted her to have a slow, soft, sensual climax.

Maolíosa had a soft and gentle touch as she caressed my head and shoulders and when she came I felt a wonderful tingle go down my back. It was a magical moment.

We then made love, and it truly felt that our two bodies were one. As I came inside Maolíosa, it was a truly inspirational feeling of physical pleasure and emotional delight.

For the first time since Sophia and I had broken up, I felt complete as a man. I felt strong again. More than that, I felt that I had a future and a purpose in life.

Afterwards, Maolíosa and I laid together intertwined, holding and caressing each other before we slipped off to sleep in each other's arms.

**

I awoke and was surprised to find that Maolíosa was not in bed next to me. Somewhat alarmed, I looked around the room for her, and she was sat naked on the settee in the room, staring out of the window at the sun rising over the fields at the back of the lodge.

It was a truly beautiful sight, as was Maolíosa herself. I got out of bed to sit next to her and she put one arm around my neck.

As we looked at the sunrise together, I kissed Maolíosa gently on her cheek and saw that there were tears were falling down her face.

"Why are you crying?"

"I'm upset because it can't always be like this," she replied.

"But there's no reason why it can't always be like this. Unless, that is, you have a secret husband or lover somewhere that you haven't told me about."

Maolíosa smiled and said,

"You're very sweet but it's not our destiny to be together, and anyway, you are the one who's married, not me."

"Look you, I'm only married on paper, and I haven't even spoken to Sophia for nearly six years, never mind spent any time with her. Now provided that you have no major objections to having a relationship with a divorced man then I just don't see what your problem is."

"It's not that that bothers me."

"Well, what is it that does bother you?"

"It's as I said. It's not our destiny to be together," she replied.

"I don't believe in destiny, not if it stops us being together. We make our own destinies in life, don't we, Maolíosa? You're the one who's always going on to me about coming to terms with the past and looking to the future with optimism, aren't you?"

"It isn't that straight forward."

"My God, you are so bloody enigmatic!"

"You don't believe in destiny now but one day you will. Some things are meant to be, and some things are meant not to be," replied Maolíosa.

She then turned away to look out of the window at the rising sun, the tears still rolling down her cheeks.

"Tell me more about yourself," I said trying to lighten the situation.

"Such as what?"

"OK, have you ever done anything that you've regretted in life?"

"Nothing that comes to mind"

"Nothing at all?" I asked.

"I led a remarkably dull life completely devoid of any controversy or misdemeanour," replied Maolíosa.

"You must have done something. Even someone as goody two shoes as you!"

Maolíosa laughed at my comment and then thought for a while before saying,

"There is one thing. It wasn't actually something that I regretted doing, but it did cause a great deal of concern and distress for others which I never wanted to do."

"What?"

Maolíosa paused and with me expectant for some sort of revelation, she said,

"When I was eleven-years-old, I went on a holiday to Galway with my parents and sister at Easter. Ma was very sick, and we all knew that it would be our last holiday together. Despite her illness, or maybe because of it, it was the most wonderful holiday of my whole life. I didn't want it to end and to go back home to Dublin. It was almost as though while ever the four of us remained in Galway then we would always be together as a family, and we would always be happy."

She paused before saying with a smile on her face,

"Happy together in Galway…"

Maolíosa's words trailed off as her mind seemed to drift to another place.

"But I don't understand why *you* caused such concern and distress for others though," I said.

"During our time in Galway, Ma and I went together to a place called Ardfry House. It was a quite splendid deserted old building in the loveliest of locations, overlooking the ocean and the sailing boats in the bay. I'll never forget Ma saying that the place was so beautiful that she wanted to be buried there."

"Was she?"

"It wasn't possible. Ardfry House had no cemetery and no one knew who owned the house or the land. When we got back to Dublin, and she became sicker by the day, she told me that Ardfry House was a place where her soul would always be at peace."

"It still doesn't explain the distress that you caused for others."

"Less than two months after we returned to Dublin, Ma died. The cancer ate away at her, taking something from her every day. It was terrible to watch her fade away in front of my eyes. She had no quality of life at all in the end. After her death, I tried hard to come to terms with it but I missed her so much. In the end, I raided my small savings account and took the train to Galway. I walked all the way from the station to Ardfry House to find Ma. It was very selfish in hindsight. I didn't think about anyone else as I made my way across Ireland. Da was frantic with worry. Thankfully he guessed where I'd gone and came over in his car."

"It's astonishing that he knew where you'd gone. You must have been really close as a family," I commented.

"Yes, it's like a sixth sense has always existed between us. When Da arrived at Ardfry House, he found me watching the sun come down over the bay. I didn't find her, but I did sense her presence. I knew that she was finally free of the pain that had haunted her and that she would always be there for me."

"D.H. Lawrence once wrote that the dead don't die, they look on and help," I said.

Maolíosa smiled before saying,

"Sometimes they do more than that! Sometimes maybe they can even change things for the better. Maybe…"

I held Maolíosa in my arms as she continued,

"Anyway, by the time that Da arrived, I felt so much better and was ready to move on with my life. Da was very understanding. He gave me a big hug and asked me to come home."

"You really loved your mother, didn't you?"

"Completely. She wasn't an educated woman, but she was intelligent. There was a warmth and simplicity to her that I loved. She

300

was very understanding of human nature and its frailties. There again, she needed to be as she had such a terrible time with her own father. He was involved in a bad accident and became an alcoholic. Ma spent years looking after him, caring for him, but she was always philosophical around it. She always said that if it hadn't been for looking after him then she probably wouldn't have ended up meeting Da. But it hurt her dealing with her alcoholic father. I know it hurt her. She always worried that his soul would never find peace."

"My Dad was an alcoholic, it's awful I know."

"There are all these funny Irish quotes about alcohol and drinking but there's a darker side. I once ready a quote that drunkenness is nothing but voluntary madness. And alcoholics spend their life like that. It's a madness that destroys them and brings down everyone around them."

"I saw it, I guess that I was lucky that I was at boarding school and didn't have to live with it all the time. It's still a wonderful story about you and your mother though," I said.

"You are the only person that I've ever told about this other than Da. I never even told Aoife about it. So, that was my summer in 1979. Can you remember yours?"

I had to think for a minute.

"Oh yes, I remember. I was miserable most of the time. But I did have an unforgettable weekend with my Dad playing tennis and cricket. And we had an Irish housekeeper. Annie was her name. I've never really thought about it until now, but she changed my life by getting me to write to my friend David, whose parents ended up adopting me. Strange how such small things can have such a massive impact on your life?" I said.

"Did you like Annie?" asked Maolíosa.

"She was great!"

"That makes me very happy!"

"Why?" I asked.

"It just does."

Maolíosa smiled brightly. It was a smile to melt the most cynical of hearts.

I kissed her softly on her lips.

We went back to bed and laid together until it was time to vacate the room.

It had been a magical, mystical, remarkable night.

**

301

Steve said his goodbyes to his companion of the night and the five of us assembled in the car park before driving around the countryside in search of a proper old fashioned village pub.

Suitable pub found, and with drinks and lunch bought, the five of us sat outside in the August sun joking and laughing. Even David seemed at peace with life and was, unusually, drinking orange juice.

He asked Steve,

"How is training at Sheffield Wednesday going?"

"It's fantastic working with such quality players. You learn so much. I'm playing for the reserves tomorrow night."

"Why on earth didn't you tell me, Steve?" I demanded.

"Because you never asked!"

"Wow. I'm over the moon for you," I said.

"We'll have to come and watch you," said Maolíosa.

"What? You can stay over?" I asked.

"Yes, if you drop me off at Stansted on your way home. I'll sort out the flights and make my way up by train tomorrow."

"Come back with us tonight!" I said.

"No, the car's full enough. and I don't know how long it's going to take to sort everything out. It's easier this way!"

"You're right Maolíosa! All you need to do is make your way to the Sheffield Wednesday ground tomorrow night and give your name at the player's entrance. I'll tell them you're coming and there'll be no problem," said Steve.

The Fateful Night

I made my way to the ground at Hillsborough to watch Steve, the man of the hour, perform in the blue and white stripes of Sheffield Wednesday. I'd been to the ground on several occasions but never gone in through the players' entrance.

Once inside, I was taken aback at how plush the surroundings were, very different from those for the average paying spectator.

I walked into the players' bar area, and Maolíosa was already sat there, again in a white t-shirt and jeans, looking relaxed and rather delightful.

I kissed her on the lips.

"So you found your way here OK then?" I asked.

"Easy peasy, lemon squeezy," she replied.

"So how do you feel the day after the morning after the night before? Any regrets?"

Maolíosa looked me straight in the eye and said,

"There were things that I would have changed about my life given the chance again but Saturday night wasn't one of them."

I instinctively hugged Maolíosa tight.

"How long can you stay for?" I asked.

"As long as is necessary."

"I'm finally going to sort out a divorce with Sophia."

Maolíosa looked seriously perturbed, almost upset, with my decision.

"We should talk about it later when we're on our own," she said.

**

It was time to focus on the match, and I was more nervous about the game than Steve, who had been calmness itself. Before leaving to get changed, he'd confidently predicted that he'd score at least twice.

Steve's comment could have been viewed as arrogance or bravado, but for me it was simply born of genuine self-belief.

And his words again were proved to be correct as that night, in front of 400 spectators or so, Steve scored a thrilling hat trick in a 4-2 win for

Sheffield Wednesday reserves. He was taken off with 20 minutes still left to play – the sparse crowd all giving him a standing ovation as he left the field.

After the game, all four of us cheered the conquering hero as he entered the players' bar area, match ball in hand.

"Why were you taken off with around twenty minutes of the game remaining, are you injured or something?" I asked.

Steve, smiling from ear-to-ear, replied,

"The manager wanted to save me. I'm in the first team squad for the opening game of the league season."

"What, the Premier League?"

"Yes, the Premier League! What else?"

"My God, I don't believe it!" I replied.

I was absolutely delighted, shook Steve's hand warmly and put my arm round his shoulder. I actually wanted to hold him aloft as I couldn't have been more jubilant if it had been me playing for Wednesday's first team.

I shook my head in disbelief and said,

"Bloody hell, my house mate is going to be a Premier League footballer!"

I'd actually remembered my camera this time, and I took some pictures of Steve along with the whole group of us. However, Maolíosa seemed very uncomfortable in having her picture taken and, worse still, she just wasn't communicating with me as usual.

I left her talking with Steve as I went over to see Sue and David. Sadly, despite Sue's presence, David was knocking back drinks again at a truly alarming rate.

"Must go for a tom tit!" he announced before disappearing.

"David has always been a drinker. During university, he went through a particularly dark and difficult time. But I'm more worried about him now than I've been at any point. He was calmness personified yesterday, drinking orange juice but look at him tonight," I said to Sue in his absence.

"I'm so worried about him. During the early days of our relationship, I was able to control his drinking but now I never know what I'm going to get with him. It's awful watching him tonight. Problems, problems, problems!"

Sue was becoming increasingly distraught and started to cry.

"There are other problems?" I asked.

"I'm pregnant," she replied.

"I noticed that you'd put on some weight when we were at the concert but…wow – speechless! I don't know what to say."

"I'm sorry, but I had to tell someone but please, please promise me that you won't tell David."

"OK, I promise but you've got to promise that you'll speak to David about it."

"I can't. I don't know what to do. If I tell David he might leave me but if I had an abortion and David found out then he might leave me anyway."

"David won't leave you; I've known him long enough to know how much he loves you," I replied.

Sue smiled through her tears and gave me a big hug before saying,

"I don't expect him to leave Stef as I fully understand the difficulty of his situation with his job and everything. But there's such a pain and unhappiness to him. He hates his life. All he wants is to be back home in Devon working on the family farm."

I was silent.

"I do love David, you know," continued Sue.

"That's very obvious to anyone who sees you together."

"That's as maybe but I don't think that anyone realises how much I do love him. Both my parents died some years ago, and he's everything to me. I would do anything, literally anything, if David could only find some happiness in life rather than seeking consolation in yet another bloody drink."

I simply didn't know what to say.

As David returned from his toilet visit, Sue turned away from him and wiped her eyes.

"Come on, love; let's go to a club in town with Steve!" he said with a drunken slur.

"Can't we go back to my flat in the nurses' home?" asked Sue.

"How can you say that on such a night of celebration for Steve?"

"All right then, I'll come with you," she said with a weary sigh.

"Good girl."

I went over and said to Maolíosa,

"They're all going into Sheffield to a club but I'd rather we went back to my flat. It would be nice for you to see where I live. Plus, I want to talk to you further about what I mentioned earlier."

"I'll come with you. I agree, it would be good to talk!" she replied.

We all left together and before getting into David's car, Steve asked me,

"Can I borrow your camera?"

"No problem!" I said.

David was driving. As Sue was about to get into the passenger's seat next to David, I said to her,

"You will speak to David, won't you?"

"I promise I'll talk to him tomorrow when he's sobered up."

**

It was a muggy summer night. A thunderstorm was in the air, and the 'heavens opened' as Maolíosa and I drove back to my apartment.

The road conditions were awful and concentrating on driving safely helped take my mind off the fact that Maolíosa was saying virtually nothing at all to me.

Back in my flat in Hathersage, I made a cup of tea for the two of us and as soon I sat down together with her on my settee, Maolíosa said,

"You're wrong to divorce your wife. Your relationship could still work if only you could forgive her for what had happened. You should sit down and talk with Sophia, not divorce her."

"For God's sake, woman, how many times do I have to tell you that any relationship with Sophia is just impossible after what she did? I don't want to talk to her. What I want is to spend more time with you and I can't expect you to do that while I'm still officially a married man. Can't you understand that? And whether you want to see me or not, Maolíosa, I'm going to divorce Sophia and that's that."

"I'm tired. It's been a long day. Can't we talk about it in the morning?" she asked.

"If you want, but I'm not changing my mind!"

Once in bed together, Maolíosa was asleep in seconds, whereas I laid awake thinking.

**

At around two in the morning, the telephone rang.

"J.P., it's David, there's been a terrible accident!"

"What?" I said.

"Fucking get down here!"

"Down where?"

"The Northern General Hospital, you idiot! Now. Gotta go, sorry!"

Maolíosa woke up at this point.

"What's the matter?" she asked.

"It's David. He says that there's been a terrible accident!"

"You go."

"What about you?" I asked.

"Oh, I'll be fine. I can look after myself. Go!"

As I drove, all I kept thinking was why didn't I stop David driving when he was clearly drunk again.

**

I parked my car and ran to the Accident and Emergency department as fast as I could. Once there, I was confronted by the usual early morning mass of humanity with their scrapes and bruises of a night's drinking.

I went to reception to inquire about Steve, Sue and David and was met by a dour middle aged woman, who looked up at me over her spectacles with the sternest of faces.

"I'm here to see David Pritchett. He phoned me to say that he was involved in a terrible accident this evening."

"Are you relative or friend?" asked the receptionist.

"I'm a friend."

"Can you please sit down; someone will come and talk to you in due course."

"But why can nobody come and talk to me now?"

"We're very busy tonight; there's been a major accident with a bus and a car."

"Yes I know, it was probably my friends who were in the car in the accident," I said.

"And if you sit down then somebody will come and speak with you in due course," repeated the receptionist.

"Why for God's sake will nobody tell what has happened to my friends?"

"I'm sorry sir but unless you calm down then you will be ejected from the hospital."

So I sat down and waited and waited and waited with all manner of thoughts going through my mind – was someone killed, critically injured, hurt, what? It was the not knowing that was eating away at me.

**

I heard shouting and screaming. It was clearly David's voice.

"Why won't you let me stay? Jeez, for fuck's sake!" he screamed.

A few seconds later, he was brought through reception with a policeman by his side. David's face was scarred slightly but otherwise he was all right, physically at least. I went over to the two of them and asked the policeman,

"Can I speak with him?"

"Yes, but only for a couple of minutes," replied the policeman.

307

"What the hell happened?" I asked David.

"We were hit by a bus at the Ponds Forge roundabout. It wasn't my fault; you have to believe me, J.P. Sue's in intensive care in a coma; in a fucking coma, for fuck's sake. They did an emergency operation on her for three hours, and the doctors said they believe it was a success, but she's still in a coma. And they don't fucking know when, or if she's going to come out of it. And the police won't let me stay with her because they breathalysed me and found that I was well over the legal limit, and they insist on taking me to the cells for the night."

"Shit! What about Steve?" I asked.

"Steve's going to be all right but his leg was very badly broken in the crash. You do believe me that it wasn't my fault, don't you J.P.?"

I didn't answer David.

"You've had enough time. Sorry, sir but we have to go," said the policeman, and he led David away.

I needed a cigarette. I asked around reception whether anyone had a cigarette that I could buy.

A kind middle aged lady who had been sat there patiently with a cut in her head ever since I'd arrived, and very probably long before, smiled at me and told me that I could have a cigarette from her for free. I thanked her and went outside to smoke in the night air still trying to come to terms with everything.

After my much-needed cigarette, I didn't feel able to drive. Unable to move, I sat around reception for another hour, maybe longer; my mind a complete blur.

**

I looked at the clock. It said twenty to five in the morning, and I saw two people coming through the reception door together.

At first, I thought it was some strange, bizarre hallucination. I couldn't believe my eyes. I looked again disbelievingly.

It was my mother. Her hair was now grey and short and not the curly dark locks that I remember from my youth, but that aside, she was exactly as I remembered her. And it was definitely Man Mountain with her; he didn't seem anywhere near as big as I remembered him, but it was him nonetheless.

Neither of them noticed me as they went straight to reception and announced that they were the parents of Stephen Dalton and asked if they could see their son.

"My God, Steve's my half-brother," I said to myself.

Suddenly all the comments that Steve had made to me about his family whizzed through my mind. I realised that he hadn't been talking to me about the complications in his family; he was actually talking about me as being the complication.

I immediately went up to my mother and asked,

"Can I come through with you to see Steve?"

My mother smiled at me and said, as though we'd last spoken together only the day before,

"Of course you can, Jonathan."

Feeling utterly bewildered and disorientated, I sheepishly followed my mother, Man Mountain and the doctor through to the room where Steve was.

Once in the room, Steve was still awake but his whole left leg was in bandages. He smiled brightly when he saw us.

"I'm sorry that it's taken so long to get here. After the game tonight we booked into a Sheffield hotel. It took ages for the police to find us," said my mother.

"No worries!" replied Steve as relaxed as ever.

"How is he?" my mother asked the doctor.

"He's suffered an extremely bad compound fracture of his left fibula and the tibia was broken too. We will need to operate on it," replied the doctor.

As I stood in the room a whole host of contrasting feelings ran through me. I watched my mother fuss and dote over Steve the way that I remember her looking after me when I was ill as a child. But I felt a stranger in the room, as though I was intruding on a private family moment to which I didn't belong.

"Do any of you know what happened to everyone else in the car?" asked Steve.

"Sue's in intensive care in a coma." I replied.

"And David?"

"The police have taken him away to the cells for the night."

"But it wasn't his fault."

"That's as maybe. But the facts are that he was drunk, and the police know that."

"I only hope that some good can come out of all of this. It's certainly fantastic to see the four of us all in the same room for starters," said Steve.

"I really should go. I've had no sleep and need to go home," I replied.

"Should you be driving? You look exhausted," asked Man Mountain.

"You're right, I am."

"Do you want a lift back to where you live, Jonathan? I've had five hours' sleep, and I'm fine," he said.

"That would be very kind. I'm sorry, but I can't remember your name."

"It's Craig."

"Thank you, Craig."

Craig and my mother took me back home, and I finally slept a little in the front seat. When we arrived back at the flat, I felt it only right that I invite the two of them in for a drink. They both said that they'd be delighted to accept.

I walked in the living room and there was a message on the table from Maolíosa saying that she'd moved to the Travelodge in Attercliffe on the edge of town.

"Fuck, shit, just what I needed!" I moaned.

"Is there anything that we can do?" asked Craig.

"Thanks but you've gone to enough trouble already. There's nothing can be done about it now anyway. I'll make you both some coffee."

Whilst the three of us were drinking, there was a knock at my door. I opened it to find Brian and Alison there.

"Thank heavens you're in, Jonathan. We've driven up straight from Devon as soon as we heard news of the accident," said Brian.

"We've been shifted from pillar to post for the last couple of hours. We were sent from the hospital to the police station. And then when we got there, we were told that we wouldn't be allowed to see David until nine o'clock," added Alison.

"More than two hours to kill then," I said.

"We thought about going to see Stefanie but felt it better that we came to find you instead," said Alison.

"A very wise decision," I replied.

Brian said to my mother,

"Mary, I'm very sorry for what's happened."

"Don't worry, Brian. You've no need to apologise. The important thing is that we sort all this mess out."

As I listened to their conversation, I had the very strong sense that Brian, Alison, Craig and my mother were friends, and that they had known each other very well for some time.

Not for the first time that night, I felt an alien in my surroundings – this time in my very own home. I shook my head in disbelief, thinking that I would at some point wake up and find that this had been some very, very weird dream.

**

I cooked breakfast for everybody.

After eating, Brian said,

"I never knew you could cook. That was really good."

"My mother taught me," was my instinctive response.

My mother smiled at me. I smiled back at her more in amusement at the sheer absurdity of the whole situation.

After breakfast everyone went their separate ways.

Brian and Alison to see David at the police station whilst Craig and my mother were heading back to their hotel before going to the hospital to see Steve.

I desperately needed some sleep and then hoped that I could sit down calmly and try to come to terms with events.

**

As I drove to find Maolíosa at her hotel, I was still struggling to come to terms with the fact that my great friend, training coach and flat mate, Steve, was, in fact, my half-brother.

I remembered back to my childhood and couldn't help but laugh at the utter bloody irony, black humour almost, of how I'd hated him as a baby, both as he grew inside my mother and then, later, after he was born – yet, ultimately, had ended up loving him as a friend.

With all this going on inside of my head when I did finally arrive at the Travelodge to see Maolíosa, I had no idea whatsoever of what I was going to do or say to her.

She was sat outside on the pavement in front of the main entrance to the hotel in a flowing light blue summer dress and matching flat shoes. I had the sense that it was almost as though she was sat there waiting for me.

"How are you?" I asked.

She smiled at me and replied,

"I'm fine. It's nice to see you."

"Why did you leave?"

"I didn't want to be in the way!"

"Good decision as it happens. It was like Paddington Station in the flat this morning!"

I held Maolíosa tight, and she kissed me gently on the cheek.

"There was a bad accident last night involving David, Steve and Sue. Their car was hit by a bus. Sue's in intensive care in a coma, Steve needs an operation on a compound fracture but David's OK – well,

311

physically at least. He's spent the night in the police cells. But it wasn't his fault. Steve agreed," I explained.

"What are you going to do?" she asked.

"I'm not sure what you mean. Do about what?"

"Do about David?"

"I'm obviously going to help him in any way that I can."

"I don't know what happened in the accident, but he was clearly drunk when he got into the car to drive," said Maolíosa.

"I told you. He says the accident wasn't his fault, and Steve agrees with that."

"He was drunk, and harm came to people. You know how I feel about that. Drunkenness is voluntary madness, and alcoholics drag all those around them into their madness. And David is an alcoholic, isn't he?"

"It wasn't his fault, how many times do I need to tell you."

"How do you know? You weren't there," she countered.

"I don't want to argue, Maolíosa. This isn't the right time and place. I have so much that I want to say to you."

"Maybe you're right. Maybe you need some more time and space to think about things, and we should meet up tomorrow to discuss things further."

"I need time?"

"Yes, you need time," she said.

"If that's what you want."

"It's not about what I want, it's what you need. I'm leaving on Thursday morning. Why don't you pick me up tomorrow around eight in the evening?"

"OK, I'll be here."

**

I drove back home and met up again with Brian and Alison. I was delighted to see that David was with them.

The three of them talked through the events of the past hours. David had been charged with drunk and dangerous driving, and he would have to face trial. The bus driver was claiming that the accident was David's and if proven, it could very possibly mean imprisonment for him.

"All I want is to be with Sue," said David.

"What are you going to do about Stefanie?" I asked.

"I'm going to leave her. I should have done it long ago, but I feared for my job. The bitch didn't even come to the police station to see me – says it all!"

At this point Brian interjected,

"Look lad, whatever you want to do and whatever happens, your mum and I will be there to support you. If you lose your job and go to prison, we still love you and we'll do whatever we can to help."

David started to cry, only the second time in all the time that I knew him that I'd seen him do so. Alison went over and held him tight as he sobbed. Brian and Alison had always made me feel part of their family, but I felt that I had no right to be there at such a private and personal family moment.

I made my excuses and went to buy some milk.

As I walked to the local shop, I thought of the sad symmetry to David's tears. He had first cried all those years ago at being told by Brian to leave the farm and find a different future. Now he was crying at the consequences of that future.

I then thought about Sue being pregnant. Without doubt, it wasn't a good time to tell David about Sue, but I decided that he still needed to be told.

When I arrived back at the flat from the shops, David, Brian and Alison were sat silently in my living room. David, however, was at least in a slightly better frame of mind.

I took a deep breath and braced myself before saying,

"David there's something that I need to tell you."

"What?"

"Sue's pregnant."

"Why didn't she tell me, for Christ's sake?" he demanded.

"She was going to, but she was frightened of losing you if she did."

"Is this truly what I've become?" asked David.

He put his head in his hands.

Brian and Alison were silent throughout. What should have been a celebratory occasion in hearing news about their possible first grandchild was instead a mess of monumental proportions.

"Right, that's it! Will you drive me to see Stef, J.P.? I'm sorry to have to ask you but in no fit state to drive, and I'm not sure if I'm allowed to anyway," said David.

"Of course I will."

Aftermath & Revelations

As I was driving David to his house in Fulwood, he was clearly a man in torment.

"What I could have been, oh, what I wanted to be. I never wanted any of this shit. I only wanted to be a farmer like my Dad. Why didn't Sue talk to me, why didn't she tell me?" he asked.

"I guess because she loves you more than you can imagine."

"You will come in with me when we get there, won't you? You'll enjoy what I have to say to Stef."

"Look, it's between you and her, nothing to do with me."

"I can't do this on my own, J.P. If Ron's there it'll be two against one. You've don't have to say anything. Just be there. I'm truly sorry to have to ask you this when I've clearly created such fucking chaos with Maolíosa here."

"David, I'd all but given up when you came and found me in Coventry and gave me a job and helped me rebuild my life. So if you say sorry to me again, I'll thump you. If you really want me to come in with you then of course I will."

"You wouldn't hit a drunk down on his luck would you?" joked David.

"I will only if he starts feeling sorry for himself."

David smiled a weary smile.

**

When we arrived at the house, as David had expected, Old Man Barton's Jaguar car was on the drive. We walked together towards the front door.

"This fucking place is nothing more than a monument to the folly and artifice of my life," said David as put his key in the lock.

We went into the lounge, where an ashen faced Old Man Barton was sat with Stefanie.

"Ah, here he is finally, my wonderful husband," said Stefanie.

"Why didn't you come to the police station to see me?" demanded David.

"That would have been so demeaning. A police station, dear oh dear! Someone of my calibre and position in society should not have a husband arrested by the police."

"Your attitude says it all about our relationship, or more to the point, our complete lack of relationship," said David.

"I can't believe that a failure and a drunk is lecturing me on *my* attitude to our marriage!"

Old Man Barton, who had been silent up to that point, gave Stefanie a 'look'. As always, he was the one person who could even remotely control his daughter, the one person who Stefanie actually treated with respect.

She changed her tone,

"I've talked with Pater and have agreed to stand by you."

David looked Stefanie straight in the eye and said,

"I don't want you to stand by me. I've met someone, and she was badly hurt in the accident. She may not recover but whether she lives or dies, one thing is for sure, the current Mr and Mrs Pritchett have no future together."

"I know all about your affair with your little tart. Anyway, I've been shagging someone from the tennis club for the past six months. At the end of the day it's only sex," replied Stefanie.

"Go on then, tell me, purely out of morbid curiosity, who have you been shagging?" asked David.

"Richard Sadler!"

David laughed loudly before asking,

"How can you compare someone who loves me to someone who has shagged half the female members of the Tennis Club?"

"I'm not going to argue. Don't be stupid David, you've way too much to lose," threatened Stefanie.

"Don't threaten me. If that's the case, I resign with immediate effect. I love Sue. I want to be with her."

"How can you get emotional over a mere nurse? It's so pathetically bourgeois. I'm disappointed in you. No, more than that I feel sorry for you. You're nothing without my father and me."

"I realise that someone who's as bloody pretentious as you, whose only emotional trait is vindictiveness, will never appreciate that two humans can truly care for each other. However, understand that Sue's carrying my baby, I love her and that's more important to me than you, Barton's, anything," replied David.

"You stupid man, you stupid pathetic little man," cursed Stefanie.

Stefanie turned to Old Man Barton and told him,

"Not only should you accept my pathetic husband's resignation with immediate effect, but you should also fire that hanger on of his too."

"I work harder in a month than you ever did in a year, Stefanie. I've always done everything that has been asked of me and more. I'm David's friend, but I'm no hanger on. Have me fired if you want but at least, for once in your sorry, miserable life, show me the respect that my efforts and performance warrant," I interjected.

Stefanie turned to Old Man Barton and said,

"I can't understand why you've tolerated such a couple of no hopers for all this time. That's why the company is in such a mess. If you get rid of them then we can start again."

"Stefanie, the company is my company and not yours and I will decide who stays and goes. And the company is not in a mess. The only reason why profits are down stems from your colossal blunder and not from anyone or anything else," said Old Man Barton.

"I can't believe you're saying this. You're pathetic as a man, and you're pathetic as a father."

Old Man Barton did not respond; instead he gave Stefanie another 'look'. Even the dreaded Stefanie responded to Old Man Barton's stare, and she calmed down.

"I think that you all should please leave now," said Stefanie.

Her manner was remarkably polite and civilised manner and the three of us shuffled out of the house and towards our cars as directed.

Once outside, Old Man Barton pulled us to one side.

"David, if you want to reconsider your resignation, then you still have a job and my full support. And Jonathan, whether David stays or not you also still have a job. I apologise for my daughter's behaviour. It's my fault, a case of too much money and too little love. I've spoilt her too much in life and stood up to her too little."

I shook Old Man Barton by the hand and thanked him. David was more demonstrative and put his arm around him and said,

"I'm sorry, Ron."

Old Man Barton smiled and replied,

"Look after yourself, son."

**

When David and I walked into Sue's hospital room, it was a terrible sight with tubes and machines everywhere, seemingly monitoring every possible vital sign.

316

Sue's face was badly bruised and her head was still bandaged from the operation. A nurse was checking up on her and writing notes on her chart.

"Can I come in and stay with her?" asked David of the nurse.

"Yes, as long as you want," she replied.

"How is she?"

"Stable."

"And the baby?"

"Fine, as far as we can tell."

"J.P., can you leave me alone with her?"

"Of course."

David shook me warmly by the hand and said,

"Thanks for all your help and support today."

"You've nothing to thank me for."

"So much for my Master Plan, eh!" said David.

"We're still the Two Musketeers though."

"Dumb asses, the pair of us."

"Speak for yourself," I replied.

David smiled.

**

Steve and I had a chance to talk in his room before Craig and my mother arrived.

I immediately told him about the events with David and Stefanie and he laughed. And as the two of us talked and laughed more that afternoon, I thought how lucky I was to have Steve as my half-brother. Although thirteen years younger than me, he was in many ways far more mature and balanced than myself.

Before my mother and Craig were due to arrive, Steve became more serious.

"I'm sorry that I never told you that I was your brother. I tried to on a number of occasions, particularly after you won the tennis. But the words would never come out, or the time didn't seem right."

"I know. I remember that I ranted about my mother and then went to bed and passed out."

"Ever since I was poorly as a young boy, I wanted us to meet and be proper brothers. It's why I came to Sheffield. Why I joined Hathersage Cricket Club. Why I moved in with you. It's like a dream come true for me. The thing that I wanted most of all has actually happened."

Tears filled my eyes as I replied,

317

"I hated you when you were a baby and look at us now. I'm lost for words."

Steve smiled.

"One favour?" he asked.

"Anything!" I replied.

"Will you speak to Mum?"

I sighed heavily.

"For me?"

"I'm so glad that you're my brother, I really am. But there's too much history between her and me," I replied.

"You said anything, remember? Will you at least try though?"

"OK, OK, for you, I will. But I don't think that we have anything to say to each other though."

Steve smiled a very broad smile.

A few minutes later, Craig and my mother arrived. My mother smiled and gave me a kiss, and Craig shook me warmly by the hand. Out of courtesy, I hung around the room for a short time and then made my excuses and left.

As I left the room, Steve asked me,

"Remember what we agreed?"

"Yeh, I remember."

**

I woke up around at around nine o'clock the next day and went out for some cigarettes. Upon my return to the flat, I found my mother, dressed in jeans and a jumper, sat alone on my doorstep in the early morning sun.

When I saw her, I breathed a sigh of frustration. It was the last thing I needed at that point.

"Can we talk?" she asked.

"Come in for a coffee."

After making the coffee, we sat down in my lounge together – her on the settee and me in a chair.

I nervously lit a cigarette.

"You're so like your father," said my mother.

"That would explain why you left the both of us then," I replied.

"I can understand your bitterness. You can't imagine how much I wish that things had been different. I loved your father, and we were happy for quite some time. Both of us wanted to have more children, but your father had a very low sperm count, and it was the days before IVF. We tried and tried for a second child but it never happened."

318

"So what?" I asked.

"Not being able to have more children made me very sad. But I read something once that said what's gone and past help should be past grief. I came to terms with the fact that you were my only child. After all one child's better than none at all, and I do truly love you. I did then, and I do now."

"It's from *Winter's Tale* by Shakespeare," I said.

"I never knew that, all I knew was that it made sense to me. Your father though was very different. He couldn't move on, he couldn't let go. His reaction was to become increasingly distant and instead throw himself into work as if more money and a bigger house would somehow compensate for the fact that we couldn't have more children."

"Is that why you left him then, because you couldn't have more children with him?"

"No, of course it wasn't. It was the fact that no matter how much I loved, nagged, begged, cajoled, pleaded with and reassured him that it wasn't important; nothing would bring him back to me. I did love him, but I could no longer deal with his continued rejection of me. In the end, it was as though he was totally absent from my life."

"You're right. He was never there. Both before and after you left."

"It's odd that you should say that. I always thought that it was me. It always felt that my presence only seemed to serve to remind him of his own physical shortcomings. I wasn't able to make him happy no matter what I did. His rejection was tearing me apart. I simply couldn't keep living that way. And when he began to continually question me as to whether he was your father then for me that was the point of no possible return."

"He's your son, Robert, but only when it suits you," I said remembering the words of years before.

"I knew that he'd lost all touch with reality when he started saying that. Of course, you're his son. I offered to do tests, anything to prove to him that you were his. But he wouldn't listen, he didn't want to know. All he wanted to do was drown in self-pity. He was mentally ill and needed professional help, but he wouldn't listen on that either."

"You said the words when you left. 'I love you so very, very much but I cannot continue living like this," I said.

There were tears in my mother's eyes as she replied,

"You remember."

"Of course I bloody remember"

"I felt that I had a right to be happy in life but that there was a price to pay for that happiness, and that price was you. I desperately wanted you to be part of my family after the death of your father but when

319

Steve was diagnosed with leukaemia, it was very difficult. Craig and I had started our own gym, and it was a lot of work building the place up. Craig told me that he couldn't cope with the gym, Steve's leukaemia, and your coming to join us. I didn't agree but when we met at your father's funeral, it was clear that it was better for everyone that you stayed with Brian and Alison. All I hope for now is that you and I can make our peace and move on."

There were tears rolling down my mother's cheeks by this point.

I went to sit next to her and gave her a hug.

"Maybe. Let's see. At least we're talking," I said.

My mother gave me the broadest smile through her tears.

For the next couple of hours, we chatted about what I'd done over the previous 18 years of my life. I was staggered by how much my mother knew, how much she'd been in contact with Brian and Alison, how many events that she'd attended, such as my graduation, without my being aware.

Most remarkably of all, my mother had even attended my wedding.

"With Brian and Alison's help, I sneaked in un-noticed at the back of the church," she said.

"I didn't see you at the reception though."

"No, but Brian made a tape recording of all the speeches for me."

"Astonishing. Absolutely bloody astonishing!"

I laughed aloud.

"I loved your speech. It was obvious how much how you loved and adored Sophia. I was so sad when I heard about Melissa. It was nice to be a grandparent."

"I never thought about your being a grandparent."

"It's not important in the whole scheme of things. What's important is that you and Sophia split up. It seems such a waste to me. She came to visit me after you broke up."

"What, Sophia came to see you?" I asked.

"Yes, she wanted to try and understand why you were as you were after Melissa died."

"I guess that I behaved just like Dad did with you. I blamed her for Melissa's death – at least in part. However, what's gone and past help and all that."

"Jonathan, you are your father's son but you are not your father. Similarly, Sophia and you are not your father and me. She still loves you."

"She still loves me? Still?"

"She certainly did when I last saw her around three months ago. We meet up every now and again. I guess you give us a common interest," replied my mother.

I laughed at the absurdity of it all as my mother continued,

"She's a very interesting and attractive woman; very intelligent, no doubt. Love is strange. Every couple and every relationship is different. Every woman is different, not that a lot of men understand that. I remember Sophia saying to me that the nature of a woman defines how she is loved, and she's so right. You gave her something – something that she's never found before or since."

"She always talked about a sense of belonging," I said.

"Yes, she said that to me. And you made her happy. I don't think she's ever had true happiness in her life other than with you. You should talk to her. I'm not saying that you should get back together but at least talk to her."

I shrugged my shoulders.

**

Around midday, my mother and I went to the hospital to see Steve but he wasn't in his room. We asked the nurses where he had gone. The sister on the ward said that Craig had taken him in a wheelchair to see David and Sue.

When we got there, Craig was waiting outside as David and Steve were talking in Sue's room.

"Let's go for a cup of coffee," said my mother to Craig.

I went into Sue's room. She was still bandaged around her head with machines and tubes everywhere.

I sat down next to Steve and David. Other than his leg, Steve was looking well and in excellent spirits but David looked awful, as though he'd not been to sleep for two and a half days.

"Any change?" I asked him.

"No."

"You should try to get some sleep."

"I won't rest until Sue comes out of her coma."

"Sitting here won't help her."

"But I feel responsible," he replied.

"I thought that you said the accident wasn't your fault."

"It wasn't but I still feel responsible."

"It wasn't your fault. I was there; you might have been drunk but, without any doubt, it was the bus that was to blame for the accident," interjected Steve.

"What about the baby?" I asked.

"Fine at the moment from what the doctors say; they told me that some women have given birth after spending virtually the entire pregnancy in a coma. But I can't even start to get my head around that right now. All I want is that she comes out of this coma, and that's she's all right."

Steve and I were silent.

"Why don't you take Steve back to his room?" suggested David.

As I pushed Steve in his wheelchair through the corridors of the hospital, he said,

"This will either be the making or breaking of David."

"Sadly I think that you're right. On a more positive note, I talked with your mother this morning, and it was better than I thought it would be – much better in fact."

"Don't you mean our mother?" asked Steve.

"You're right. I mean our mother."

The biggest smile imaginable crossed Steve's face.

"Having my leg decimated by the accident is a small price to pay if you and Mum start talking again, if somehow there's a way that we can get on as a family. I don't think that you can imagine what that would mean to her. It would be like the missing piece of her life was finally in place."

"We're hardly bosom pals yet. It'll take time," I said.

"I know. But at least you've finally made a start."

"That's what I said earlier."

Future Promises and Past Words

As I arrived at the Travelodge, once again Maolíosa was sat outside on the pavement in front of the main entrance to the hotel wearing the same light blue summer dress as the day before.

I parked the car and walked over to her. She smiled and kissed me on the cheek.

"We really must stop meeting like this," I said.

"I'm sorry for yesterday," replied Maolíosa.

"It was an emotional day."

"I know. Ma's father had a drink problem, and I know how much pain it caused her. But I'm fine now. What's happening is all part of the journey."

"So what do you want to do tonight?" I asked

"I don't know."

"Do you like Indian food?"

"You eat. I can sit with you."

**

As the waiters brought the poppadums and pickle tray, Maolíosa was still hardly saying a word.

I eventually plucked up courage to ask her,

"What about us?"

"How's everyone?" retorted Maolíosa.

"Steve's in good health, both in body and mind apart from his leg of course. Sadly, Sue's still in a coma."

"And David?"

"He's going to leave his wife. But he's in such a terrible state over Sue."

"He's lucky to have a friend like you."

"It's the very least that I can do. I owe him," I said.

"Maybe if you'd been as supportive and understanding with your wife then the two of you would still be together."

"That's different. Surely you can see that."

"Not from where I sit. I think that you owed your wife at least as much as you owe David now. The difference is that your wife hurt you directly, whereas David didn't. If you were one of Sue's relatives or badly injured in the accident like Steve then you'd probably feel differently," replied Maolíosa.

"Sue has no relatives that I know of, and Steve doesn't feel any hostility towards David."

"Yes, but your brother is both understanding and forgiving. You're not, Jonathan."

"I don't remember telling you Steve was my brother."

"You must have done."

"I think I would have remembered. It's not exactly a minor issue in my life."

Maolíosa was silent.

"Anyway, whatever. The important thing is that Steve persuaded me to talk to my mother, our mother. You'd be surprised at how understanding and forgiving I was with her."

"Even if that's true, I still don't understand how you can be understanding and forgiving with your mother and not with your wife. And I don't think it is true, by the way."

"What's not true?" I asked.

"What you say about you and your mother."

"Yes, it is."

"I don't believe you when you say you forgive your mother. Showing some understanding maybe I can believe but forgiving no. Did you apologise to her for how you behaved towards her?"

"No," I admitted.

"Redemption comes from genuine forgiveness. It doesn't come from mere understanding."

"I don't believe this, Maolíosa. I've come along this evening in the hope of talking about my relationship with you. You still haven't answered my question of what about us. All you do is go on and on and on about my mother and my ex-wife. I haven't come to see you to talk about my mother, and I certainly haven't come to see you to talk about my ex-wife. I want to talk about us."

"She isn't your ex-wife. The two of you are still married," replied Maolíosa.

I banged my head on the table in utter frustration and in doing so I managed to knock the contents of the pickle tray and mint yoghurt all over the table and much of my face.

At least, if nothing else, it brought a big smile to Maolíosa's face as she wiped my face clean with her napkin.

324

Still smiling Maolíosa said,

"What you need is time."

"I don't need time, you said that yesterday. I know what I want. I want a chance at a relationship with you. I want a chance to look forward not back. It was you who told me in Dublin that there's no gain in life without pain, and that I need to look forward in my life and not back. Can't you see that I'm trying to do that for God's sake?"

"You're sweet. As stubborn as a mule and quite unforgiving, but you are definitely sweet in your own strange way."

She leant over the table to give me a kiss on the cheek.

"With all this continued analysis of my life, I've lost my appetite. So what do you want to do?" I asked.

"I'd like to spend the night with you. I don't want to make love, but I do want to be with you."

"Your place or mine," I said smiling.

"Yours. It would be nice to spend some time with you in your own space."

"No problem. And tomorrow I'm off work this week and can take you to the airport if you want."

"No need. Just take me to the train station first thing," she replied.

"Are you sure?" I asked.

"Completely."

**

Neither of us was able to sleep much that night. The two of us hardly spoke at all either. We stared into space alone with our thoughts.

Daylight began to shine through the windows of my bedroom, and we got dressed to go to the train station in the middle of Sheffield.

As we were approaching the station, Maolíosa said,

"I've come to some conclusions."

My mouth suddenly went very dry.

"What conclusions?" I asked.

"Do you remember where and when we first met?"

"Of course I do, April seventeenth in the bar at the Midlothian Hotel at eight o'clock."

"And if you were to be in that same hotel bar at the same time on the same day next year then who knows what might be there to greet you."

I pulled into the drop off area by the station and stopped the car.

"My God, why do you always have to be so enigmatic? Maolíosa, that's nearly eight months away. So much can happen between then and now."

"Exactly! You said to me last night about looking forward and not backward. That's right. But everyone, and probably you above all, needs time to come to terms with the past before they can move forward with optimism. I've told you that repeatedly, again and again. I think that you're still obsessed by your past. It's not that so much can happen; it's that so much needs to happen."

"Like what?" I asked.

"Like fully resolve the issue with your mother, and I mean *fully* resolve, not where you are now with her. And genuinely sit down with your wife and talk WITH her rather than serve her with divorce papers. And let's not forget the situation with David. I think that eight months is the right length of time to address all those issues," replied Maolíosa.

"It's more than enough time if you ask me. That's so unfair."

"And why should any woman have to deal with a man with all your unresolved issues? Is that fair?" asked Maolíosa.

I was silent.

"And one more thing, David should make a promise to you that he will never, ever drink again. You're supporting him as his friend in his hour of need, and that's the least he should do in return," added Maolíosa.

"Can't I even write to you or telephone you?"

"The eight months will soon pass. You've a great deal to do. I don't understand your problem; we've barely seen each other for seven days in the past four and a half months. It's not as though you're used to seeing me every day. I've never lied to you, Jonathan, and I never will. You do trust me, don't you?" she asked.

"Of course I do. Anyway, do I have a choice here?"

"No," replied Maolíosa with a smile.

I sighed.

"You're essentially a good man but you have to sort yourself out. You need to start helping yourself and not expect that things are always going to work out for you in life. They don't. Things go wrong, it's what happens."

I sighed again.

"Look, I must go. April seventeenth in the bar at the Midlothian Hotel, eight o'clock. Remember?" said Maolíosa.

"I'll be there, you can absolutely guarantee it."

She kissed me gently on the cheek, got out of the car and walked into the station.

I just sat there. Eventually, one of the staff working at the station asked me to move on.

**

Following my discussion with Maolíosa I called in to the hospital on the way home to find David. As expected, he was still in Sue's hospital room and looked even more drained and exhausted than the previous day.

"Any change?" I asked.

"No, none," said David with clear sadness in his voice.

"I saw Maolíosa last night."

"How is she?" he asked.

"She's OK but not interested in seeing me until I've resolved what she sees as all my issues with Sophia and my mother."

"She's right, not that I'm in any position to offer advice on relationships considering what a fuck up I've made of my own life!" replied David.

"Maolíosa also said that you should promise me that you'll never drink again. And she's right on that too."

"I will never drink again if Sue recovers."

"But what if she doesn't?" I asked.

David was silent and looked at Sue, lying motionless in her bed attached to all her tubes and monitoring devices.

"This is important to me," I said.

David sighed and then looked me in the eye.

"I'll never drink again."

"Spit on your hand and swear it on the honour of the Two Musketeers," I demanded.

David spat on his hand and again looking me in the eye as he shook my hand with a firm and purposeful handshake, he said the words,

"I swear on the honour of the Two Musketeers that I will never drink alcohol ever again in my life."

"David as much as I love you and for all that we've been through and for all that you've ever done to help me in life, if you ever let me down on this then I'll never speak to you again."

"J.P., I've promised you and I will honour that promise."

**

I arrived back home to find a message on my answerphone,

"Hi Jonathan, this is Ted Sadler. Can you please give me a call?"

I made myself a cup of coffee and sat down; the flat seemed very empty and quiet without Steve. I played some Oasis records for a while, but it just wasn't the same without him around.

327

For want of something better to do, I returned Ted Sadler's call.

"Hi Ted. It's Jonathan."

"Thanks for calling back. There's a great opportunity for you. Yorkshire are playing Essex in the County Championship Final at Wimbledon next weekend, court number 1. Somebody's had an injury and, based on your current form, Richard and I have pushed for you to be in the squad. Looks like it will go ahead. Great news, eh?"

"Wow…wow – normally Ted, yes. Normally this would be beyond my wildest dreams but my brother Steve's in hospital, and David's in a mess. His girlfriend Sue's in a coma. I don't know. Honestly I don't know."

"Yes, I've heard from Richard about everything that's gone on. But, Jonathan, this is probably a once in a lifetime opportunity for you. At least think about it."

"I know. Can you just give me twenty-four hours?" I asked.

"That should be workable."

**

I went to see Steve whilst my mother and Craig were busy in town buying some additional clothes for their extended stay in Sheffield.

I arrived at his room to find him propped up in bed and full of his usual positive spirits in life.

"How are you?" I asked.

"Getting there, the surgeon's set a date for next Tuesday for the operation to put a metal plate in my leg."

"What did he say about your leg?"

"He told me that the likelihood of ever playing professional football again was virtually non-existent. But I knew that already. What's been going on with you?"

"I've possibly been picked for Yorkshire to play in the County Championship Final next weekend at Wimbledon," I told him with no real enthusiasm.

"That's fantastic. Once I've had my operation next Tuesday, I reckon with Mum and Dad's help I'll be able to come and watch you play if you're selected."

"I'm not sure that I want to play."

"I can't believe that you're saying that. It's a once in a lifetime opportunity."

"Ted Sadler said that."

"For fuck's sake, if you're picked you should play and enjoy every minute of it. If what's happened to me proves anything, it shows that sometimes you only get one opportunity in life. This is your opportunity. You'll regret it in years to come if you don't take it," said Steve.

"I just feel bad playing when your leg is in such a mess, David is in such a state, Sue is in a coma. You know?"

"You're beginning to annoy me, bro. You owe it to me to play. It was my pep talk that changed the course of the final. Remember?

"How on earth could I forget that?" I said smiling.

"Yes, and that whole day, that remarkable comeback and victory would be diluted if you don't play. I'm going to be there next weekend with *our* Mum and the two of us expect to be watching you. And not only watching you, but watching you play the best tennis of your life."

"I've not been selected for sure yet. And I might play complete shit even if I am chosen."

"You will be chosen, trust me. And if you play shit, it doesn't matter if you enjoy the day and, most of all, if you do your best. Anyway, the form you're in there's no way that you'll play shit. White Line Fever, right?"

I laughed and said,

"White Line Fever indeed! OK, you've talked me into it. I will play, and I will do my best. I'll do it for you, brother."

"I'd like you to do it for yourself as well," replied Steve.

He smirked at me and a broad smile filled my face.

I went home feeling more positive and called Ted Sadler to confirm my availability. I was told that I'd been selected.

Steve had been right. For all the on-going traumas, I was delighted upon hearing the news.

**

Later that evening, I received a call from David.

"Sue's out of the coma," he said.

"Wonderful, wonderful news! I'm delighted for you both. My God, I'm so relieved. How is she?"

"She's still in intensive care but the signs are increasingly positive that she'll make close to a full recovery."

"And the baby?"

"Seems fine."

"Is Sue conscious? Did you tell her that you know about the baby?"

"Yes and yes. And, I also told her that I was going to divorce Stef and leave Barton's."

"What did Sue say?" I asked.

329

"She can't speak. She needs speech therapy. But she cried and made a movement with her hand that told me that she loves me. For the first time in years, I feel truly happy. I don't care what happens to me now. They can throw the book at me, send me to prison; I don't care. Everything I prayed for I've got."

**

Steve's operation was a resounding success, and he was given the all clear to come with my mother to watch me play at Wimbledon.

Before travelling to London, I took the Friday off work and spent all the day practising at the tennis club with my team mate for the weekend, Richard Sadler.

It was an inspirational day with him – a brief glimpse into what my life could have been but for the 'good' Reverend Brownley's intervention in my life.

As we drove down together to London in Richard's car, I enjoyed his company – he truly loved tennis and, whilst the local tournament at which I'd recently beaten him was not a major issue in his life, playing at Wimbledon in the County Championship Final clearly was.

I was taken aback by how nervous he was about the weekend ahead. It really mattered to him.

En route, we very briefly discussed Richard's liaison with Stefanie. He had a mere five words to say,

"Dreadful person, great in bed."

I laughed and thought to myself that it was some consolation that David, in the early days at least, had obtained some value from his marriage to her.

Richard and I joined the other two members of the squad, Eric Porterfield and Dan Scaly, on the Friday evening.

It was agreed with the team management that Richard and Eric would play the singles whereas Dan and I would play the doubles on Day 1.

**

Richard lost his match. It was a match that he could and should have won, but he ended up going down in a tie-break in the deciding third set.

Whereas he had been philosophical at losing in the Sheffield Tournament Final, this time he was furious and inconsolable as he threw his racket against the dressing room wall in frustration.

330

Eric then lost to the opposition's best singles player, Peter James, and we found ourselves 2-0 down in the best of five. If we lost the doubles then there would be no point in turning up on the Sunday.

Dan and I won the toss and chose to serve.

My first serve sailed out and the toss on my second serve was all awry, and I netted my serve for a double fault.

I laughed to myself and saw Steve in the crowd. I knew to stay positive, to think of the game in 'White Line Fever' terms. The next three serves were aces.

The match was a tight one with the first two sets shared one apiece – both decided on a tie break.

Dan and I worked well together despite the fact it was the first time we'd met, never mind played as a doubles pair. I loved grass as a surface – it suited ideally my natural serve and volley game. I began to find my range and timing in the third and final set and together with Dan secured the vital rubber win.

**

We met as a team with the selectors on the Saturday to review matters and plan for the second and final day.

The view of everyone was unanimous; our problem was how we were going to beat the opponent's best player, Peter James, if we were going to win.

Richard was clear in his thoughts,

"The way I'm playing I have no chance. I think that Jonathan should play."

"I agree. He carried me out there today in the doubles," said Dan.

"No way," I protested.

"If Richard's comfortable with that, I agree. I definitely think that it's the best decision," added Eric.

"I want this medal and, assuming you win your game, Eric, which I'm sure you will, there's only one person in this room on current form with the slightest chance of beating Peter James and that's Jonathan," reinforced Richard.

The selectors concurred.

Eric did win his rubber to bring the overall match back to 2-2.

The deciding rubber was to be myself against Peter James.

**

Sport is a strange thing. Some days you turn up and everything goes absolutely right, and that afternoon was such a day for me. My fitness was excellent, my mind-set right, and everything about my game was at its best.

I took the first set 6-4. My team mates suddenly started to believe.

I played the second set as though in a dream. Everything seemed in slow motion – the ball seemed bigger, my racket seemed bigger, every audacious shot came off.

A thunderous ace; my thirteenth in only nine service games sealed a 6-1 second set win and with it the rubber, the match and the championship.

I raised my left arm in triumph and looked over at Steve's smiling face.

Peter James shook my hand and said,

"Remarkable. Well played. Who the hell are you?"

My team mates then descended upon me to congratulate me before we were presented with the cup and individual medals.

I couldn't stop smiling.

As I collected my medal, I heard a voice say,

"Well played, son."

For the entire world, it sounded like my father's voice speaking the same words that he had said to me in our back garden all those years ago.

I even looked around expecting to see him.

**

After the Final, I went to find Steve.

As I climbed the stairs of the stand to find him, I thought of how Steve's crying as a baby had ruined my chances in a School Tennis Final but now how he, more than anyone, had enabled me to truly fulfil my sporting ambitions in life.

Sadly, in the meantime, all his sporting ambitions effectively lay in ruin. It was the bitterest and sweetest of bittersweet realisations.

When I found him, he was sat in his wheelchair with my mother beside him. They were both smiling brightly as I approached them.

I immediately gave my winner's medal to Steve.

"I've had the best day of my sporting life. And none of it would have been possible without you. I want you to have my medal."

Steve accepted the medal, shook me firmly by the hand and said,

"I can't tell you how proud I am of the way you played today, bro. That second set, shit, it was like you were on a different planet!"

332

My mother joined in,

"I'm so proud too."

Emotion welled up within me and I embraced the two of them.

Any negative feelings I still felt about my mother were temporarily forgotten as we crouched, hugging, over Steve's wheelchair.

It was a great, great moment.

The Trial

It was my 30th birthday. There were cards from Steve, my mother and Craig and all the family on the farm in Devon.

Steve rang me up to wish me a happy birthday in person.

"Happy birthday, bro!" he said with customary zest.

"Cheers. How are you doing?" I asked.

"It's going to be a long process but time flies quickly enough. Before you know it, I'll be giving you a thrashing again on a squash court."

"In your dreams!"

"Are you still training and exercising hard?" asked Steve.

"Of course I am. There's not much else to do other than work if I'm honest. I miss my sparring partner."

"Tell me about it, it would have been cool to stay with you but with my leg I need to be here. You should come down to Norwich!"

"I will, but I've a lot on at work at the moment with David leaving and not being replaced," I replied.

**

In the middle of October, I made the long trip down to Devon. It was good to be amongst friends again.

As soon as I saw David I was struck by how in six or seven weeks the benefits of his changed lifestyle were very evident. He looked younger and more relaxed. Most noticeably of all though, he was clearly happy; particularly when he was together with Sue.

"This is my second chance in life, and I'm going to take it," he told me.

It wasn't only David who was in fine spirits. Although her speech was still limited, Sue was able to write without problem and she gave me a short note:

Dear Jonathan,
I'm sorry that I can't say these words to you.

All I've ever wanted since first meeting David is for him to be happy. Not only has he now found that happiness but I'm there to share it with him.

I will always be grateful for your support in helping us find our New Dawn in life.

All my very best wishes,

Sue x

I was very touched by the note and thanked her. Sue gave me a 'big hug' full of human warmth.

Everything in the garden seemed thoroughly 'rosy' except for the not so small matter of David's trial. One of the major difficulties was finding the money to hire the top quality lawyer imperative with the possibility of David being sent to prison. Sue's redundancy money was relatively small and any insurance money for the accident was not going to be seen until after David's trial.

Brian made the position very clear when he, David and I talked about it in the evening.

"We've no assets other than the farm itself. I've discussed with a local bank about the possibility of re-mortgaging or selling it."

"I'll never speak to you again, Dad, if you sell the farm. It's taken me over ten years of my life to get back here where I always wanted to be. Our family's been here for centuries, and I'm not about to have someone else own the farm," replied David.

"All right, selling's out of the question. But we could re-mortgage. It would even have some tax benefits to boot," said Brian.

"So why haven't you done it before?" asked David.

"Because we've never needed the bloody money before, that's why, David," retorted Brian.

With that David stormed out, clearly upset by his father's words. Brian sighed with frustration.

"I always say the wrong thing, don't I?"

"You love your son, and he knows that. He'll calm down in the morning," I replied trying to play down the situation.

"You're probably right. But the problem of the money will still be there."

"There are other options," I suggested.

"Like what?"

"You could release the remaining £10,000 from Dad's trust fund to help finance the trial."

"It's actually nearer £15,000 because you've not touched the money for eight years. But there's no way that I'd let you do that."

"Brian, that money will be mine in less than five years' time anyway, and I've no idea what I'm going to do with it. I don't need it. It's much better to put the money to good use now," I said.

"But I promised your father," countered Brian.

"Sod the promises to my father. David's been the best friend to me that I could ever wish for in life. He's always been there for me when I needed him most. This is my chance to repay him."

There was silence from Brian. I continued,

"I'll never forgive myself if I don't help David. Releasing this money for him is as much about saving me from guilt as saving David from prison. I am his friend, and I should have said and done something about him always driving after he'd been drinking. But I never did."

"If I agree, it's only on the condition that we pay you back."

"Didn't you tell me years and years ago that friends don't have to pay back those things that are given freely?"

A broad smile crossed Brian's face as he said the words,

"I did that."

"So are we agreed?" I asked.

"Yes we are and thank you very much. Do you want a whisky? I never get it out when David's around because…well, you know."

**

The following Monday, Old Man Barton and I had over a pub lunch together at work. The whole unfortunate episode had clearly taken its toll on him and he had visibly aged with the entire trauma.

I spoke with him about David's trial. He said little at the time, but four days later he called me into his office.

"Jonathan, I know that I can trust you with some confidential information. Quite honestly, there's no one else here that I feel that I can talk to. I'm going to find a buyer for the company provided they commit to keep all the staff. The truth is that my heart's not in it anymore since David left. All the fun that made it worthwhile has gone."

"Won't you miss working here, Mr Barton?" I asked.

"I won't miss the bloody Information Technology, laddie," was the gruff response.

"But you have excellent IT skills."

"Aye, they're not bad. But I bloody resent that that's how we have to do things these days. It's the bloody exchange of data, nothing more. My twenty-five years in business have been about communicating with people, other warm blooded human beings, not a piece of sodding software. I want communication, not information in my life."

I laughed.

"And laddie, call me Ron. I'm fed up with bloody Mr Barton. If anything I prefer Old Man Barton."

"How did you know that we called you Old Man Barton?" I asked.

"Laddie, if a mouse farted at the company, trust me, I'd know about it."

"What are you going to do now then, Mr Barton?"

Another of Ron's withering looks came my way.

"Sorry, Ron."

"You know, long ago and far away, before I married Beth, I was a young lad full of too much testosterone and too little sense, and I fathered a son by a young woman called Sally. We never married even though I wanted us to do so."

"So you have a son?" I asked.

"Aye laddie, in one of life's great bloody ironies, Sally rejected my marriage proposal because, in her words, I had no prospects. No bloody prospects, eh. I'm a bloody multi-millionaire now."

"What happened?"

"Shortly after the birth of the baby, Sally had married some ambitious young guy, and they emigrated with the sprog to Australia. My lad's name was Peter and I've not seen sight or sound of him since he was eighteen months old. It's actually Peter's thirty-fifth birthday on April 25 this year and Beth and I intend to be there in Sydney to celebrate the event. I'm now nearer sixty than fifty and I've never been a father to Peter but once I've retired, I intend to change that."

"Absolutely bloody marvellous!" I said.

"Aye, laddie, it is. It's never too late! Remember that in life. And this issue with David, I gave him a shareholding in the company and I'll gladly release some of the money up front to help with his trial."

"David told me that there was nothing in writing regarding his shareholding. It'll certainly come as a very welcome and much needed surprise for him."

Ron looked at me with disdain.

"I don't see why David should be surprised. I promised him a shareholding, and I'm a man of my word. David should know that by now."

"I'm sorry; I didn't mean to insult you. He thinks what with everything that happened between him and Stefanie," I replied.

"I know David behaved like a complete idiot, but being married to Stefanie is potentially going to do that to any man. David's asked me to be a character witness at his trial, and I'm going to do it. Stefanie's said that she'll never speak to me again if I do it. I'll have to remind her of that the next time she asks me for some money."

We laughed and Ron continued,

"Aye, it's funny but it's also sad. All my money has ever done is to create a monster in Stefanie. What she needs is some 'tough love' as the Americans call it – love and discipline in equal proportion. It's partly my fault. I always gave her money, but I hardly gave her love and I certainly never applied enough discipline."

"Isn't that how you should deal with savage dogs? Fifty per cent love and fifty per cent discipline!"

"It is, laddie. The truth of the matter is that I've failed her as a father. But maybe, just maybe, it's not too late. I reckon that the best thing that I can do for her now is to make her stand on her own two feet and start living in the real world."

**

A few days later David rang me and told me that Old Man Barton had sent him a cheque for £25,000 along with a recommendation for Elliot Brown as, quote unquote, 'the meanest son of a bitch of a lawyer who's so good that he'd probably have got the Yorkshire Ripper out on probation'.

**

Autumn became winter and David's trial was upon us. As demanded by the court, Steve was a witness in the trial, and he needed to be in Sheffield.

Craig and my mother brought him around to my flat. My mother and Craig didn't stay long and went off separately to a hotel in Sheffield.

It was wonderful to see Steve as I'd not seen him for some three months, though obviously I wished that I could have been seeing him in better circumstances. I was incredulous at the progress he had made. He only needed a walking stick and could move around the flat almost as easily and as fast as I could.

As soon as my mother and Craig had left, Steve said with clear hurt in his voice,

"I thought that you'd forgotten about me."

"Don't be daft. Of course I haven't."

"You never phone."

"I'm not a very good talker on the telephone," I replied.

"You could have come down to Norwich. I asked you enough times."

"It's a long and arduous journey, and I've not really had the time."

"Bro, you're so full of shit sometimes," said my brother.

"OK, OK. I'll be honest. I'm still not comfortable with your father or my mother. Sorry *our* mother...*our* Mum...whatever. You know what I bloody well mean."

"Yes, I do know what you mean, but I also know that you'll never be comfortable as long as you avoid spending time with the two of them. The longer you put off coming down to see us, the more difficult it will become."

"You're right. I owe it to you to make an effort. I promised you after all."

"You did. Right, done, agreed. I've not come all the way here from Norwich to argue, let's talk about something else."

"I'll drink to that!" I replied.

We put Oasis' *Acquiesce* on at full volume with me on 'hair brush vocals' and Steve on 'walking stick air guitar'.

Once again the music sounded so good in my flat.

With beers in our hand, we talked about all manner of things until the early hours of the morning.

Despite the rapid progress Steve was making with his leg it was going to be a long, arduous haul back to fitness for him.

"I've decided to take a year out of university and focus on my physiotherapy and walking unaided again. I was two years ahead anyway so losing a year is no big deal. Plus, I do need a degree now. "

"So you don't think that you'll ever play top class football again?" I asked more in hope than optimism.

"No way, that's been pretty much clear since day one after the accident. One leg is going to be slightly shorter than the other. However, provided I put in the work there's no reason why I won't still be able to do loads of things – like beating you on a squash court!"

**

The next day was a cold miserable Friday morning in December. It was raining, and the wind was blowing as it can only blow through the hills of Sheffield.

The fact that it was Friday the 13th only served to increase the sense of impending doom. As I walked to the courthouse, the rain seemed horizontal.

I saw David briefly before the trial. Despite the fact that the next few hours could possibly land him in jail, his body language was positively defiant.

"Best of luck," I said.

"Thanks, I'll need it. Sofe's going to be here, by the way. She wanted to come, and she's still my friend if not yours."

"That's your issue, not mine. Just don't expect me to talk to her."

**

David's defence was based around his genuine remorse, the fact that he was actively seeking counselling to address his drink problem and, most importantly, that the accident wasn't actually his fault.

Sadly, I had been called as a witness for the prosecution and told the truth of that fateful evening as I was forced to under oath – of how much David had had to drink.

I desperately hoped that it wouldn't cause too much harm.

Thankfully there was much to support David's cause. I was a character witness as was Old Man Barton as he had promised. And there was David himself, who was both credible and sincere in his remorse; quite movingly so in fact.

It was very clear how much he regretted what had happened, though adamant that the accident was not his fault, and his desire to change his life. Communicating those things to the strangers that make up juries is not easy but David did it without question.

And critically there was Steve, who categorically reinforced David's story that the accident was not his fault – that the bus has skidded into David's car and not the other way around.

And above all there was Elliot Brown, who truly lived up to Old Man Barton's pre-trial billing. Words in the hands of Elliot Brown became weapons, as I was reminded of the classic old Douglas Adams' quote. If it would help win the case then Elliot Brown was the type of man who would convince you that black was white and then gleefully watch you be killed on the next zebra crossing.

The crux of the case was the testimony of the bus driver himself as he had claimed that David was to blame for the accident. Watching Elliot Brown cross-examine him was akin to seeing someone being dissected alive without anaesthetic.

As the driver's testimony continued he was increasingly put under enormous pressure from Elliot Brown, who, supported by various issues from the driver's private life, such as his debts and troubled marriage, not unjustifiably accused him of lying over the matter for fear of losing his job.

He put the driver on trial, accused him of committing perjury and, worse still, of leaving Sue, a poor woman badly injured in the accident, still without proper speech, to bring up a child on her own with the child's father in prison simply because the driver did not have the basic human decency to tell the truth in this matter.

Elliot Brown was relentless, utterly relentless and finally, reluctantly, the driver admitted that he had skidded in the accident.

The driver left the witness stand in some significant state of distress.

I looked around the public viewing gallery and there was Sophia. Quite simply she looked absolutely gorgeous in a short blue skirt and high heels. Her figure and brunette hair as compelling and stunning as the first day that I'd met her – and wedding and engagement rings were still on the finger of her left hand.

It was a struggle not to keep looking at her.

**

It was time for the verdict to be delivered.

David was found not guilty of dangerous driving albeit, as expected, convicted of drunken driving.

The judge subsequently announced that David would also be banned from driving for three years and fined £1,500. But none of that mattered. David didn't have to go to prison and, down on the Devon farm, he had no need to drive anyway.

**

There was a celebration party held afterwards in the hotel where David, Brian and Alison were staying and what a party it was, running through the afternoon and into the evening.

David was on orange juice and led most of the fun. Ample proof if any were indeed needed that a love of life doesn't need to come from a glass of alcohol.

Sophia also attended the party – sexy short blue dress, magnificent vertiginous blue shoes and all.

She came up to me smiling. Butterflies filled my stomach, and I did not have the faintest idea what to say. Thinking that I was ignoring her as usual, Sophia's smile disappeared.

I rushed to the toilet to try to regain some composure.

When I returned I found that Elliot Brown had moved in on Sophia.

"I like your dress," said the lawyer.

"Well thank you, Mr Brown. It matches my underwear."

"That would seem to be a matter worthy of further investigation."

"I'm a married woman, Mr Brown," said Sophia.

"I've a lot of expertise in divorce cases. And please call me Elliot."

"I'm sure you have, Mr Brown, though I'm sure it must be very tiresome being named as the correspondent so often in such cases."

The 'mighty' Elliot Brown, master of all he surveyed hours before, was struck dumb.

I stood there smiling at the magnificence of my estranged wife.

**

At around nine o'clock, David shouted to everyone in the room that he had an announcement to make.

"I've asked Sue to marry me and, much to my delight, she's said yes."

The whole party seemed to descend on the two of them to give their congratulations, except for Sophia and me. The two of us stood back from the melee and caught each other's eyes for the umpteenth time that day.

Sophia smiled at me.

I closed my eyes and looked away.

It was time for me to leave. For all the celebrations, I wanted to be on my own and was able to make my exit without anyone other than Sophia noticing.

I'd not smoked since the traumas of August earlier in the year, and I bought a packet of cigarettes in the hotel reception. It was a cold winter's night, and I starting walking, without consciously heading in any direction.

**

I found myself at the university Halls of Residence area. I stopped to sit on a bench outside Halifax Hall where Sophia and I first made love.

I lit a cigarette and spoke the following words to myself – words of a song that were imprinted on my soul:

342

'The first time ever I lay with you
I felt your heart so close to mine
And I knew our joy would fill the earth
And last till the end of time, my love.'

Afterwards, I wandered to the botanical gardens, where Sophia and I had kissed for the first time, and stayed there all night to watch the semblance of a sunrise, oblivious to the December cold and wind.

I took a bus to pick up my car from where I'd left it in town and then drove to work at Barton's unshaven and with the previous day's clothes still on.

As I arrived to find the company site deserted, I'd been completely unaware of the fact that it was a Saturday morning.

Happy Families

I drove back to my apartment and went to bed for some sleep only to be awoken by the sound of loud knocking on my door.

Craig, Steve and my mother had called to see me. Casually dressed and smiling; they were all wide awake and full of energy. The same could not be said for me.

"You'd better come in. My apologies, I didn't get much sleep last night," I said trying but failing at being hospitable.

"Where did you get to last night?" asked Steve.

"I needed some space."

"We're sorry to get you out of bed. We were wondering what you were doing for Christmas and if you wanted to spend Christmas with us in Norwich?" asked my mother.

"I don't know at this point what I'm doing."

Steve looked at me with anger in his eyes.

"I could come to Norwich, I suppose," I said.

"None of us would be offended if you want to do something else", said my mother.

"No, I won't be doing something else. I'd be delighted to come. It's very kind of you to invite me. Now can I please go back to bed to get some sleep? I'll see you all in ten days' time."

"We'll get on our way," suggested Craig.

Some good words of sense I thought, and I crawled back to my bed.

**

All four of us exchanged presents on Christmas Day.

Steve and I both laughed at the fact that he'd bought me *Different Class* by Pulp just as I'd bought it for him

My mother used the perfume that I bought her straight away whilst most of the bottle of whisky I'd bought for Craig had been consumed by Boxing Day evening.

Craig and my mother had bought me a new running top and tracksuit bottoms.

That morning as we opened all our presents, warmth ran through me.

I asked my mother,

"Can I help you prepare the Christmas lunch?"

"Of course you can," she replied with a sense of real delight in her voice.

As we set about our task with the stuffing and trimmings, I remembered the days of my youth as my mother and I had worked together in the kitchen in Taplow to prepare food that my father never seemed to come home and eat.

"I have one great memory of Dad," I said.

"What's that?"

"We played a tennis tournament in the back garden one day. The whole court was marked out properly and there was even a cup presentation at the end. It was astonishing what he did!"

"When your father put his mind to it, he could be a kind and generous man."

"You're right, when he put his mind to it. Sadly it wasn't that often," I replied.

"He was not a well man mentally."

"I know. I realise that now. But that day was special. I remember him saying to me when I won the tennis match, 'Well played, son',"

"I've thought a lot myself about your father during the past three or four months," admitted my mother.

"The strange thing is that I heard the same words after the tennis final at Wimbledon."

"You never know. It might have been him. If it was then he'd have certainly been very proud of you."

"Do you think so?"

"I know so."

I smiled.

"I've been reading a lot of Samuel Johnson recently. I know that both you and Sophia shared a love of literature together. Do you know any of his works?" asked my mother.

"Not particularly. Although talking of Sophia, didn't he write that 'love is the wisdom of the fool and the folly of the wise'?"

"I believe he did! Which are you, the fool or the wise?"

"The fool!" I replied.

We both smiled at each other before my mother continued,

"I can't remember exactly the words but Johnson wrote about a person's spirit appearing after their death."

"What did he say?"

345

"His concluded that although all logic was against it, all belief was for it."

I smiled again before asking,

"What do you think?"

"Oh, I would always take belief over argument."

"I've never thought about it but I would as well probably."

"Steven says that you've something going with an Irish woman?"

"Maolíosa? I'm not sure whether there's 'something going' as you put it but yes, we have a relationship of sorts. Time will tell, I guess."

"Your father was from Dublin!" said my mother.

"What?" I replied.

I was genuinely shocked.

"Yes. He was orphaned at a young age. It was a terrible tragedy. His father, your grandfather, was killed in a road accident because Robert chased a ball into the road, and his father was hit by a car as he pushed Robert out of the way. And then his mother had a miscarriage a few days later and died."

"My God, that's awful," I said.

"I know. So your father was brought over to Manchester by his grandmother, and she was the one who raised him. She was a very, very cold and uncompromising woman. I only met her twice, and she showed no love or affection whatsoever towards your father. I think that's why your father and I got together in the first place. I had my sister, but we were never close. Your father and I were two lonely orphans. It was actually quite touchingly sweet for a while."

"I think he committed suicide," I said.

"So do I. I've always felt that. One of the main reasons that I left him was that he was past help and past hope. When I left your father, he'd given up and no longer accepted any accountability or responsibility for his own life. He wouldn't talk about anything. He wouldn't talk about you, how he felt about not having more children, other things."

"Like what other things?"

"Shortly before his grandmother died, he went to see her on his own. He came back in a dreadful, dreadful dark mood. I've never thought about it until recently, but looking back I think that's when a lot of our problems started. He never would tell me what was said between him and his grandmother. He flatly refused to discuss it. Maybe she blamed him for her daughter's, his mother's death, I don't know. His grandmother always gave me the feeling that she was angry with your father about something. Anyway, whatever was said, your father shut me out on the matter and then when we learnt about the situation with his sperm count, he ended up shutting me out on everything."

"I think he shut everyone out. He certainly did a lot of the time with me," I said.

"After I left, I felt that it was only a matter of time before he took his own life. You've got to want to change in life, and he didn't. All he did was drink. The only effort he ever made was to fight for custody of you. That annoyed me so much at the time. I had no chance of winning with that bloody lawyer of his."

"I didn't like him either; the greasy, slimy Mr Bennett."

"Horrible odious man. So once I lost custody of you, I always tried to drum into Steven that you have to take accountability and responsibility for your own life. If you're not happy in life then do something about it. Awful things happen to a lot of people. It's how you deal with the difficulty that's important, not the difficulty itself."

"Maolíosa said pretty much the same thing to me."

"She's right."

"After you'd gone, Dad and I had a housekeeper. Auntie Annie, I used to call her. She was really kind to me and she told me always to remember that the Lord helps those that help themselves. Not that I believe in God," I said.

"I'm not sure I do either but I do strongly believe that life helps those that help themselves."

At that point, Steve popped into the kitchen for a drink of water. After he left, I said,

"I think you did a great job in bringing up Steve."

"Thank you. I'd like to think so. We certainly had help though. With his leukaemia, he couldn't go to school and through a very lucky quirk of fate we were able to find him the ideal personal tutor."

"I remember Steve saying, some professor or something wasn't it?"

"Yes, Professor Peter Ellis was his name. I felt so sorry for him as both his wife and his only son died of cancer within around a year of each other. He was a real academic, a renowned expert in child psychology, but he ended up leaving his post after what happened. He had so much money that he didn't need to work. He used to come to Craig's gym every day, and they got talking. When he heard about Steven, he agreed to become his tutor in exchange for free gym membership. Best deal of our life in hindsight. Peter always said it helped him too, that his time with Steven was part of rebuilding his life. I went to his wedding last year. It was so good to see him find happiness in his life again."

My mother laughed.

347

"Why do you laugh?" I asked.

"Peter said when he finished as Steven's tutor that he was fourteen going on forty."

I laughed as well before saying,

"He's right there. I can't believe he's only seventeen."

"I'm very proud of him. I'm very proud of you," replied my mother as she continued to chop up some potatoes.

"Mum, I'm really sorry for how I behaved towards you for all those years ago," I said.

"It doesn't matter now," she replied.

"Yes it does. I'm genuinely sorry."

I looked over at her and there were tears running down her face. I went over and gave her a hug. She cried some more, and I felt tears start to run down my own cheeks.

She then said to me,

"You've no idea how much I've dreamed of this."

**

After lunch, I talked with Craig whilst my mother continued in the kitchen, and Steve went through his daily exercise routine in his constant battle to return to some sort of normality with his left leg.

Craig and I were sat in the living room drinking a glass of whisky watching some rubbish or another on television as Craig said,

"I'm sorry. I never congratulated you on how well you played at Wimbledon."

"Thanks. I could easily have never had the opportunity. But for a rain interruption that helped me win a club championship a few weeks earlier, I would never have even been considered to play. That and Steve's remarkable inspired pep talk during the rain break."

"But life's like that. The key thing is that you had the opportunity, and you took your chance. Not everyone does that," said Craig.

"I suppose not! I don't remember seeing you at Wimbledon."

"I was there but I tried hard to stay out of the way so that you, Steven and your Mum could have some space. I tried too hard with you all those years ago. I wanted you to look upon me as a father, but I know now that's never going to happen. But I'd like to think that we could at least get on well together in the future".

"I think that we will."

"So do I," he replied.

We raised our glasses and touched them.

At the end of January, I went down to Devon to see David and Sue for the weekend.

David had insisted that Brian and Alison go away for their 35th wedding anniversary, their first holiday away from the farm that I'd ever known.

Sue very much looked as though she was more than eight months pregnant and her speech was showing a good improvement even if she was still some way from fluency.

David, Sue, Graham and I spent a very pleasant evening, eating a takeaway pizza with Graham and I drinking some wine.

As we worked our way through our second bottle of wine, I watched David gently sipping on a glass of orange juice and felt obliged to ask the question,

"Doesn't it bother you, David?"

"Does what bother me?"

"Graham and I drinking in front of you."

David simply laughed and replied,

"It bothers me a lot less than Dad always trying to sneak a glass of whisky when he thinks that I'm not looking. I've told him, but he takes no notice the silly old bugger. The fact is that I've made the decision that I needed to take and the last thing I want is for the world to treat me differently because of that decision. I mostly drank because I was unhappy but now I'm very happy. I don't feel the need anymore; it's as simple as that."

Sue smiled at David as he said the words.

**

I awoke with a start. Mayhem was breaking out around the house. I looked at my travel alarm clock and it was 2.53.

I quickly came to my senses and realised that the commotion was due to the fact that Sue's waters had broken, and that David was panicking about the fact that Graham was not able to find his car keys.

I quickly threw on my clothes and offered to drive Sue and David to the nearest hospital. They took up my offer without hesitation leaving Graham looking suitably sheepish and embarrassed.

I broke every speed limit, not worrying for a minute about how much wine I'd drunk a few hours before, and we made it to the hospital in less than 20 minutes.

David went in with Sue and I was left, not for the first time in recent months, hanging around a hospital reception area waiting nervously for news.

I waited and waited and waited until around three hours later David came out to see me. He was clearly highly emotional and in tears.

"Mother and wonderful baby boy both fine and healthy," he said.

"Absolutely bloody marvellous, many congratulations!"

"You know what?"

"What my friend?"

"I couldn't half murder a drink," said David.

"The best I can do at this early hour is a cup is tea at Greasy Eddy's. If he's still there, that is."

"Brilliant, bloody perfect in fact – Greasy Eddy's it is then!"

I drove David into Barnstaple town centre and parked so that the two of us could cross the River Taw on the old Long Bridge and get some much needed air into our lungs.

The sun was rising as we crossed the bridge, and David put his hand around my shoulder.

"I can't believe all this has happened to me. Less than six months ago I hated life and worst of all I hated the person that I'd become. And look at me now," he said.

"I'm just glad I'm here to share it with you," I replied.

"Always the Two Musketeers, eh!"

We both smiled.

And to add to our considerable delight, Greasy Eddy was still there in his same old place. As we walked in together, to our considerable surprise, Eddy was clean shaven, his hair had been combed and, perhaps most remarkably, the normally omnipresent cigarette was not dangling from his lips.

Eddy greeted us like long lost friends with an enormous smile,

"Well bugger me backwards, it's the dynamic duo!"

"It's good to see you, Eddy," I said.

"What brings you to my fair abode?"

"We're here to celebrate David's first child, a boy!"

"Bloody marvellous, the teas are on me!" said Eddy.

As he prepared the teas, Greasy Eddy let fly to one of his trademark 'passing motorcycle' farts.

"Terry Hennessey, 1-0!" said David and me in unison.

Eddy laughed.

"You've stopped smoking, Eddy," remarked David.

"I have. I finally met a woman. Who'd have thought it after all these years? I was convinced that I'd be a bachelor all my life but then

Shirley wandered in here one night, and it was love at first sight. Who'd have believed it? Never been happier."

"And it was Shirley who insisted that you stopped smoking?" I asked.

"Not quite. She said that she'd tolerate one of my frailties in life, and that's all. Farting, smoking and my non-existent relationship with my mother and only one could stay. What with my dear old Dad, I couldn't possibly stop farting, so I had to sort out the other two?"

"So you've made your peace with your mother?"

"Took ages to track her down but track her down I did. Best thing I ever did bar meet the missus. I made it up with her, and it felt great. Life's too short, you know."

"It is indeed, Eddy!" I replied.

"Your tea's still shite," complained David.

"That's why I give it away. I still do the best fried breakfast in Devon though. Can I tempt you both?"

"You bet," said David.

"Me too!" I added.

**

Once back at the farm, David needed some sleep after the excitement of the night. Although tired, I decided that it was time for me to go home and leave Sue and David some privacy with their new baby boy.

I had plenty of time on my hands and after the events of the night, I made a detour to visit Melissa's grave in Reading for the first time since her funeral over seven years previously

I arrived at the cemetery in Reading and I was able to find Melissa's grave relatively quickly.

The grave had been kept in an immaculate condition and there were fresh flowers on the grave along with a note.

Written on the note were the words:

I think of you and miss you every day.

All my love,

Mum

As I read the note I cried.

The Argument...and a Wedding

I received a formal invitation for David and Sue's wedding.

David and Stefanie's divorce had come and David and Sue had decided to get married in Barnstaple Registry Office at short notice on April 12th, five days before I was going to Dublin.

David asked me to be best man and added that he hoped that I would actually be able to make his wedding this time!

Steve had also been invited, and I arranged to collect him from Norwich a couple of days before the wedding so that the two of us could make the long journey down to Devon.

However, Ron rang me later the same day up to tell me that he had been invited to the wedding too, much to his delight.

"Why don't we attend the wedding in style, laddie? We can drive down to Barnstaple in my Bentley."

"I'm sorry, Ron, but I've arranged to pick up my brother from Norwich as he's still somewhat incapacitated by his leg."

"That's no problem I don't mind going via Norwich. Beth's showing solidarity with Stefanie and won't be attending David and Sue's wedding. I can't complain. Beth's willing to travel to Sydney to meet my son, and that's what most matters to me. I'll be glad of the company on the drive down."

**

Despite the hundreds of miles we had to travel, Ron, Steve and I were at the farm by the late afternoon on a glorious early April day.

As we drove into the farm, David was mucking out the pigs with great relish.

After saying hello to everybody, Ron took Steve in the car to the accommodation at the local inn whilst I stayed with the whole family catching up with all the events of the past couple of months.

Much had changed on the farm in a short space of time since Sue had given birth. Graham and David were now running it jointly. Graham still didn't have a wife, but he'd always seemed happier milking cows than chasing women and perhaps, as David had jokingly suggested, the combine harvester was his true love in life.

Sue was helping them both, particularly as her speech had now all but fully recovered, allowing Brian and Alison to settle into a well-deserved retirement.

The new baby had been christened Alec and was in excellent health. Sue gave me Alec to hold, and as I held the tiny smiling baby in my arms, memories of Melissa consumed my mind.

I was filled with poignant sadness.

The six of us, Graham included, talked most of the afternoon. The laughter and banter were as it used to be, the only difference being that it was Sue and not Sarah who was there.

Sarah did arrive later, together with her husband, and was clearly pregnant. She looked fulfilled as a woman. As Sarah sat with her husband in the kitchen of the farmhouse, clearly very content with her life, I thought to myself that in the same way that some sons become their fathers, then some daughters also become their mothers.

I stayed at the farm for an evening meal. As soon as I'd finished my last mouthful of food, Brian invited me next door to the sitting room for a drink.

At that point, Sarah's husband made his excuses and left whilst David stayed in the kitchen to discuss the wedding with Sue, Alison and Sarah.

After pouring me a very large whisky, Brian said to me in a serious tone.

"I pushed and pressured David into what I wanted him to do with his life rather than what he wanted to do, didn't I?"

"You only wanted the best for your son, Brian."

"I did that. But I was still wrong. Looking at how he's been so happy in the past months, I know that I was wrong."

"I have a friend called Maolíosa who says to me 'no pain, no gain' and the fact that we should look forward, not backwards."

"That friend of yours is probably right," said Brian.

"I know it's a cliché but all's well that ends well and, as you say, David's now the happiest and strongest I'd seen him since his early teens."

Brian smiled and said,

"I've a video to show you."

The video was of an advert featuring David talking about how his alcoholism had resulted in him no longer having his job and, more importantly, nearly killing his future wife and child.

It was a very powerful advert as David's genuine remorse came across clearly and strongly on screen.

"Tens of people have joined Alcoholics Anonymous around here since they started running it on local television. It's been such a success that they're talking about going with it nationally. I'm so damn proud of him," said Brian.

It was the most emotional that I'd ever seen Brian.

David walked through the sitting room door to join us.

"I invited Sofe to the wedding, by the way," said David.

"No problem! I keep telling myself that I should speak to her."

"It's about bloody time that you spoke to her. Jeez, J.P., she's still your wife!"

**

I walked to the Star & Garter Inn where we were staying. It was a homely and welcoming Devon pub in the finest tradition. As I was checking in at the bar, I saw Sophia and Steve talking together.

My hands started to shake.

I immediately left my suitcase with the person at the bar and went outside. I had an old packet of cigarettes in my coat pocket and lit up to try and calm my nerves.

As I stood in the car park staring blankly into space, I felt a tap on my shoulder, and the surprise made me jump. As I turned around it was Sophia, dressed in blue jeans and a baggy black jumper.

"Hello stranger," she said.

"I'm sorry, but I just don't know what to say to you," I replied.

Sophia smiled at me before saying,

"That explains it then."

"Explains what?"

"It explains why you've not said anything to me for nearly six and a half years. Which is a little strange considering we are still man and wife – technically anyway. Don't you think that it's a little strange?"

"I meant to do something about starting divorce proceedings last year. Thank you for reminding me, dearest wife."

"Why do you always have to be so bloody rude and unpleasant with me? If you wanted to hurt me for what I did then you've most certainly succeeded over the past six and a half years."

I said nothing in reply.

"Can't we call a truce and talk together like adults, please," pleaded Sophia.

"I've nothing to say to you," I replied.

I started to walk away, and Sophia pulled me back by the arm.

I could feel the adrenaline of excitement and sheer animal lust run through my body.

"Tell me, husband dearest, why did you never ask me why I ended up having sex with one of my work colleagues?" demanded Sophia.

"OK then, just why did you fuck someone who you worked with?"

Sophia looked me straight in the eye.

"It was because the man I loved more than anything in the world showed no affection, support or sympathy towards me after our baby died. He shut me out totally. Because the man I loved and who had once so adored me no longer held me in his arms, never mind made love to me anymore. That the man I loved made me feel unwanted, unloved and worthless. And worst of all, he blamed me for the death of our baby, whom I loved just as much as he did. That man made me feel a failure whereas once he had made me feel the most loved woman on the planet."

I could see the tears start to form in Sophia's eyes as, still looking straight at me, her voice became increasingly emotional,

"I know that none of that excuses what I did but you have no idea of the aching hole that you left in my life; which you still fucking leave in my life. You've no idea how much I've missed talking to you, not only for the last six and a half years; I missed talking to you for the last twelve months that we lived together."

"Who are you to talk about holes in people's life? When I found you shagging on the desk that evening it was like having my guts ripped out. I wasn't sure I could carry on breathing. I didn't even want to carry on living. Part of me died that night," I shouted back at her.

"Hallelujah, at last some bloody emotion from the man. If only you had let your emotions out seven years ago then we wouldn't be in this ridiculous and farcical position now. Why did you bottle everything up inside of you instead of talking to me? I was your wife. YES, YOUR WIFE. Didn't that mean anything?" Sophia shouted.

Before I could answer, Sophia continued,

"Why whenever you are hurt do you cut the people who love you most out of your life? I just don't understand why you do this. Does it give you revenge? I know only too well myself how effective your silence is in hurting the people you love. But what I don't understand is the fact that, in hurting other people, you also so totally succeed in hurting yourself and making yourself even more reclusive, melancholy and downright bloody miserable in the process. Why do you do it? For goodness' sake, man, lighten up."

I shrugged my shoulders like a naughty five-year-old schoolboy that was being told off by his teacher.

"You're right. It's how I am, it was how my father was," I replied.

"But it doesn't have to be like that. I still love you, Melton. You're the only man that I've ever truly loved despite your pig-headedness, stubbornness, vengeful nature, emotional retardation and all your numerous other personal frailties and foibles. What am I going to do with you?" she asked.

There was more shrugging of shoulders.

"What I do know is that this is David's wedding, and I ruined his last one because of you. Not this time. It's his day not ours. I'm going to bed. I'll see you tomorrow," said Sophia.

"OK," I replied.

**

When we arrived at the Registry office in Barnstaple the next day, both David and Sue were dressed more as though they were attending a meeting than a wedding.

This was very much in keeping with the ceremony itself, which was very business-like and over in less than 20 minutes.

As David and Sue kissed at the end of the short ceremony, I found myself looking over at Sophia, dressed all in white and looking stunning as always, and was all too aware that her eyes were also fixed on me.

We traipsed out of the Barnstaple Registry Office passing on our way the next couple waiting outside ready for the 'marriage conveyer belt', and it was back to the farm for the wedding reception.

The guests at the reception were divided almost equally between the drinkers and the non-drinkers, virtually all of which were David's friends and associates from the local branch of Alcoholics Anonymous.

I hardly drank at all. The same, however, could not be said for Brian and Ron, who started to drink as though there was no tomorrow.

Although there was no formal wedding breakfast, I was asked to give a speech as best man.

"Sadly, I missed David's first wedding, and I'm delighted to have a second chance. David has been my friend for close to twenty years, through thick, through thin. He was always there when I needed him most. For a long time, he was the brother that I never had but, in recent months, I've found that I'm lucky enough to actually have a great brother of my own."

My eyes caught Steve and he smiled at me.

"And what can I say of Sue? She's a caring woman of kindness, compassion, sincerity, modesty and substance who genuinely loves David. In fact, Sue is the complete antithesis of David's former wife, Stefanie and therefore I have absolute faith that David and Sue have a relationship that's truly made to last."

Brian and Alison cheered and anyone who knew Stefanie at all laughed heartily, no one more than Ron himself.

"So to David, the best friend that any man could have and to Sue, the woman who makes him so very happy and is made just for him, I wish you both, along with your new born son, all the very best. So, ladies and gentlemen, please raise your glasses to the bride and groom."

"The bride and groom", said the assembled party in unison.

David followed with his own speech.

"Life is strange, you know. Sue met me on a grass verge in the early hours of the morning when I was going through a period of, how shall I say, permanent intoxication. She's seen the worst of me, Jeez, *she's seen the very worst of me* but now she's hopefully seeing the best of me. The marriage vows say for richer, for poorer, for better or worse, in sickness and in health, and I know I have a woman who lives and breathes those words in everything that she does."

There were assembled 'aahs' from all present.

"I'd like to thank my parents and my family for their steadfast support in the most trying of circumstances, my ex-father in law Ron for his phenomenal support and friendship, my old friends, my new friends at AA and, of course, my very best man, the one and only Jonathan Paul Melton. But most of all, of course, I want to thank Sue. She has given me a son; she has brought a happiness to my life that I never ever thought possible and now she is my wife. I love you, Sue, more than words will ever be able to say."

David embraced Sue and kissed her. I could feel the emotion well up inside of me. I looked at Sophia and she looked at me. We both smiled at each other.

It was the first moment of affection between us in over six years.

**

After the speeches, John Tasker and his wife, Katrina, came over to talk to me. The passing years had been kind to them both, particularly Katrina, who looked as attractive as ever.

"It's good to see you, Jonathan," said John.

"You too, John."

"David told me about your day at Wimbledon. It must have been very special."

"It was. I was finally able to show what ability I had. However, without my brother it just wouldn't have happened. I still can't believe it. It was like a dream come true."

"I can imagine."

"Do you still play cricket?" I asked.

"I finally packed in last year. I had a shocking season. Anno domini, I guess."

"At last, I have him to myself at weekends in summer," said Katrina.

Katrina gave John a big hug and she asked me,

"How long is it since John and I came to your wedding?"

"Over eight and a half years," I replied.

"Sophia still looks amazing."

John then visibly gave Katrina a dig in the ribs.

"What are you doing that for?" she asked.

"Because Jonathan and Sophia are separated," replied John.

"I don't believe you. I watched Sophia looking at Jonathan during his speech. It was the look of a woman in love let me tell you. John's got it wrong, hasn't he?" she asked me.

"No, he's right."

"But that fabulous groom's speech you gave all those years ago."

"That was then, this is now," I said.

"But she still loves you."

"Katrina! I can't take you anywhere. Leave the poor man alone. It's his life," interjected John.

"But it's such a waste," insisted Katrina.

At this point, John was frantically trying to drag Katrina away to talk to someone else but Katrina still had one parting shot for me.

"She still loves you I tell you. I know these things, I'm a woman."

I decided to go over to speak with Sue, who was standing alone.

"Thank you so much for those kind words in your speech," she said.

"They were absolutely true and therefore no thanks are necessary."

Sue was silent but smiled.

"How are you finding things on the farm?" I asked.

"It's like a dream come true. Alison and Brian make me feel so welcome. They treat me as though they were my own parents."

"I know. They've always been the same with me. Although Mum and I get on well now, I'm grateful beyond words for what Brian and Alison did for me, particularly in my teens."

At that point Alison wandered over to join the two of us with an enormous smile on her face and said,

"I loved your speech, Jonathan. Everything you said about Sue was true. It's everything a mother could want to have her son finally settle down with such a wonderful woman."

Sue visibly blushed at such a tribute.

"Are you all having a good time?" asked Brian, forcing his way into the conversation.

"Yes," the three of us replied in unison.

"It's a lot better than the pretentious nonsense at David's last wedding. I hated that bloody wedding reception."

Ron was clearly in earshot. Alison, Sue and I visibly cringed at Brian's words.

Ron came over to join us and said,

"I hated it too, Brian. To make matters worse, it cost me £25,000."

"Wading in again, Dad?" said David as he came over.

"No," replied Brian.

"Yes he was," said Alison.

"Can I have a word with J.P.?" asked David.

David and I wandered together into the old barn, our old meeting place from days gone by.

"This old barn doesn't change, does it?" I asked.

"Jeez, the discussions we've had in here. The barn doesn't change but hopefully we do. Thanks for today, J.P."

"It was nothing but an absolute pleasure."

"You wouldn't be offended if I made Ron Alec's godfather, would you? Sue and I are planning to have more children, and I'm very sure your chance will come."

"No problem. Ron's a great man, a truly great man."

"You're telling me. He gave me a cheque for £150,000 as a wedding present. He told me it was my shareholding. I can't believe it. Any immediate financial issues with the farm solved in an instant."

"He's been good to me as well, really looked after me. Made sure I still have a job with the new owners and everything," I replied.

**

At around five in the afternoon, David and Sue were leaving for their honeymoon – a short couple of hours drive to spend five days on the south coast of Devon.

"Enjoy Torquay!" I said to him.

359

"Enjoy Dublin, though Lord only knows why you're going there when the love of your life is stood over there," replied David.

"On your way, Pritchett!" I said with a smile on my face.

David then gave me an enormous hug and said,

"Thanks again for everything, J.P."

As everyone at the reception waved the two of them on their way, Sophia came over to talk to me.

The two of us had managed to avoid each other all day or more's the point, I'd made a point of avoiding Sophia all day.

"Look, here's my business card. Maybe, just maybe you might want to give me a call," she said.

"You're right. We should talk more," I replied.

"I'll meet you any place, anytime – Sheffield, Paris, London, New York, Dubai, Singapore even. I'd like Singapore, I've never been. You name it, I'll be there."

Dublin in the Rain

April 17th had finally arrived, and I felt full of optimism as I set off from home to catch the early afternoon sailing from Anglesey.

The argument with Sophia after all those years had finally cleared much of the emotional debris from our relationship. I knew that I wanted to be with her again. As the ferry made its way across the Irish Sea, I realised how much I still both loved and was in love with Sophia.

I now so wanted to have that second chance with her.

My time with Maolíosa had been wonderful and more than anyone, she had made me see sense on the key issues in my life; Sophia, my mother, my attitude to life itself.

As Maolíosa had said, it had been all about confronting and dealing with the real emotions and genuine issues in my life.

Maolíosa had also been right that it wasn't our destiny to be together; that some things in life are just not meant to be. Even so, I was really looking forward to seeing her again.

There was so much I wanted to tell her from the last time I'd seen her, so much that I needed to talk with her about.

**

I made sure that I was in the bar at the Midlothian Hotel on time.

As the clock in the hotel reception chimed eight times to mark exactly one year to the minute, there was no sign whatsoever of Maolíosa. She was never usually late, and as the seconds and minutes passed, doubts were beginning to creep into my mind.

After 30 minutes, I wondered whether I had the right day, the right time and the right place. And when three quarters of an hour had passed and still no sign of Maolíosa, I started looking around the hotel for her, but she was nowhere to be seen.

I went to reception to check whether there were any messages for me, but there were none. The young man who was working on reception had the misfortune to be wearing a particularly ill-fitting red, purple and green hotel uniform and I asked him,

"Does Maolíosa still work here?"

"Maolíosa who?" was the gruff response.

"I'm sorry, I don't know her surname. She definitely worked here in April and July last year."

"I've only been here six months."

"Is there anyone else around who might know?"

"I could ask the duty manageress I suppose," he said.

"That would be very kind of you," I replied.

Cussing on his way, the young man went in search of the duty manageress. However, she couldn't remember any Maolíosa either. She inspected the hotel records, but there was no Maolíosa on file, irrespective of surname.

I rubbed my hands through my hair in frustration. The duty manageress took pity on me.

"Betty will probably know. Betty knows everyone who has worked here. I'll go and get her."

Some five minutes later an elderly woman wandered up to me.

"Are you the gentleman looking for Maolíosa?"

"Yes!" I replied.

"I remember her. You can't trust the hotel files, you know. Information's always getting lost," said Betty.

"You do remember her though," I said.

"Yes, Maolíosa O'Connor. Lived down Elgin Avenue I think."

"You wouldn't know what number, would you?"

"Sorry, no. I'm not even sure it was Elgin Avenue."

"Don't worry. You've been an enormous help. Thank you so very much."

The next few minutes were spent frantically looking through the local telephone directory. Inevitably there were literally hundreds of O'Connors in the telephone book but none listed as living on Elgin Avenue.

I tried telephone directory enquiries, but they told me the same story – that there were no O'Connors listed on Elgin Avenue.

I'd come this far and wasn't about to give up just yet. I borrowed a city map from the hotel reception and checked the whereabouts of Elgin Avenue. It was only around a ten minute walk from the hotel.

I ran there in less than five.

When I arrived there, I was very relieved to see that there were only about 20 Georgian town houses on the relatively short Dublin backstreet.

All I wanted to do was to find Maolíosa, to speak to her, to understand what was going on.

I decided to knock at the first door where I could see a light on.

A pretty young woman around the same age as Maolíosa answered the door and without any introduction, I immediately asked her,

"I'm sorry to interrupt your evening but do you know whether Maolíosa O'Connor lives around here and, if so, where I can find her?"

Sadness was evident in the young woman's face.

"Do you know Maolíosa O'Connor?" I repeated.

"I did. I knew her from when I was a little girl. She was my best friend. Maybe you should come in."

I felt that I was finally making some progress. I followed the young woman down the entrance hall and sat opposite her in a tastefully decorated living room with an impressive high ceiling.

"I'm Fiona," she said.

"Hi, I'm Jonathan."

"I don't remember Maolíosa mentioning a Jonathan."

I was disappointed that Maolíosa hadn't mentioned me to her close friends.

"We spent some time around Trinners together," I said.

It was the best that I could come up with, and it seemed to put Fiona at ease.

"Look I don't know how to break it to you but Maolíosa went missing with her sister, Aoife, and her Da, Peter. Almost exactly a year ago come to think of it. They were sailing in Galway and there was a freak bad storm, and they were never found. I'm surprised you didn't hear about it. Their old house across the way has been empty for the past year. Thank the Lord it's finally been sold, and someone's going to at last move in. It's been downright creepy at times. It's as though there's something still restless there, something that's not quite at peace. Does that sound weird to you?" asked Fiona.

"Not at all," I replied.

Tears were in Fiona's eyes.

The mention of Aoife's name sent a shiver down my back and my brain seemed to be working at 100 times its normal speed.

"Do you have a photograph of Maolíosa? I would be good to check that we're talking about the same woman," I asked.

"Sadly I don't," she replied.

"Can you describe her to me?"

Fiona now looked at me very suspiciously. I could sense her discomfort as she asked,

"How did you come to meet Maolíosa again?"

"I met her at a concert. I was a bit of a lost soul at the time, and she took pity on me. We had some fun together, and she told me to look her up the next time I was in Dublin. She was one of the kindest, most sensitive people that I've ever met. OK, sometimes Maolíosa could be a little brutal, but she was always well meaning. And wonderful blonde hair, how can I forget that! " I said.

Fiona smiled and then laughed.

"That was Maolíosa all right, kind and sensitive, but not afraid to speak her own mind. And she was definitely one of the great matchmakers of all time. It was her who introduced me to my fiancé, and I can think of at least two other couples where their relationship was significantly 'helped along' by Maolíosa's grand schemes," she said.

"Did Maolíosa ever have a boyfriend herself?" I asked

"No, that's the remarkable irony. For all her successful dabbling in other people's relationships, Maolíosa never seemed to find love herself. She was always too busy looking after her Da. Sad because she was such a wonderful person, but I guess you already know that."

"Yes, I do. She was. Many thanks, Fiona. You've been a real help."

"No problem. I'm so sorry to have to give you such bad news. I still can't believe it myself; Peter, Annie, Maolíosa and Aoife O'Connor, all of them sadly no longer with us."

"What did you say? Annie?" I asked.

"Yes, Annie was Maolíosa's Ma. She died from cancer. Must be going on twenty years ago now."

Fiona smiled before adding,

"She was lovely too. We all used to call her Auntie Annie when we were little girls."

**

I wandered back towards the hotel in a trance.

My mind was working frantically trying to make sense of the remarkable discussion with Fiona; my thoughts analysing all the events over the four months I knew Maolíosa.

As I walked through the Dublin streets, the rain was by now belting down. I didn't care. My mind was in a complete whirl.

En route, I found a cafe that was open and sold cigarettes. I bought a packet and lit up.

Next to the cafe there was a bench in front of an old church. It was quiet and peaceful. I decided that I needed to sit there to try and find some calm.

Fog started to come down to add to the rain.

It didn't matter. I was trying desperately to gather my thoughts, but all I did was go around and around and around in circles in my head, unable to comprehend or rationalise what had gone on.

I just wanted to talk to Maolíosa one more time, hoping that she could provide an explanation for everything.

It was a forlorn hope.

**

After an hour or so, maybe longer, I looked down at my hands and saw my wedding ring on my right hand.

Something inside of me told me that it was time to stop thinking, pontificating and analysing and start doing.

I thought about how I'd spent too much energy in life worrying about things outside of my control and not given enough time and energy to things that I could influence.

It was a long overdue time for change.

I took my wedding ring from my right hand and put it back on the correct finger.

"I'm going to get me a woman. Not just any woman but my woman! Life helps those who help themselves" I said to myself.

I starting walking back to the hotel as the Dublin rain continued to fall. It was as though the rain was cleansing me.

I felt fresh with all my negative energy and thoughts washed away. All the feelings around Dublin and its rain that had seemed to be part of my DNA were now gone forever.

As I walked through the rain and the fog, I passed an oldish woman, coming in the opposite direction, who said,

"Good evening to you, young sir. No mistaking that summer is around the corner."

"It certainly is," I replied.

Redemption

As I walked through the entrance of the Midlothian Hotel, I thought of Maolíosa's words of 'who knows what might be there to greet me'.

Then, quite unbelievably, as I entered the reception area, soaking wet, there was Sophia sat there waiting.

As soon as she saw me, she rushed up to me, hugged me and kissed me on the cheek. She then proceeded to talk very frantically,

"I'm sorry for being late. I had everything planned to be here by eight as per your message. But the damned plane was over three hours late. It's now nearly eleven o'clock, and I was sure that I'd missed you."

"What message?" I asked.

"The message that you left for me at work this morning – the one that said to meet you at the Midlothian Hotel, Dublin at eight. I was sure you'd ring after David's wedding so when you did, I just dropped everything. I've been so worried for the past half hour what with being late that you'd given up and gone somewhere else. But I checked with reception and found that you'd booked a room for the night. Reception said that you'd gone looking for some woman, and I assumed that it was me."

"So, let me get this right. I rang you at work and told you to meet me here at eight?" I asked.

"Yes!"

"Did you actually speak to me?"

"No, but you left a very clear and detailed message. And it said not to call you back because you were in a meeting."

"And you didn't think that was odd?"

"Yes, it did strike me as a little odd. But I thought what the hell; I've nothing to lose other than the price of an air fare. I jumped into a cab and went straight to the airport."

"Are you always late, by the way?" I asked.

"No!"

I looked at her incredulously.

"Mostly, I suppose," said Sophia.

"Sadly I think that we've both been part of some mischievous matchmaker's plan to get us back together. It definitely wasn't me who left the message at your work."

There was a massive look of disappointment on Sophia's face.

There was a silence between us. I looked at her, all fully made up and all in black – a black jacket, a matching sexy knee length black skirt with magnificent black stiletto shoes.

She looked sensational.

I had to remind myself that this was actually my wife.

"You look nice, particularly the delectable and sumptuously vertiginous shoes. Actually, it's really good to see you. I was just thinking about you and here you are," I said.

"Well thank you, husband dearest. They're my work clothes, that's all."

"You always go to work dressed like that?"

"Mayhap, I might have changed my shoes. I always keep these in my drawer at work; one never knows when they are going to be needed."

"They lose their magical properties if worn too much, right?"

"They do and I might also have bought some different underwear in Duty Free at the airport waiting for my plane. But yes, they are my work clothes."

There was another brief silence and then we both laughed together at the absurdity of the situation.

"Look, I'm soaking wet but if you give me five minutes to change, what I need more than anything now is a drink and I most certainly do NOT want a drink in this hotel. Do you fancy going somewhere?" I asked.

"Where?"

"I don't know," I replied.

"I simply adore a man with a plan."

I quickly changed, and since the rain had temporarily stopped, Sophia and I set off walking towards town. As natural as anything, she tucked her arms inside mine and smiled a smile to light up the world.

I felt as though I was walking on air.

As we walked, Sophia asked me,

"You've changed where you wear your wedding ring?"

"Well I knew a woman some years ago seeking a love so amazing, so divine, one that demands her soul, her life, her all. She said that the position was sadly vacant at the time. Although perhaps a little tardy, I was considering making an application. Assuming of course the position is still vacant, that is."

"Mayhap it is."

"Has the woman had many applications, do you know?"

"The usual mixture of stray dogs and totally unnecessary and overrated dates," replied Sophia.

"No pedigree pet, a man who dares?"

"David found this strange man in Coventry with only a deckchair to his name and somehow, against all my better judgement, I knew that he was the one for me. There is no reason when it comes to love, after all."

"That's pretty much what Jean-Baptiste Poquelin said."

"Who?" asked Sophia.

"You mayhap know him as Molière. 'Reason is not what decides love' were his exact words, I believe."

"Hidden layers, Melton, I've always liked that about you. With so many men, there's less to them than meets the eye. But never so with the erstwhile First Bard of Sheffield, I feel."

"Erstwhile? Erstwhile!!"

Sophia laughed and pushed me playfully.

"Anyway, we digress. Pray tell, this strange aforementioned man in Coventry, who also had three pieces of cutlery and an old CD player I must add in his defence, was he mayhap pig-headed and stubborn?" I asked.

"Undeniably, and with the most terrible vengeful nature. Totally retarded emotionally, of course. Not to mention all his other personal frailties and foibles."

"Such as?"

"Oh, far too numerous to mention! Stupidity and anal retentiveness immediately come to mind, but I'm sure I can think of many more given the opportunity," replied Sophia.

"I'm sure you could. So what happened to the woman in the meantime?"

"She was cast either amongst the promiscuets, which was, by and large, unsatisfying, or the celibates, which was even worse. She had psychotherapy, hypnotherapy and even, goodness me, acupuncture, but the good old fashioned method of going to church and telling herself that 'This too shall pass' always worked best."

"Good word, promiscuets!" I said.

"Yes, I like it. I've always felt that a collective noun was appropriate, the celibates have one so why not the promiscuets?"

I laughed.

I stopped in the street and pulled Sophia towards me.

My heart was pounding.

The two of us kissed; a passionate kiss that seemed to last forever. I was absolutely lost in the moment as adrenaline pumped through my veins. For an instant I was back in Nice in the pouring rain on our honeymoon.

I was scared to open my eyes in case it was all but a dream.

After kissing, we looked into each other's eyes, and Sophia smiled at me.

I smiled back and said,

"I've been such an idiot. Or even, as David has often referred to me, a nail-on 24 carat idiot! I can't even begin to apologise for how I've behaved. Really, I can't."

"Better late than never, I suppose! I'm sorry too. You could never know how much I regretted what I did."

"It's doesn't matter now, my love. What matters, hopefully still, is that I love you and that I want to be with you."

Sophia threw her arms around my neck and said,

"And I love you more. I have kind of missed you as much as it pains me to say it. All those hidden layers, I guess. Would sir mayhap like to go back to the hotel?"

"No, I want to go dancing!" I replied.

"Dancing? Did you say dancing?"

"Yes, Irish dancing. I think I might surprise you!"

"More hidden layers! I should have known, I guess. This, I simply have to see!"

As we carried on walking towards Temple Bar, Sophia asked me,

"David told me that you'd met someone?"

"Yes, I did."

"What happened to her?"

"She died, I believe."

"That's sad."

There was a brief silence and then Sophia said,

"That's when I fell in love with you. When my grandmother died and you said the D.H. Lawrence quote, 'The dead don't die. They look on and help.'"

"Maybe they do. Maybe they do more than that. Maybe even sometimes they change things," I replied.

Time briefly seemed to stop as a whole myriad of emotions and thoughts passed through me in an instant – sadness, bittersweet poignancy, gratitude, happiness, joy, elation, forgiveness and, above all, an overwhelming sense of redemption.

A smile crossed my face and disappeared in the twinkling of an eye as Sophia asked me,

"Do you remember the day in Endcliffe Vale Park when I recited from *The Rainbow* and then you asked me if I knew what the last thing out of Pandora's Box was?"

"Of course I remember, and it's Hope."

We looked at each other and laughed.

"Life is for living, life is for loving," she said.

As we walked through the streets of Dublin arm-in-arm, it started to rain again.

"How I love Dublin in the rain," said Sophia.

I smiled, this time the broadest of smiles, and replied,

"Me too...me too."

Printed in July 2021
by Rotomail Italia S.p.A., Vignate (MI) - Italy